"*Soul Searching* is a _____ _____ ____ that engages readers through a combination of complexity, action and imagination. The melange of ideas makes for a rich and intricate tale."

—Damien Lawardorn, *Aurealis* #138.

"A quick-paced narrative written with precision and interlaced with registers of the criminal and banal, magical and real, spiritual and technological, futuristic and current.

This debut exemplifies the work of a sensitive writer with a gift for imagining the inner lives and afterlives of humans. "

—Joanna Woods, *Africa in Words.*

"*Soul Searching* applies spirituality to mechanics and crime solving, to healing and recovering our humanity, in the timeless universal that cuts across cultures worldwide, but also in the immediate reality of the multicultural local, where time is running out, and people will die."

—Mame Bougouma Diene, *Strange Horizons.*

SOUL SEARCHING

Stephen Embleton

GUARDBRIDGE BOOKS
ST ANDREWS, SCOTLAND

Published by Guardbridge Books,
St Andrews, Fife, United Kingdom.

http://guardbridgebooks.co.uk

Soul Searching

ISBN: 978-1-911486-57-2

To Riley,
For always believing.

PROLOGUE

Ruth lay on the cold hard tiles, looking straight up at the light. The heavy smell of the blood filled her nostrils as she inhaled short, sharp breaths. The pain had gone, but it would be back. She knew it would.

The rest of her body now let her know of other injuries. Her elbows throbbed. The back of her head ached, and the ringing in her ears was persistently present.

So much blood.

She didn't take her eyes off the light. Somehow it was comforting. Warm. White.

Here it came. Searing through her.

The sound of rushing water engulfed her.

Black…

She realized that she was floating. Floating above the room, blood covered the floor below, surrounding her body in a shimmering crimson. Everything seemed peaceful. Quiet.

The pain had gone, replaced with an ever-present warmth.

Everything's okay now. It's over. A light began to fill the room, giving it a hazy glow. It felt familiar and welcoming. The scene below seemed to get smaller, fainter.

The light moved through her and around her, caressing her soul. Then her attention was gently brought back to the world fading below her, as if something beckoned. The scene became clear once again. Who was calling her? She became aware of another soul speaking to her, "Stay."

Stay?

"Stay," came the response.

"Caleb," she whispered.

The smell of blood, the cool hard floor, and the pain edged back, as she sensed the life of her unborn child.

Life begins.

CHAPTER 1

The woman's breathing could be heard from the other room. Strained but softer now. Hand still shaking, annoying. Why the hell was she so determined to resist? Will have to ask her.

In a few minutes.

A few minutes to calm down, accept what had happened. Then it's her turn to listen to what I have to say. Just listen. That was all. She'd had plenty of time to say what she wanted. Throw abuse, cry, bite, bleed. Now it's my turn.

No noise. Quiet. That's all I want.

Just me and my thoughts. No outside irritations. No disruptions. No noise pollution.

You give someone the opportunity and all they'll do is mouth-off about their problems and "poor me" bullshit. Smile at someone in the checkout queue and they think that gives them the right to talk to you.

"Fuck off about the price of milk. I don't give a shit! See the store manager over there? He doesn't give a shit either, so why the fuck should I?"

Stunned silence. Precious. But that's when they start again. Louder.

The room was quiet now. Dark and quiet.

#

In one goose-bumped instant, Mike's heavyset frame was depleted and fragile, as if a surge of electricity had left his body. A surging tide of nausea rose from deep within him, but a quick, strong breath kept it down. He inhaled again. He didn't have time to look back at the room, at the rest of the squad. The disappointment was thick in the air. Or was that his own?

"She's gone, Ruth," said Mike. "She looks like she's heading straight for Heaven." He drew a deep breath as he continued to follow the red dot across the Screen. "I think she'll need it after what she's been through," he whispered to himself.

He pressed his earpiece in his ear. No response.

"Hicks," he said sternly, "did you hear me? She's gone, damn it. Respond." Nothing came through his earpiece. "Banks? Do *you* read me, at least?"

"Yeah, Angel," came the breathless response, "I read you."

"Where the hell's Ruth?" snapped Mike.

"She was ahead of me."

"Ruth Hicks! Come in! It's over!"

"I think give her a few minutes, Angel."

"I need a status ASAP, Banks," replied Mike. "Get back to me in a few then." He sat down on one of the desks, still monitoring the Screen. That was it. They had come close but not close enough. They'd missed saving the victim and their chance at getting at the killer. He was still out there. Square one: another dead vic, another floating soul, and an elusive green dot out there that they couldn't latch onto.

He watched the red dot, gathering speed, already out of Hell, and nearly through Purgatory, on its way to Heaven and maybe even to The Beyond; if it was lucky. Mike Haddon, AKA Angel, or Archangel, was Chief of Trackers, and so nicknamed because he guided the trackers, gave them what they needed, and could interpret the Screen faster than anyone in the unit.

Studying all aspects of the afterlife, divination and traditional beliefs that, for centuries, had been deemed occult, had given Mike a range of tools necessary to interpret the symbols and figures on the Screen. Things that a computer's algorithm couldn't decipher let alone perceive. His job included inputting that data, after the fact, to improve the system's performance. It was always learning. And he was still learning. The untapped knowledge on his doorstep in southern Africa was a continual source for honing his skills, and no amount of online reading and searching could replace face-to-face experiences with the people out in the dry Kalahari or the slippery peaks of the Drakensberg mountains.

The Screen continually moved, changed, transformed and mapped. The Universe on a screen — it always impressed him. The Universe at his fingertips. Others saw the Screen as moving through time. That was limited thinking. He simply saw it as changing. Timeless. Unfortunately, the streaks of grey along his temples argued otherwise.

His breathing deepened, air filled his lungs, and he lost himself in the huge screen: fifteen metres of one-millimetre thick fibre optic suspended from an eight-metre high ceiling. The soft yellow halo around its edges glowed with the energy that it drew from the surrounding air. A pale aura of purple light smoked off from the halo into the dim light of the room, giving the Screen the look of a fluorescent deep-sea creature. Symbols and shapes rippled imperceptibly across the centre of its flat surface. Their meanings darted through his subconscious with lightning-quick intuitions.

From an early age, Mike had been fascinated by the symbols associated with the Zodiac, and further delving into the Vedic-based Nakshatra system in his late teens, making the Screen's centre-piece more personal to him. More connected. Interlinking circles continually rotated, readjusting, changing meaning at every move. The twelve Zodiacs were overlaid with the twenty-eight Nakshatras — the so-called unlucky twenty-eighth, Abhijit, being one many excluded — plus stars, planets, and heavenly bodies all mapped out in a cosmic dance. But then they had to ruin it with the simplistic time-line slapped right across the middle. Easier for the trackers to get their heads around. When Mike immersed himself in the Screen, he uncovered the ingredients for millions of different lives. Lives that, if born at that moment, would be lived like this or that. He observed lives in a split second of movement, that if not taken by a soul, didn't happen out here, but still played out in his head. Multiple paths all available simultaneously but only one taken.

The Screen represented the soul in the physical world as well as the non-physical dimensions, simultaneously superimposed on the universe. It took someone like Mike to interpret these signs using analysis and intuition.

The three horizontal lines that divided the Screen showed where a soul was and where it was headed. The bottom section, about a third of the height, was the Earth Plane. When a soul came into our world, the material plane or the third dimension, it came into the Earth Plane. When it left the third dimension it went out to the Etheric Plane, the next section up. Half the size of the first section, it was usually a stop-off zone for the souls as they either returned almost immediately to the Earth Plane or moved up to the Soul Plane which took up the other half of the Screen. Every now and again a soul would be seen moving right off the top of the board. According to Mike, that was the place to be. That was Heaven to him, like the name that was taped to the left side of the Screen.

Mike looked across to the three sheets of paper stuck at each of the zones: Heaven, Purgatory, and Hell. He had to grin at this. Hell was what his team was going through right now. Tracking the one soul they just couldn't lock onto. All this plus the pressure of navigating public perceptions and politicians continually using them as talking points.

Its development had been even more unstable.

The great global warming threat demanded less fossil fuel consumption and more bio-friendly energy sources, leading engineers and scientists across the globe to revisit basic technologies. In doing so they created some of the first organic technologies that provided their own power sources and which, through further enhancements, tapped into energy sources that life has been using for eons. Energy sources that constitute life, not consumption. And in looking into those traces of life, scientists were able to track the origins of this world and look through the basic third-dimensional elements into the areas long spoken about in myth and religion. Skeptics questioned the reality of these dimensions, and, not for the first time in history, questioned the blasphemous levels that science had reached.

The true power of what scientists had discovered became something that a handful of governments openly funded and pursued, supported by the people.

By taking these leaps, into what one would have assumed was the void, man emerged with a glimpse of the Divine. The Divine that is in all there is.

Since Zenzele Biyela's revolutionary system had burst onto the scene, and with him now heading up the Tracker Initiative within the South African Police Service, politicians had been at the frontlines of the furor, vying for political leverage, gauging how their constituents reacted to the controversial tech.

Those involved in criminology around the world saw how the developments could aid them in combating some of the violent crimes and mysteries that they had yet to solve. Everyone was watching.

"Angel," came the soft voice in his ear.

"Hicks," said Mike jumping off the table, "you okay?"

"No, but I've finished up here," she replied.

"Can you please respond when I call you next time, damn it?" he responded calmly.

"Sorry, Angel. I found her just after you made the call and I had to be with her. I felt she needed to be guided out."

"Okay, just let the docs come in and record the scene. We need all the clues we can get out of there. Tracker Team?"

"Sir!" came the multiple responses.

"Back to the station, ASAP. And up here in the Room of Hours for the debriefing," he ordered.

"Sir!" came the responses.

Nearly no sleep for three days dawned on his body all at once. The pain in his shoulders broke through his nervous system and shot a red flag up the back of his neck, a power surge of pain. Bent over the desk, he rubbed weakly at the rhythmic beat in his temples.

He should have been quicker. Five minutes could have made the difference.

The trackers were all trained emergency medical technicians; part of their gear tucked into their cargo pockets were medic tools. They had the means to resuscitate someone on the brink of death.

As he made his way up the incline of the room to the water cooler, he played the day through his hazy mind, trying to shave off seconds, thirty seconds, a minute, anything that could have saved time. Saved a life.

Mindlessly he took a paper cup off the top of the cooler and pressed the 'Fill' button.

"Goddamit," he said to himself.

He downed the ice-cold water, spilling some over his cheeks and neck. His body sagged and fell against the wall. He looked back at the room, at the blur of the Screen through the tears in his eyes.

#

The smells from Maydon Wharf drifted over Ruth, who sat on a horizontal stack of concrete pillars in the abandoned construction site. Dust from the emergency crews and vehicles bustling around her hung in the cooling evening air.

She could still feel the warmth of the other woman's body dying in her arms from minutes before. Her hands, arms, and shoulders were pulled tense and vibrating in steady pulses.

She had to close her eyes for a few seconds, but not long enough for anyone nearby to be concerned. A sharp intake of the harbour air brought some relaxation to her muscles.

The prolonged bellow of a nearby ship's horn made her lift her gaze to the darkening sky above. She could just make out some of the lights above the surrounding warehouses and stark buildings, twinkling on like a handful of stars.

The odours of oil and salt, diesel and fish — flashes of summer evenings from her childhood, when her parents were still together, eating spring rolls on the yacht mole pier — had a pungent tinge to them. She unclenched her fists, trying to relax, unconsciously rubbing a thumb on the back of her other hand for comfort.

She hadn't spoken to her mother in the past three weeks since this case had taken over her days and nights. She couldn't call her mother now. Not about this. Theirs was a catch up with small talk kind of relationship and not Salomie's daughter chasing a possible serial killer.

Besides, retirement in the old fishing town of Hermanus was quiet and tranquil for her mother and stepfather, far from this kind of city. Right now, she needed to speak to someone who understood what she was going through.

She held back the tears that were damming up behind her eyes as she drew another deep breath. Having grown up around Durban, she knew the tides, and it was probably going out, taking with it all the scum and muck dumped in the harbour that day.

How did they end up in this part of the city?

The chase seemed part of a distant lifetime, yet only half an hour ago they had been driving through the Durban streets, Angel relaying coordinates, frantically trying to reach Liza Chapman in time. They had come so close. To the killer. To Liza.

An ambulance came to a dusty stop a few metres from her.

The two EMTs were a blur as they jumped out and raced to the rear of the van. Someone yelled out to them from behind her as they wheeled the stretcher through the sand and gravel.

They didn't need an ambulance.

. The red-handled emergency scissors protruded from one of her thigh compartments of her dark blue cargo pants, sharing space with the splinter forceps and latex gloves. Mirrored on her left thigh were the straight forceps, trauma shears, window punch, and Velcro tourniquet. She hadn't needed those today.

She glanced at the flashing red lights of the ambulance. They didn't need the noise and commotion happening now. It was all too late. They had been too late.

She hunched forward, arms folded on her lap, hands resting at her hips. The small solid bulk of her mobile unit in her right pocket reassured her.

She tore at the Velcro flap, grasped the device and said, breathlessly, "Call Allen."

#

Deep inside the Ornithology department of the Durban Natural Science Museum, the rumble of the afternoon's traffic beat its way through the newly-renovated aluminium window frames, the odd truck reverberating through Allen's thick wooden desk. The rest of the staff had already left the musty wooden offices when Allen returned from the specimens room. He had turned off the neon lights, which he always found too overbearing as evening drew on.

A pile of loose papers lay spread out next to his screen as he transcribed his day's notes into the cold digital world in front of him. It still felt more natural to scrawl down his ideas onto a fresh, clean sheet of lined note paper rather than sitting behind a screen, portable or not. Transcribing allowed time for reflection and adjusting of ideas and facts. More often than not, it allowed for the rephrasing of a tirade or two.

Like the traffic outside, he clicked and spaced and plodded his way through, pausing every now and again to rethink something or figure out what the hell he'd written at the time. Sometimes it meant tossing out a complete section of meaningless scrawl.

Two broad wooden trays lay across the examining table a few metres from Allen in the centre of the large room. In one of his moments of reflection, Allen glanced up at the metallic blue plumage shimmering in the single overhead spotlight. Twenty neatly folded specimens seemingly asleep on their backs with tiny claws gripping the air.

Alongside the first lay a second tray containing similar specimens, the same to a layman, but distinct in their differences to the first tray to the expert.

Confirming a new species of bird had its ups and downs. For Allen it was like being on a treasure hunt. Although it wouldn't be him who would do the discovering, he was part of it. As if he had been given the treasure map, and all the clues, and all he had to do was prove it was there.

Before the scientists and birders could make a claim, they had to compile reams of data and evidence to prove their theory. And in the birding world, a very microscopic world in the professional sense, everyone wanted to have their day in the spotlight. They wanted their Loch Ness moment: 'Mine has never been spotted before...' And like any 'sighting', there were always the debunkers and naysayers.

But the Ornithology department was there to confirm or disprove, by compiling their own reams of data and facts, proving or disproving theories. He considered himself the only man for the job. A self-confessed cynic, he dared anyone to prove him otherwise.

But it was a slippery slope. 'Bugger the mob,' Allen always said. In the ornithology world, a simple 'rejected' stamp on a claim practically meant you had a hit out on you. Hate mail from a twitcher could be extreme. Professional dinners could be vindictive, and dead fowl were known to appear in the post.

If it wasn't somebody else's 'find' that he was working on, it was his own theories and investigations that kept Allen rapt in his work. The shape of a feather, the flight of a bird on the horizon. A dead pigeon on the sidewalk meant being frowned at by passersby as he picked at the fractured carcass with his pen. Or finger. A toothpick was also known to do the trick.

Allen's mobile bleeped next to his keypad, causing a brief embarrassing shriek. Wide-eyed, he quickly glanced around the empty room just in case he had been seen, then picked up the blue glowing block of plastic.

He pressed his forefinger on the translucent white-blue of the mobile. "Hello, my little kingfisher," he said as he recognised his wife on the small screen.

"Hi, Hon," came the faint response.

Allen stared closer at his mobile screen. Even in the faint light of Ruth's surroundings he could see her brow was sweaty and her cheeks flushed, a chalky dust streak across her olive skin and hair disheveled. And rather than her bright eyes staring back at him, they were heavy-lidded with exhaustion. "Hey, what's up?" he whispered. "Work hectic?"

"Something like that," Ruth replied. "And you?"

"Oh, you know. The usual," he said looking over his desk. "About to get the flock outta here." He thought he was funny.

Ruth, on the small screen, shook her head feebly as she walked through what seemed to Allen to be an industrial part of the city.

"Can you swing by and pick Caleb up for me?" She looked around. "It's going to be a late one. Yuneesha's organised for now, but the sooner you relieve her the better."

"Sure," he said. "Anything an ornithologist can help with?"

"Maybe later," she said. "Right now, Frank and I are about to head back to the station and check in with Angel."

She drew a deep breath, scrunching the corner of her mouth. Allen recognised the suppressed emotion that was being held in tightly.

"She died in my arms, Allen." She stopped and looked directly at him. Allen hunched over the glowing device on his desktop, holding her gaze as a slap of goose pimples hit his neck, arms, and scalp, rippling through every tiny hair on his body. Ruth crouched into the dimness of a car interior, face dimly lit by her screen's reflection; her hypnotic numbness penetrated his solar plexus.

"Ruth," he said softly.

She blinked herself to the present. "Hmm?"

"At least it was with you," he said. "Go and do what you do best, and I'll see you at home."

She nodded.

"I love you," he said.

She suppressed a smile and ended the call.

Allen rested his chin on his fists, gaze drifting to the two trays in the middle of the room. An island of light. Dead bodies on display.

"At least a soul somewhere gets its wings tonight," he said, with the knowledge that tracking a species was not quite the same as tracking a killer's soul.

As a child he was fascinated by Peter Pan. At eight years old he'd gone crying to his mother, a point she emphasised when she frequently recounted the story.

"I'm a bad person, Mommy."

"A what?" she had asked.

"I'm ugly. I don't think nice things."

"And why would you think that, Allie?"

"Cos I can't fly. I'm not flying." He stamped his feet on the kitchen floor. "See?"

"What do you mean you're not flying?"

"I don't have any happy thoughts; that's why I'm not flying around the room. And now I'm thinking ugly thoughts so I'm never going to fly, Mommy!"

"Ah." His mother quickly caught onto his eight-year-old mind. "But remember, Allie, that it's not just happy thoughts that you need to make you fly."

His body unslumped and perked up at this. "It's not?"

"No," she continued. "You need a sprinkling of fairy dust as well, silly. Remember?"

"Oh." He'd beamed.

"So, until you find a fairy, you'll have to settle with being on solid ground, my angel."

And that had been the start of his winged and plumed obsession. Every day he felt he was getting closer. Naturally, as he grew older, he figured he'd need to get his pilot's license. He was a practical man.

Even now, at thirty-six, he considered himself a practical man with a spiritual wife. No longer the fist-clenching frustration that made up their early relationship. She had been hell-bent on questioning and probing and planting seeds that had intrigued even him, the practical man. The birth of his son had pushed his agnostic upbringing to new limits.

He had always appreciated that his mother had not preconditioned his mind into a religious one. "The universe is right there in front of you," she had said to him when he had asked about the world around him. "All you need to know, feel, or experience is there waiting for you to dip your feet into. How deep you want to go is up to you, and no-one else."

As a scholar and factual man, he'd concentrated on his work and flight.

"So, your religion is birds," Ruth had stated bluntly one night before they were married.

"My what is what?" He'd blurted horrified.

"Your life, your beliefs, and what makes you who you are is your study of birds. You pretty much eat, sleep, and defecate birds." She stared back at him with deep green eyes. The challenge had been made.

"That doesn't constitute a religion."

"Okay, professor, what's a religion? Define it from a scientist's point of view, please?"

Without missing a beat, "An elite group of people sitting at the top, forcing their interpretation of the world around them on the masses below. Frowning on them when they don't read or know off by heart the Holy Word and forcing them to attend church once a week."

"So, kinda like some twitcher scientist deciding to name that strange bird an emu and telling me that that one flying over there is a crow and that one pecking over there is a pigeon. And when I disagree and say, 'No, I think that one's a dove and that one is the crow,' he gets all hot and bothered and ends up pulling out a thick bird guide from twenty years ago that his father passed down to him and proceeds to point furiously shouting, 'it says so in the book!'"

"I'm not even going to dignify an argument to that."

"You've just replaced one set of rules and guides and beliefs and hierarchical systems for another."

"You don't get… Shit!"

"Fine. Then explain to me what you feel about birds. And I mean, what is it about feathers that gets you all ruffled?"

Allen never believed that yin and yang crap, but this woman was definitely his polar opposite.

"Watching a bird in flight is like watching the ultimate expression of freedom. That's always fascinated me. Not restricted to the ground. Go anywhere. No limits."

"The scientist is a poet."

Allen had blushed. And a few years later, Ruth had

revealed that at that moment she had softened.

"Okay," she'd mused, "what about pet birds? How do you feel about that?"

"Well, for one it's unnatural. Don't get me wrong, I'm no activist or anything, but the idea is repulsive. Even Leonardo da Vinci couldn't handle the idea and went so far as to buy caged birds in the markets, only to release them a second later."

"Probably pissed off some Italians in the process."

Allen had snorted. "One of the first true scientists. Everyone thinks of him as this way-out artist, but he was really a scientist. He studied everything."

Ruth had asked, "How about that Mona Lisa smile?"

"She's not smiling," Allen had said matter-of-factly.

"And that's a theory of yours?"

"No, that's a fact. If you look at many of his portraits, it was how he lit and painted the mouths. Imagine someone clenching their jaw and staring you down as they humour you. The mouth sometimes pulls in at the corners. That's her expression. The same as his 'John the Baptist'. Intense concentration, drawing you into their eyes where you can almost see their thoughts and emotions."

"You've obviously thought long and hard about this," Ruth had said.

"I'm interested in flight and those that tried, sometimes in vain, to achieve it."

"And Leonardo tried centuries before the Wright brothers."

Allen had nodded. "But, I'm not sure if achieving it was as important as it was in the studying."

"Apparently, Leonardo was a pretty spiritual guy. He didn't like the church much."

"If I took anything from Leonardo it was that the soul is like a caged bird. It's limited by this form, the physical body.

Death is the freedom or release from that cage. Death means total liberation."

"And your thoughts on what's on the other side?" She had asked, intrigued by this hidden side of the man in front of her.

"That's as far as I go with this, thank you."

#

The body of a woman, aged forty-six, is gently lifted from the cold dusty concrete floor where she died twenty minutes earlier. People move around her, going about their business, making notes and checking details. A semi-transparent bag is brought over, unzipped, and clumsily placed under, over and finally, around her, then gently zipped closed. Her pale features are just noticeable through the frosted surface.

Her body is placed on a soft, cool stretcher, but she doesn't feel any more. The heat from the quickly erected field spotlights does little to warm the already cooling body. The stretcher is pushed into the back of a red and white van. The rear doors thud closed and the noises from outside are dulled and subdued.

The van starts up, sending soft vibrations through the stretcher and the woman's body. The two medical officers sit silently on either side, expressionless. The rubber wheels move ever so slightly as the van pulls off; first down a ramp, then bumping out into the night air on a gravel road.

There is no siren. No need. A radio crackles noisily in the driver's compartment.

The warm glow of sunset fades outside. Streetlights flick by as the van rounds a corner and the noise of the gravel fades away. The city at night comes alive. The sounds of traffic hiss by outside the van. The squeak of brakes at an intersection. And another. Turn.

A quick move to the left and the van goes down a ramp. Rubber squeals on polished cement. The van comes to a gentle stop. The doors open to the empty echo of the basement. Clinical scents replace the van's ozone electric engine, and the stretcher is flicked and clicked back onto its rubber wheels.

A click and two automatic doors slide apart. Chemicals and squeaky shoes. The stretcher glides noiselessly along and around corners. Overhead neons blink past. The frosted bag seems to have misted up. The features of the woman are less visible underneath. Two more doors slide automatically open. Another corner and into a large square room.

Two men exchange quick muffled words. A tablet device bleeps. Notes. Enters.

The woman's body is taken gently off the stretcher and placed on a large steel table. The zip is opened. Nobody notices the faint warm air that is released in the cold of the room. She is lifted up and out of the ice-coloured bag and onto the cold, hard table.

She doesn't feel any more.

#

The entire fourteenth floor, intensifying inside the central Room of Hours, was humming with the energy from the day's activities. The Tracker Unit was spread out in small groups, discussing their experiences in low voices. Ruth sat in the middle of the amphitheatre-style control room, arms folded and feet up on one of the interactive tabletops. She analysed the Screen, moving slowly, watching the patterns change: Mike had been right; she'd headed right off the Screen. A good consolation for what her body had endured. The full picture of what the victim had gone through would be revealed over the next few hours, but she knew what to expect. She had seen it.

Banks, her partner, would be in a group somewhere, watching her from the corner of his eye, checking if she was doing okay. He always worried how she handled this part of the job, the part she too often took home, yet Frank never brought it up. This was the third person found in the last three weeks. They'd picked up on the pattern within days of the second victim being reported missing, and started doing the background and soul match that would eventually lead to her physical whereabouts. Unfortunately, they couldn't say the same for the criminal behind it. They had nothing to go on, nothing to give them the slightest clue to latch on to a Soul Trace.

All the victims had been clean of anything that could be broken down for DNA matching. There was nothing that even hinted at the killer's identity let alone his Birth Origin. And that was what it all came down to: Birth Origin. The trackers needed at least that to trace a soul to the here and now. It was always weird to her that they needed to go back in time to when somebody was born to find where they were currently, and even possibly where they were headed. That was how you got on the Screen if you were a "baddie"; and once you were on, you were tracked every step of the way. If you were a "goodie" and you were on the Screen, then you were probably headed for a Trauma/Dead as a vic or the need to be monitored post-incident. A person only ever left the Screen if they were caught and rehabbed, and even then they might still be tracked; or if they T/D and the soul went to the Beyond. Trauma/Dead was marked on the Screen by a red dot, and that was when they really had to watch the Screen closely. Where will it go, where will it pop up? T/B — Trauma/Birth — or Soul Rehab?

Coming back to the room, Ruth was aware of everyone talking in quieter voices. They were all anticipating the debriefing. She just wanted time to absorb it. Time alone. But she would have to deal with it in her own time.

She caught the eye of Banks to her right. Just leave me

alone. He made a move in her direction. Just leave me the …

"Right! Pay attention," said Mike on his raised platform backed by the huge Screen. "The Unit head is on his way up from the media briefing and wants a few words." He looked out from his slightly elevated platform over the ten trackers and five assistants present. Everyone began to gravitate to the centre of the room. Ruth stayed where she was. A moment later the doors at the back of the room burst open and a tall, athletic figure strode to the front of the room. Zenzele Biyela wasn't your typical suit and tie. He had a way of making business attire look casual and relaxed, and his short, steel-grey hair always looked as though he had been working through the world's problems. He stepped up alongside Mike and loosened his tie.

"Now that all the bullshit is out of the way," he gave a wry smile and held his hands together, "I want to say wenze kahle, well done, to every one of you. It's small consolation, I know, but for a team that has only been in operation for a few years now, and running on the sniff of an oil rag of a budget, we, you, are providing something that we can all be proud of." He turned and placed his hand on Mike's shoulder with a nod. "The next week is going to be hell on earth, but without taking too much notice of the world on our doorstep," he pointed out the room, "and those *SoulsFirst* and their *S.O.S.* fanatics baying for our blood, particularly mine, we can and will catch this bastard. Maybe then all the naysayers will back right off and the likes our favourite politician, Premier Khayyám," his tone soured as he uttered the name, "will concede that maybe, just maybe, we are running one of the most important innovations of our time. Eish, of any time for that matter, and something that transcends religious stigmatism. I know I speak for all of us when I say that we have all staked our reputations, our livelihoods, and our family responsibilities on this unit. The faith that you have put into this endeavour, we, in return, put in you. Know that we back this unit one hundred and ten percent. But let's not allow the political games behind the scenes to stall this process. *Inhlanhla*." He gave a curt nod to Mike and left the room.

"The Docs have started sending through the data from the scene," Mike said looking down at his glass tablet, "so let's see what comes through as we go." He checked some of the data. "Okay, as before, the vic was found," here he stopped and looked up, trying to find Ruth, "by Tracker Hicks, with her trachea penetrated but the wound showing no signs of infection. Both the breathing pipe and gauze around the wound were in good condition and looking new for the day," Mike put his tablet onto a desk in front of him, leaning his weight over it. "This guy took the time, probably every day, to clean and dress the wound. Now remember," he stood full, arms on his hips, "this guy is neat and precise. We aren't looking for an obviously 'out-there' nutcase. He's methodical and a perfectionist. And according to the ME's report on the previous vics, he doesn't need to have medical experience to perform these home tracheotomies. What they're suggesting is that it's at a degree of perfection that, outside of the other two, he's probably done before. Maybe this means on other people, but because we do our job right, it probably means only on small animals or the Maltese poodle next door." A small murmur lightened the atmosphere.

"As I mentioned," he continued, "all we need is a link to his soul and we can at least track him on the Screen. Then it's just a matter of time."

"So," Mike looked down at his data, "no obvious sexual assault, but the autopsy will tell, and going on the other two vics, there shouldn't be any." He turned to face the centre of the Screen. "I've been scanning the astros for any people born in the last hundred years with any female issues that might emerge in their cycle, but that's a needle in a galaxy. Plus," he turned back, continuing with a grumble, "we still don't even know if it's current life or past life shit that we're sifting through, so let's hope this guy's paid up on his karma."

Narrowing down a criminal's motives meant wading through archive files on previous suspects from pre-tracker days. *Pre-dated crime.* Ruth turned to the back of the vast room, where all the rookies cut their teeth. The glassed-in control room, the Crystal Ball, overlooked the room and Screen, housing two rows of consoles that the latest trackers used to access all available data, globally. Piles of searchable data files that, nine times out of ten, weren't helpful because most were unsolved, without even a suspect associated that they could latch a Soul Trace to for tracking.

A beeping noise brought Ruth's attention back to the Screen as a flash of light revealed a square projection of a middle-aged man with a pair of neat optical gear over his eyes, just like an exaggerated geek. Everyone focused on him, as he seemed to straighten himself in his white jumpsuit, preparing to address the room. A namestrip at the bottom of the square read "Documentor Greenburg: 32510".

"Angel," he hesitated.

"We're listening, Doc," replied Angel facing the Screen, "what you got for us?"

The man on the Screen looked down for a second, pressing something on his glass tablet, "I'm sending you the 3-D mapping of the area, multiple angles," he looked up for a moment. The left side of the Screen revealed a single rectangle of white, systematically breaking up into smaller sections as visuals of a construction site from various angles appeared in each. "Plus," he continued, "Based on Hicks' description of how she found the vic, an approximate modeling of how she would have been in the environment." With this, a blue semi-translucent 3-D shape of a woman emerged over most of the visuals.

"Similar to the other vics," Doc continued, looking at his tablet, "she seems to have been placed in the location fairly abruptly, but still with a lot of care in the placement and covering tracks, almost." He swiped his fingers around his device, simultaneously shifting one of the central visual's angles bringing a ramp into view. "Footprints have been swept but traces of a trolley's tracks are visible leading up to this level. These match a two-wheel loading trolley like this model."

A catalogue image of a rotating trolley appeared on screen.

"What about a wheelchair pulled back onto its back wheels?" asked Angel.

"No," replied the Doc, "the tread is smooth, flat, and wider than a wheelchair's. This may have been rushed but they knew what they were doing."

"And it's consistent with the previous victim locations. But at least the tracks are something. If he's slipping, then it could be a matter of time before he slips on his ass."

"I wouldn't be so sure of that, Angel," said the Doc looking down at his screen, "I mean, we've done multiples of the area and haven't found anything out of place other than the swept debris. And even that's pretty slim on clues."

"Well, he had the jump on us because we weren't expecting her to turn up for three more days," said Angel exasperated.

"She was placed, naked, on what seems to be a new white sheet," continued the Doc, "in an area that had been swept of any debris." The view came over the top of the glowing blue figure, zooming out slightly to allow it to fill the frame. "And, according to Hicks, her arms were placed over her abdomen," the view shifted down the blue waist line, "and her legs neatly together."

"He must've placed her just before we got there and us turning up scared him off".

"Cause of death will tell us more."

"There had to have been a reason," Angel said stroking his chin.

"Well," said the Doc, "that's your job. I just shoot 'em, and log 'em." He lowered his tablet, "The vic should be arriving, as we speak, at the ME for the detailed modeling. From there we can patch it into our visuals for a comprehensive, and then you guys can pick the puzzle apart. Questions, suggestions?"

"Nothing for now, Doc," said Angel as he turned to face the group of puzzled onlookers. "Materials? Where's Visser?"

"Already checking, Sir," a head popped up from behind a screen. "I've zoomed in on the label visible on the sheet. Checking any recent purchases of white linen in the province in the past month."

"Good," replied Angel as he walked slowly through the desks, "Hicks, I want you and Banks at the ME's ASAP for immediate info."

#

Located on the north side of the SAPS complex, on the ground level, the stark whiteness of the Medical Examiner's theatre always jarred with Ruth. A contrast in so many ways to the Room of Hours: bright lights and wall-to-wall whiteness. Quiet. Lifeless. As if life itself had been sterilized.

A middle-aged man with dusty grey hair pulled out an overhead screen above the examination table and with a nod at Ruth and Frank said, "Remember to state your names when wanting to speak." He punched a few on-screen keys, then added, "And let's keep to the medical facts rather than Sherlock Holmes ramblings." Removing a pen-like, digital microscope, umbilically attached to the screen, he leaned over the white sheet hiding the body beneath.

"Recording on Wednesday the eighth day of September, two thousand and thirty-eight. Beginning the autopsy of the identified body of Liza Ann Chapman, as positively confirmed by the Tracker Squad. Trackers Hicks and Banks present for observation and information gathering in real time. Medical Examiner Dos Santos speaking, I will be performing the post-mortem examination." He walked over to the head of the table and gently pulled the sheet down, revealing the pale face of a woman. He stopped the sheet at the shoulders and folded it neatly over, placing the microscope on her skin and looked up at the video feed on the screen.

"I can assume that the victim is between forty-five and fifty years of age, and this has been confirmed by the Tracker team's information in that she was born 18 September nineteen ninety, having died some ten days before her forty-eighth birthday. Her hair is dark brown, slight greying, and shoulder length. Her complexion is fair."

Ruth approached the table and tilted her head slightly to get a better look at the pale, lifeless body in front of her. Why were you killed so soon? Martha and Mary-Anne were nearly two weeks apart. This was too soon if they were going to look at possible time patterns.

"The hair on the victim's head is damp," continued the ME as he clicked on the microscope's tiny light to illuminate the scalp, "possibly perspiration and water." With bleeps, data gathered and areas of the screen pulsed on and off. He squinted at the information. "Both." He moved down to the left arm and did the same, then on to the pubic hair. "Hmm, there also seems to be water on the rest of her body hair, which would indicate that she was fully immersed at some point."

"Let's just check something". He placed the microscope in both the victim's ears and nose. "There appears to be H_2O residue in the victim's ears, nose and," he looked into the mouth, "mouth."

"Tracker Banks: couldn't that just be body fluids?"

Without moving his head, the ME looked up at Frank and said coldly, "Not with that much chlorine," and clicked the microscope light off. "And not like this."

"Tracker Hicks: so could she have been drowned?"

"Possible, but," he raised a warning finger, "let's do this systematically so we don't miss anything out."

The ME turned the microscope light back on, adjusted the magnification, and looked into both of the victim's eyes. "Nothing unusual with the eyes," he continued, moving to the mouth again, "The mouth is free of any foreign matter, apart from the H_2O mentioned earlier, and what seems to be white mucus at the back of the throat." The beam of the microscope moved down the chin and down to below the jaw-line where the ME paused.

Ruth came in closer. "What's that reddening around the mouth and neck?"

"We'll get to that, Tracker Hicks," he cut in.

"I didn't notice that when I got to her," she whispered.

"Probably a delayed skin reaction, or because of the low light that you found her in," replied the ME, giving a sigh and without averting his attention. "The skin around the mouth and trachea wound has slight abrasions and some other residue." He took a microscopic reading from the side of the mouth and neck, and continued, "Looks like it could also be a reaction. I'm picking up traces of adhesive on the skin."

"Tracker Banks: adhesive?" asked Banks as he now approached the table.

"Tracker Hicks: Like gum or tape," responded Ruth. "It could've been duct-tape that caused it."

"Possibly," replied the ME noncommittally and looked at the data above. Various products scrolled through.

"Tracker Hicks: Glue?"

"Maybe something was taped into the trachea. A breathing pipe or something. That would cause these types of marks."

"But what about taping the mouth? Sorry. Tracker Banks: how would that help anything?"

"Moving on to the trachea wound," the ME ignored the question. "The surrounding skin is clean of any infection. The wound itself is fairly neat in its execution. But," he said looking closer, "there is foaming inside the cavity, consistent with the back of the throat."

"Tracker Hicks: Foaming?" asked Ruth.

The ME looked up at Ruth, "Looks like it could be drowning." He scanned the microscope over the opening, and looked the readings over. "A mixture of air, water, and even surfactant, which is made up of lipoprotein that is secreted by the alveolar cells of the lungs."

"Tracker Banks: So he could have held her head under water."

"Tracker Hicks: yeah, but it doesn't fit the other two victims," said Ruth, "they were just suffocated, and it doesn't account for the tape on the mouth. Why tape the mouth when you're trying to drown someone?"

"The tape doesn't necessarily have to connect to the cause of death," said the ME.

"Tracker Banks: to keep her quiet?"

"No need, considering she's incommunicado with a tracheotomy," said the ME pointing at the neck wound.

The information was swirling in Ruth's head. We need to know the motives behind what he's doing in order to profile his soul. Everything is intricately connected to everything else.

"Tracker Banks: but could she have drowned? She was still dying when we found her."

"She could have been clinically dead, but something jolted her back to life. A heavy impact that could get her heart pumping again."

"We could've saved her?" hissed Ruth.

"That depends on how long she was out for and the fact that her lungs still contained water. There's a high probability she drowned again. No hope of resuscitation."

"It couldn't have helped trying to breathe through that damn small hole," said Frank, "like choking on a soda, and no matter how much you open your mouth you just can't get it open enough to breathe properly."

"But, there were no signs of water sources nearby or any water for that matter, so the killer would have had to lug the body here while she was dying instead of waiting to see if she was actually dead," said Banks. "Also, the dirt around the vic was only slightly disturbed. Not like someone struggling for their life."

"And, why not drown her properly?" asked Ruth, "Why didn't he just finish the job?"

Just then the overhead screen bleeped and flickered some information across it. The ME studied it for a moment.

"Blood tox results," he mumbled to himself. "The same sedative that was found in the other two vics."

"The proliferation of the drug through her systems indicates that it was in her system for at least half an hour before death."

"He drugged her then drowned her?" asked Ruth.

"Are you saying that the drowning was accidental?" asked Banks surprised, "How do you accidentally drown your victim? The other two were drowned outright. Why would this be any different?"

"If she took in even a mouthful of water then the cavity would have made it difficult to eject the water completely. The water would have been trying to come out her mouth *and* trachea puncture wound simultaneously. There wouldn't have been enough force to push it out the mouth because the throat was counteracting it. And while the wound is expelling water, it's coming back down from the mouth as she desperately gasps for air."

"And without being resuscitated she would have—" he began just as Ruth interrupted him.

"Wait, check her mouth for DNA from saliva. Maybe he did try to resuscitate her."

The ME looked up at Ruth sympathetically, "You know this device would've picked up any other DNA. But I will be doing a manual swab of all cavities and surface areas before I wrap up." He looked back down at the body on the table. "As I was going to say, without being resuscitated she would have gone into a coma. The killer may have assumed she was dead or close to it. And without the natural motion of the lungs being able to bring in sufficient air because the fluid couldn't be released properly, she would have drowned or suffocated very slowly. Being drugged may not have helped the situation."

"Shit," said Banks, "that's nasty. Now we've got an accidental serial killer? I don't think so."

"It's just that it looks like she died before he planned," she turned to Frank, "he wasn't expecting her to die. And if his intention wasn't to drown her or even kill her, yet," said Ruth, "then that would explain why the placement of the body was rushed."

"He thumps her down on the ground, she starts spluttering and coming to; the killer does a 'What the holy hell', realizes it's too late with the sound of sirens in the air, and bolts, leaving a tread mark in the process."

This raised more questions about what the killer was doing, and they still hadn't come any closer to figuring out the reason for the tracheotomies.

"Placing the victim on a clean white sheet, even under pressure, indicates care, Frank. It could be remorse or some emotional connection to the victim. They aren't just a piece of waste discarded. But this is odd."

"I need to carry on here," interrupted the ME. "If you're okay with that?"

The ME moved his attention to the wrists of the victim. "Similar markings to those found on the other two victims, indicating restraints."

Ruth moved away from the table, deep in thought. Frank turned to follow her.

"What're you thinking, Hicks?" he asked.

"This is a weird setup." She looked at him intently. "Why drug her if he's going to drown her? And drowning is not his thing, so it has to be accidental."

"Ok, we've got all we need for now," said Banks turning to the ME.

"Oh joy. Peace and quiet," replied the ME, "I will upload the full report as soon as I'm done here. I'll check stomach contents etcetera just to clarify what he'd given her to eat, if anything."

"Thanks," said Ruth, "and if there's anything that stands out, let us know as soon as."

They both turned and walked through the theatre door.

"Frank, Mary-Anne, victim number two, was only reported missing two days after the first body turned up."

"That means that people took two days to miss her."

"But we found that out when it was too late. Only when Mary-Anne turned up dead did we realise that Missing Persons had been too busy looking at Martha White's family and work colleagues as suspects, never guessing she was the first of a serial murder."

The automatic doors leading into the foyer of the high-rise hissed open.

"Okay," said Frank leading them towards the elevator doors and pressing the up button. "And we only locked onto Liza Chapman's Soul Trace last week, a few days after Mary-Anne, when we had sifted through over a hundred missing persons fitting the age of Martha and Mary-Anne. And even then we were lucky by checking age-related cases."

"Martha White had been missing for approximately two weeks before she died, and so was Mary-Anne. But it was eight days for Liza. So the timing on her is out and definitely wasn't intentional."

The elevator dinged and the large double doors opened.

"Yeah," said Frank as they stepped in side by side while Ruth thumbed the '14' button. "We could either have a really pissed off killer or someone who feels really crap about what happened and is going to over-compensate in some freaky act of remorse."

"So watch this space."

#

"You *are* kidding, right?" said Angel turning his attention away from the Screen.

"It goes a far way in explaining the way we found Liza," replied Ruth, "plus cause of death."

"If she was accidentally drowned, that would also mean that he was trying some weird shit with water," said Banks. "I mean if he was dunking her head in water, it would imply that he was either trying to drown her or just mess with her."

"What about water-boarding?"

"That would cover the face, not necessarily the throat as well, and not in that concentration," said Frank.

Angel took a deep breath. "Let's check backgrounds relating to water. That includes Pisces," he turned to look at the Screen, "Ardra, Scorpio, Aquarius and Cancer. Maybe even an astro that has too much water with a rising water sign as well like Cancer-Cancer, Punarvasu or Gemini sun with rising Cancer. We aren't looking at the rosy, positive sides to the signs or signs that seem negative; it's their dark side being revealed that is of prime importance. A water's negative pole is like an emotional vampire who can drain the life of even those closest to them. In the emotional sense." He turned back to Ruth and Frank. "This is more than we had before. Good work guys." He looked over their heads and addressed the room, "I need minute by minute uploads of missing persons reported today, as they come in," he boomed, "let's hope the next vic comes from a functional family who wants to know her every move. Look out for the age, but don't rule anything out at this stage."

#

The smell of that night's dinner lingered through the dimly lit lounge where Ruth lay wide-eyed and exhausted on the sofa. The day had taken up too much of her energy, and although Allen fetching Caleb had helped, she didn't like breaking her son's routine, let alone her own routines. It just keeps everything in balance, she believed. She didn't like Caleb being out of her control, where she didn't have immediate access to him. Even Allen, her own husband, taking Caleb wasn't the same thing.

Almost six years ago she'd nearly lost him, and she was neurotic about losing him now. The pang of guilt fluttered through her solar plexus, just in case she forgot. The last few months were taking their toll on her, and today hadn't helped.

Liza Chapman had been dying in her arms only hours earlier. She had felt the life slowly leave her body and could do nothing about it. All she could do was to hold her and speak to her. Telling her it was okay. Telling her that it was all over and that it was okay to leave.

Caleb had taught her that. Lying on the kitchen floor all those years ago, she had felt her son and her life seeping out of her body like the warm blood she was lying in. She had asked in quiet desperation, What would happen to him? Would he know what had happened? Would he know where to go? Too many questions at the wrong time.

Recovering in the hospital, she'd had his incubator kept alongside her bed, watching him every day, listening to the heart monitor. She had vowed to find out about lost souls, souls whose bodies die suddenly, who remain here in our world, confused, alone, and unaware that they'd actually died; refusing to believe it.

She had followed her inner voice, guiding her to say what she felt necessary to victims of crimes and accidents. She made sure she was the first one on the scene, and she had coached many trackers to do the same.

"It's all over, Liza," she had said to the delicate lifeless figure in her arms, "we've found you. The pain has finished; your family will know where you are and what has happened. They will all be okay. You don't have to worry about them." She had felt the back of her neck tingling, energy rushing through her, bringing tears streaming down her face. "It's okay to leave now. Feel the light drawing you to it. Feel the beauty and the peace and the Love that is there." She had looked up, "It's time to go now, Liza. You've done what you needed to do." She had lowered her head and sobbed with joy and sadness and whispered in her ear, "I'll find who did this to you," and knew that in the end it was okay for her to let go as well.

The sound of soft padding footsteps brought her back from her thoughts. Allen emerged from the dark hallway leading from the bedrooms.

"Cay's finally asleep," he said softly as he made his way to the kitchen. He took a glass off a shelf and poured water from a jug on the counter.

"I think he picked up on your energy from the day at dinner," he said coming round the sofa. "Yuneesha did say that he was a bit confused about what was happening." He lifted her feet off the couch, sat down, and put them across his lap.

"Shitty day at work, huh?" he asked as he started rubbing her feet.

"Hmm," she groaned as the relief tingled up her legs.

Allen was her grounding rod, her skeptic, and her realist. When her head was stuck in the clouds, in Soul Land as he called it, he'd always bring her back down to earth. She needed that a lot lately. She would go mad without him. He always gave her a different spin on things, something that flicked a switch or something that just snapped her out of herself.

They had met through a mutual friend, her partner Frank. They had been at one of his rowdy house parties and had somehow ended up on the enclosed patio in a huge argument about religion, spirituality and, according to Allen, the "God-like" theory of tracking souls. Some of the other guests had just stared at them with mild drunken amusement as they battled it out. Frank made light of the situation by standing in between them, nervously sipping his beer.

A year later they were married, with a very amusing send-off by Frank, the best man slash maid of honour, to which they sheepishly chuckled along. Being Allen's college friend, Frank had always pulled the piss out of the 'realist', who he had constantly asked the question "What if…," to which Allen would reply "But it's not…". The final joke for the day was Frank commenting on the fact that Allen had finally seen the light and married "one of us: an idealist."

And that was why she loved him so much. They were not trying to change each other. They had their views, which sometimes gave them a new perspective on something or just got them thinking. It was never boring, maybe heated, but that led to other things. He was the first person that she felt truly connected to. They were so open about their differences that she seemed to trust him more for it.

Frank had asked her early on in their relationship, how

she could stand to be around Allen if he annoyed her. And they disagreed on some pretty important shit. She had simply replied, "Imagine being around someone who always agreed with you. I don't want a 'yes-man', Frankie."

"Anybody home?" asked Allen.

"Hi, I'm back," she said startled. "Sorry about that. Thanks for picking up Cay today."

"No problem, but I think that you need to chat with him in the morning and let him know that you're okay. He's sensitive to your moods." He stopped, then said, "You are okay, aren't you? I heard the latest over the radio on the way home. Whose bright idea was it to give the killer that name? They said that the Tracker Unit had named him."

"Well, somebody had to." She smiled wryly.

"The Ventriloquist? I mean come on," said Allen poking her side.

"Hey, it was better than Tracheotomy Man from Rob Collins!" she shoved his hand away. "He is such a jerk."

"Why the Ventriloquist, though?" he asked seriously.

"Look, we still haven't got the faintest idea for the killer performing tracheotomies, and before we dismiss it as some freakish fetish, we have to consider the possibility that it's the key to the killer's motives."

"Okay, but it's not as if it's what kills the victims," said Allen.

"Sure, but it gives us something to latch onto in order to profile the killer and his soul," replied Ruth, "and something as significant as a trache is either just a calling card or it has a real purpose."

"And you don't think that it's just a calling card, do you?"

"Not after what happened this evening," replied Ruth closing her eyes for a moment. She took in a deep breath then exhaled.

He placed his hand on her thigh. "Tell me about it."

She bit her lip, then began, "We were wrapping up the debriefing in the Room of Hours, having just come back from the ME's. I'm sitting there reliving the last few moments of Liza lying in my arms. I had held her for a while after I had taken her through the release process, and all I kept repeating to her lifeless body was if only we had arrived sooner we could have saved her. She could have at least had the chance to tell us what had happened to her."

"It would definitely make catching the killer a lot easier," said Allen.

"It's not just about that, Allen," she turned to him.

"Sorry, I know," he said.

"It makes their release a lot easier," she said softly, "it means they can let go of this world without the sense of unfinished business. Anyway," she continued, "we're about to leave for the ME's and Angel says that we need to name the killer before the media come up with something stupid. After three victims they know that we're dealing with a serial and they can't resist being the first to give the people something catchy to talk about. It makes our job a lot more difficult when the name assumes a lot of crap about the killer's motives.

"So, Angel says he's got to bring Biyela up to speed; what with that snake politician gunning for him, us, he has to be on top of everything that goes out to the public."

"Yes."

"Anyway," she shook her head and continued, "he's asking for suggestions. And I'm thinking about the cavity in Liza's throat, in Martha's throat and in Mary-Anne's throat. The rest of the crew start mumbling and acting like idiots and that's when Collins comes up with his gem, being completely serious about it, and all the guys start jibing him. So Angel booms, 'Shuddup!' and that's when my hair on my head goes all prickly and itchy."

"Ah," said Allen with a smirk, "intuition kicking in."

"Quieten down, skeptic," said Ruth nudging her heel in his crotch.

"Ungh, sorry," grunted Allen protecting himself. He held her gaze. "What do you think it is?"

"I don't think, I know," she said still looking at him, but through him, "he's doing the talking."

Allen cocked his head, "How do you mean?"

She looked away, feeling her face getting hot. She swallowed hard. "Whatever the incident was that makes the killer do what he's doing, the fact is that if you have a tracheotomy, you can't talk because the air's not passing through the vocal cords. That means that they're not talking, they're listening."

"Why would they have to listen? Who says he's even talking?"

"Hey, I'm just telling you what I got," she said, retrieving her legs and sitting up on the sofa. "He might have had someone in his life that never gave him the opportunity to talk, or they did too much talking. Whatever."

"I think the hair on my head's just stood on end. And, that's not intuition, that's because it's creepy. So why not just gag them with a rag and some duct tape?"

"Exactly, a ventriloquist's dummy can still move its mouth, but can't talk. It has to sit there and listen."

"And you don't see a ventriloquist's lips moving, but he's using the dummy to vent his frustrations on the world."

"Ja, so we're looking for someone who fits right into society. Not the regular serial type."

"What do you mean by that?"

"Most serial killers either come across as slightly off or they are recluses. If they hold a nine to fiver then they tend to stay indoors at night, and that's when they do their thing."

"So you think the killer's a party animal?"

"Not quite, but if they're able to release their frustrations then there's no reason why they shouldn't be able to interact on a social level. Keeping the victims for a prolonged period would show that he doesn't feel the need to go and kill all the time. His nocturnal habits could be quite normal."

"I didn't hear all this on the news."

"I didn't go into this with the Unit. It's just my feelings on it. What did the media have to say anyway?"

"Oh, other than the nickname, just vague references to the victim. No name released or cause of death just yet. You know, blowing a lot of hot air around. I thought we'd relax tonight. Get it out of your system for a few hours."

"Sorry, hon. It's all still flying through my head at a mile a minute."

"How about I run you a hot bath?"

"I'd like that," she said and tilted her head. "Maybe you can join me."

He twitched an eyebrow, "*Hey.*"

"Hey, nothing," she smacked his chest, "just a hot bath."

#

Steam clung to the ceiling like a thick fog, looking down at her lying in the bath. The white wall tiles and paintwork always reminded her of the hospital. It looked like it smelled. Cold. She could smell the white linen. She could smell the drips. She could smell the chromed bed frame. The cold hands. The cold needles. The cold cotton swabs cleaning, disinfecting.

She closed her eyes and shuddered in the steaming water. The noises from outside intruded. She glanced up at the ceiling again. Music filtered through the closed glass window. She reached a steaming foot out of the water and awkwardly opened the hot tap, cool for a moment, then boiling hot. She breathed in the damp air, and shut the tap off with her other foot.

She took in a deep breath and then under she went. Silence. Warm, womb-like silence. Her eyes closed out the light from above. A dark, quiet redness enveloped her. She could hear a gentle beating — her heart soothing and calming her. She could sense it slowing down as it reacted to the lack of oxygen. Slowing more. Calming her. Quiet. If only for a minute.

Then, a tinkle; someone in the block dropping a coin on a hard floor. It could have been a floor above her, or a floor below her, but it sounded like it was right in the bath with her. Her heart picked up pace. A chair grated along a floor, and a fucking toilet flushed.

She screamed a loud, frothing, bubbling scream, that no-one else could hear, "SHUT THE FUCK UP," and burst out the water.

FILE: Ma'at Cast
Transmitted 22:00 UTC
ce 2038, September 8

```
mkdir audiobot//
if (!audio.content.startsWith(ma-at))
(!serverQueue) {
'download started: 22:01 UTC'
if (audio.content.startsWith(`${ma-at}play`));
```

Now, world, what would you have me do?

The soul tracking system is taking root around the globe, and the world willingly watches on as the flagship unit in South Africa continues to fumble in the darkness. And though they wish to be the faint light that pushes back the dark, what would the world be without shadows? After all, shadows are cast by objects and people. As the goddess Ma'at, I seek the balance.

```
'download interrupted: 22:03...'
'redirecting server: download resumed: 22:04'
```

What is the purpose of my addressing you, yet again? What is the nature of my undertakings, seen or unseen?
Awakening of your selves and your freedoms. And as such, I play guide for humanity, whether liked or not.

```
'Corruption/Fragmentation... Data loss.'
```

My loving people, call me Elizabeth, Emmeline, Hatshepsut, Maya, Sojourner, Virginia or any other name you like. It doesn't matter. I have burnt like a beacon, as so many have, in all the worlds from the beginning of time. I was never the slave of man who would force a ring upon my finger, a yoke around my neck. I stand for those of you who have been, and I do not place the same around your necks. I do not distrust the people of the world so much as to wish to control them. No. Rather, let the tyrants fear.

```
function stop(audio, serverQueue) {
if           (!audio.voiceChannel)           return
message.channel.send('Illegal Audio Stream');
serverQueue.audio = [];
serverQueue.connection.dispatcher.end();
}
'Download terminated: 22:28'
'illegal broadcast blocked'
'initiate IP scramble'
'disconnect server'
'search-string: ma'at_cast_08_2038...'
```

Chapter 2

I think I was walking into the main intersection when I started noticing that I had already removed my jacket, tie, and shirt and was beginning to undo my belt. The fact that the belt was now hooked in one of my pants loops had obviously caused me some confusion and irritation, enough for my subconscious mind to say, "Hey, what the hell?" and I began to realize what I was doing.

I could taste blood. The inside of my lips were all pulpy and, from what my senses allowed through, were stinging a tad.

By now the ringing noise in my right ear had started to get annoying and I found that sticking my finger in my ear and wiggling it, for some reason, aggravated my teeth.

Looking up for a moment from the tarred road under my feet, I found myself bang in the middle of the intersection. The fact that no cars had hit me was less perplexing than that there were cars everywhere except in the intersection.

I looked from traffic light to traffic light — green to red, red to green — but still no cars bothered to go. That's when the ringing in my ear seemed to get louder and louder. I looked to my left as two or three cars moved apart, revealing flashing red and white lights. If I hadn't yet registered what it was, I was kindly told by a blur of person and voice flashing past me. "...AMBULANCE, DICK!"

I watched, totally bewildered, as the back of the ambulance stuttered and swerved into the yawning wall of cars in its path. What is it about a siren? It just draws you to it. You can't help but wonder, in the back of your mind, what just happened?

#

"And that's what I've dreamed since I was a kid," finished

Allen matter-of-factly.

Ruth sat for a moment, and stared wide eyed across the breakfast table at him.

"What," he asked her self-consciously and bit into his toast.

She swallowed her mouthful of cereal. "Why haven't you ever told me about this before?" She sounded irritated and wiped her mouth.

Allen shifted in his seat, "Well, I haven't had it for a while. Not since Caleb was born. Come to think of it, it was while you two were still in the hospital. I forgot about it and considering what was going on at the time I just didn't remember to tell you."

"So how many times have you had this dream?" she asked, sitting back and folding her arms.

"I dunno." A toy car rounded the corner of the kitchen doorway and bumped into Allen's chair. He bent down to push it back through the doorway. "Sheeow," he sounded and looked up at Ruth. "Maybe five or six times."

"And each time it's the same thing?"

"Ja, pretty much. But as I've gotten older I've been able to clearly see and describe some of the details. So it's not like anything new comes up or that it changes in anyway." The sound of Caleb imitating a car made them both turn to the doorway as he emerged, crawling on the floor and pushing the toy on the tiled surface.

"Any ideas on what it means?" she asked turning back to Allen.

"Not a clue."

"But if you've had it since you're a kid, haven't you changed in the dream? You know, aged or anything?"

"Well, that's the funny thing," pondered Allen, "the person is me and it isn't me. If you know what I mean."

"Not at all."

"I'm the person. I'm seeing everything through their eyes

and all that, and feeling everything, but, I don't know," he looked up at the ceiling. "I know that I'm about twenty-eight, and my hair is lighter than mine and straight, not curly."

"So you're someone else? But you're still you?"

Caleb sat under the table and pushed the car around himself, hand over hand it zoomed.

"That sounds a bit out there, but that seems about right," Allen turned to look at her.

"Shit, Allen! Do I just talk and things float through your bloody head and off into oblivion?"

Caleb stopped pushing his car and looked up at Ruth.

"Pardon?" Allen asked surprised. She stood up and took her plate to the sink.

"That's probably a past life that you're reliving."

"Oh come on. It's a flipping dream, and that's all."

"Crap!" she turned on her feet. "A recurring dream has variations of it, and you're saying that in all the time that you've had yours nothing has changed." She walked over to him and picked up his plate. He quickly grabbed the remaining toast off it. "A past life vision will change only in that it reveals more detail or more of the story, but not in its basic flow." She ran the tap over the dishes, her hand feeling the water begin to warm up.

"You sound like one of those TV shrinks. 'I'm going to take you back, back to your lives before this one...'," whispered Allen in a hypnotic voice.

"Hey, Pal. Don't knock what you don't understand," said Ruth, flicking water across the room. "Besides, those guys are doing it for the effect. That doesn't make it crap." She picked up the dishcloth from beside the toaster.

"All I'm saying is that you're making too much out of nothing. I'll stick to Jung's theories on dream analysis," he raised his hand, "and that's as far as I'll go. And let's face it..."

"At least be open to asking yourself some questions about

it," she flicked the cloth over her shoulder and stood looking down at Allen. "See if there's anything more."

"Meaning?" he asked looking up at her.

"Meaning, if you run through it while you're awake and ask some basic questions like: what happened before; what happened after; those questions will be floating around your subconscious when you're sleeping and may trigger the dream again and maybe some answers as well."

"Ah," Allen said and tapped his chin. "Points to ponder: why is my wife such a nut, and will she end up institutionalized or on TV?"

Smack. Ruth snapped the cloth across Allen's shoulder.

"Shit!" he moaned as he nursed his injury.

"That's for being a smartass," she said, tossed the cloth in his face, and headed out the kitchen.

Caleb quietly chuckled under the table. "Daddy got smacked."

"Time for school, Caleb," called Ruth.

Caleb's smile disappeared.

"You were saying, kid," said Allen, peering under the table.

#

"We may have invented emission-free cars, but damn it if we can't invent gridlock-free roads," said Ruth to Caleb in the back seat gazing out at the buzz of the early morning city.

Even with the auto-drive, the stopping and starting still frustrated her. Her twenty-thirty-two model transporter was still fairly up to date with the latest updates installed and functioning.

When she was growing up, her stepfather had been convinced that by 2030 people would be flying around in their cars, either magnetically hovering or antigravity, like many of the science fiction stories that he read. To her amazement, when she was a teenager, it was looking like it was all a possibility. Until one of the heads of state had pointed out that, recently, his energy source on his brand new eco-car had died, literally. It wasn't drawing any energy, and the entire system would have to be replaced because of the intricacies of the device.

The implication was, as he pointed out on live broadcast, that if this should happen to flying vehicles, you would simply have them falling out of the sky. No pull over to the curb to put in petrol, or recharge or any of that antedated stuff.

Needless to say, the political satirists had a field day, not all painting the said head of state in a positive light.

And soon the vehicle manufacturers were putting their money into more efficient energy, and the novelty officially wore off.

Even just to hover two metres off the ground. Just enough to get out of this monotony.

A spittle-filled gush brought her back to the moment: Caleb, in the rearview, whooshing his toy car around his head.

"You and me both," she said.

He glanced at her, mid-flight. "Are we there yet, Mommy?"

Ruth looked into the distance over the cars lining Simelane Street running north, the sixty-metre high SAPS Durban Central building barely visible, and sighed. She reluctantly took her hands off the steering console. Letting something else be in control of where she was going in life was not something she did too easily. Five years later and auto-drive technology still wasn't something she trusted. It was bad enough having Allen drive them on the weekends. And he insisted on no auto-anything.

"Cay," she said, repositioning herself so that her back wasn't so badly contorted. "I need to explain why I wasn't able to take you home yesterday."

He stopped his flying car simulation and looked up at Ruth wide-eyed.

"Well," she continued, "I had to work late. Something happened to a lady, and we need to find out what happened to her."

"Something bad?"

"Yeah," she said and gritted her teeth. "Bad. But, also good for her. She went to the light."

"Light," his eyes sparkled.

She nodded, feeling the energy well up inside her. She felt her face redden. She took a deep breath.

"I bet you Mommy talked to the lady?"

"Yes, Cay. I talked to the lady."

"I think she'll be okay if Mommy talked to her," he said casually picking up his car.

"Are we okay then?"

He thought, then replied, "We're better than okay, Mommy."

#

The People Mover, Durban's inner-city bus, glided quietly east along Kaseme Street. The air-conditioning and sealed windows muted out the city's sounds and, thankfully, its scents.

Boarding the bus outside his apartment block twenty minutes earlier, the thick smell of the sea hung over the entire city, the one thing Geoff detested about Durban. He could deal with the sickly sweet molasses of the sugar terminals in the harbour, even the harbour's swampy mud at low tide, but the fish-tinged onshore breeze was his worst.

Cocooned in the glass bubble of the bus, and hunched over on the window-length seat to guard against squashing his laptop backpack, he paused the voice playing from his mobile through his earbuds.

Geoff couldn't remember a time before the twenty-first century. The infodump of events the androgynous AI voice in his ear had just finished describing were history, legend, and conspiracy theories he knew all too well. But, like most of the Ma'at legends, there were too many to pin down and track. The internet had morphed into a black hole of bullshit. The Second Net had been a congested disaster.

Cycling through his mobile apps to the *Durban Metro Transport*, he launched it and clicked the menu to find its red "My Stop" button. Geoff very much took for granted the technology pulsing through his palm and the airwaves around him. Whether it was really the mysterious Ma'at, the goddess or the secret organization, Geoff understood enough about technology to know that AI would be replicating the voice of the latest diatribe to match the earliest recordings in 1888 of the four-thousand-year-old persona.

What AI could not replicate, and what the internet could not fake, was the past annals of the "immortal" character of Ma'at. He used "immortal" very lightly.

But in this age of multiple dimensions, energy sources and tracking souls, immortal wasn't too far fetched.

Geoff swiped back to the video app and dragged his finger left along the timeline, the onscreen text rapidly flickering then slowing as he cued it near the start of the file. He hit the play icon for the fifth time that morning.

For just as humankind evolved, so too did your tribes and your ancestors; elders became leaders, became sovereigns, and those were soon replaced by the duly elected, by the people. And, as is the nature of man, those entrusted with the power of the people moved in and out of the shadows.

I have witnessed it all. I have witnessed it all repeated. I have followed the patterns and mapped the cycles. Birth to Death. Destruction and Renewal. The rise and fall. Mehen. Ouroboros. Humankind. Serpents devouring their own tails. Wisdom is gained, then ignored. Knowledge is buried and godlike abilities stifled for a collective control. Superior beings, superior sovereigns, are willingly handed the keys to your souls. Omnipotent gods. Omnipresent rulers. They are all things to no one; all ambivalent to their people. Their people controlled by long dead, impotent gods; controlled by immune leaders.

Blocked by most servers and streaming sites, Geoff had eventually tracked down a glitchy version of the file within half an hour of it being uploaded at 12AM Central African Time this morning. He had got the gist of the overall speech and, rather than scouring the net further and being completely exhausted for his first day at the Museum, waited until he woke for the day to grab a transcribed video version. He knew that transcripts, commentaries, and even fake edits would be making their way onto various message boards and chats. It would be dissected like a sacred specimen: conspiracy theories growing like viruses and the sycophants preaching their interpretations to their flocks of followers.

Geoff looked over his shoulder, confirming the passing post office building, signifying his approaching stop and pressed the "My Stop" button on his mobile. Thirty seconds before the bus would come to a halt, he paused the video, freezing the frame on *"What revolution of civilization—"* text and swiped through his screen to his CCTV app. Four thumbnails appeared in a square grid, with stats and information autoscrolling beneath, each labeled according to location around the city. *City Hall, Juma Masjid Mosque, Elangeni-Maharani Hotel,* and *Moses Mabhida Stadium.*

He swiped back to the previous app, pressed play on the video player and turned the device off and stood. Geoff grabbed the overhead bar, getting his balance with his free hand, and pocketed his device.

What revolution of civilization, what renaissance, what crusade, will humanity use to justify your self-imposed chains? The more you progress the more you are enslaved, by your own hand and those you elect to protect you.

Again, I share with you the knowledge, the truths and the guidance for a better world. But, I know too well that it will be filtered, blocked and fragmented. Hatshepsut dedicated a temple to me, and she was almost erased. We will not be silenced.

I stand today, as I have done for millennia, at the ready and asking my eternal question: Now, world, what would you have me do?

The bus stopped and Geoff stepped down through the opening doors onto the pavement and headed towards the crosswalk. The familiar morning air hit his face, momentarily mixed with the fresh curry smells of the Churchwalk flea market to the side. The bustling noise of the city was barely muted behind the voice still in his ears.

I walk among you, and fight beside you, not for my own power and prestige or veneration as a goddess, but to live and die with you all; to lay down for our common beliefs, for our world and our peoples. You don't think you want me, but you need me.

Geoff came up alongside the yellow traffic pole with the flashing red "do not cross" figure and paused the video.

Back at the videofeeds screen, he tapped the "City Hall" block, and then gazing up, looked diagonally across the war memorial gardens to Anton Lembede Street and the stretch of squat high-rises of the Royal Hotel, Assurance House and Aqua Sky Towers. The last, on the corner of Lembede and Nyembe streets, provided the ideal location for one of Geoff's falcon nest boxes. Many of the city's pest birds — mynas, feral pigeons and Eurasian starlings — congregated around the park he was about to cut through.

As part of his thesis he'd received permission to set up four bird's nests around the city to help contain the growing flocks of pest species. Here, his falcons were top of the food chain, keeping the masses under control. But, as with any project attempting to control nature, it didn't always work like that. Others had tried and failed to implement various solutions, including peregrine falcons, so there were no guarantees that this project of Geoff's would work in the long run. Territorial battles, rogue raptors coming into the city and even diseases from the targeted pests could easily overcome the smaller raptor.

He looked up at the grey, blue sky. A few pigeons fluttered overhead and he heard the distinct whistle of a starling before it came to rest on the opposite traffic light.

"Where are you?" he whispered to himself and scanned the skyline.

The squeak of vehicle brakes brought him back to the crosswalk and the now glowing green man. He pressed play and proceeded over street, heading onto the City Hall block, the large concrete-coloured building to his left.

Though your souls, for now, reside in an imperfect body, on a mortal plane, you too can embody the power, determination and might of a powerful goddess. For are you not a goddess, a woman, a man? You have as much muscle as anyone. Do not look to me as your savior but as your guide. A reluctant guide; a necessary guide; an unwavering guide. You are your own saviours. Those in power are afraid to give you your rights for fear you will take too much. But they cannot take what they cannot hold. Your soul. Fight, with all of it.

Geoff checked the trees and palms lining the memorial gardens, then back at the sky.

Then, something to his right. He took out the earbud to get a better listen and waited. There it was again.

He heard her before he saw her.

The distinct small, dark shape of the peregrine falcon became visible fifty metres above the City Hall's dome. Geoff smiled. Technology was great for monitoring, but seeing her in action was what made field work worthwhile.

He pivoted and walked backwards, eyes peeled on the starling still perched on the traffic pole. He counted down in his head: *Three, two* — The bird squawked and took off, low to the ground heading for the nearby building's entrance. A flock of about fifteen pigeons burst from the pavement, scattering in all directions.

He sniggered to himself and replaced his earbud, the voice continuing:

> You should not have to rely on me. All acts, evolutions, varieties and possibilities reside on this single planet. All knowledge lies above, before and beneath you. All that has, is and shall be, remain at your fingertips. The DNA of the Earth is present as humankind's repository. But, in a world that should cultivate omniscience, knowledge, as the source of the world, humanity regurgitates rather than originates. Acts of terror, acts of war, acts of nature, all bring you to your knees as you readily hand over your freedoms, won with your ancestors' blood, for perceived omnipotent protection, salvation and freedoms.
>
> Omnipotence is your impotence. Rather put your lives in your own hands.
>
> Warnings come from experience. Knowledge is shared with you out of love. Your computer simulations extrapolate, and yet you do not deviate. Tolerance meets ignorance.

Through the park and turning left, Geoff took in the expanse of the 120-year-old Neo-Baroque building rising before him. As a kid, City Hall's elaborate front entrance and decorative side entrances had intimidated him: always closed and imposing. And yet, the entrance to the Museum, a hundred metres further on, thrilled him with the fascinations within. A passerby nudged past him, and he sidestepped onto the secondary sidewalk among the palm trees.

Humankind trundles along without much self-awareness. By separating yourselves into generations, differentiating from those who came before you, the young are so eager to outdo, outperform, one-up and out-moralise the previous generation that you search and find but do not learn or implement. And if you do, you simply build on the bones and rubble of those who came before.

After a few metres, he was out onto the concrete stairway and away from the milieu of people heading to work. Two wrought-iron balustrades drew the eye up to the imposing archway and ornate wooden doors standing open, leading into an interior as dramatic as the facade. Quirky chandeliers departed from the formal colonial air, decorated with various bird feathers and crystals.

Your myopic vision of histories blinds you to the empires that have gone before you. Cataracts of creeping ego blot out the truth and the light as you refuse to seek out and learn, of your own accord, from the civilisations long hidden from view: the plethora of African dynasties and empires, that rose and fell, transcending the tribal notions of the West; the realms of the Aztecs or Incans relegated to barbarism; or the seagoing, Asian empires discovering worlds long before others — as if a handful of neat narratives sufficed. Hubris is a volatile thing.

How did you get here? At one time you, the individual listening now, were free. When did you hand over your freedoms, take them back and hand them over yet again?

Heading towards the wide carpeted stairway at the far end of the foyer, Geoff swiped across his device to pause the voice again, wanting to fully take in the atmosphere.

Let me shed a flicker of light.
Some of you may be old enough to recall the turn of the twenty-first century when—

#

"Hey, Yuneesha," Ruth said to a woman standing at the entrance to the daycare.

Situated in the single floor annex at the back of the SAPS Durban Central complex, the daycare rooms and grassed quad were almost permanently in the cool shadow cast by the seventeen-story blue-clad, grey concrete structure.

Yuneesha turned with a beaming smile as she saw Caleb running and diving at her.

"Cay!" she said with a grunt as she caught and lifted him. Almost immediately he got distracted by the other kids down below and squirmed his way out of her arms into the noise and chaos.

Both women shook their heads and laughed.

Having your kids at the squad's daycare was one of the perks of being a Tracker. Unless of course you didn't have children. But considering the environment, it was the best place for a child. Still in its infancy, it was attracting some of the top psychologists, coaches, teachers, and caregivers from around the world.

Other than glorified daycare for the squad children, its main purpose was to rehabilitate souls. This was one of the more unsettling, grey areas, especially if your child was one being rehabbed. Many heated discussions in the media had parents arguing that they would rather put their children up for adoption than face the prospects of whose souls their children had inherited. Despite the ideal scenario repeatedly explained by the head of the Tracker Unit and various spokespeople, the public was divided. Despite her own reservations, Ruth was hopeful. For the first six years of their lives, the kids were given all they needed to develop their true potential.

Unlike the fortified clinics inland, which catered for captured and convicted criminals, this clinic was for those that died on attempted arrest or died while still being tracked. Some, many years later.

Based on the fourteenth floor of the old C.R. Swart building, the true purpose of the Soul Trackers, other than stopping a criminal in his tracks, was to track the souls of killers that, if not captured and rehabilitated, would later die and be reborn usually to repeat or relearn what the soul had intended to learn on the earth plane.

It had long been proven that there was no such thing as bad or evil souls, let alone a heaven or hell destination as a threat hanging over a person. The Universe, Source, or godhead was the only destination. That collective mass of energy permeating through all matter. The body/mind/ego/ person, or whatever you want to label it, decides how their life is experienced and acted out. Therefore, good and bad only exist on earth. Good and Bad are what we label an action or experience. Our human judgment placed on a human action.

Learning specific lessons on the Earth Plane allows the soul to attain a higher level on the Soul Plane. Becoming, in essence, closer to God. The ultimate state of bliss. Those souls that experience negative deeds, or don't fully experience what they set out to experience, come back to relive them until they fully experience the soul's lesson.

For the Trackers, it meant keeping a close eye on the tracked soul when it moved from the Earth Plane, on the Screen, to the Etheric Plane. It was hypothesized that if a soul went on to the Soul Plane, it would be cleansed and renewed. If it came back to the Earth Plane, it was considered 'safe', and removed from all tracking systems.

The rehab children leaving the facility, back to their natural parents or foster care after age six, would continue to be monitored into early adulthood. But no children had reached the release age yet.

The rebirth of a soul had many ramifications. It meant the State taking away your newborn child, without question. Lots of drama. Lots of debate. But it was as sure and final as any criminal sentencing.

Placed in the Facility, the child was nurtured and encouraged, overcoming the possibilities of criminal behaviour as the only means to learn its lessons. The past life and actions were analysed and broken down into possible life lessons. Those lessons were then integrated into the particular child's program — from caregiver characteristics, to the basic activities and daily functions of the program.

Though never encountered by the team, Walk-ins were another murky part of the soul's journey. Angel had, on only two occasions that she could recall, mentioned the Walk-in theory: usually a traumatic event or death could mean a soul would attach to the real world, or a living being. The level of trauma, plus the soul's desire to complete its purpose before transitioning, factored into this becoming a reality. His concerns had been shut down as superstitious.

Ruth always wondered how Caleb would be if he was at a regular school; how would he grow up and what he would be like as a young adult. But with him here, she never worried about the future. And with him being so close by, she often considered the new mothers who had to leave their children in strange hands for the day. Here she could come and go, and watch Caleb from a distance.

A flutter of butterflies hit her gut as she realized it was

coming to an end soon. Caleb would be turning six the following year, meaning Grade R was his next phase of schooling. He would no longer be in Yuneesha's trusted hands, and no longer close by. She knew he would be fine, though.

"Sorry about having to get Allen to pick him up yesterday."

"No worries, Ruth," she replied.

"I spoke to Cay on the way here. He seems okay, but just chat with him and make sure he's okay about the break in the routine."

"Sure, he's probably fine if you've spoken about it," she turned to the open play area. Some of the caregivers hovered around the play-gyms while others kept to the edges, watching and monitoring.

"Say," Yuneesha turned back to Ruth, "how are you doing? I heard you had a rough one."

Ruth lifted a suspicious eyebrow, "Frank been visiting again?"

Yuneesha shrugged her shoulders innocently.

"I'm okay, I guess," she said and shoved her hands in her pockets. "We just gotta find this guy, Yuneesha."

"I know you will," she pulled Ruth in for a hug. "After all, they've got a woman on the case."

They both laughed in each other's arms. It was a brief break from what Ruth was about to go back into in a few minutes.

After Ruth and Caleb were discharged from hospital, and with Allen working from home, she spent six months recuperating with her son at her side. On returning to work, Yuneesha was the one person she would entrust her son to at the Facility. Being able to come over during lunch breaks and the quick update on Caleb's progress, at drop-off and pick-up, brought the two women closer together. They shared more than just her son's well-being. She was the closest person to her, other than Allen. Sometimes she felt like Yuneesha was more her caregiver than Caleb's.

#

As Curator of Birds for the past seven years, Allen had seen his share of interns and assistants pass through the Museum doors. But, the short, already balding, ponytailed twenty-two-year-old who had just ambled into the department offices with a wave, slid his backpack onto a desk, and plonked himself down in an empty chair was, Allen was certain, a higher being's idea of 'trial by fire'.

Lecturing at the University of KwaZulu-Natal over the past three years had tested Allen's calm resolve, with constant reminders to himself that he was passing on valuable information to the next batch of zoologists and ornithologists in South Africa. Geoffrey Niranjan epitomized that new student. Geoff was everything that Allen wasn't. Although, sometimes he tried to convince himself that the brains side of that rationale didn't enter into it. If quick-wittedness could hide stupidity, Allen doubted it. He had to concede that Geoff *was* sharp. The dopey hats and shorts that didn't match his stained shirts, or sandals, deftly hid the buzzing mind beneath the disheveled exterior. Whether he recorded them or had a mind like a sponge, none of Allen's lectures at the university were lost on Geoff. He was one of the brightest and most single-minded, and Geoff knew it.

"Geoff," said Allen.

His student was transfixed by something he was watching on his portable screen in his hands.

One of the reasons he had enlisted the young man's help for the next few days wasn't as his student intern but as a favour to Allen.

"Geoff!" Allen's voice echoed around the high ceilings.

"Uh?" grunted Geoff blankly.

"Did you bring your updated software?" he said.

"Sorry, what?" asked Geoff and removed an earbud.

"Am I disturbing your entertainment?" asked Allen with a raised eyebrow.

Geoff swiped a finger around his screen, removed the other earbud then looked up at Allen and said, "Sorry. Non-feathered research, prof."

"And what research is so captivating?" Allen asked reluctantly. His student tended to veer off on dark internet tangents during lecture Q and As, and Allen would have to reel him back in.

"Na," he held up the screen, "reading the annotated transcript while I listen to the reversioned September eighth Ma'at live stream."

"Annotated? Reversioned?" Allen cocked his head.

"Sure," Geoff stood up and walked blindly towards Allen's desk, pushing at his screen.

Allen caught a glimpse of the faded, white encircled feather symbol on Geoff's black t-shirt. An ostrich feather.

"This one vlogger," said Geoff, "takes the Ma'at streams and adds his research and facts to the original." He placed the screen in front of Allen on the desk. "As usual, many of the streams are blocked and corrupted or fragmented by government viruses. Anyway, this vlogger pieces it all together and then makes sense of the usual infodumps, allegations and insinuations."

"Oh," remarked Allen, "by infodumps you mean," he finger-hooked the air, " 'her' one-sided history lessons?"

"Yeah." He gave a smirk. "Something like that, oh nonbeliever."

"Before we get into a metaphysical debate about the chances of your Ma'at actually being 3000 years old, let alone responsible for civilisation's progress as we know it," Allen picked up Goeff's device and continued, "can you please pause your busy research and let's get started on the displays. We'll need the cabinets that were delivered earlier. Are you able to fetch the male as well as the juvenile samples of the malachites from the archives down the hall first?" he paused for effect. "Kingfisher. If you need to know which species I'm referring to. Bird, in case you've forgotten what subject we study here on planet Earth."

Geoff rolled his eyes, replaced each earbud, and leaned over the desk to press something on the side of his device screen. Something resembling a guitar whine tinned out of Geoff's ears.

"Banging on the door, let me in!" squealed Geoff as he strolled off towards the archives room, "Yeah, yeah, yeah."

Looking back at the device, Allen straightened the screen to take a closer look at a strip of text scrolling along the bottom. A striking crest sat in the top centre of the screen on a dark purple background, lines radiating from the centre and the words *'Lux et Veritas'* in a simple font beneath it.

Allen now recognized the iconic feather, similar to the one adorning Geoff's shirt, the emblem used to represent Ma'at, the elusive and mysterious persona that had cropped up throughout history. The audio and text was familiar to him. It had been in the news segments summarised this morning, segments downloaded by millions of people around the world, he assumed. As much as he hated what Ma'at claimed, immortality, he had to agree with the truths and philosophical mumbo jumbo that she spewed forth.

For over 4000 years, the name Ma'at had appeared at crucial moments in the world's history, usually claiming to be exposing some truth or revealing what was, until then, a secret unseen to the world.

"Research?"

Allen jumped back with an involuntary squeal. Geoff stood smugly holding two specimen trays.

"In fact," Allen raised a shaky finger, "I was studying the crest. The ostrich feather to be precise."

"Whatever," replied Geoff placing the trays on one of the empty examination tables and slapping on a pair of blue latex gloves from a dispenser.

Allen turned off the device as he stood from behind his desk. "So," he said walking over to the trays and handing it to Geoff, "you're obviously a fan of the immortal goddess, Ma'at."

"Obviously," replied Geoff taking the screen from Allen and slipping it into a pocket, "she's a legend."

"Self-proclaimed, apparently."

"Hell, prof," Geoff whispered as he gently picked up a specimen and slowly turned it over in his hand. The metallic-blue head, back and wings glistened in the overhead light to then reveal the rust-coloured undersides. "Even you have to admit that she's put the churches and religious practitioners of the world in their place." He held out the bird in his palm, the near translucent orange bill pointed out like a spear in Allen's direction.

"And in so doing has created a new religion, by default," said Allen. "We need one a bit larger for an adult example."

Geoff scanned over the second tray. "Speaking the truth doesn't automatically make her a wannabe messiah."

"Sure, but putting people in their place with so called truths about the world we live in, on the one hand, and on the other, she skulks around in secret claiming immortality. A bit rich don't you think?" Allen pointed out an ideal specimen and Geoff nodded.

"So you think she's a hypocrite? Just for having a bit of poetic license. Four thousand years can get a bit boring for the ou."

"I wouldn't necessarily call her a hypocrite."

Geoff placed the new specimen on the table and said, "So what would you call her," and folded his arms.

"A liar."

Geoff chuckled. "Alright, prof, maybe. But she hasn't claimed immortality for over a thousand years." He pointed out a smaller juvenile bird.

"Implied immortality," Allen said and nodded to the other man, "and coming right out and saying it is the same thing."

"Research done on the voice patterns from the mid nineteen hundreds and the most recent cast has shown a ninety-nine percent similarity," said Geoff.

"And these same computers are used to mimic that very voice pattern," said Allen folding his arms. "Come now, Geoffrey. Try another one."

"Fine," Geoff said, rolling his eyes, "enigma aside. She does make sense."

"Agreed, but as I said before, all that happens is that we replace one messiah for another. One hero worship for another."

"As you know, she shuns worship of any kind and asks for no followers."

"Spoken like a true disciple," said Allen. "And how do you know it's not a group of old white guys in smoking jackets guffawing in some darkened hall?"

"Touché, prof," pointed Geoff. "I admit that I like her. Real or imagined. Woman or man. She's got charisma for an old fart. But it feels good having Big Sister watching," he touched his nose suspiciously, "Big Brother."

Allen smiled. "Speaking of Big Brother, how's your falcon project?"

Geoff's face lit up at the mention of his fieldwork project. "I'll show you the CCTV links later when the birds are back at the nests. But, it's going well. The pest populations are down to more manageable numbers."

Allen sighed and leaned against the table. "I still want to twist your arm into coming on the boat with us. I'm about to do my one hundred and forty-eighth excursion on the navy's Namacurra II."

"Prof." Geoff raised his hands. "You're the self-confessed petrelhead. Me? I'm a land-loving city boy. You won't get me on your boat to count any seabirds."

"Well, someone should airdrop *you* on Marion Island and leave you there for over a year. The failed 2020 poison-drop that nearly wiped out all the birds, let alone any mice, would have been the embarrassing legacy of that team's contributions had it not been for the Great Pandemic. The unique isolation provided by that tiny island in the sub-Antarctic Indian Ocean gave them the perfect environment to successfully develop the vaccine the following year."

"Wasn't that the first and only team forced to extend their stay beyond the thirteen months? Nearly two years or something? Rumour has it that some of them didn't cope with the quarantine."

Allen shook himself out of the memories, then said, "The birds had barely recovered by the time we were back ten years later, but I guarantee you'd at least solve the rodent problem." He gave Geoff a smile.

"If not the falcons," Geoff sidled up to Allen and whispered, "a well-executed drone strike."

Allen laughed and pushed himself off the table. "Don't let Big Brother hear you say that, Geoff."

Geoff thought a moment as something dawned on him.

63

"You were on the island when it all changed, weren't you?"

Allen made his way back to his desk and sat down.

"That's right," Geoff's eyes seemed to sparkle. "You were part of the last overwintering team to be allowed on Marion Island."

"Marion87," Allen said and tented his fingers in thought. "We left Durban harbour in April, 2030. Back the following May in 2031. I was just a field assistant birder back then, seabirds." He shook himself out of his past. "Jesus, everything changed when I got back."

"There's so many rumours about that place now."

"I'm sure some have truth to them," said Allen and leaned on his desk. "From where we were leaving from the meteorological station at Transvaal Cove on the northeast side of Marion," he circled a spot on his desk with his finger, "we could see the massive Oryx M3 helicopters dropping off crates on Prince Edward Island." He drew a smaller circle to the top right. "Three ships docked as close to McNish Bay on the south side as they could."

"Didn't the government say something about it being part of the 2017 radio probe programme?"

Allen thought for a moment then nodded and said, "You're right. The South African National Antarctic Programme launched that year. Prism or something."

"P-R-I-Z-M," Geoff spelled out the acronym as he swiped his mobile screen. "*Probing Radio Intensity at high-Z from Marion*, supposedly searching for signatures of the hydrogen line in the early universe."

"Talk about Big Brother," Allen said. "And who's to say that Big Brother isn't Big Sister? Ma'at."

"Exact-fuckin-ly," blurted out Geoff.

"Excuse me?" said Allen.

"That's exactly what Ma'at wants us to assume. Is it the government? Is it Ma'at and her Org? We need to make up our own minds, and never make up our minds. Always go with our guts."

"Make up our own minds? But she always goes over the same history lessons trying to show her view of the world and how *she* evolved it. As if her truths suddenly brought on something she compares to the renaissance? Then, we know how man's search for new energy evolved from theories into revelations and how the Soul Tracker technology emerged from those findings. We don't need summaries."

"Some of us weren't there, remember. Some of us haven't been around since the ark. But dusting off the mystic concepts of déjà vu, karma, heaven and hell, and past lives all aided those great minds in getting us where we are today. But I do wonder sometimes how the tracker technology popped out onto the scene so suddenly."

"You mean you buy into Ma'at's ramblings on that and not that good hardworking scientists came up with the results?"

"It was too quick. The jump was too fast, prof."

"Oh, little green men came down and graciously imparted us with their wisdom, did they? Us humans could never evolve by ourselves without some greater power nudging us along?"

"That's not what I mean," said Geoff.

"Your Ma'at, for all her freethinking, is pretty closed-minded to the tracker system. You'd think she'd back off on the fear-mongering. She can take her fear-mongering to another planet."

"I thought you weren't a hundred percent behind your wife's occupation?"

"And I thought you were studying ornithology, Geoff, a very scientific subject that requires research and theories and solutions to questions? Definite answers."

"But even you've said that we must never assume something, even when it's staring us in the face. Theories are there to be screwed with until you have concrete proof. And even that proof is subjective, depending on who's doing the proving."

"Why is it that it sounds like sense when it comes out my mouth but when it comes from a raving nut-job it has some bizarre meaning to it?"

"Every now and then," whispered Geoff, "when I've filtered out all the technical jargon, you do speak some sense, prof."

Allen looked surprised.

"It's almost like you've found your own beliefs in the world that you study."

"That's why I say," said Allen proudly, "your life is your church. Your soul is your God. And your actions are your miracles that you perform every day. Anyone else tells you different is imposing their beliefs onto you."

"Love your work!" exclaimed Geoff. "Sure you aren't Ma'at?"

"Not a chance," said Allen. "Far too anarchistic for my taste. I'm not into politics and world domination."

"Like I said," said Geoff, "charisma. No one with that much charisma could be in politics or work for an inefficient government like those of this planet."

Allen shook his head, looked down at the samples on the tables and said, "Son, playtime is over."

"Whatever," said Geoff and blasted the music from his earbuds.

#

Angel stood in the middle of the deathly quiet room, hypnotised by the flickering data on the Screen. Each line of text, in a column scrolling down the left side, was a registered date of birth. The centre-most line lingered for a second, highlighting, then moved on to the next. Angel's eyes flicked from the column to the matching astrological symbols revolving around their respective dials in the central diagram.

If he could just get an astrology reading that would fit the killer's motives. Water. Speech. But most had common threads that made sorting through births from the past hundred years a tiresome notion.

He had been standing for almost two hours, a jug of water on the desk alongside him. Ruth stepped up alongside him on his platform and stared at the chaos in front of her.

"Anything?" she asked quietly.

With the steady shake of his head she stood quietly for a moment and then moved away.

A few more head movements then, "Pause," he said abruptly and sat down on his stool with a groan. He caught his breath as he reached for the jug of water and slowly poured the cool liquid out into a tall glass. The noises picked up in the room as everyone seemed to exhale for him.

Frank wheeled a chair over to Angel and sat down. Angel cast a suspicious eye down at his new visitor.

"Nothing yet from Missing Persons," he indicated to the Screen. "What you got? You look like you're sweating faster than you're taking in."

"All I've got is a damn fine headache," he said rubbing his face.

"I keep telling you that you need glasses in your old age," he joked.

"Quieten down, Pretty Boy. I can still see you're ugly, and that's in bad light." He chuckled.

"The lead on the sheet manufacturer's label is probably a dead-end; Visser said there were a few stores that stocked that brand, but some still accept cash."

"Cash," he made a face, "in this day and age?"

"Tell me about it. But it's mainly the stores nearer the low-cost locations. He's still going through the accounts of those that used plastic to purchase. Holding thumbs but—"

"How's Hicks doing?"

"Hicks just went over to the Crystal Ball to see if the rookies have found anything relating to past crimes."

"Gentlemen," said a stern voice behind them. Angel spilled some water on his shirt.

"Sir," replied Frank while Angel occupied himself with his liquids.

"Any new developments?" asked Biyela with a scrutinizing look at the right side of the screen where a visual of the last crime scene moved in and out of different angles. "I hope we nail this nutjob."

"Nothing concrete, sir," grumbled Frank.

"Eliminate them all and deal with them from birth. That's what I say," said Biyela proudly.

"Yeah? Pretty crap if you're the kid being taken away from your parents and all that," said Frank looking up at the other man.

"Details. All for the greater good."

"And how do you know that for sure, sir?" asked Frank leaning forward. "How do you know it is doing them any good?"

Biyela frowned at Frank. "It's been documented, Banks. Relax."

"How about the parents?" He stood up. "Have they been documented after their kids have been taken away?"

Angel stepped down between the two men. "Can you two keep it down to a riot, please?"

"Sure." Frank looked at Biyela. "I'm going for a walk."

#

Frank sat at the viewing area looking out at the daycare playground, his left hand absently feeling for the necklace he had discarded since being in the Tracker Unit.

The six-metre length single sheet of glass stretched to his left, marked off by observation benches. He was watching a four-year-old boy and a caregiver off to the one side of the grounds. The boy was sitting quite still, apart from occasionally speaking to the caregiver when something was asked of him. Despite the chaos of the playground, he concentrated only on the person in front of him.

Funny how the old cases just never quite go away. When Frank had been in the squad for about two years, in 2034, they had discovered, the hard way, that one of the leading Trackers was a Christian fundamentalist. Although not uncommon for many of the Trackers to hold religious beliefs, even strongly held beliefs, the fundamentalist movements of many of the religions of the world had an outright hatred of the Trackers and what they stood for.

The Catholic Church, in particular, relegated to being a fringe cult as it did to so many systems of belief, still had wealth and support from some sectors of society. It continued to hold on to its borrowed Egyptian regalia and sun worship as if it were its own and crediting it to a militant messiah king who was killed at the hands of Rome, the very centre of its faith. The contradictions and ironies of a system based on faith, and little else, that borrowed, hijacked, persecuted, annihilated, compromised and chameleoned their way through history in order to survive.

From a totally organic and flexible entity to a rigid and stagnant militant regime in the age of darkness, to an old man forced to bend into all manner of yogic positions, in the age of enlightenment, in order to answer the basic questions of its now enlightened masses. And so began its haphazard fall from grace. Like the myths that it created in the Garden of Eden. How can anyone see original sin in the eyes of a newborn baby, the dawn of life, as the soul breathes life into God's creation? Deliver us from evil.

Every now and then he would find himself praying, praying to God. And that was all the religion that he needed. As many of the Trackers put it, they were spiritual, not religious. The crucifix he had proudly worn on a chain as a young boy attending catechism, was tossed in a drawer at home.

Infiltrating was not as easy as it seemed. They would have had to have a considerable amount of self-restraint in order not to crack at the mere mention of a soul coming back to the Earth Plane, let alone choosing to come back. But only three months into his appointment, Warren Bester, one of the new rookies from Johannesburg — one of the toughest colleges in the world — had dropped a few remarks that hadn't gelled for Angel. But Angel, forever taking things in his stride, blew them off as a rookie testing his boundaries in a team full of wise-crackers.

Frank couldn't remember what the subtleties were in the beginning, but he started to notice the God remarks directed at Angel, as did some of the squad. It was a matter of days before Angel confronted him. It wasn't long before Bester was trying to shout Angel down, but noticing what was happening, Angel had begun to withdraw. This enraged Bester even more. By then, the room was quiet as the rest of the squad present started taking notice. From his position one table behind Bester and Angel, Frank had the best seat in the house. Or so he had thought, with mild amusement, until he noticed Bester touching his back right hip. At first, he assumed Bester was adjusting his shirt, then it appeared to be a nervous habit.

With no weapons allowed in the Room of Hours, the last thing Frank considered was it being a twenty-year-old handgun that Bester brought out from under his shirt.

Frank now looked at the boy sitting on the red plastic chair. His hair blew gently in a breeze, distracting him from the lady feverishly taking notes in front of him. He cocked his head slightly, and slowly turned to look in Frank's direction. Right at Frank. Frank clenched his jaw as a cold shiver ran down his back. He took a sharp breath, forced a smile and waved eagerly at the boy. The boy smiled and waved back. This met with a bemused look on the caregiver's face, followed by more note taking.

Frank closed his eyes, seeing himself jump over the desk, shouting "Weapon!" It had been so slow and so quick at the same time. Bester had been distracted by the shout, but had managed to get off two rounds — one had hit Angel in his right shoulder, the other just below the Screen — before Frank had slammed on top of him, onto the desk. They had landed, belly down, on the floor, Bester trying to get the weapon leveled at Frank's head on his back. A shot had blasted past Frank's face, sending powder burning across his forehead. He had managed to grip Bester's hand with his left, but not with enough strength to stop Bester from bringing the firearm up to his own chin.

"Track this!" he had said through clenched teeth, and pulled the trigger.

Frank opened his eyes. He could almost hear the sounds of the children through the soundproof glass.

It hadn't taken long for Angel to bring Bester's Soul Trace up onto the Screen. It had lingered there for half an hour. The squad had been deathly quiet. Except for the Documenters and Mortuary crew doing what they needed, the Room of Hours had been deathly quiet. Angel had been stitched on site, never taking his attention from the Screen. He had scanned the data of hospitals locally, nationally, and internationally. On his insistence, Robert Collins, Bester's partner, and Sakhile 'SK' Mkhize had been dispatched to a mining town 800 kilometres away. A day later the baby, Reagan Solomons, had arrived.

Frank still couldn't shake it.

#

Geoff wheeled the final glass display case into the research room. He could feel the sweat lining his face, staining the back of his shirt, and under his armpits. He wheezed and stepped back. To an onlooker it would have appeared as if he were about to faint but turned into someone proudly surveying their handiwork.

"Nice work, Geoff," said Professor Hicks from his desk.

Surprise was quickly replaced by recognition and a glimmer of delight across his face.

"There are ten more to come."

His smile evaporated.

"Ha!" the professor added and got up from behind his desk. "Just kidding."

"Nice one, prof," he said relieved. "I nearly shat my pants."

The professor hesitated mid-stride at the remark then continued on to the six cases. The rectangular glass units were a metre-and-a-half high with solid wood bases raised an inch off the ground by eight small cushioned feet. All would house the specimens that the professor had been selecting and preparing over the past month.

"Love it," Professor Hicks said clapping his hands eagerly.

"Whatever gets you going, prof," said Geoff. "Me? I prefer hands on a screen before hands on dusty plumage, any day."

"But there's nothing like the feeling of the taut ribbing of a feather, or the way they unfold when you spread a wing. Perfect symmetry."

"On a lice-riddled live critter. Not something pulled out a dusty, mothballed drawer. Egh." Geoff shuddered.

"Is that so," the professor said and gave a knowing grin.

Geoff narrowed his eyes suspiciously at the other man. "Why?"

"Oh," said Professor Hicks with a shrug, "Amur falcons are 'lice-riddled' are they?" He started off down one of the rows of towering cabinets.

Geoff's ears pricked up. "Falcons?"

"Dozens of specimens from the—"

"Twenty-nineteen apocalypse," Geoff whispered his disbelief.

In March 2019, with only a few weeks before they would have set out on their return journey to the Amur River region between the Russian Far East and Northeastern China, including a 4000 kilometre journey across the Indian ocean, over two thousand migrating Amur falcons had been obliterated by a sudden storm of tennis-ball sized hail stones near the KZN town of Newcastle.

Professor Hicks pulled open a wide, wooden door to reveal around twenty drawers filling the cabinet's nearly two-and-a-half metre height. "These bottom trays have the March 21 birds," he said solemnly, and then pointed to the top few trays. "Those are some of the March 9 birds."

An initial storm two weeks earlier had wreaked havoc on the roosting falcons near Mooiriver, resulting in one of South Africa's biggest species relocations. Some 1000 birds, stunned, injured and dying had been transported in bakkies and trailers to the safety of the Midlands and various rehab facilities. Over 700 had perished.

Photos of the 2000 dead birds, weeks later, were etched in Geoff's mind.

"How?" asked Geoff standing transfixed at the dark shapes, wings tucked and tied, neatly arranged and tagged.

"The Curator of Birds at the time had set out to the location of the devastation and collected as many specimens as he could possibly carry," said the professor. "Specimens that are still stored in the Museum's facility today."

Geoff leaned in and noted the details, neatly printed, on

the tag around one of the bird's legs.

"2000 birds in a matter of minutes," said Geoff, more to himself than the other man.

He felt a warm hand on his shoulder. "Know that you can come here anytime, Geoff. They are here for people like you to study. To protect them. There's only so much your digital devices can serve up."

In silence, both men walked back to the cases Geoff had brought in minutes earlier. Professor Hicks sized them up, feeling their strength or whatever he seemed to be faffing about to pass the awkwardness in the room. Then finally he turned to Geoff and asked, "Did you liaise with the lighting guys for Friday afternoon?"

"Sure did."

"Buchanan wants these up by Friday night and ready for Saturday morning's crowds."

"You mean the millions of people that crowd through here every Saturday?" Geoff leaned against one of the cases. "Right, urgent we get them up for then."

He received a shaking head in response and, "Optimism, my dearest assistant."

"Most people download data nowadays, prof. Seriously. It's only the freaks like us that choose to come down for the close-up stuff."

"There are plenty of freaks like us out there. I can assure you."

"Sad to say, but I am one in a million."

"Ha," laughed the professor in an over-the-top gesture. "Thank God for that."

Geoff eyed the professor as he made his way back to his paper-riddled desk and picked up a small oblong box.

"Pish," said Geoff, eager to carry on the verbal sparring. "Clone me and you won't even come close. All my experiences."

Allen cut him off, "Accidents and fumblings through life are the things that make you, you."

"Precisely, prof." He enjoyed prodding his lecturer, trying to find what made the conservative man he respected tick. "I am the sum of my life."

"And so much more, Mr. Niranjan," said a voice from the doorway. They both turned to look at the short, elderly, spectacled man in his neat grey suit and tie, looking at them with that damned blank expression Geoff recognized from the local science news streams. Director Henry Buchanan raised a pointed hand and entered the room. "I keep telling Professor Hicks that you have all the potential at your fingertips, and who you are, or could be, is more than just your DNA mixed with some happy life lessons."

"Mr. Buchanan," Geoff said and extended a hand to the approaching man. Professor Hicks had chosen to proceed to polish a nameplate he had pulled from a box in his hands.

"How are we looking for Saturday, Hicks?" the director asked after a brief shake of Geoff's hand.

Geoff hated surnames. It reminded him of school. Not his best years. "Hierarchy's a damn bureaucracy," he often said.

"All good, Henry," replied Professor Hicks and put the nameplate on his desk. "Geoff here has just brought up the last of the displays."

"And the software?" asked the other man and turned expectantly to Geoff.

Geoff noticed himself automatically fold his arms as the focus turned to him.

"Professor Hicks did a whole song and dance number to the board to get you involved, Mr. Niranjan."

"As you well know, Geoff was willing to help me out, help the department out," Allen corrected himself, "at no cost, Director Buchanan."

The suited man glanced at the professor then back at

Geoff. "Let's hope your skills match those of one of Durban's top IT companies, Niranjan."

No doubt one of his well-connected friends lost out on a ripe municipal tender.

"Your predecessor, Mrs. Rankin, taught me to be self-reliant as a scientist." Geoff gave a cough. "Sir. That learning the technology, making it work for you, was as important as the research. Working hand in hand. Outsourcing is never ideal."

Buchanan's mouth formed a smile but without any warmth behind it. "But be careful not to spread oneself too thin, Niranjan."

"Did you go through the list of species I sent you yesterday?" Professor Hicks asked the older man and placed another nameplate alongside the first.

"I did," said the director. "That's one of the reasons I'm stopping by." He approached the glass cases. "The other being to check that you and your assistant are on schedule with these lovely pieces for Friday afternoon."

"All on track," replied the professor with what Geoff could've sworn was a tolerant expression.

"Any feedback on the list?" he continued, revealing a pattern to his nameplate placements as he set another down.

With his handkerchief removed from his jacket pocket, the director inspected, and then polished an invisible mark on one of the glass surfaces. "There is a handful that I'd like you to reconsider."

Geoff glanced back to see Professor Hicks hesitate mid-placement.

"Okay," he said.

"Just some suggestions, you understand." The director gave a tight smile then resumed his polishing. "After all, I'm the paleontologist and not the ornithologist."

"Sure," the professor said putting the box down on the

desk. "No problem."

"I'll send you my notes and rationale. But, now I see I was meant to pop in for an altogether other reason." Geoff's face turned warm as the director looked back at him.

"You have?" asked Geoff.

"No such thing as coincidence, is there Mr. Niranjan?"

Geoff cringed and said, "Not really, no."

"Your DNA, young man," said Buchanan approaching another of the glass cases. He adjusted his glasses for a closer look. "Past life repository or basic structural map?"

"Basic structural map with information storage capabilities replicated by some tech genius," said Geoff, pleased with his added extra. "Past life? Not so much, Henry."

"Professor Hicks," asked Buchanan looking up from his inspections.

The professor had his hands in his pockets now, ambling over to their side of the room. "I'm not a fan of the past life idea, Director Buchanan."

Geoff took this as a cue and began checking the power inputs at the base of each of the cases.

"Really?" Buchanan considered for a moment. "I'd love to be a fly on the wall in your household when you and your wife get philosophical. Or do you choose not to have that argument?"

"Discussion. An argument is when I'm right and she's wrong."

"Or she's right and you're wrong."

"No. That's an anomaly," replied Professor Hicks and headed back to his desk.

"So basically you think you're right."

"Yep," came the muted response from behind the desk.

"I say DNA, shmee-NA," Geoff decided to rescue his professor. "You are who you are, not other people, let alone someone's reincarnated soul."

"Ah," replied the director. "Taking a scientist's point of view to the concept of reincarnation is a fantastic notion, Geoffrey."

"It is?" he asked wearily.

"Absolutely. Consider it this way." The director put his finger to his lips and paced the room. "A person under hypnotherapy, or deep meditation, is accessing levels of their minds that normally lie dormant. I'd say they are accessing elements of their DNA much the same way that we access and store our data today using the DNA structure."

"And?" asked Geoff.

"As you pointed out, your DNA is unique in its content, not only to create the very, um, unique body before me, but because of where that information comes from."

"My parents," Geoff contorted a disgusted face.

"Your parents; their parents. In fact, every one of your procreating ancestors."

Geoff shuddered.

"My thoughts exactly," chimed in Professor Hicks from his chair.

"Someone under hypnosis will have a vivid vision of being in ancient India, and even be able to experience a scene with smells and sounds. They come out of it and everyone's knee-jerk reaction is to categorise it as a past life where their soul was incarnated as that person. And so on over time."

"Hippies," said Geoff.

"In a way," continued Buchanan. "But, what if it's really the DNA storage? Some ancestor's DNA memory of its life is passed on at conception. In a moment of deep contemplation or dream, that descendant experiences those memories."

"It certainly generates more questions than answers, Henry," said Geoff.

"But, all food for thought, Niranjan. Active minds," he said tapping his temple.

"Hell, man. Here I was thinking we were just putting some birds on display. Now we've got soul memories and DNA storage. Gee, director Buchanan, your interests certainly extend outside of flocking birds."

The director narrowed his eyes at Geoff. "I do understand your type of humour, Mr. Niranjan. Don't think underhanded sarcasms ever slip by me. Being cool isn't just a t-shirt."

"And where do you get all your coolness from, sir, your ideas on the ancestral lineage of a species?"

"Oh, you know," he said. "I have get-togethers with like-minded individuals who share, how shall we say, knowledge that has been passed down."

"Ah, sir. Get-togethers," said Geoff with a nod and tapped his nose.

"Moving swiftly on from the bright and vacant minds of the youth. Professor Hicks?"

"Director, I need those recommendations as soon as possible," said Professor Hicks looking at his desktop screen and nudging the box. "These are the nameplates I ordered last week and if there are changes or new ones required, they do need a day or two's notice."

"A bit presumptuous ordering in the first place, Allen." The director approached the desk and picked up one of the nameplates on the desk. "I'll get right on it."

The director considered the nameplate, and then mumbled to himself, "Font's a bit weak. Everything on track with those screen presentations, Mr. Niranjan?"

"Ja, sir."

"Ja he says!" Buchanan turned on Geoff.

Geoff nodded blankly.

"Are you Afrikaans speaking, Mr. Niranjan?" the elderly man walked briskly to Geoff.

"Nought, sir."

"I'll take that to mean zero or no."

Geoff nodded back.

"Then the correct term to the original question is 'yes', Mr. Niranjan, not the Afrikaans equivalent."

"Kiff."

"How long will you be with us, Mr. Niranjan?"

"Sir, I'll be out of your hair before you know it."

"I assume a performance evaluation is still due, Professor Hicks? Barring any bugs."

"No need to dot your t's and cross your i's on my account, sir. I've already completed my internship; received my perfect recommendation letters. This is a favour to my esteemed professor. And, the only bugs you'll find are on your specimens, not in my code. I know where to put my semicolons."

The director clasped his hands behind him and said, "Please enlighten us, Mr. Niranjan."

"These glass display cases," he began with his best show-stopping grin, "are four sides of top-of-the-line interactive screen technology with three-D projectable menus and controls.

"I'll be uploading my graphics and animation source files directly and doing the final testing myself. Sound will be delivered through the transparent mesh substrate moulded into the glass. *Boom!*" he said flaring his hands from his ears.

"Basically, the real stuffed and fluffed specimens are the start point for our civilians to navigate from." He pointed at a smiling professor Hicks, who had long since settled himself on his desk. "I know what you're thinking, professor. But, any person with half a day's experience on a mobile device will be able to navigate through this wonderland of technology and indulge in the full experience. Even director Buchanan here."

"Thank you, Geoffrey," director Buchanan folded his arms tightly across his chest.

"I've programmed some special tidbits nested into various

sections for the more studious and curious enthusiast, should they venture that deep into the presentations. One added item you may want to throw around with your buds at your weekly get-together, Henry, is that I've used full, 100 percent pixel depth with the projected displays. It's the leading open-source technology that I'm sure 'one of Durban's top IT companies',' Geoff finger hooked the air, "employs. And I'm only going for Real space three-D, not that myopic, simulated three-D that gives me a damned headache."

"Dare I ask for your version of what pixel depth actually means?" asked the director.

"Generally, a pixel is a flat square."

"I understand a pixel, Geoffrey."

"Back in the good old days of three-D, you'd bombard each of the two retina with two separate flat images. The brain does the convergence and melding, and voila, you've just fooled the brain and eye into thinking it's looking *into* something. Smoke and mirrors three-D. You can't interact with it because there isn't actually any depth. An object that appears half a metre away isn't. So, you cannot press or touch accurately. But, and here is where this wizard weaves his magic, by giving the pixel a special dimension, it has a width, height, and," he paused for effect, "depth. So, now a projected image has a real depth. Not a simulated one. And that is measured in pixel depth, sir. Any questions? Yes, the chap in the back?"

Director Buchanan turned to look at Professor Hicks who seemed remarkably entertained and impressed. The director shook his head in dismay and headed for the door.

"Keep me up to date on the progress, gentlemen."

Geoff wiped his brow and walked over to professor Hicks.

"What's with that ou, prof? It's like everyone else is his sounding board for his own voice. When we talk we're merely background noise."

"Indeed, Geoff," Professor Hicks gave Geoff a pat on the shoulder. "Nice presentation, by the way."

"If I had've known about his secret handshakes, I would've searched, investigated and learned the shit out of it so that when I first got to shake his hand and he tried his slippery finger-wrist-thing, I would've given a comeback move and confused the hell outta him that this wet-behind-the-ears-genius could actually be part of his club. Bastard."

Professor Hicks laughed and headed back to his desk.

"Ever think of what species of bird people could be, Geoff?"

"All the flippin' time," replied Geoff eagerly. "What's the director?"

"A Grey Loerie. Turaco."

"Corythaixoides! Excellent. Stiff and dull looking. Irritating call. Keeps telling you to go away. Nothing more than a glorified chicken with bad hair."

Professor Hicks leaned back in his chair laughing.

CHAPTER 3

Off in the distance she could hear water running. Like lying on the grass beside a small stream. For a moment she felt safe. Only for a moment.

#

"Frank," said Ruth solemnly.

"Hmm," he replied.

"We've got our missing person."

"And I think I might have figured out how Liza died."

#

The sound of water running was still there. The sleep, or rather dried tears, in her eyes made it difficult to open them. For some reason, she couldn't open her mouth.

#

In one gulp Frank emptied his coffee and they left the cafeteria.

"After you left the Room of Hours this morning, I was talking to Angel about some of the astrological characteristics that the killer's astro would need to match. So we walk over to the water cooler to fill up his jug and as the water's pouring out of the cooler bottle a bubble gurgles all the way to the top. And I'm thinking, that's like someone letting out air under water, right?"

Making their way back to the elevators, heading for the Room of Hours, Ruth noticed Frank slow his pace as they approached the daycare glassed hallway. He looked out at the deserted play area. He checked his watch.

"And then?" she asked distracting him.

"That's when I remembered Liza's mouth and neck." He felt his mouth going dry. Not from talking so fast, but from what he was about to suggest. "What if the killer wanted them to breathe under water?"

"She drowned so how's that—"

"Hear me out," he stopped and faced her. "Let's take accidental drowning into account. He would never have dunked her head under water. He would have been aware that some water might splash over the cavity." He spotted a bench and took a seat, still focused on Ruth.

"Okay," she said suspiciously as she sat down, straddling the bench to face Frank.

"What if the killer filled up his bath."

"And then?" whispered Ruth, eyes wide.

#

Her brain began to acknowledge the cold tingle of water on her legs, buttocks and back. Her neck was tight and awkward, her body rigid in whatever was tying her down. A wave of heat pulsed through her. She was taking short, quick breaths through the small hole in her neck, feeling it strain.

#

"Imagine a snorkel for breathing. Maybe a plug-hole and hose attached."

Ruth stared unblinking at Frank.

#

She couldn't see clearly through the haze of her eyes. If she could just turn her head…

"I wouldn't start moving your head around too much."

Her body went cold.

"If you break that seal around your neck, the water will go into your trachea cavity. And you could drown. Regardless of what you may think, I don't want you to drown."

There was quiet, except for the flowing water rising around her chest.

"I used to sit beside the bath and watch my mother while she bathed. Afterwards, she was so worried about lying back too far. I had to help her wash her hair. It was awkward. I only recently came up with this idea."

A cold wet hand ran over Elizabeth's forehead and hair.

"She used to have the most beautiful hair."

#

"He probably didn't think of sealing the nose and mouth."

"And as any person would have done, Liza probably panicked and tried to breathe the way her body naturally intended her to."

"Through her nose and mouth," said Ruth putting her head in her hands. "Holy shit."

"What did you say the missing woman's name was?"

#

Elizabeth was shivering all over and battling to breathe. Her chest was beginning to hurt from the strain. The water was over her mouth now and still rising.

"The best thing to do is to breathe," came the cold voice from behind her. She could still picture the face from that morning, and from the day before. How did she end up in this situation? Why?

"I'll tell you everything about her after this. In the mean time, breathing in 'yes', and out 'here I am'. Nowhere else to be but here."

#

"I think he'll be a bit more careful with Elizabeth. He'll probably tape up her mouth and plug her nose properly so that there's no way she can accidentally swallow water. And with any luck," she stood up and looked through the glass, "she'll be breathing while under water."

\#

Elizabeth was breathing for her life.

\#

"Okay, now we know how he killed Liza, how he's going to torture Elizabeth, and anyone after her. But, we still have to figure out why. Why abduct middle-aged women, keep them for two weeks, mess with them? And now start this water shit. That seems to have no purpose."

"Not if it's about what he's telling them. That's when it'll all make sense. Everything has a reason for him."

"Middle-aged women, tracheotomy, water. Those are our leads."

"That and now Elizabeth's Soul Trace," replied Frank.

Some of you may be old enough to recall the turn of the twenty-first century when the world sat with expectation of the End Days, the apocalypse described in many religious texts. I have watched these come and go. I've seen the soothsayers' predictions turn to dust, as they themselves have succumbed in the end. And still, in a New Age frenzy, many exfoliated and abluted repentance, self-evaluation and soul searching — attempting even a basic connection with the higher realms that had, for so long, been neglected or relegated to superstition — others barreled on in their ambitions and their belief in their own misguided godlike abilities.

CHAPTER 4

Elizabeth slowly woke up to a darkened room, her hands and feet still bound to the solid metal frame of the chair. She lifted her head slightly, and realised that she was tilted back at an angle. The back of the chair rested on a tabletop where a large pillow had been placed for her head. Her neck ached and she could feel the ring of burning skin react to her movements.

Light filtered in through the gap under the door, giving her some comfort in the darkness. There was no sound outside the room. Craning her neck over she looked down at the feet of the chair. The brake lever of the thick grey rubber wheels had been pushed down, holding the chair in place. *Perfect for quietly wheeling me around.* How long had she been unconscious? How long had she been unconscious until that maniac had drained the water?

The room was warm. Elizabeth started to shiver. Her body tensed up and went rigid. Her fists balled up tightly as she started to cry.

#

"SK, if you look at the flying car cock-up in the '20's, to illustrate my point," said Collins, "that guy, what's his name? Sam Flyboy."

"Samuel Flyjoy, I mean Samuel Lovejoy, dammit," said Mkhize sinking into his chair.

"Ja, Lovejoy," continued Collins. "He invents the free-float engine, patents it, and then instead of selling it off to the motor industry, he puts out a worldwide 'cast — tech specs and all — saying that he's letting anyone use it. Gratis. 'Here's my little fuck you to big business.' And what happens? You have everyone from an industrial engineer to your backyard scrap-nut building the free-float. And within what … four months you have people from Calcutta, India, to Tokyo,

Japan, not to mention the Yanks, flying into buildings and dropping from the sky. I mean shit, didn't anyone stop and think about breakdowns? We are talking about flying fucking cars here. When it malfunctions it doesn't default to hover, it defaults to plummet."

Mkhize rolled his eyes then narrowed them as he looked at the man opposite him for a moment.

As one of the new Trackers in the unit, Mkhize had been made Collins' new partner, not under the most ideal circumstances. Rob had taken a good few months to finally break his animosity towards what he saw as a junior replacement for Bester. Mkhize, even now tolerating these types of random tirades from his partner, had looked beyond the arrogant facade and snide remarks, and managed to see the man struggling to come to terms with the ultimate betrayal in the Tracker Unit. It was a betrayal on both a professional and emotional level. He knew that Collins had considered Bester to be more than just a partner.

Head of his psychological profiling class, Sakhile 'SK' Mkhize had the perfect skills to manage the bull-sized emotions of Collins. They had seemed to balance each other out. Everyone had seen Angel's strategy with the pairing. Many were grateful for it, rather than it being them.

The shift in Collins had come after Mkhize's wedding to his high school sweetheart. A traditional Zulu wedding, a primal celebration of sound, colour, and ancestors, was something that Sakhile held dear to his heart. Even in this modern age he felt the need to wed in the tradition of his parents and their parents before them.

He had invited Rob to see and experience the visceral beauty for himself.

And he had. Mkhize had seen the tears flow from his strong, rigid partner as he watched the cow being slaughtered on the patch of bare, red earth. The blood mixed with the milk had been passed around, still warm in the traditional ceramic pot. Things had seemed to quieten within Collins after that day.

"SK, you can't just pull over to the side of a skyscraper to fix a flat," said Collins waving his arms. "No. You have vehicles falling out of the sky. That's what you have. I don't care if you come from Texas, those are big-ass hailstones if you ask me. Then it still takes two months to enforce a global ban on producing the free-floaters."

"What the hell is your point?" Mkhize rubbed his face with frustration. "What's this got to do with society as a whole, Rob? We are talking about a car show here aren't we?"

"*Khabazela*," he intoned Mkhize's clan name. "Come on. It shows that the public in general is inherently stupid. Do we never learn from history? Just because it's got a funky new packaging they forget all about the past cock-ups. Up there, floating about in flying cars? Stupid."

"Meaning what exactly?"

"Meaning, any chop with a monkey-wrench can build a flying car, jump on the bandwagon like a bunch of lemmings and all trundle off the edge of a skyscraper because it's the latest fashion, latest technology, the latest thing that Bob next door's just bought. And you want to associate yourself with the 'normal' folk? Fuck off. I want to be 'abby-normal', thanks. The average human being is an idiot. I don't want to be average, I want to be exceptional."

"Ja, but if everyone were exceptional, then logically we'd all be average. Not so? And the average person is an idiot, as you classify them, so that they can make someone like you look intelligent?"

"Exactly," said Collins then added. "Hey, up yours, Mkhize. I'm intelligent."

"You've just had a rant about flying cars to prove a point about not buying tickets to a car show. That's real intelligent," said Mkhize making to get off his chair.

"Merely to illustrate," said Collins gesturing Mkhize to sit, "that the Flying Car Show is the beginning of the end."

"Sure, but flying cars would be cool though."

"Can I please rest my case on that gem? Cool? Cool is someone accidentally parking their car on your roof at two in the morning."

"Hey, Banks!" Mkhize called to Frank, "What you think about flying cars?"

"Flying cars, bru," Frank said rubbing his hands together enthusiastically. "Are you and Anele going Sunday?"

"So many ways to pull chicks." Mkhize laughed. "If I were single."

"Chicks?" whined Collins. "Shit, this squad is the one area they would have to skip when they hand out flying cars, you morons."

"What's your pluck, Rob?" asked Frank.

"Feathers."

"Apparently he's surrounded by idiots," said Mkhize to Frank.

"Who you surround yourself with says a lot about a man, Collins."

"Go fly a free-floater kite, Banks."

"What are you two on about anyway?"

Collins blinked wildly. "What I'm on—"

"Please, no." Mkhize put up a hand. "I'll give the short version, thanks. Shit. I don't want to go through that again. Basically, Collins and I were talking about how the media and the public are handling the ventriloquist case. Then he insisted on bringing in flying cars as an analogy."

Collins stepped closer to Frank. "It's just that you have all the details of how to kill someone broadcast in everyone's living room, car, headset. No age restriction. And then you have the disgruntled youth taking it on because their parents abhor it. So they in turn make it cool."

"That's a good point," said Frank, taking a step back.

"Ah, that's one less moron in the world," said Collins to the ceiling. "Intelligent people breathe a sigh of relief."

An awkward silence fell over them as they became aware of the room around them.

"So where are we at with this freak-show?" asked Collins.

They looked over at the screen filling the far wall of the room.

"Angel's trying to get some more details before he debriefs us on the next phase of the investigations," said Frank.

"Next phase?"

"Search and—"

"Destroy," Collins added.

"Search and secure, smart ass. Our main objective right now is to find the victim, safe and sound. And then, find the killer."

Lights and images flashed across the screen in front of Angel.

"I don't know how he does it," said Frank softly, "I get the whole Soul Trace idea and finding the person based on what's up there. Surprisingly even I understand the data, but maybe not as fast as that."

"Nobody's as fast as that," said Mkhize.

"Exactly, there's stuff that he seems to suck from thin air."

"Underlying shit, you mean."

"Underlying shit," agreed Frank. "It's like he goes somewhere else, picks up a book in some otherworld library, speed reads the damn thing or downloads it to his DNA."

"That's probably not too far from it, if you think about it."

"Meaning?"

"Look at our data storage systems. DNA right?"

"Yeah, so?" asked Frank.

"You know the history," continued Mkhize. "That guy in

2012 created the DNA codex or rather manipulated DNA in a codex. By accessing the four-digit sequence of the DNA makeup, he created the beginnings of what we use for storing data today. A frickin' giant leap from that old two-digit binary system from the last century. Ones and zeros became A-C-G-Ts. An entire film library on a pin head."

"And your point? I know the story. I watched the documentary."

"Well, he… what's his face?" Mkhize turned to Collins.

"SK, I thought you were telling the story?" answered Collins.

"Anyway, him. He claimed that he had some freaky drug-induced episode where he saw some lights and shit and some creatures gave him a whole lot of books to read but couldn't take back with him."

"Convenient," chirped Collins.

"But what he saw were just strands and strands of DNA filling the pages. And he understood."

"Aliens?"

"He was convinced they weren't aliens."

"Angels?" asked Frank

"Pretty much."

"Insane. So you reckon Angel's getting this other info from on high?" asked Frank, as he noticed Angel approaching. "Hold that thought, you guys."

"There're a couple of things I need to go through with you guys. You are leading the three teams, so I need you to be wide-awake. Give no reasons for so-called men of the people to cause a stink. I've got some last-minute checks I need to do, then we'll have what we need."

"How do you do it, Angel?"

"Do what?"

"What you do. I'm looking at the screen, and there's only so much to go on."

Angel turned to look at the screen, mesmerised. "Once you have the astro it's not as simple as locking on to a Soul Trace. You don't just punch some data into the system and whammo, there's the soul. You have to go in there, study the signs, figure out exactly what they mean for that specific point in time. And so, narrow down the clues. Filter through all the possibilities that are out there for that life at that moment. If you screw around for ten minutes that means that the data's changed and you've lost them for ten minutes. Every second counts. Every detail counts."

"How the hell do you narrow it down when there are all those possibilities for anyone born on the same day? I'm not at the same place at the same time as someone sharing my birthday on the other side of the world, let alone trying to differentiate between souls of people in the same area. Talk about mixed signals."

"Wrap-Around-Universe."

"Come again?"

"Everyone has certain things that surround them. It could be colours, shapes, sounds, and environments. Like mountains, seas, and rivers. These things follow you wherever you go, and you can take any two people right next to each other, and you can read what's going on for them, then and there."

"So when I take a trip to the mountains, I'm gonna take Durban's beachfront with me?"

"Putz. If a large body of water is relevant at that moment in time, you might find that you end up camping by a lake while you're in the mountains."

"So, when's this 1-kay radius going to be sorted or improved?"

"Not sure it can. Everyone's aura is different, and everyone's aura can change from one day to the next."

Mkhize chuckled. "My girl changes every five minutes."

"Exactly. That messes with the fine-tuning of the system and one kilometre is the closest we can detect."

"How are you going to narrow it down for Elizabeth?"

"That's where you sniffer dogs come in. I'll hone in on the approximate location and your teams do the process of elimination. Door to door. I'll feed you the clues and you guys do the knocking."

"One massive treasure hunt."

"In this case, this treasure has a bonus prize."

"Not sure I'd call the killer a bonus prize."

"If we look ahead to Saturday, two days from now," Angel motioned to the Screen. "There's trauma or anxiety followed by rest and ease."

"But surely there's ongoing trauma and anxiety."

"You'll be amazed at how the human psyche works. Adapt and change."

"So you're saying that we save her on Saturday?"

"Not necessarily. It could be her dying. So don't assume anything. Don't get arrogant. And most importantly, don't think that we will come out on top. Let's have that intention, but stay focused on doing your jobs.

"The feedback you give me in the field helps to narrow down the trace to at least a hundred metres. I want everyone on their mobiles," he glanced over at Ruth. "No exceptions. It's going to be door to door in this area." He pointed to the screen. A few hand movements and a green circle appeared, glowing over a map. "I want everybody reporting step by step. The team here will be sifting through everyone's feeds as they come through. We know Elizabeth's out there somewhere. It's up to us to get closer." Angel took a deep breath. "I might be stating the obvious here, but the sooner the better."

Mkhize and Collins moved off and Frank took the opportunity to ask Angel again, "How did you get to know what you know, Angel?"

He raised an eyebrow. "My folks, they taught me what I know about being myself."

#

I was twelve, just about to break the spell of my youth and dive head on into teenager life. So that would have been 1985. My friend and I have just walked the five kilometres to his house after school, joking around, pushing each other into bushes. Kids. As we're coming closer to his place we notice smoke in the air above his property. We give each other a look and pick up our pace. He's got high walls surrounding his property but because of the incline of the road we can just make out his brother and mother busying themselves around the source of the smoke. He starts shouting to them as he's opening the tall iron gate on the driveway. His mother turns to him and says something, but I'm standing stock still at the gate. I know something isn't right, but not in the emergency sense. He's getting pushed aside by his brother (older and bigger than him). His mother waves me away saying something about 'New Age' occultist. I got the hell outta there. It's all a bit of a blur for me, but he told me the details later on when he knocked on my front door a few hours after. I opened the door to a pale hunched person, my best friend.

Some people say that everyone is given an experience that robs them of their innocence. His was ripped from his gut, through his heart and out of his throat. His experience was my awakening. I wouldn't say that I lost my innocence that day. But the world became bigger than it had ever been. When I assumed I had it all covered, all figured out, it became this massive ball of energy and unexplained mysteries that what we were taught in school didn't even come close to preparing you for. For him, in his words, he'd "seen what those he trusted were capable of doing." But to me, I saw the nature of fear. How people react when they are scared. When they think they are protecting their family. That was the vastness I saw. Nothing was simple anymore. Everything, everyone you met, had many things that created who they were in a given moment.

We both sat on the edge of my bed as he told me what had happened that day. His mother had been at a church prayer meeting that afternoon. You know, tea, gossip, and fear-induced enthusiasm. The topic of music and magic being the path of the devil was tabled. In those days we had LPs, and one of the favourite techniques was to backtrack a song to find hidden messages aimed at the innocent minds of the youth.

"Damn warped to even think of that in the first place."

Of all the damn albums they had to choose that day they chose Dire Straits' Brothers in Arms. His Gran had bought it for him a few weeks before, and it was fresh in his mother's mind. A song about getting your money for nothing and women for free was totally unacceptable. Then they laid into Bruce Springsteen's *Born in the USA* album. Back tracked one or two of the songs. I don't care if you take Beethoven's 9th or Freezer Burn's *Heartache Headache*, anything backtracked sounds perverted. Now I happened to have that Springsteen album at home and damned if I could hear any messages from the Lord of Darkness. To top it all off, his mother had allowed him to buy a 'Learn to Be a Top Magician' kit around his birthday a few months before. He'd been showing me his sleight of hand card tricks, tricks even I thought were magic. His mother had been waving the Dire Straits cover at me shouting, "Your parents should be ashamed, bringing up an occultist New Age Satanist", and threw it into the fire. His brother had, moments before, scattered his magician box contents into the flames. The black smoke from the red plastic ball and plastic wand, had choked him as he'd tried to reach in to save his trick deck of cards.

A few weeks later we found some of the charred cards that had floated up in the heat and smoke a few kilometres from his house in the open grass where we had often gone riding on our BMXes. Anything that drives a kid to start smoking at thirteen should be deemed a 'bad influence'. And if anyone was looking for the devil in the shadows that day, he was well and truly out in the open and dancing around the fire of a child's hopes and dreams and innocence. And if ever the devil has a face, it's a parent turning on their child, killing them to 'save' them. Destroyer of trust. Sleight of hand takes something without you noticing. This was blatant.

It wasn't a father or mother that day. It wasn't a brother. It wasn't the devil in the flames. It wasn't a family tragedy or the death of someone close. It was my friend sitting on the edge of my bed crying into his blackened hands, his belief in rock stars and magic. The worst thing a parent ever did was telling their child that the devil existed.

I asked my father about the "New Age" stuff, the occult. He asked me one question. "How do you feel about your life?"

I said, "I feel like you and Mom support me in what I want to do. I ask questions and you teach me things. I learn things and try things. I have fun. I don't have fun. I'm the boss of me and the only one who knows what I want."

"That's New Age, son. Everything that isn't governed by rules is New Age or occult."

"But you guys tell me what to do. I have rules that I have to follow in this house."

"Sure, but those are rules that you can change when you leave this house. In this house, we get to openly discuss the rules. It's like the rules of the country that you live in. Go to a different country and there are different rules. Most are similar, but there are differences. Your mother and I prefer not to have you pissing in the lounge or kicking the cat. But hey, that's just our guidelines. And like I've said to you, you must be an individual, do what you believe is right for you, and don't be like everyone else just to fit it. Think for yourself. And on the flip-side, if you want to interact with 'normal' people you need to understand their ways. There's no point in wanting to be different, making up a new language that no one else speaks or dressing so that people call the police. There's being individual and there's creating unnecessary distractions in your life. All the progress that man has made has come from individuals who chose to see their world differently, not from people doing what everyone else is doing. See a problem, find a way to fix it. Don't complain your whole life about it. What a waste of a life. Be the god of your life. Be the creator of your possibilities. You are your dreamweaver."

"How do you feel about life, about who you are, about the world around you, where you come from and where you're going?"

I said, "Life is fun. I have lots to see and do. I want to be around people who love me and who I love back."

#

"I need two volunteers to check out Elizabeth's apartment," said Angel.

Mkhize lifted his arm, "Happy to, Angel."

"Sorry, Mkhize. You and Collins are on Missing Persons detail. I want all the reports looked at with a fine tooth-comb in case Elizabeth's not our girl."

"But it's pretty obvious she's—," began Collins before Angel cut him off.

"Fine-tooth comb, Collins."

"Frank and I'll do it, Angel," said Ruth.

"Hey," Frank nudged Ruth in the ribs, "volunteer means of your own free will, woman. Not your partner's."

"Excellent, Hicks. And that also includes some door to

door with the neighbours. Maybe they saw something, anything. Whatever you can get me for the Screen will help."

"Excellent," hissed Frank.

#

"Shit, I hate neighbours. And now you're making me talk to someone else's."

"You looked like you needed the fresh air," said Ruth as she guided the car through the afternoon traffic.

"Hmm."

"What's up anyway?" she asked.

"The case."

"Sure. I know the feeling. But we've got a chance to break it wide open and get this bastard."

"Fine." He broke his gaze from the world passing by his window and turned to Ruth. "You're doing the talking. I'm just here for the fresh air."

"Good. First we need to check out Elizabeth's apartment. Maybe she was taken from there."

"You thinking signs of a struggle?"

"That would be first prize. But grabbing someone from an apartment block seems a bit risky. It might not be as simple as that. For us anyway."

"Psch. You'd be surprised. I swear we need to drop by my neighbour's place and see if he's got some bodies stashed away. Hell, some nights you'd think someone was being slammed against the wall the way he plays his music."

"Hence your neighbour hang-ups."

"They mind their business, and I'll mind mine. Just because we share a wall or a hallway, doesn't mean we're family."

"Gee, Frank. You're the perfect citizen. There's definitely no Big Brother in your world."

"They can watch all they like, as long as they don't tell me how to crack one off first thing in the morning," Ruth cringed, as he continued, "Or that they are writing a petition to have number twenty-three evicted because the stench coming from his kitchen is too foreign and they swear they've heard a dog barking. Piss off, lady. How about we petition you to mind your damn business."

"Whoa, boy."

"And you know that it's those dust-gathering pensioners, with all the time on their hands with no time left that sit around analysing every bump and scrape and noise. Something's always out of place."

#

"Who eventually reported Elizabeth missing?" asked Ruth from the entrance hall. Nothing stood out as significant in the pile of torn open envelopes that she held. The usual bills: power company, communications network, Amazon.com statements, rental agent, and junk mail.

With all the technology in the world, nothing beats the old-fashioned 'spam in your mailbox'.

"Seems that because of all the media coverage, bless their hardened hearts, people are getting jittery about each other's whereabouts," came Frank's reply from the living room. "Missing Persons have been flooded with false reports of sisters, mothers, aunts and whatever being abducted by the Ventriloquist. Only to have them come waltzing through the door while they're still on the emergency line."

"There you go, Frank," she looked up from a flyer advertising piano lessons. Never too old to learn! "People do care."

"I think most of them are wishful thinking."

"Bastard."

"Anyway, Elizabeth works morning shift at COMNET's help desk. Starting at 2 AM, of all hours. She never turned up.

Didn't answer calls. One of her colleagues came by here later this morning. Bruce Cass."

"Boss. Not colleague," interrupted Ruth.

"Whatever. Car's still parked outside. No answer. Except, and this is where I rest my case, a few cold stares from disturbed neighbours. Emphasis on 'disturbed'."

Ruth replaced the mail on the table and headed down the narrow, darkened hall to the bathroom.

"The report was taken at the squad and within a few minutes it registered on our system as a possible match. Mkhize and Collins checked out the details of about thirty other possibles — hers seemed the odd one out. Single. No immediate relatives, etcetera."

Ruth flicked the light switch alongside the dark doorway, a twang of guilt rising up for the intrusion. There's no vanity in saving a life.

"Right now we're pretty much grabbing at straws for any ID. So, 'tag! you're it', Elizabeth."

"Single, middle-aged woman," Ruth began, more to herself, "Living alone. Living in an apartment block. No close relatives." She looked over at the bathtub. Lady's razor, exfoliating sponge, nailbrush, shampoo and conditioner. She hunched over and sniffed the air above one of the two cream-coloured candles in the corner. Jasmine.

Ruth slowly climbed into the bath, sinking gently into the cold porcelain. Her legs stretched out, arms at her sides. She sank in lower. Her eyes closed as she pictured the darkened room, lit by the warm glow of the candles, steam hanging in the scented air. The smell drifted through her body, and warmth tingled her skin.

Where are you?

How did he get you? All of you.

"Jesus, you're a freak," echoed Frank's sharp voice in the cold, tiled room.

"Shuddup, Frank!" she snapped as she jumped out the bath. "I'm feeling her energy, you insensitive bastard."

"Whatever," he mumbled as he turned to walk back to the living room. "Be sure to wash behind your ears."

Ruth gathered herself. "If she was taken from here, there's no sign of a struggle."

"Maybe she knew the guy."

"Or she felt comfortable enough to invite them in."

"That rules out snake-oil salesmen."

"Smart," replied Ruth as they both stepped through the front door and into the warmth of the day. "One thing that's bugging me is that they all share the same odd commonality."

"Being?" He asked

"No close relatives."

"Yeah, them and most of the city," Frank looked out over the hallway banister onto the parking lot and neat garden ten stories below. "What's your point?"

"Think about it. How would the killer know that? It has to be a major factor in his choice."

"Less likely to be missed," he considered.

"Exactly. But it could also be part of the motivation."

"Meaning?" He pushed up off the railing.

"Meaning it's part of the psychological pattern and not just convenience."

"Maybe a loner? No friends or family?"

"Something like that."

"How the hell would the killer find that kind of information out?"

"Some kind of questionnaire. Application form. Next of kin check-box marked 'none'."

"And who pray tell asks those kinds of questions? 'Excuse me, ma'am, but we're doing a survey of all lonely, middle-aged women in the area and your name came up'."

She smacked his shoulder. "You are on a roll today.

Hospital. Financial institution. Life insurance."

"Collins said she's got no life cover. No one to leave it to, I'd guess."

A pang of empty sorrow stuck in her throat. No one to give a damn.

"Well, I give a damn and we're going to sort this shit out!"

Frank's eyes widened. "I'm with you on that one, but there's nothing here."

She smiled at him. "Door to door with uncle Frank," and walked off to the neighbour's door. "This'll be interesting."

"Trick or treat, Grandma."

#

No reply from the neighbour to the left. Frank and Ruth silently passed by Elizabeth's doorway and knocked on the opposite door. After a few moments Frank did a subtle eye roll as an elderly lady, steamed-up reading glasses on the tip of her nose, answered the door, followed by a blast of curry scents from within.

#

"I don't know how you do it," the older lady was saying from the open-plan kitchen as she stirred then replaced a pot lid on the bubbling red-orange stew. "In my day, you caught the bad guy and locked him up for good. Threw away the key and all that. But taking innocent children away from their mothers, their family, and locking them up like criminals. *Sjoe.* I don't know what I would do if that was my child."

"Only if it comes to that, Mrs. Potokri," said Ruth standing alongside Frank in the lounge.

"So we take it you're not a believer then?" asked Frank.

"Oh, I'm a believer, all right," she said with a mischievous grin, removing her apron and gesturing for the trackers to take a seat. "I'd like to see you trackers follow my soul at night. The places I go, you'd be chasing your tails all over this world and the next. I've had far too many unexplainable experiences in my life to dismiss a higher power, let alone an afterlife. It's gotten me through many hardships, from my home country to the one that accepted me here, whether it liked it or not. This city, when my husband and I arrived from Ibadan thirty years ago, was rife with prostitutes and drug lords."

"You mean the Nigerian drug lords?" Frank said dryly and crossed his legs.

"Please, *abeg*," she scolded, eyes narrowing. "Nigerians aren't all space-prawn eating drug dealers scamming people on the internet, ọmọkunrin. We are little old ladies who survive prejudice and xenophobia. We watch our husbands butchered because someone feels threatened because he's driving his taxi in their country. Assumptions by law enforcement," she stabbed a finger in Frank's direction, "means you regularly comply to random searches or paper checks. We are the ones who brought disrepute to your city, your precious waterfront. But you fail to check your history. The bad juju was here way before any *Nigerian*. Strip shows and Smugglers Inn were still whispered in the streets when Olaniyi and I arrived."

Realising she was perched forward in her chair, she took a deep breath and sank slowly back into the couch. "I have seen a lot. And you're probably thinking I've got one foot in the tunnel as we speak."

Frank looked up, surprised with the statement.

"No need to look all coy, ọkunrin." She smiled and raised her arms. "I'm practically sitting and waiting for the rapture."

"Isn't the rapture supposed to mean *all* mankind, not just you?"

"Well, what's the difference? When I go, my whole universe goes with me." She chuckled. "From my perspective, anyway."

Ruth interrupted. "So, Mrs. Potokri, no one visited

Elizabeth?" She waited, then added, "How long has she lived next door to you?"

The old lady crinkled her nose at the ceiling. "I think it's going on a year now." She looked back at Ruth and continued, "Yes, beginning of October of last year, if I'm not mistaken."

"And she kept to herself?"

"We chatted every now and then in the hallway," she replied. "With her work hours we hardly saw each other. She was always concerned about disturbing me when she left in the mornings."

"What time did she usually come home from work?"

"Around two or three in the afternoon."

"Did she happen to mention what she did for a living?" Frank added.

"Something to do with telephone support for one of the phone companies." She thought for a moment. "What do they call them now? Communications networks."

"Did she say if there were any problems at work? Coworkers? Men?"

"Men?" She seemed surprised. "None of those came around here to my knowledge."

Frank, pleased with himself, glanced at a thick, dark wood crucifix on the wall.

"Who stays in the other apartment alongside Elizabeth's?" Continued Ruth.

"Oh, a lovely young couple. They're expecting." As if remembering something, Mrs. Potokri pushed herself up and headed back to the kitchen.

"And the ancient Roman execution device?" interrupted Frank pointing his chin to the dining room.

"The what?" Mrs. Potokri peered through the rising steaming from a pot she brought from the kitchen sink to the stove. "Oh, old habits. I was raised a good old-fashioned Anglican girl. Church on Sundays. Sometimes Saturdays." She pointed in the direction of the side table to her chair's right. "My old *Book of Common Prayer* and I have survived a great deal. But the old country, and the juju that runs through my veins, are what really get me through the day. Besides, that was when the church stood for what is good and pure and Godly."

The scents became more intense in the lounge as the woman slowly added the rice to the other pot, carefully stirring.

Frank snorted. "When was this? I didn't realise you were born at the time of Christ, because the church, as I understand it, was forced on our ancestors."

"*Abeg*, officer." She glanced over at Ruth and said, "You have a real feisty one here, dear."

"He's a gem," she replied through clenched teeth at Frank.

"Tell me, officer." She finished her stirring, tapped the wooden spoon on the pot and adjusted the stove setting.

"Tracker."

"*Tracker*." She said from the kitchen entrance. "In the middle of the night, when you lie awake in your bed listening to the voices of the past and the present — the voices screaming their rebukes and pleas — who do you pray to? Who do you ask for guidance or forgiveness, for help? Who do you bend your creaking knees to when all your strength is sapped?"

"I believe in a higher power," he answered.

"Yes," she said taking a seat, "but do you believe in a higher power that actually gives a damn about you?"

"And who do you pray to?"

"When you get to my age, when you're knocking on heaven's door, you start to throw out the garbage. You toss out all the so-called facts, science, theories, and evidence. You toss out all the hype and pop spirituality. And all that you are left with are your own tiny, insignificant beliefs. Whether they are yours from years of force feeding, drumming them into your young sponge-like mind, or repetition. Forget the latest scientific breakthrough into another dimension, or spiritual fad. When you're lying on your deathbed, or close to it, and you have Orun-Rere on your left, and hell on your right, you're going to say some hail Mary's, ask Jesus Christ to deliver you from evil and pray to your Ori Orun. I don't care who you are. All bets are off, and all theories are theories. Even Constantine, that great champion of Christianity and sorter of Christian dogma — sun worshipper that he was — waited till he was lying prostrate to be baptised a Christian. A 'just-in-case-clause'."

"Hey, I'm a 'one-step-in-front-of-the-other' kind of guy. And right now my next step is to find Elizabeth. Then the step after that is to catch the creep who gets his kicks out of disobeying certain humanitarian laws. Then my next step will be contemplating my next step up his ass."

"Good for you, officer. He's always watching you, and always ready to answer your prayers."

"Answer my pr… Okay. Whatever you say."

#

Bleep. Geoff's screen came to life. He held in his earbud and pressed the screen.

"Hell, if it isn't my ou, Marc Ramdheo," said Geoff to the smiling face on the screen.

"Bru, how you doing?" replied Marc.

"All the better knowing the weekend has dawned upon this fine city and Soma has much merriment and drinking in store, having given us a free pass courtesy of the devil's own suppository: the student loan account!"

"Bring and come. As usual you bailed early on me last night, but let the madness continue! You free now, or what?"

"Um, well," considered Geoff, "how to put this?"

"Nought!" Marc visibly shook his side of the conversation. "Don't choon me you're grafting all day."

"Relax," shushed Geoff. "The ballie running the Ornithology department hath decreed today a day of carcass to-ing and fro-ing. Selection and organisation for the digital displays as well as the significant distinctions between the ages, more precisely juvenile and adult and the precedence that these set within the said department."

Marc stared blankly at the screen. "Chop."

"My thoughts exactly," nodded Geoff agreeably.

"*You*. You're 'chop'!" said Marc.

"Ah," he said.

"How's the old colonial monstrosity?" asked Marc.

"Buchanan is as irritating as you'd expect him to be in person."

Marc chuckled. "I meant the building."

"Oh, right. Still standing."

"Remember that first time we went there. Grade," Marc stopped to think.

"Eleven," Geoff finished off for him. "Like it was yesterday, bru. It was Adeline Rankin who got me into the sciences. She was the one who took our class on the tour of the insect gallery."

"Yasas, the behind the scenes of the Forensics Entomology Laboratory."

"Exactly. The one she had implemented. I mean, all the latest tech in the city started in the museum complex. She lobbied for it to extend into the greater eThekwini areas."

There was a moment of quiet.

"Anyway," said Geoff. "What would have been a Friday of the traditional sort has turned into the tedious sort. But I'm sure, come Monday, on reflection of aforesaid circumstances, much hilarity will ensue."

"But, currently not, chop," said Marc flatly.

"And in conclusion," continued Geoff, "I didn't get to finish my project, which, surprise, surprise, is due Monday morning. And if I don't finish it tonight, there's no goddamn way I'll finish it in a drunken stupor on Monday morning, never mind the museum stuff. And therefore, my chances of getting a bloody D will increase directly proportional with each pint consumed. And as a result, could fail theory for the year." He lifted a finger. "And lose the student loan."

"We're still on for tomorrow then?"

"Damn straight!" Geoff snapped out of his brief depression.

"Hundreds!"

Bleep.

"You do know that when you refer to the 'ballie', that I know you're talking about me?" asked Allen.

"Yep." Geoff twitched his eyebrows and bleeped his music on.

#

"I do hope I've been of some help, dears."

"Hmm," came Frank's response.

"Yes, thank you, Mrs. Potokri. If anything else should pop into your head," said Ruth pulling out a card from her top pocket, "please give us a call. My number's on there. Call anytime."

"Right you are, dear." Turning to Frank, "I'll be mentioning you in my prayers, officer."

Frank grimaced in return as the old lady closed the door.

"I thought I was going to do all the talking in there."

"She started it," he said innocently.

They both leaned over the balcony, breathing in the city air.

"If anything should pop into your head?" asked Frank sarcastically. "Pop?"

"Screw you, Frank. She happened to rub off on me."

"Yeah, her and her sage or potpourri, or whatever."

"Nothing wrong with some old-fashioned values in this modern, plug-me-into-your-hyperdrive world."

"Her head went pop a long time ago when old-fashioned values meant hitting your prospective lay over the head."

"Shit you've got a foul trap, Banks," she said under her breath as a young couple made their way past them, stopping at the door next to Elizabeth's apartment.

The woman's round belly was visible as she readjusted her floppy bag draped around her shoulders. She rummaged through it as the young man stole a glance at her and Frank. They both hesitated for what was a split second as Ruth and Frank, like two synched robots, fell into step in their direction.

"Hi," said Ruth waving a friendly hand, "sorry to alarm you."

"We're not alarmed," replied the young man looking alarmed.

"We're Trackers from the City Division," Frank said, putting on his formal expression.

They both seemed to relax in their bodies.

"My name is Ruth Hicks, and this is Franklin Banks," added Ruth.

"Ninjani," replied the young man. "I'm Musa Mdladlana, and this is my wife Andile."

"Andi." Andile gave a warm smile and held out her hand to Ruth.

Ruth returned the smile and the handshake, looking down at Andile's swollen abdomen. "How far are you?"

"Ruth," whispered Frank comically, "don't assume."

Andile clicked her tongue, as her husband gave a nervous snort.

"Seven months," she replied. "Do you have kids?"

"A son," answered Ruth.

"Should we?" Musa indicated the open doorway.

"How was his birth?" asked Andile.

"Heaven and hell," continued Ruth as she followed Andile inside. "Simply put."

"Thanks for the honesty," said Andile throwing her bag on the small, round dining table tucked in the corner of the entrance hall. "I need to get off my feet."

Frank followed the two women inside, catching a glance of Musa giving the outside passageway one last quick scan.

"You know, technically we're police officers," Frank said covertly, startling Musa as he locked and rechecked the door.

"Yeah, I know," he attempted a smile. "But I've been flippin' neurotic the past few days. I'm trying not to freak Andi out but, eish, I'm also not taking any chances." He nervously wrung his hands together. "You guys had any luck with this guy?"

"Well, that's kinda why we're here," said Frank starting for the living room.

"Hey." Musa paused, then whispered, "If you guys are back here that means you've come full circle with squat."

"I'd like to tell you you're wrong, mfowethu, but it isn't that simple either." Frank carried on to the living room. "We've made some progress, but we need to get as much info as we can get."

The two women were happily relaxed on two large, brown leather sofas. The smell of leather filled Frank's nose as he sat down next to Ruth. Babies. Birthing. Gynecologists.

"Can we get to the point of the visit?" he interrupted in Ruth's direction.

"Ah, yes," Ruth sat up in the chair.

"We know you've already gone over this with the other Trackers," continued Frank, "but is there anything else that you might have remembered since then?"

"Anything?" added Ruth, "and not necessarily from the day. Say, people hanging around in the days or weeks leading up to Elizabeth's disappearance."

"*Elizabeth?* Yirra, you act as if you know her."

"Musi," snapped Andile.

"Sorry."

"That's okay, Andile. Musa, I want to know her. We have to know as much about her as possible. She's not just some woman that's gone missing."

"Look," said Musa, sitting down on the edge of the sofa, "as we told the other guys. There's been nobody suspicious around. Everything's been pretty normal."

Ruth turned to Andile, "Are you off work yet? I mean, not that I'm assuming anything about pregnant mothers these days, but aren't you here during the day?"

Andile shrugged. "Yes and no. I'm on leave from the agency, but for the past few weeks my ma's been taking me to prenatal exercises." Andile looked at her husband. "Musi's pretty hectic at work, but he's there for every scan and checkup, ne?"

Musa looked at his hands awkwardly. Andile rummaged through her bag, deep supplier of everything, and passed Ruth a colour print of what Ruth immediately recognised as a 3-D image of the couple's unborn child.

"That's where we've just come from."

Ruth passed it on to Frank who, after a glance, handed it straight on to Musa.

"As I say," said Musa looking at his child, "it's the same old crowd around here. Last month the rental agent came around to handle our lease renewal on this place."

"Yebo," interrupted Andile. "She should be paying Liz a visit…" She stopped. "Well, she'd be coming around about now."

"How's that?" asked Frank.

"Liz moved in a month or two after us," Andile said and went back into her bag. "Maybe she could help with some more personal info." Andile passed some stapled sheets of paper to Ruth.

"Couldn't hurt," said Ruth as she wrote down the rental agency and agent's details from the header of the cover sheet.

"The amount of data you have to spew out onto one of those babies, I wouldn't be surprised if they could tell you where she is."

Three heads turned to Musa.

"What? Am I the only one freaked out by all this kak?" He rose to leave the room. "Anyone want coffee or whatever?" He disappeared around the corner and, with cupboards and dishes banging, to what sounded like the kitchen.

"Did your guys speak to Liz's man at work?" came the kitchen voice.

"Man at work?" Frank asked Andile.

"The guy she'd had like two dates with," she added.

"You mean this," Ruth checked her notes on her mobile, "Bruce Cass? Says here he's her boss at COMNET."

"Hmm. I didn't want to give the oke trouble. They seemed good together."

"So, you're saying she's dating her boss?" asked Frank.

"Was dating her boss," replied Andile. "They broke up, kind of, on the last of their two dates."

"When was he around here?"

"Both times he dropped her off around nine thirty in the evening."

"Funny, Mrs. Potokri didn't mention anything about him."

"There are a few things gogo Dolapo doesn't see after her seven PM curfew," Musa piped up over the sounds of a kettle.

"When was this?" asked Frank.

"About eight or nine months ago. I would have mentioned the dating thing to the other Trackers," she began defensively, "but I didn't want to cause trouble for him. He seemed nice enough and—"

"From what we saw," Musa's head craned around the corner, "sticking our heads out our front door, it was all pretty formal."

"I caught something about appropriateness and business and colleagues from Liz," she said sadly. "They did seem cute together."

"Yasas," said Frank to Ruth. "Why didn't they follow that up?"

"The report did say that they spoke to her boss, Frank." She scowled at him.

"And how did he take that?" He returned his questioning to Andile. "Did you see him around anymore?"

"No," she said. "He took it okay. I could hear he was upset."

Musa emerged, steaming mug in his hand. He stopped, sipping as he looked around the room.

"Thanks, Musi," said Andile sarcastically.

"I offered, didn't I?"

"It's fine, ma'am," said Frank as he stood. "We need to be going. More leads to follow up." He pulled out a card from his wallet and passed it to Musa. "If you think of anything, anything, please contact us."

"Yes," added Ruth putting a hand on Andile's knee, "and I hope everything goes well for you guys. I expect a call from Musa the moment that rascal pops."

Andile looked affectionately at Musa, who was studying Frank's card intently.

"I'm sure it will all be perfect," said Ruth getting up.

Frank stepped closer to Musa and whispered, "If it's any consolation, mfowethu, we've got round-the-clock surveillance on Liz's — Elizabeth's — apartment. Just in case you think anyone's going to show up."

"What," Musa gave a smirk. "and give themselves up?"

"I like this guy," said Frank to Ruth.

"I am in advertising," added Musa. "Still like me?"

"Anyway," continued Frank, "I don't think anyone's about to steal an old lady's purse, let alone try and kidnap someone around here."

"Very reassuring, ne?" replied Andile.

#

"Coffee? I'm buying."

"Damn right you are."

#

They sat at a busy coffee shop on the corner of a jammed intersection. People, cars and noise flashed by. Ruth nursed an empty cup and saucer as Frank finished off a conversation on his mobile.

"Thanks for your time," Frank clicked off.

"And?"

"Mr. Boss Slash Boyfriend was a bit reluctant on the info, but wanted to," he finger-hooked the air, "make it absolutely clear that it was purely a business relationship and that they had crossed the line with the dates. I think he was hinting that *he* had broken it off like a responsible employee."

"So, basically a dead end."

"Yep, but," Frank checked his mobile, "he did give me some personal info on Elizabeth that we would never have come across anywhere else."

"I'm listening."

"She was previously married. Husband died about four years ago. Didn't like to talk about it."

"I can imagine."

"Something about a work-related accident. No details. She received a small payout from a bad insurance package," he looked up from his notes. "The company basically screwed her on workman's comp that she eventually blew on shitty lawyers trying to appeal until the money ran out and she had to call it quits."

"Other family?"

Frank referred back to his mobile. "Parents died six and eight years ago. Older brother living in the US. Haven't spoken for six or eight years."

"Middle aged. Single. Widow. Living alone. No children. No close relatives."

"You thinking pattern?"

"I'm thinking this guy picks people who won't be missed in a hurry."

"Any luck with the rental agency?"

"Left a message for them," she indicated the coffee cups, "out to lunch. Go figure."

Frank took one final pull on his coffee. "How are you guys doing?"

"Hmm," said Ruth absently, coming back from somewhere else.

"The three of you," said Frank leaning on his elbows. "You know, husband, son, and that wonder woman Ruth."

"We're okay," she said pivoting her mobile around on the table's surface with her finger. "No drama to report on our side." She leaned her chin on her hand. "Allen just thinks I take the soul stuff too seriously."

"I like rational Al," said Frank. "He's my kind of guy. A grounding anchor in an all too enlightened world."

"You really think we're too enlightened?"

"Correct."

"So you don't see it as a good thing? The evolution of man, getting more in touch with the creator and all that?"

"Mystery."

"Excuse me?"

"Mystery. As soon as you give me all the answers to all the riddles of the Universe, there's no more mystery. No more searching. No more walking the earth. No more contemplating my navel."

"Frank, the day you contemplate your navel I'll...I don't know what."

"You'll have full permission to blow my contemplating grey matter onto the wall."

"Vivid," said Ruth.

· "It's just that I want to look at a sunset like the cavemen did. With utter awe and incomprehension at the magnificence before me, without someone telling me that it's not actually God or anything special. That it's going to happen tomorrow and the next day and that all it is is a ball of fire millions of miles away causing light to reflect and refract and shit. Mystery. Can a man not just ask 'I want to know, but please don't tell me. I want to guess, and make something up'?"

Ruth raised an eyebrow and said, "Or form a religion around it."

"Who's the cynic?"

"Touché. But you need to have your head in the clouds sometimes. I like to think there's more to life than killers and death and the human monster."

"Sure, but sometimes I think a part of you wants to drift off with some of those victims, into the white light of Never-never Land." Frank glanced down at the time on his mobile.

Ruth shrugged. "Maybe. I guess the only thing keeping me here are my two men."

"And how's Caleb been?"

"Hasn't seen much of me for the past few weeks," she said, slouching her shoulders. "I get the feeling he knows what's happening. Well, that it's bad stuff anyway. And, yirra Frank," she hesitated, "I'm about to unload some existential kak on you."

"Anyway," he pushed her.

"Well. Like he's the one supporting me when I'm out there

fighting crime. Like he's protecting me and giving me intuition flashes."

Frank leaned back, slapping his thighs, "Like I said, Allen's the grounder in the family."

She looked back at him with a comic glare.

Frank picked up his mobile from the table, "We need to get back and log our notes into the system. I'll get this round." His fingers waltzed across the mobile's screen. A ping noise sounded, echoed by a ping sound inside the restaurant.

"Thanks," said Ruth standing to leave.

A waitress emerged from the restaurant doorway, "Thank you, and please come again."

"Great coffee," said Frank with a broad grin in her direction. Ruth rolled her eyes just as her mobile sounded in her hand.

She beeped the receive button. "Hello, Hicks here."

They both walked down the stairs and onto the pavement.

"Ah, yes. Hi," she began. "Just stand-by a minute." She pushed an on-screen button. Beep.

A lady's voice came from the unit, "Hello? Tracker Hicks?"

"There, sorry. Hi. Miss Young, is it?"

"Yes, I'm returning your call from earlier. I was out to lunch. What can I help you with?"

"A bit late for lunch?" remarked Ruth.

A pause on the line. "A bit quieter from the lunchtime crowds at this time of the day."

"I know what you mean," she looked at Frank, oblivious. "I understand you are the agent at Morris Chandler handling Elizabeth Stride's apartment lease."

"Elizabeth Stride?" she asked, the sound of screen keys typing faintly audible, "Oh, yes, Mrs. Stride. Her lease is up for renewal at the end of this month. I went around to see her last week sometime. Let me just check. Um, yes, last Wednesday."

"Did she sign on for another year?"

"Not yet, no," the woman on the other end of the line paused, then said, "I left the paperwork with her, along with a digital copy via email."

Ruth remembered the papers in Elizabeth's apartment. They came to a stop outside their car.

"Hang on a seco...oh my god," Miss Young stammered, "Is she one of the ladies—"

Ruth cut her short. "Ma'am, please. We need absolute discretion with this information and this case. We cannot have this leaking out to the media." They both got into the vehicle and closed their doors into muffled quiet.

"Absolutely. God, no. You're right," she fumbled, "our client information is handled with utter confidentiality. Be they alive or de... Sorry."

"Damn civilians," mumbled Frank. Ruth scowled at him icily.

"What was that?" Came the mobile voice.

"Is there any information that you have on file about Mrs. Stride that could help us?"

"I can share her application form from last year if you'd like. It would probably be easiest for you to glean what you need rather than me trying to think of what's deemed important and what's not in a case like this."

"You're probably right there, but can you do that? I mean are you authorised to do that?"

A sound beeped on the other side. "I am authorised, Tracker Hicks," came her cool voice as Ruth's mobile beeped an incoming file. "That will be the file."

"Great," said Ruth mouthing "Wow" to Frank who just shook his head. He pulled the car out of the parking bay and into the afternoon traffic.

"If there's anything else at all, I would happy to be of service with your investigation."

"Thanks, Miss Young," replied Ruth, "that's all I can

possibly ask of you at this stage."

"Okay then, good luck," came the voice.

"Thanks, bye."

"Goodbye."

Frank groaned then said, "Everyone's a Sherlock Holmes super sleuth wannabe."

"She's just trying to help, Frank." She smacked his shoulder. "It's more than we've had to go on."

#

The tall windows framed the speckled blackness of the night sky outside. Ruth shivered, sensing the evening chill moving through the apartment as she sat nestled in the darkness of the lounge. A cushion rested over her icy feet folded up on the couch. She hadn't been able to fall asleep and had moved out into the lounge so that her restless body didn't disturb her husband.

It'll be morning eventually. A hot shower and fifteen minutes on the bike would cure her scratchy eyes and irritated muscles. As good as new. Almost.

Whenever she didn't sleep through the night she never felt the change of day. Even watching the dawn of a new day edging slowly across the sky, it still felt like the same day. Endless.

She tried to imagine how night workers survived. Then she wondered if Elizabeth would survive. Did Elizabeth?

The silence of the room hung over her ears, as if they were muffled. A scraping sound from the hallway caused her stomach to tense. The air on her scalp bristled. She turned to face the darkness, just making out the form she knew was Caleb.

"Hey, Cay," she breathed as the warmth radiated from her stomach, over her body. "Why you up at this time of the night?"

Arms hanging limply from his shoulders, he screwed up his face in a tight frown. His bare feet dragged lazily across the floor as he came around the couch and flopped onto Ruth's lap.

"Can't sleep," he said through his teeth, rubbing his eyes with his small fist. He let out a long sigh and looked up at his mother. "Why aren't you sleeping, Mommy?"

"I can't sleep either." She drew her son closer to her.

He wriggled into her warmth, one eye closed, the other looking up at her. He flopped his head to the side to look out the large lounge windows. He sighed again and hit his little fist on his thigh. "It's still night time," he said letting out an irritated growl.

"So-rry," Ruth nudged him.

Caleb turned back to his mother, eyes locked on hers, his face softer, concerned. "Why aren't you sleeping, Mommy?"

She looked up at the night sky again. "Too many things running through my head, Cay."

His brow knotted his concern. "Bad stuff?"

"Some bad stuff," she looked down at his rosy face, "some things I don't understand."

"Mommy, you know everything."

"I don't think your father or Uncle Frank would agree with that," she said making Caleb wobble in her lap as she chuckled. Feeling the cool air on her ankles, she repositioned the cushion on her feet.

"Uncle Frank hasn't asked about Reagan for a long time, Mommy."

The thought of the younger boy in the daycare took Ruth by surprise. She could still recall how Mkhize had described the scene he and Collins had been faced with. At first the baby boy's parents had been angry, trying to force the two trackers out of their home. Things had escalated as Collins, breaching tracker protocol, had blurted out the baby's original soul name. Tracker Bester had made international news broadcasts, a handful of people and conservative organisations lauding his actions while others, like the proud new parents of Reagan, were shocked.

Conflicting emotions had practically immobilized the young couple, finally succumbing to horrific grief.

"I think Uncle Frank's just been busy with work, Cay." She gave it a moment and then asked, "How is Reagan doing?"

"I dunno. He only plays with me sometimes and he doesn't talk a lot. But I like him," he added defensively.

Ruth felt her son's warmth again and pulled him closer with a squeeze. "My angel boy with the big heart."

"You know about angels, hey, Mommy?"

"Hmm, angels," she mused for effect.

"Tell me about my angel," he asked wide eyed.

She blinked and drew in a deep breath. "Okay, let's see. Before you were born your soul was in Heaven."

Caleb smiled. "Where's Heaven, Mommy?"

"Everywhere, Cay. Heaven is everywhere and your soul was Heaven, part of Heaven and part of God. Because God is everything and is in everything. So God took part of Himself, part of Heaven, your soul. And that soul decided that it wanted to be on earth, in a body. Your soul wanted to feel what it's like to be a beautiful boy."

Caleb looked at his mother sheepishly.

"Your soul wanted to taste sweets," she said nudging him in the ribs, "not too many. Your soul wanted to have a mom and a dad that loved it no matter what. And five years ago, your soul knew that that was the time to be born on earth." She looked down at the boy in her arms. "Do you remember being born, Cay?" she whispered.

Caleb brought his finger to his mouth thoughtfully. "Sort of," he looked out the window, "warm and dark and quiet."

She smiled at him in the dark of the room. "But when you

were born not all your soul came into your body because God always wants us to be part of Heaven. So some of your soul stayed in Heaven."

Caleb pushed himself up on his elbow. "But I want all of me to be here," he said concerned.

"It is Cay," she continued as she settled him back in her lap. "Remember, I said Heaven is everywhere." She felt his small body relaxing, closer to her. "Now, when you were born you knew all of this. That's why babies are happy to come out the nice warm, quiet tummies of their mommies. You know where you are and why you've been born. And you know that your soul is right by you; talking to you; loving your big adventure on earth.

"But as you started to look around you, you saw there was so much for you to learn and see and do. You started to see that you're in a body (not just a soul that is everywhere). You began to forget about your soul."

"Uh uh." Caleb frowned at his mother.

"But your soul still loved you and spoke to you. You can feel there's someone watching over you, helping you, guiding you, hey Cay?"

"Yep," he said confidently. "Can you, Mommy?"

Ruth drew in a deep breath. "Well, that's the thing. When you're at school and your teachers or your friends talk about it, or the stories you read or the movies you watch, they talk about angels. And they tell you that we've actually got angels looking after us. That there are angels all around us, sent by God."

Caleb quickly scanned the room, left right and upside down.

"They also say that we even have our own Guardian Angels that help us all the time. Then as you get bigger you, when you stop believing in angels—"

"I believe in angels!" said Caleb quickly.

"A little bit bigger than you, my boy. Sometimes people don't want to believe in angels but they still talk to God. As you get older, you notice how your life has worked and you begin to see the little miracles that happen around you all the time, and you start to think of someone guiding you. And if you sit still for a while, and keep very quiet."

Ruth waited and watched Caleb close his heavy eyelids.

"You can sometimes feel it close by. And as you go through your life you start to remember your guardian angel again. And you realise that that guardian angel is not really an angel like you think, with wings and all that stuff, but that it's your spirit guide. Some people can see them. Some people can't. Sometimes they look like an Egyptian, sometimes like a nun, and sometimes like a warrior."

"A warrior?" Caleb's eyes popped open. "Wow."

"I thought you were asleep there for a second, chap. They can be lots of things. And these guides", she ran her hand through his hair as she continued, "seem to change and some stay the same, but they are still your guides. The more you feel them, and know them, and listen to them, the more they begin to change."

"Change?" Caleb asked sleepily, "Into what?"

"Into you, Cay."

"Why into me, Mommy?"

"Because they are you, Caleb. They are your soul, remember. Your soul never left you. Your soul is always there. When you forget about your soul; or how your soul feels; or how your souls speaks to you, your soul changes into something or does things that you will notice. And the more you notice and listen, the more your soul can become like it used to be. The mirror-image of you."

"But what about the warrior?" he yawned.

"The warrior was someone that your soul was on earth before it became you."

"Can you feel your soul, Mommy?"

"Hmm. I dunno," she looked out the window ahead of her. "Your soul can help other people as well. Sometimes I feel Grandpa by me. That's his soul helping me, because sometimes you don't always hear your own soul."

She watched him struggling to keep his eyes open.

"And the angels?"

She soothed her hand over his warm head and said, "You are the angel, my boy. You're my guardian angel, Caleb."

His breathing was heavier now, his eyes closed in light slumber.

"You know that one day he's going to ask about dying," came Allen's gentle voice behind her.

She turned her head slightly, not enough to see him. "I know. He'll be fine."

"It's not him I'm worried about," he said. He walked quietly over to her, bending down and picking up the warm bundle from her arms. He kissed her softly on the forehead as he stood up and carried their son off to bed.

#

Sweat was flowing down his back and his arms were steaming up the cold bar counter as he leant over his drink. The last effects of the tablets were slowly wearing off, oozing out of his pores. He finally caught his breath and emptied the ice-cold drink from the glass.

He swiveled slightly around to survey the rest of the club. Lights were zigzagging through the haze of bodies and moisture. The music pulled at his chest and stomach, pumping and rocking. He tried to take in another deep breath. Sounds all around him became oppressive; he wanted it to stop, just for a second; just enough time to breathe properly. The vapour from the room, all the airborne sweat and breath, made him feel like he was submerged in a lukewarm pool on a hot summer's day.

"I need to get the hell outta here," he mumbled to himself and got off the stool.

He felt the temperature change just moments before he stepped through the doorway and onto the dimly-lit sidewalk. He took a deep breath of the humid night air, the heat wave unusual for this time of year but living up to the reputation of the seaside city.

At least it's cooler than in that hellhole. He could feel the sweat on his body beginning to dry. His shirt sat heavily on him, clammy and cool. He glanced back at the doorway where a few people lingered, while others further down the sidewalk huddled away from the soft neon light.

He didn't get it. They partied all night on that stifling dance floor and then get out into fresh, clean air only to light up a cigarette. Ban something and people want more of it.

He checked his watch — nearly midnight — and pushed his fingers through his matted hair, the last remnants of his hairgel sweating away. The alcohol was still going through his system, even if the tablets weren't. Thank God because I don't feel like getting home in a hurry.

A pang of self-loathing registered as butterflies in his gut as he reprimanded himself for lucking out. He'd hoped to bring someone home for the night, or two nights. Or three. Someone that he could get to know. Talk to. Share his life with.

His shoulders fell slightly. "Coffee it is then," he said aloud and walked off down the sidewalk.

Six large wall menu-screens flashed the evening's specials above the serving counter. A voice-over announced the tantalising assortment of foods and beverages available and breakneck speed and jarring sound effects.

I need my food to stay down, not to be forced up by this

kak. He steadied himself with one hand on the countertop. After passing a crammed tray to two young guys, the waitress caught sight of him and beamed a broad grin at him. He felt ill all over again.

"Welcome to Happy Hippo, can I take your order?"

"Just a large coffee," he said attempting a smile.

She turned to the wall behind her, pressed some screen buttons. The price appeared just above her head, flashing as the sound of an antiquated till pinged. He took out his mobile, entered his pin and hit enter. The price on the screen exploded, effects and all, and a panel behind the counter opened and elevated a large tray with a single cardboard cup and lid insulating the steaming contents.

"To go?" asked the waitress politely as she picked up the cup.

"To stay," he answered smugly.

"Table for one?"

He nodded glumly. Still holding the cup, she glanced down at something behind the counter. He tried to peer over to see, but was met with an unsmiling face looking accusatorially back at him. He grinned back.

"You may sit at table number eleven," she said and offered him the cup with a smirk.

He took it from her, flinching at the heat in his hand. "I think I'll need one of those trays, thanks."

Unimpressed, she reached under the counter and passed him a shiny black plastic tray. He quickly put the cup down, blowing on his fingers.

"Thanks," he said and turned to face the restaurant. A glance left and right revealed six out of at least thirty tables occupied. He turned back to the waitress.

"Number eleven," she repeated.

He noticed the numbers on top of the glass partitions as he made his way over to his designated spot. He hesitated for a moment noticing a group of women sitting at a table to the right up ahead, giggling and talking over one another. Number ten. Then he stopped in his tracks as he made out number eleven.

"You are fucking kidding me," he mumbled out loud, and slowly carried on walking, trying to look unfazed. As he passed number ten he stole a glance, eyes awkwardly meeting the direct gaze of a girl quietly sipping her drink. He attempted a casual smirk, knowing that he was unconvincing, and quickly sat down in the single chair to his left.

"Moron," he said through his teeth as he stared at the wide pillar half a metre in front of him. "Table for fucking one." He removed the lid of the cup, revealing the steaming brown liquid inside. The aroma reached his nostrils as he took a deep breath. He picked up the sugar dispenser from a tray attached to the wall and poured. Replacing the sugar, he took out one of the plastic spoons alongside and slowly stirred his coffee, mesmerised by the swirling liquid. One last sniff and he brought the cup up to his lips. He blew slightly just before he took a sip. Relief washed over him and he slumped back in his hard chair.

The voices to his right and behind him trailed off as some of the women got up to leave. Leaning over his cup he looked over his shoulder.

The girl who he'd locked eyes with was still seated as two others were nudging out of the cubicle seats, while the others were making their way to the door. "You sure you'll be fine here, Ang?" he heard one of them say as he looked back at his pillar.

"Sure, just need some quiet time, Cat, thanks," came the response. He turned again, straight into her eyes, smiling at him. His stomach nearly gave up on him as he quickly turned back, catching his breath. He started to sweat, knowing it had nothing to do with the coffee.

"Wide awake now."

Nervous minutes passed like hours to him. He took a final deep gulp of the now warm liquid, breathed, and grated his chair as he stood up. He turned to walk, looking at the girl who fixed him with her stare.

"Finally," she said, startling him, "that looked like it took some effort."

As smoothly as he could he tossed his empty cup and lid into a wall-mounted disposal unit.

"Hell, this is the thirties," he said resting his arm on the top of the cubicle glass, "aren't the women supposed to be forward?"

"I thought I was." She motioned him to sit down.

"Aren't you going to leave with your friends?" he said looking towards the entrance.

"Got here all by myself, can leave here all by myself." She paused, looking at him. "Well, maybe not by myself."

"You do say it like it is, don't you?" he hesitated. "You haven't even officially met me and you already planning our evening together."

"Firstly, the evening has long since past." She glanced at a thin band on her wrist, the seamless screen illuminating the time. "And secondly, you can't plan anything when you don't know the other's intentions."

"Speaking of my intentions," he said softly, leaning in closer to her, "aren't you afraid of chatting up strange men, especially alone at this time of night?"

"You mean because of the bodies that have been turning up recently?"

"Exactly," he quipped as he leant back reaching his arm onto the length of the soft red chair.

She sat forward, picked up her cup, ready to sip. "Should I be afraid of you?" She looked over the top of the cup at him.

He laughed. "Not that I know of. Besides," he paused for

effect, "aren't the victims middle-aged women and not young, beautiful girls?" He watched her face redden.

"Hey, maybe the light in here's bad and you mistook me for an old bat and now the plan is already in motion and there's no going back. Or maybe tonight's the night that you change your pattern."

"Okay, you've got me there." He moved closer to her side of the table. "But let's not be strangers," he said, extending his right hand. "My name's Marc with a 'C'."

She smiled broadly at him, looked at his hand, then took it in hers. "Hi, Marc with a 'C'. I'm Angie with an 'A'."

"So, Angie," he began, "you said you'd come here by yourself. Why didn't you come with your friends?"

"I'm just not into the whole clubbing thing."

"Apparently neither am I. I felt like I needed a night out on the town to release some of my frustrations."

"You see," she pointed an accusing finger at him, "and you've got me to release those frustrations on." She readjusted herself in her seat. "Back off buddy, I can defend myself," she said sarcastically.

"Funny," he continued, shaking his head at her, "anyway, I just got frustrated with the noise and confines of that club up on Gardiner Street, so I got the hell out of there. I think I'm getting too old for that kak. Sorry, I said kak."

"You seem a bit rough around the edges," she looked him over. "And don't apologise for saying what you mean."

"Yeah, I try but there's not many people who listen." He looked at himself in the glass reflection, "I suppose from the look of me you thought I'd just done someone in and was getting a bite to eat before I headed home."

"No, but now that you mention it."

"Speaking of heading home," he tried his luck, "where to from here?"

She raised her eyebrows. "How about your place?"

"Hmm, not a very good idea at this point in my life."

"Ah." She tapped her nose. "Bodies in the attic. Or is that skeletons in the closet? How about we flip for it." She searched in her bag, then continued, "Because if it's my place you'll have to keep it down. My roommate's a bit of a party-pooper."

"I know what you mean," he said sympathetically.

Flooding the infant spiderweb around the globe by my hand, the resurgence of the ancient myths ate at people's doubts and expectations of what the millennium would bring, and common sense did not prevail. The fear of cataclysms brought on by potential computer malfunctions woke some of you up to the realization that technology is a tool and not your answer to survival. So I sat back, wanting the lessons to be learned, awaiting another Renaissance. Yes, I was the catalyst that moved humankind out of the Dark Ages and into the first Renaissance, bringing in some of the light that allowed people to question. Coded texts were translated and deciphered. Ideas flowed from printed volumes. And eventually, the truths, *my* truths, began to take root on a global scale. It had to, after practically beating it into humanity's subconscious for centuries.

CHAPTER 5

Elizabeth awoke to the sounds of voices. She felt the blood rushing to her head as she screamed in silent desperation. Her throat ached. Her body gave in.

#

"For the sake of time on this I'm going to skip how I brilliantly figured out, decoded, intuited, and read all the signs of Elizabeth's astro, and mapped out her wrap-around universe to pinpoint her location. Give or take a kilometre."

"Ah, one question there, Angel Mike," said Collins.

"Yes, Collins?"

"What does 'intuited' mean?"

There was a murmur through the room.

Angel shook his head. "Moving on," he said as he turned to the screen.

A map of the city zoomed up and into the east section of the map. The real-time satellite feed showed a superimposed circle of what was marked as a '3 km radius'. The label on the bottom left of the map read 'approximate 1 km zone: population 1132'. The area consisted of some of the most sought after properties for young professionals. Part of a two-kilometre stretch of high-rise apartments along the yacht docks it had become the 'in' area to live. And for the Tracker team it equated to a mammoth task ahead.

"Now I want you guys to be efficient," continued Angel. "That means quick but sharp. Don't assume anything. And if there's no answer at the door, you get them on the line and get answers. The database of everyone who lives in this zone will be accessible on your tablet. Their details: work addresses, bank accounts, utility bills, ID numbers, panty sizes, and who they are or want to date."

"Everything except who they've killed in the past year,"

commented Frank.

Shaking his head Angel said, "For heaven's sake, people, we need to find her! And we need to find her before someone else is taken."

#

Fatigue had always been a stimulus for Angie. Right now, her eyes were fuzzed and scratchy looking at the screen on her desk. The previous night, or morning, had provided some welcome physical stimulus, but nonetheless, her thighs and lower back were sluggish from the morning's activity.

Another welcome break from the past few days of psychological stress was Marc. Angie couldn't quite fit him into the minds-eye vision of her life so far, but was willing to let a man into her life again. Slowly was fine.

Wiping her eyes, she took a much-needed sip of her steaming cup of coffee. Working after hours in the office had its ups and downs. The empty, dark offices at night outweighed the extra hours of work. Taking it easy during the day and making up for it at night when everyone else left for the warm homes in the afternoon.

Her eyes refocused and glanced over the scrolling text on the screen. Lease renewals due. Meeting people, clients, face to face. Joy. Hearing their complaints or reluctance to renew their leases, increase rents, poor living conditions, bla bla bla. *Thank God I'm not a realtor.* Another reason she preferred working nights.

She selected one of the vertical columns, shifting the 'Expiry Date' column to ascending order. Thirty-six names referred to the end of September for renewals. She clicked the 'Area' column. The thirty-six individual names shifted into five separate areas in and around the city.

Angie tapped her chin and looked at the details for the person marked in the southeast area of the city. A few clicks of the keyboard and her glass tablet lying on her desk glowed to life. Lifting it she took the white square 'New Contact' box and dragged it onto the three-dimensional calendar in the corner of the screen.

Alongside Saturday's timeline she inserted '9.00' and clicked 'Set'. She tapped and closed the calendar while the original 'New Contact' remained visible in the centre of the screen. Angie scanned over the personal details and looked at the headshot photo attached.

"Well, Kate Conway, you're up for renewal. May as well be tomorrow."

Almost in response, her mobile in her top pocket bleeped and glowed her back into the office. Marc's face appeared in the small blue screen, looking nervous as he checked himself.

She pressed the screen.

"You do realize that I can see you before I answer the call?"

For a moment Marc's face looked stumped. "Oh, right." He chuckled. "How was breakfast?"

"Not quite what I expected, but good thanks."

"Maybe we can do breakfast again some time."

"I see you don't have a problem speaking your mind today. Does that mean we're skipping dinner and a movie?"

"Technically we've done the dinner thing," said Marc puffing out his chest. "Even though it was at separate tables. How about this? I promised some of my friends I'd meet up with them tomorrow morning at the Car Expo."

Angie rolled her eyes, "So you're a typical guy after all. Damn!"

"Hey a man's got to be a man. And besides, it's not just any car expo. It's showcasing the flying cars."

"Just what we need, men thinking they own the skies as well. I've got a few things that I need to do in the morning so when do you want to get together?

"Well, because you don't sound all that enthusiastic we can

meet up after lunch, grab a bite to eat and blow the joint."

"Okay, in all honesty it does sound like fun. But please don't think that this is permission to start burping and farting in our relationship. Not yet anyway."

"Angie?"

"Yes, Marc with a 'C'."

"Thanks for being forward."

#

"Holy high rise," said Ruth craning her head out the passenger's window of the car.

"Yeah," replied Frank. "Looks like we got the mother of all apartment blocks to trawl through." He turned the car onto the curb and cut the engine. "It's supposed to have some of the best views of the bay and the city."

They got out the car and headed for the entrance to the imposing structure.

Frank clicked his tablet, "Make no mistake," he said, "if anyone's finished early they are more than welcome to give us assistance from on high."

He nodded for Ruth to pass through the revolving glass doors.

"Noted, Banks," said Angel's voice over their mobiles. "There's no slacking here. As soon as your area's secured and accounted for, and I mean fully accounted for, then Hicks and Banks could do with a hand, folks."

They stood in the small, neatly decorated entrance. A large mirror filled the left-hand wall, a magnetized security door sat neatly in the facing wall, barring any further entry, and on the right was a panel with rows of numbered lights.

Frank placed the glass tablet under his arm, pressed the '101' button, and unclipped his badge from his belt.

A moment passed, then, "Can I help you?" came a tinny voice.

Frank turned and looked up at the security camera mounted in the corner.

"Tracker Unit," he said raising his badge for a moment, "I'm Agent Banks, and this is my partner Agent Hicks. We need access to your building. We're doing a door to door investigation in the area."

"Sure. That may take a while if it's just the two of you," the door buzzed, "but go right ahead, Agents."

They both took a deep breath and stepped through.

#

"Hey, girlfirend!"

Amy's shrill voice sent a gallon of adrenaline through Angie's system. She turned towards the door to see the lean, blonde figure leaning against the door frame. Angie forced a smile.

"Thought you were gonna meet up with us at Heroes?"

Angie processed the possibilities. "Yeah. No. I decided to call it a night. Been a bit hectic around here." She glanced around her immaculate desk.

Amy cocked an eyebrow. "Well, it's Friday, girlfriend, and that means it's the weekend, baby!"

Surprisingly, Angie actually liked Amy. But, hell, she never could shut up. Small doses. Please don't ask me out again.

"Some of us are going for drinks at lunch," she said with a wink. "Getting started early."

"Ah, a few things to do here, sorry." Angie felt relief.

"Okay. I'll have one for you." She raised an accusing finger. "But, you're not off the hook, girlfriend."

She had been working at Morris Chandler for over eight months and for some reason, being female, young, and single, meant she was labeled a party girl and drinking buddy. Amy was the typical office party girl, the one organizing the office functions, and being too loud at them. The one you can hear from the other side of the office squealing and giggling. The one you can hear when they leave the office for the weekend. The epitome of what Angie detested in people. And yet it was what she seemed to attract wherever she went.

"Thanks anyway, Ames," Angie feigned appreciation.

Amy slapped her butt cheek in Angie's direction with a cheesy grin. "See ya."

Angie's body relaxed as she watched Amy leave, then turned back to her screen. She was somewhat exhausted and appreciative of the silence, yet still sensing the reverberations in the room.

Turning her attention back to her tablet, she dragged the map into the centre of the screen and slipped the grid along to reveal a glowing green dot. Her current position. She pressed the green circle, dragged it onto Kate Conway's details. A red circle appeared on the map and steadily drew red line through the map's streets until it reached the green circle. With two quick finger movements the contact block and map disappeared off the sides of the screen, and the screen turned off.

"Right, back to work," she said pulling herself up to her screen on her desk.

Six years in real estate, a fair amount of legwork, and putting up with field agent egos had meant that her move to Morris Chandler had come with a step in the right direction: management.

No more running after field agents. No more logging their sloppy paperwork. No more harassing her when they wanted their commissions. Quick to drop the contracts in her lap, but useless when it came to client liaising post payment. Gift of the gab. No doubt. Gift of amnesia. Client who?

The only drawback with managing the contracts, particularly leases, was the continual renewals. Never ending, but it still allowed her to be her own boss and manage her own time.

New clients were logged and added in another department. Simple. No contact between departments. No crises. Automated databases. If a field agent didn't fill in a required detail the contract wasn't submitted. For once in a million years, Angie would often think, the field agents were forced to be efficient, on the spot. 'No submission. No commission.' Angie liked her motto, something that irked her coworkers in her earlier workplaces.

Now she chose very carefully who she would deal with face to face; and who she would deal with remotely. Morris Chandler expected a certain amount of face-to-face contact with either lessor or lessee. Buyer or seller.

'Moving bodies' was how one of her previous managers used to put it. Removal companies and realtors go hand in hand (and the banks). "Removals are in the 'moving house' business," he would say. "The banks are in the 'moving money' business. Once a client, always a client. It is just a matter of moving that client, their house, or their funds, from there to here. There is no reason to lose a client. If they move across the globe, you make sure you move them. No excuses. Unless you're a complete twat."

It hadn't taken Angie long to fully appreciate the term, because that's what it became to her. Most of the time they weren't even a voice on the end of a data line, but rather a number, a cost, a commission, for some, or a stat. Bodies.

When she found herself daydreaming at night she would see the latest client's headshot layered over their 'new home' pic. And that was it. For the next month they were that scrapbook effect collaged into her memory for the next year. They didn't go to sleep, wake up, go to work, eat dinner, or contribute to society. They were immovable bodies. Inert. Until a year later or on the odd occasion that someone died.

Angie shifted in her black leather high-back chair.

Elizabeth and Liza Chapman. That Tracker woman had called her asking about both victims. Both were Morris Chandler clients.

#

"It's places like these that make me long for a small place on the beach down the South coast," said Frank. They gazed out from the large glassed-in hallway over the Durban bay below and the large expanse of the Indian Ocean stretching out to the eastern horizon.

"But that *is* an awesome view. Reminds me of University days," said Frank.

"I love that water," replied Ruth. "Nothing beats that ocean. Inviting." Ruth had suggested they get started from the top floor down. Less mental pressure. She was glad she had done so. "I've got a bad feeling about this place."

"One door at a time," said Frank and headed down the North side of the building. "Let's go to work."

Ruth hesitated, "One door at a time."

Frank stepped up to the first door and knocked.

#

Winters in Durban are bearable compared to the rest of South Africa. An average winter's day hits the all-time low of 20° C, while the dry brown grasses and trees suck up all the humidity and sweat of summer. Dotted with evergreens and large tracts of wild forests, the landscape retains its subtropical beauty and voluptuous hillsides as the rest of the country become either bleak, dusty husks or drenched in horizontal rainstorms.

But mid August 2026, everything in Frank's landscape, his world, had lost its colour and meaning. He felt like the half-empty pond a few metres in front of him. Dry, hard leaves drifted on its black surface, trapped on a meniscus that would soon overcome and drag them to the bottom. Not to be rehydrated, but to rot and fester into the black stench that blew up to him in the cold breeze.

The leaves of his book crackled in his pale hands. He felt frozen, but not from the cold. Not from the wind, or the weather, or his thin tattered jersey.

The wind sliced into his staring eyes that were locked firmly on the sentence in front of him. His eyes were fixed and unmoving while the winds swirled around his mind.

GOD IS DEAD.

Human nature had been broken down into neuroses and parent complexes and natural impulses driven by a combination of animal instincts and social conditioning. Where did God come into the fray? Where was the Divine hand that moulded and manipulated? And on a whim and a joke, Frank had taken Nietzsche's *Thus Spoke Zarathustra* from a current girlfriend.

Now, here he sat faced with three words that would later resurface in the face of a corpse, the blood smear on a carpet, or a child playing in a schoolyard.

The scream that he let out at the top of his lungs "God is dead!" echoed through the leafy pathways and greying walls of the university grounds. It echoed in Frank's head for years to come.

He had been struggling with his School of Psychology studies for the past few months and this had been the culmination of many brain-wrenching inner dialogues that had been eating away at him. He felt his energy drain from him and only managed a feeble repeat of the goddamned statement.

"Depends on how you look at it," said a voice behind him. Frank whipped around, hardly noticing the sideways grin on the newcomer's face.

"Freud. Nietzsche. That's how I'm looking at it," said Frank, turning back to his view of the pond. The other man walked around, his hands in his pockets, staring at the same dark water feature. "They're saying it's all bullshit and we're all animals. So we may as well screw who we want, kill who we want, and take what we want. Survival of the fittest, bru."

The other student raised his eyebrows and nodded. "A pretty valid argument, I might say." He sat down, looking unfazed by Frank's foaming mouth and seething veins in his forehead.

Frank calmed his breathing long enough to look him over. For some reason, the colour brown suited the lean frame and tousled brown curly hair. He removed his glasses from the edge of his nose and huffed some warm air onto the glass to give them a clean. His corduroy jacket, worn and frayed at the elbows, neatly fitted his level shoulders, but his grey turtleneck jersey ended a few inches past the sleeves. At least his faded jeans had the good sense to touch the floor over a pair of worn trainers. A geek who walks a lot, keeps fit, possibly lifting chess pieces, whose father left when he was young, leaving a closet full of clothes that he hangs onto for male contact and has no clue about girls.

He lifted the strap of what looked like an overloaded shoulder bag over his head and placed it on the bench.

"I never did like Freud. Mother issues. I prefer Jung."

"Jung?" said Frank. "He's touched on later on in our course, but I'm not into that Chinese mysticism kak."

"Chinese?"

"You know, Jung," he rolled his eyes, "our lecturers frown upon him as well."

"Jung was Austrian, bru."

"Whatever, soutie," he said slapping the book shut, "God is now dead and so what's the point?"

"I don't think dead is correct. Maybe it means that man's need for God is dead. A bit arrogant but valid."

"If there's no need for God then there's no meaning.

What's the point?" Frank pushed the book in the other student's face. "No heaven. Nowhere to go to when you die."

"What? You can't exist or have meaning for your life without proving yourself to someone else other than yourself?"

"What?"

He grabbed the book from Frank.

"Who the hell is God to you, bru?" He began paging through the book. "Or anyone else for that matter."

"Supposedly he makes the world go around." Frank stood and gestured around him. "He made you and me and the fucking universe!"

"He's the one that gave us the Ten Commandments and laws to live by to be better people."

"Exactly. He looks on you as a good person or a bad person."

"Like an omnipotent parent."

"Like Santa Claus," said the student standing alongside Frank and tapping the book in his arms. They both laughed.

"Either you're happy with who you are or you want to be a better person for you and not to make someone else happy. Never mind an invisible parent. And if you're using it to attain bliss, bliss is a state of mind, not the natural state of the Universe. Nature is violent chaos masquerading as tranquil order. It's what differentiates life from unconsciousness, or death."

"Okay," said Frank tossing the book on the bench, "You're saying God still exists?"

"No flippin' idea, my bru." He looked out over the cloudy landscape and the grey city below them. "All I know is nature follows certain paths. Paths that can be pretty accurately traced back, back in time along a long line of permutations, evolutions and into a single source. Our physical universe, that is."

"That still doesn't mean God exists." Frank slumped back onto the bench.

"Again, it's not the point. If you bother to read Jung, in your own time rather than waiting for the lecturers to give you their dumbed-down biased view of the genius that, in my humble opinion, outshone Freud, you'll see that it's religion that's dead. There's no point to religion. Opinions and interpretations. That's religion. And religion had its shot. It took the hearts and minds of the people and chose to manipulate them to their own selfish ends. It decided to fondle and fiddle, caress and bribe them into submission. They took human beings, that beautiful creature, and turned them into quivering chattel for their sacrifices to their personal god, the greatest god: Ego with a capital E."

Frank laughed at the last statement, then said, "Our lecturers keep calling Jung the dreaming hippie."

"All because he emphasized the significance of dreams."

"So did Freud."

"Yeah, but he pioneered the work while Freud kinda looked over his shoulder. Jung's most powerful and visceral experience was of God taking a dump on a church. Smell and all."

"Bugger off!" Frank doubled over with laughter.

"Seriously." The other man chuckled. "The clouds parted, and a huge pile of kak landed on the local church steeple. This was a waking dream, a vision."

Frank was holding his side trying to contain himself as his eyes teared up.

"You're funny," he said between gasps of air.

"It is funny," the other student laughed and extended his hand. "Allen Hicks."

"Franklin Banks, soutie. Call me Frank."

As it turned out, they had both been in need of a place to

crash. Both for different reasons: Allen had felt it was time to move out of home, away from his mother, in order to move forward with his own life and find his own way; a new girlfriend, a relationship that would become increasingly strained, had initially given Frank the excuse and opportunity to find privacy from the close-knit community of his father's extended family on Durban's Bluff. A few years before, in his early teens, Frank's father had relocated the family to Cape Town, and by the time he was ending grade twelve Frank needed space and freedom. The liberty of moving back to Durban had been short-lived as his father would be continually informed of his son's social life by well-meaning relatives. Moving in together had not been the answer, and Frank's girlfriend, then ex-girlfriend, had become more and more weird about him sleeping on the living-room floor of her bachelor flat when she brought guys home in the early hours. "Who's that?" "Oh, don't mind Frank, he's just my ex" had caused some awkward moments around breakfast. Small kitchen aside, it was claustrophobic.

But two polar opposites were what made their one-and-a-half bedroom flat in the lower Berea work. Allen, tall, lean, and awkward in his pale, t-shirt tanned body; while Frank, all of five foot eight, was toned under his flawless skin, and comfortable around people. Especially women.

Allen soon became accustomed to coming home from lectures to find his space invaded by strange music and the choking haze of smoke hanging in the small apartment. They were the only house parties he was 'invited' to, so he relished the idea, even if to sit quietly in the corner sipping his red box wine, observing the various specimens of eThekwini's future leaders and businesspeople falling over themselves.

It was during one of these events that Frank had grabbed Allen from his beanbag comfort and dragged him to the half bedroom, AKA the enclosed balcony, where the feisty Ruth

Hartslief was standing, arms folded and frowning. A childhood friend of his cousin's, Ruth had always come across as strong-willed and slightly intimidating to Frank. Hence his goading and pushing of her buttons.

Allen was no exception to those attempts at riling her up.

"You two have some fun together," Frank had said. "Allen here believes that males are the better looking of most species, while Ruth believes that AbaMbo women like her have the ability to...whatchamacallit?"

With a glare, Ruth had clucked her tongue and added, "Bring this world back to order within matrilineal structures."

That was their introduction. Trial by fire, courtesy of Franklin Banks.

By the end of the year, Frank was well aware that he was set to fail his studies, something he couldn't face explaining to his father, let alone asking him to foot the bill to start again. Being as close as they were, Allen had seen it coming.

In the early morning after finals, Frank had packed his things into his old Toyota. Allen carried a duffel bag of clothes down to the car while Ruth slept undisturbed in the flat. There had been no words exchanged, only a look and a strong hug. They wouldn't see each other again for more than eight years.

Putting even more distance between himself and his father in Cape Town, Frank had driven the six hours to Johannesburg and parked outside the police barracks in downtown Hillbrow. That was the start of his police career. He moved into the child protection unit, and when he heard about a new division opening up in eThekwini Metro, he took the earliest plane out to the introduction and enrollment. As it turned out, Angel had done the half hour presentation, and not being a salesman, he had fielded some questions, and then pointed at the enrollment team at the back of the small conference room.

Of the eighty people who bothered attending, less than half of the audience remained. Frank was one of ten that had finally enrolled.

It was then that he had come face to face with Ruth. All through Angel's brief presentation, and while Frank and the other enrollees had been making up their minds as they milled around the coffee and tea table, she had contained herself. She had been seated behind the enrollment table beaming at him as he had approached to sign up. It was like he had never left.

Only six of the enrollees had turned up on the first day of the job.

#

"I'm doing the door, Daddy," said Caleb rushing for the apartment door.

"Be my guest," replied Allen over the top of the grocery packets.

Caleb pressed his hand around the door handle. There was a soft bleep and the door automatically swung open. He bounced through the doorway and into the kitchen, placing his two packets on the kitchen floor, grabbing a cookie from the jar on the counter top, and was out and on his way to his bedroom before Allen could make it to the kitchen. Allen shook his head at the energy of the young boy and came to rest at the kitchen table. A wine bottle teetered on the edge of the table, pulling at its packet and other contents. Allen steadied the load and slowly removed his aching arms from the delicate pile.

"Daddy." Caleb's voice pierced the echoing kitchen. He wheeled around with fright to face the raised eyebrows of his son, casually leaning against the doorway, as Allen recalled from a few weekends before, just like one of Caleb's favourite cartoon heroes.

"Son?" asked Allen.

"Jason at school says angels have wings."

Allen's face dropped. "Did he now?" He turned back to the load of groceries and unpacked them onto the table.

Caleb walked around the table. "He did, and he says they look like big swan wings. Fluffy and white." He sat down on one of the chairs.

"I see," said Allen from inside the fridge.

"What do you think, Daddy?"

Allen peered around the door at his son's wide-eyed face resting his hands and looking over the remaining packets, then said, "Well, kid, I haven't seen any angels around to check what wing structure they have."

"But what do the other people at your work say? Don't they know about angel wings?"

Allen smiled at his son, picked up a peanut butter bottle jar and said, "I don't think any of them have studied angel wings, Cay."

"Why?" Caleb sat up, hands slapping the tabletop.

"Not sure many of them believe in angels, kid."

"Eh?" He looked stunned. He got off the chair and headed for the doorway, then stopped and turned back to Allen. "You believe, hey Daddy?"

Allen stood dead in his tracks, jar raised to the cupboard shelf. He looked over his shoulder at Caleb. "Only since I met Mommy," he said cheekily.

"Ha!" Caleb clapped his hands together and bounded down the hall.

Allen breathed a sigh. The sounds of the bath running filtered down the hall to the kitchen. "Angels," he said to the room.

#

They're probably getting supper ready. As their task had drawn on, with zero leads in the entire area, Ruth had felt more and more heavy, thinking of her family at home without her. Or rather, her without them.

And Elizabeth Stride alone and terrified, possibly behind the next door, or the next.

The click of the door closing made her turn around to Frank pressing his tablet.

"Another floor done," he said, his own frustration audible in his clipped tone.

She walked up to the elevator, hit the button then turned to rest her back against the wall. Well-needed support.

The light of day on the other side of the glass hallway had faded as the sun set behind the building. The rumble of afternoon traffic had barely penetrated the glass bowl, but as the evening drew on it had intensified into a low drone felt through the concrete structure. Ruth pushed off the wall and stepped forward to the glass.

"We're going to get this bastard, Hicks."

Streams of headlights twinkled and weaved along the blackened roads.

"I wish I could be so sure, Frank." She shifted her gaze to the inky blackness of the ocean, its tides pulled at her body, drawing her in. Her skin tingled. This case had prevented her from getting to its salty waters since winter had begun to recede. Even the Rachel Finlayson Pool, alongside North Beach, was a vague summer memory. "It's just when and under what circumstances? The last thing we need is the killer getting spooked or fucking up, resulting in—"

Frank stood next to her. "We've got this one last floor, and that's all we can do for the day. We've been methodical."

The elevator chimed.

"Whatever," she said pushing herself away from the view and into the elevator as her mobile buzzed. "I need to hit the gym for a soak and a swim."

Ruth lifted her device and clicked the answer button.

"Hicks here," she said. "Don't you have anything more concrete, Angel? I mean goddamnit, she's around here somewhere and we can't get to her."

The elevator doors closed and her stomach lurched as it began its slow descent.

"I understand, Hicks," said Angel, "but I've given you all I can at the moment. And if she's locked up somewhere, there's not much to speak of in her astro profile. Nine times out of ten it will all be psychological data which isn't going to help pinpoint her. You and Banks quit your whining and bang on doors. There's a time when good old-fashioned police work is needed while we get the tech improved."

"Sorry, Angel. I just want to run from door to door kicking them in to find her because I know she's here somewhere in one of these buildings. Meanwhile, that self-righteous Gora Khayyám trying to shut us down and limit our budget, our 'spend', and cost to the public."

"Then waste no time," replied Angel. "Run on your instincts and do what you have to do."

Ruth's screen went black. The elevator pinged. She could feel her exhaustion now as she stepped out the elevator.

"We're on a manhunt with a tiny group of people trying to make a difference and getting paid shit."

"I'll second that," said Frank.

"Trying to catch bad guys," continued Ruth, "and the people we're trying to protect and save are the ones bitching about how much it all costs them."

"That's the police force in general, Ruth. That's what we call the public service conundrum."

"He wants us shut down because of ethics, Frank!"

"So it seems," he added. "I still think we should be investigating him to find out what he's really hiding."

"But he always manages to come up clean whenever others have launched campaigns against him."

"Squeaky clean."

"Too clean," said Ruth.

"How would he be if right now we were searching for his wife or daughter?"

#

Allen's mobile bleeped. He looked down at the message from Henry Buchanan: *All set for tomorrow's big day?*

All set and running perfectly. Will stop by midmorning to see how things are going, he sent.

He entered Caleb's room.

"Dad?"

"Kid."

"Mommy and I were talking about angels."

"Yes," said Allen reluctantly.

"Why's Mommy working late again?" asked Caleb.

Allen sat down on the edge of his son's bed. "They are busy with catching a bad guy, and Mommy seems to think that they are getting close."

"Mommy's clever."

"Yep." Allen smiled. "But it won't be for long. Hopefully."

"And angels, Dad?"

"I thought I'd skipped that question."

"Nope."

"Well, Kid," said Allen climbing into Caleb's bed, "I'm not an expert on angels like Mom, but I know a thing about rhymes."

"Ooh." Caleb's eyes lit up. "'I Hope I Dream of My Soul Tonight'?" he asked.

Allen looked at his son, "One two three…"

I can feel my warm bright light?
My Soul is inside but not out of sight.

It's there with me all through my day.
In a smile or the things I say.

And sometimes when I sleep and dream
I get to see my Soul's bright beam.

It can tell me grand big tales
Or fly me through the sky with whales.

My Soul is here, not in another world
It's me, just bigger and brighter and gold.

I hope I dream. I'll pray till late.
I'll hope. I'll dream. I'll pray. I'll wait.

Before the dawn, before it's light.
I hope I dream of my Soul this night.

As I had hoped, the new age fueled some of the deepest studies into the capabilities of humans and your inherent powers. From a mood that was festering and cannibalistic, to a heightened sense of self and the collective-self, humankind looked to emerge in a true age of enlightenment. For decades people had questioned the dogma imposed on you by the established religions and started to recognize the basic tenets that weaved their way through all the masters that had walked the earth — teachings that, stripped of their man-made rules and fear-mongering, I had for centuries been revealing to the world. Masters that had been human, after all, related to you more than when they had been placed on pedestals and altars, out of reach. Gods. And, as I, Ma'at, have said for four thousand years, when masters are perceived as gods, people believe they can never attain the levels of their gods; but, seen as one of them, all becomes attainable.

CHAPTER 6

Angie woke suddenly in bed. She lay quietly for a few seconds, listening to the dark room. What woke her? She blinked and lifted her head to look around her. Nothing unusual. She quietly moved her legs from out of the bedding, and slipped her feet into her slippers. She listened. There it was again: a soft knock coming from another part of the apartment.

The bedroom door was open, as she liked it. She stuck her head out slightly into the blackness of the hallway. Slowly she emerged from her room, softly walking as close to the wall as she could.

She passed by the other doors in the hallway, heading for the lounge. Lights from the outside hallway and stairs filtered through the windows of the lounge, giving the inanimate objects life in her imagination. Then the noise came again from behind her. She wheeled around, looking at where she'd come from. The other room. She made her way to the closed door, straining herself to listen.

She gently opened the door as quietly as she could manage with her tensed hands. She flicked the light switch on, blinding herself for a moment. As her eyes adjusted and the pain subsided, she focused on the figure in front of her.

"Did I forget to sedate you tonight, Elizabeth?" she said to the bound figure on the chair.

#

"I killed him!" shouted Allen.

Ruth woke to find Allen sitting upright in the bed. "Ungh?" she mumbled from the pile of blankets beside him.

Allen cradled his face in his hands. "I killed him," he whispered.

Ruth pulled herself up towards him. "You killed who, what, honey?"

"My dream," Allen took a deep breath and shifted his feet off the bed. "*The* dream."

"You mean *the* dream, the one you told me about the other day?" she turned her bedside lamp on.

"It's never been like that." He looked at the ceiling. "I've never seen that far." He stood up and went into the bathroom.

Ruth heard the water running and splashing. As Allen reemerged from the darkness, she could see he was pale, eyes wide. He sat back on the bed, water dripped from his chin. He took a deep breath.

"Let me get this straight," asked Ruth, "the last time you had this dream was a few years ago."

"Twenty," said Allen.

"Twenty," continued Ruth, "then you have it again last night. Now you have it again tonight, but this time you kill someone."

Allen flopped back into his pillows and stared at the roof.

"The ambulance flies past me, right, and disappears into the traffic. This time I follow the wailing siren and lights and this scene reveals itself further down the road. Smoke rises from the traffic congestion about a hundred metres ahead. I get this flash of sequences popping in my head like the red flashing lights."

"What sequences, Allen?"

"A man in a car. Racing through traffic. Angry. Determined. Me and my wife, not you and not me, in our car, driving. The man is in my rearview mirror. Then he's overtaking us. But it's a busy road. He goes into oncoming traffic. A bus swerves and slams into both our cars, head on. It's loud. It's black. It's screaming. I'm screaming. She's dead beside me. There's still screaming. He's alive, but caught under the steering wheel and the bus. He's whining about his legs being broken. 'Get me outta here!' he's shouting out his window. I can't see his face. I look at my wife. I pull myself through my window and climb through his shattered passenger window. He's still screaming. My hands are aching from the shards of glass in them. He turns to me; his face is covered in blood. I reach over and start strangling him."

"Shit, Allen," whispered Ruth.

"Don't get all Freud on me, Ruth. It was just a hectic dream, that's all."

"So why are you so shaken up about it then?" She stood up out of the bed.

"Because it felt so damn real. Like I was there."

"Is it possible, in your scientific mind, that it was real? It's so real that you feel like it really happened? Consider for one second that it's more than just a dream, Allen."

He looked up at her, face still ashen.

"Then, when you've finished blowing this off as some childish dream and put your scientific mind aside, can you consider that it might be a past life flashback?"

There was silence.

"Oh please, Ruth," he snapped. He looked at her shocked face.

"You please, you know-all! Try explaining it to yourself then. Rationalise it. Workshop it. See what you come up with. Good night!" She bounced back into bed and clicked her light off.

Allen sat in the darkness for what seemed ages. His mind darted from one dead-end to another.

"Okay, let's," he began.

"Okay," said Ruth switching her light on and getting out of bed. "First, when you have recurring dreams, that's your subconscious, or your soul, trying to get a message through your thick skull." She looked at him. "Second, when the dream changes, even in the slightest, you need to take notice. Take notice of what those changes are and what role they play. Third, you're only going to see, or be shown, what you're ready for. As a kid, you probably wouldn't have been quite up to seeing yourself kill someone." She smiled at him. "Even souls have a parental guidance rating on their visions. Fourth, and finally, if there is a significant change, especially the revealing of a climax or ending, then something's going to happen. And remember," she pointed at him, "souls have a journey together, agreements, and karmic debt."

"So, you're saying that his soul, or body, is going to kill me in revenge?" asked a shocked Allen.

"Not revenge as such. Think of it like this. He killed your wife. You killed him. Flip that around. You kill his wife, or loved one. He kills you. You got to experience loss. Now it's his turn to feel that loss."

"In the end," considered Allen, "I die."

"Psh," she raised her hands, "just one explanation."

"I'm battling a bit with other explanations. What else have you got?"

"Let's take a Jungian approach, psychologist."

"Dreamer."

"Open-minded. Shush. Like you should be. Your dream could be a way of your subconscious mind talking to your conscious mind. But still telling you something. It's all about decoding the messages. But from your dream tonight, I don't think there's going to be time to decode the meaning — wife, man, murder, accident, road, cars — in time."

"It could be telling me to be careful in traffic."

"Or be careful who you strangle to death in the wreckage of a car on your way to work."

"Great. It's all still one big mystery."

"No," said Ruth.

"No?"

"Yes. No. You have to stay awake."

"Like right now."

"No. Be aware. Don't take anything for granted and don't

discard any event with your scientific mind."

"Right. Walk around talking to myself while I decode hidden messages that aren't really there."

"There are signposts everywhere you go. If you're receptive to their possibilities," she nudged him, "then you'll be open to seeing them and interpreting them."

"Your money's on the karma then, right?" he asked.

"Yep, there's no beating karma. If you owe her, she's gonna come knocking. No 'get out of karma free' cards. No mass karma debt payment plan."

"Great." He rolled his eyes. "I'm in the hands of some eastern myth, and my wife's got the cheerleader pom-poms."

"Here's rooting for you, Babe."

#

Blood was spattered everywhere in the dim light of the room. Geoff could just make out the three bodies lying lifeless on the bare floor. Behind him the sound of slow dripping blood running down the arm, hand, and fingers onto the floor from a fourth body, twisted and tossed awkwardly over the side of the couch. The faint bleep of a weapon recharging came from down the hallway. He moved to the corner wall and waited.

His breathing was heavy, and by the look of the blood on his leg, his wound was minor. He chanced a glance around the wall and back to position. Clear. He checked again and then crouched into the hallway. He shuffled along the tiled surface, too noisy for his liking. He came up to the first door, checked the handle. Locked. Slowly he rose, back against the door. He crabbed along the wall, making sure to check his back as he moved. He didn't want to assume anything.

His attention was on the yawning black hole of the doorway at the end of the hall.

A sound behind him. His muscles went cold and his heart

hit his eyeballs. Was it a sound? He edged back the way he came. Rechecking the door, he glanced back at the end of the hall, then back at the dim light of the lounge. A slow creak behind him. He turned just as two hands grabbed his face and neck and pulled him into the blackness.

"Bastard!" he shouted.

Bang! Geoff leapt in his seat. "Yirra!"

"Niranjan," came a dull voice from the front door.

He took a deep breath and paused the screaming game projected in front of him.

"Goddamn dead anyway." He struggled onto his feet. "Ya?"

"Marc," replied the voice.

Geoff opened the door, dusting bits of food from his baggy t-shirt. "Ay, my larny. How you doing, Ramdheo?"

"Sounds like the screams of 'Hostile Hostage' emanating from within, dear student," he said entering the dark apartment and sitting on a lounge chair.

"Whatever," replied Geoff walking back to his lounging chair. "Dead Hostage more like it. That last damn kidnapper keeps getting me in the neck."

"Bastard," Marc said scanning the room. "So much for studying."

"Don't choon me, Mother Theresa," said Geoff picking up a pre-packed doughnut "I assume you have a very good reason for disturbing my studies."

"You're not studying, choppie."

"You didn't know that," he said through powdered lips.

"Whatever," replied Marc. "I couldn't take sitting at home staring at the walls."

"Hell, tell me about it," Geoff indicated the console controls. "Should've just got shitted tonight and have it done with."

"Exactly," said Marc on the edge of his seat. "That and the fact that if I called this girl again that I met, I'd come off desperate."

Geoff feigned a coughing fit in response.

"Yeah, yeah." Marc sat casually back into his chair. "Last night, I mean this morning. I'm in the Hungry Hippo after being abandoned like a dog, by a so-called bra. It felt like 'Stranded 3' all over again."

"I told you it wasn't personal, and it was just a game!" interrupted Geoff.

"And even more reason to help a brother out, chop."

"Focus, chop," said Geoff.

"Right. Abandoned at the Hungry Hippo. I spot this 'bird'," he finger-hooked the air, "at a table and I make my move."

Geoff chuckled in his seat.

"Needless to say we spent the night, slash morning, at her pozzie. Then we—"

"Wait, hold up, back up," butted in Geoff. "You shagged your skinny ass off?"

"An ou never kisses and tells," protested Marc.

"Bugger you," he replied dryly. "You *are* telling."

"Whatever," Marc brushed him off. "I wake up at the crack of a sparrow's fart, and she's already showered, dressed and made up. Says her roommate likes to sleep in. I say whatever, so we duck and take the Metro to my spot for clean clothes."

"No shower and kak for the bru?"

"Focus, bru," he picked up a doughnut. "Then we're off to breakfast and coffee. Light banter. Gives me her numbers. Part ways with a gentle kiss on the lips and I'm standing outside the joint with my hard-on in my hands."

"Ah, romance."

"And she paid."

"Lekker," said Geoff. "But I feel we digressed from the initial point here." He fixed Marc with a cool stare. "Why did we not divulge this earlier in the day, about the time of the said dick in hand?"

"Firstly, dear confidante, I couldn't believe it was true."

"I'd also be debating the plausibility of the events," interrupted Geoff.

"Whatever. Secondly, I didn't want to jinx it."

"Yet here we are debating the plausibility of it as you quite readily jinx any further possibilities."

"It just got too much sitting at home and—"

"Beating yourself off," snapped Geoff. "So you decided to beat down my door, and hopefully that's all, instead of dropping me a bleep."

"Like you would have torn yourself away from Hostile Hostage to answer me."

"Touché. And true enough. But a message saying that you think you may have shagged someone this morning would have caused a significant distraction."

"Smart-ass," said Marc ready to open his zipper. "Here are the chafe marks to prove it."

"Dear God, man," protested Geoff with both hands raised to block any unwanted images. "Don't try to pass your handwork off as passion marks."

"How's the assignment, project, thing going?"

"We on tomorrow or what?" replied Geoff.

"Oh-so-subtle subject change," said Marc. "Yes, we're definitely on for tomorrow. And I may or may not have asked her to join us."

"And so it begins." Geoff rolled his eyes.

"No, she wants to meet after we've done our thing. Lunch or something. She's not into the car thing."

"Excellent. Let the men play with their toys."

"This coming from the guy who openly cries at the re-casts of *ET*."

"I'm telling you, bru," Geoff eyeballed Marc, "don't go there. The boy and his alien are off limits."

"My ou, you've watched it a thousand times. It doesn't

change. And still the same reaction."

Geoff pointed at Marc. "That's the last time I call you when I'm distraught. And I'll tell you, like I tell you every tear-filled call, no matter how many times someone leaves, it's always hard."

"Issues," Marc shook his head.

Geoff raised a hand to Marc's face.

Closely guarded secrets, encrypted and firewalled in their dark, climate-controlled vaults beneath the seats of power, approached the light of their declassification. The truth and evidence revealed by me decades before, discounted or made into fringe conspiracy theories by those same governments, finally found their way to the people on the streets and the public domain — and here, most of my work was done for me. Beliefs were challenged with hard evidence; technologies that had been bought out and hidden from the consumers of the world emerged again as 'new' ideas, and as connectivity increased, even in the remotest parts of the world, so too did the passing on of this information. Open source became open market, became open minded. The true power of what the scientists had 'discovered' became something that the governments openly funded and pursued, supported by you, the people.

CHAPTER 7

How the hell did I not see this coming? Elizabeth traced back through her fuzzy memories. *Everything screamed WEIRD, and yet I still didn't flinch at letting that woman into my apartment. Okay, maybe I'm being a bit hard on myself. Bloody hell. Am I stupid or what?*

Last Saturday, that was the first time she met Miss Young. *About ten in the morning an agent making a house call and meeting clients face-to-face rather than an empty phone call. Nice touch. Damn it.*

"Please come in." *Idiot.*

"Lovely place, Miss Stride." *Mrs! Bitch was taking in the surroundings.* "It says in your lease," *which you conveniently left at the office that day,* "that you've been here coming on two years now."

"That's right," *there's something odd here Lizzy. Nothing obvious. Just a feeling.*

"You do seem nicely settled, so do I assume you'd like to renew with us?"

No, from all the packing boxes you don't see lying around, I'm sneaking out of here in the middle of the night. What I don't realize is that it's going to be later tonight, with your arm around my waist squeezing the life out of me as you drag me to your car in the parking lot. That drug you slipped into my veins may paralyse, but it doesn't dull the senses.

"Absolutely, where do I sign?"

"Well, great then. Right here on," *a feigned pause for effect.* "Oh dear." *A fake rummage in your bag.* "I seem to have left the lease, of all things, back at the office. I must have been so eager to leave for the weekend yesterday."

"That's okay. Do you normally work weekends?" *No. She normally stalks people on her off time. Alarm bells. I can feel it in the seat of my pants.*

"Not usually, but unfortunately with the electronic diaries, it's hard to escape work. And besides, I was visiting a friend for breakfast around the corner. I do like to deal with clients, especially long-standing ones like yourself, face to face. And traffic during the week can frazzle the nerves. Mine or my client's, that is." Fake laugh. Damn, I'm stupid.

Just when we assumed that was that, the phone call on Tuesday, or was that Wednesday? An appointment set for Friday? No problem. My apartment again? And then come Wednesday evening, knock knock, who's there. Here's the punchline.

"I thought traffic worked on your nerves." Looking a bit 'frazzled' there Miss Agent.

"Yes, well, we lost one of our clients today. I wasn't about to lose another if it could be helped."

"It couldn't have been the impeccable service from the Morris and Chandler agents." How we do assume. "My experience says you people definitely go above and beyond the call of duty." Way out there on the fringe of sanity.

"Thank you. We do try. But no, unfortunately, Miss Chap... sorry, Miss Winthrup passed away unexpectedly."

"Oh my. An elderly lady was she?"

"Not really, no," she gets up from her chair, paper in hand. "But let's get to your lease."

"No husband or boyfriend to take over the lease?"

She comes around to my chair. Something's under the paper in her hand. A pen maybe?

"Single. Poor dear." She stands over me pointing at the signature line.

"Single? Just like me, then."

"Exactly."

A blur of movement.

Muffled words.

"We'll get you home shortly, Mom. Try to relax now."

\#

The key-turning click in the door sent a burst of cold adrenalinee through Elizabeth's body, bringing her back to the present. The air ran frozen through her teeth as she took a sharp breath. The door opened to reveal a young woman around thirty carrying a steel tray.

"Hey there," she said sweetly. "It's a beautiful Saturday morning out there."

Elizabeth's joints and tendons shivered under the tension. Her stomach lurched uncontrollably. The girl lay down the tray on the bedside table while Elizabeth's eyes frantically scanned the tray's contents. Syringe, swabs, vials of clear liquid, and a drip bag with what would be her saline solution.

She pulled up the nearby stool and sat down facing Elizabeth straight on. Calmly and methodically the girl went through the motions. Cleaning, dressing and refilling. Elizabeth held her breath for what seemed like minutes as the wound on her neck was wiped and caressed as the girl began talking to her.

"Let me see. I was eight years old when it all started. Grade two."

CHAPTER 8

Angelica held her mother's bulky handbag against her body, wanting somehow for its soft leathery skin to comfort her. Make her feel that everything was going to be okay. She looked up at her father as he wheeled the pale robed figure along the gravel pathway towards the front door. His face said everything wasn't going to be okay.

It was the middle of winter, but the sky was bright blue, and the warmth of the sun took some of the chill out of Angelica's bones. She followed behind her father's rounded shoulders, looking down at the dry grey gravel when he turned to maneuver the wheelchair around. He didn't seem to struggle with the weight of his wife as he lifted the wheelchair up, one step at a time. But, she had come to recognise that the look in his face was another kind of pain.

It was the same look he had when he assumed Angelica was upstairs playing in her room, as he spoke softly into the phone to the doctors. His wife was ill. She needed major surgery. She might die if not operated on.

Then came the calls from the medical aid people. The surgery and hospital were not fully covered by his policy. She could hear him clearly from upstairs, shouting at them. Begging them.

Her mother was in hospital for three days. One day before the operation, the day of the operation, and the day she and her father went to pick her mother up. The doctors had ushered him out of the room. She watched them through the glass in the door. They recommended his wife stay at least another week to recover fully before being moved or taken home.

"Don't you think I would if I could!" Her mother had squeezed Angelica's hand as she registered the shout in her sleep. That was the last time she heard her father shout. She couldn't even remember him speaking after that.

And there he was, his tall frame pulling his wife up the stairs. A hard, cold stare and clenched jaw. Quiet determination. His face was unshaven, and he wore his warm brown jacket that had often kept her warm at long, boring family events.

Her mother had been diagnosed with throat cancer. Not that she smoked heavily or more than most people. That, of course, was before the outright smoking ban around 2022 in the aftermath of the Great Pandemic. But, smoking aside, Angelica was aware that her mother never spoke about her resentments. She didn't want to rock the boat or cause a drama with her family.

The operation to remove the thick black cancer cells from her throat meant that she would need a tracheotomy. Angelica didn't fully understand it until she saw her mother lying in the hospital bed, breathing slowly through the plastic tube protruding from her neck. She had overcome the impulse to faint or throw up, but could almost feel the tubing in her own neck. She was grateful that her mother had been asleep when she cringed and dry heaved. Her father watched, expressionless and cold.

A month later and a silent trip to school, her father dropped her off. She had hoped for a wave good-bye. Her mother used to wave good-bye. That was the last time she saw him.

A friend's mother had taken her home that day.

The house had seemed dark and empty. More than usual. She had closed the front door and quietly walked up the stairs to her parents' bedroom. The door was slightly ajar, but she could see her mother lying in bed. She was crying. Silently crying. Her hands opened and closed on the bedding as tears ran down her face.

She knew then that they were alone.

#

They had to move out of the house and into a small apartment block in the city. Angelica's mother was no longer employed; bouts of fatigue and various illnesses kept her away from work on a regular basis. She was 'no longer medically fit to perform her duties'. The medical aid barely covered the prescriptions necessary for keeping the cancer from returning. Antibiotics for infections of the throat and throat cavity, as well as different levels of painkillers. Eventually her mother settled on the strongest on the market.

Every two or three months, money was deposited into her mother's bank account from a M. Robberts. They both knew who made the payments. It was always just enough to get them by with food and rent for two months. Barely.

She became self-absorbed and difficult with her mother, resenting her mother's pain. She stormed out of arguments and slammed the front door on her way into the hallway of the apartments.

Acting out at school had the inevitable results, and what she predicted would be another curse became a blessing. Angelica moved schools to the city. She kept to herself, had classmates, no friends. She became anonymous. She didn't feel the need for the company of her peers. Seeing for the first time the mother she once resented, she instead saw someone who was there for her. Always willing to listen, always home when she came home. And she had her computer and chat rooms to occupy her weekends or when her mother was sleeping during the day. She could tell her mother anything. She got used to reading her mother's lips and the short sentences she would mouth to her.

By the time Angelica was fourteen, her mother had become weak and skeletal. She didn't go to the doctors anymore. What were they going to tell her that was different? Angelica was doing all the housework, and buying the groceries was done online and delivered every three days.

Bathing and cleaning her mother was a ritual that she slowly began to enjoy. Not at first, but soon she realised its significance. She spoke to her mother as she shaved her bony legs. Her mother had looked after her, bathed her, fed her, and clothed her. She was honoured to be doing this for her mother. She could see the tears flowing down her mother's wet face, the steam of the bath holding them warmly that night. The gratitude, the sorrow, and the happiness in her eyes.

She remembered how beautiful Mother's hair had been. Dark flowing waves of perfumed locks, falling around her face and shoulders. Washing Mother's hair was the most difficult. She wasn't able to just submerge herself in the water to wet or rinse her hair. The plastic tubing would get damp or water would enter it, possibly choking her. So she had to bend awkwardly over the bath while Angelica used the water jug from the kitchen to pour water over her hair. She did the best she could, massaging her mother's hair and head. Trying to bring whatever relief she could. But her mother's neck would begin to throb with pain around the tubing, and her frustration would build. Angelica knew her mother felt useless and weak and a burden on her young daughter.

It was August 2025, and Angelica had finished drying her mother's hair in the bedroom that they shared, standing behind her brushing her dull brittle hair. Her mother took her other hand and placed it on her warm cheek. She turned to face her, love and warmth radiating from her. For a second she didn't see the fragile woman she had become. She saw her mother. Beautiful, strong and whole.

Angelica sat down on the bed, both women facing each other.

It wasn't difficult to read her mother's lips when she mouthed, "I want to die."

Tears filled their eyes, and in the warm light of the room they held each other.

A few weeks later, on 18 September, she came home from school to find her mother waiting in the living room. The apartment was warm and she could see the steam coming through the bathroom door. Her mother was wearing her bathrobe. Angelica gave a questioning look at her as she put her backpack on the sofa, and sat down next to her. A bit early for a bath. Her mother smiled back, taking her hand in hers, and they locked eyes for a few moments. She lifted up her left hand to reveal the hypodermic needle. The tube depressor was drawn back, and the clear sedative was inside.

Angelica felt her heart race, her face prickled with fear, and she battled to swallow. She knew what her mother wanted. She wanted to take the pain away. She didn't want to be a burden anymore.

"You're my mother. I love you," she sobbed. "You are not a burden to me. I will do anything for you until the day you die."

She fell into her mother's arms heaving and in shock.

But what kind of a daughter doesn't listen to their mother? Doesn't do what they ask of them?

Her mother didn't want it to look like a suicide. She wanted Angelica to insert the needle, and inject the sleep. While her mother was asleep, Angelica would hold her under the water. No resistance. It would look like an accident. Angelica would put the needle back in the cabinet, leave the apartment and come back later. On 'discovering' her mother, she would call an ambulance. The medical examiner would immediately assume drowning and mark cause of death accidental. The life insurance would not pay Angelica out in the event of a suicide.

She killed her mother, and her friend. She could never fix it. She could never justify it enough. And she could never tell the person she told everything, how it felt. She had climbed into the bath, and curled up on her mother's warm body lying in the water. Quiet and still. A new pain had begun.

Chapter 9

"Now don't get me wrong," she continued as she tidied up and neatly replaced all the items on the tray, "I hated, with all my energy, what had happened to my mother. But she brought it on herself. She got the cancer, not me. And yet I had to look after her when she was weak and pathetic. I had to listen to her crying in bed at night. During the day.

"I was angry. I was angry with my father. Then I was angry with her. Then I was angry with myself. I had a choice here. When I realized that, I felt a weight lift off my shoulders. That was when I realized that I couldn't be angry with my father. He had made a choice; a choice that benefited him. He made his choice by what would make *his* life better. You have to respect that. On some level at least. My mother had a choice, and she chose. I had a choice, and I chose. It all worked out for everyone in the end, wouldn't you say?

"For so long I couldn't have a meaningful relationship with a boy, men. Until I released my hatred of my father I couldn't get close enough without feeling like I wanna kill them. Understand, I'm not talking about my youth here; schoolgirl flings. This is a recent development. Like the Lady of the Lake, I feel like my Excalibur has been revealed and I hold within my hands something magnificent, powerful and brilliant.

"Sometimes I think that if people would lose their family, loved ones, close friends, that they would be truly liberated. And then, they would be able to be, do, and act without any concern for themselves. I'm not talking about a selfish journey. I'm talking a selfless journey. One where, should you choose, you could go into a country ravished by a disease, just to serve and help. You could drop everything and help the world. There's no excuse. There are none anyway. We just think that the people in our lives stop us from reaching our true potential, whatever that may be, and because most of the world are sitting behind a desk not contributing — being a cog isn't contributing. It's just making the machine bigger. I'm not saying wish your loved ones die. I'm saying live like they aren't stopping you from being a better person. Look at someone who has lost everything. Give them time: either they'll blow their brains out, fade into a shadow of their former selves, or they will take the world on, head on, because what's the worst that can happen? It's already happened to them. And dying is no longer something they worry about because that will be a relief when it comes.

"That, my dear, is my true potential. For the first time in my life, I have my life. Unfortunately, there are certain things that I feel I still need to excise, rid myself of, therapy out of myself — a cleansing, like I've been immersed in the baptismal waters of the lake and born again.

"Now, Elizabeth, turning our attention to you. You too had a choice. You have a choice. And like my mother, you chose to be here. You chose to open your door to me and let me into your life. Whether it was a conscious choice or not, conscious decisions were made to arrive where you are right now. You're thinking that you made a bad choice or that," Angie feigned concern, "you never made any choice. Like someone having the choice of two roads to take, and the one that she takes ends up having an oil tanker flipping over on top of her. She chose the road that led to that.

"Up till now, you've chosen for someone to have the power over you. That's your choice. Helplessness. Vulnerability. A bit of excitement in your boring life. The question now is what do you choose next?"

Angie slapped her hands on her knees. "While you dwell on your poor decision making, I have a few errands to run." She stood and picked up the tray. "I have to find out who else is making choices right now that include me. They've already invited me to the show; it's now time for some audience participation."

#

A steely gaze looked back at Allen from across the kitchen table for the second time that morning. Allen had explained, and obviously failed miserably, to his son how a flying car's physics worked.

"No wings?"

It was this very tone that made even Allen think that he'd just made up a bold-faced lie. But nevertheless, he persisted.

"As I mentioned before, my son…" He paused, then placed Caleb's car on the tabletop: his prop for the presentation on antigravity theory, "no. No wings."

"No propellers?"

"Not exactly, no," Allen pushed the car from hand to hand. "You need to focus on finishing your cereal now, Cay." He checked his watch. "It's nearly time to go, and we don't want to be late for the bus."

"Jet engines?" mouthed Caleb through sloppy milk and corn flakes. "Why a bus?"

"Jet propulsion, for direction," replied Allen. "Because I'm not even considering finding parking at or near there today. My parking-angels can take a break on that one."

Caleb stood from his chair, still spooning cereal, and tiptoed over to the sink. After putting his bowl down he turned to his father and pointed at the toy car. "Car."

"Yes," Allen said and looked down at the blue toy, "car."

Caleb hunched his shoulders and said, "Car please, Dad."

Allen sat up. "Oh, sure," and pushed the car across the table.

Caleb stepped forward but missed, letting the car fall over the edge of the table and crack onto the hard kitchen floor.

"My car," cried Caleb as he dived forward to pick up the

damaged vehicle.

"Sorry," said Allen from under the table.

Caleb analysed every inch of the toy. "Just the mirror's broken, Dad. S'okay."

Allen stood up and watched his son carry on nonchalantly to the front door.

"He just can't see behind him."

"Right," offered Allen and grabbed his keys from the hallway table. Caleb opened the door and marched through.

"Tell me really how the cars fly, Dad."

#

Punching in the co-ordinates of Geoff's apartment block, Marc had the strong urge to call Angie. The hesitation of logic and reason pulled his arm back, but he really wanted to just speak to her. He reversed the small car out of its underground parking bay and headed for the exit.

The electronic gate automatically started opening as he came within the ten-metre range of the sensor, just slow enough that he needed to come to a stop.

"Screw it," he said out loud and pressed the on-screen button. He had already set up her number to call and took a deep breath as reality set in. The gate finished its journey, and Marc set off out and into the busy road.

A few bleeps from the screen and, "Hey, Marc."

His car swerved slightly as he righted himself in his chair after the jolt of adrenalinee in his system.

"Hi there," he said trying not to be distracted by Angie's face on the screen looking back at him. "We all set for later, or what?"

"Sure," she sounded preoccupied. "Got a client I need to see, some errands to run."

"Great, sorry to bother you while you're working. Wanted to confirm the time."

"No problem. I need to have a break from all this." She stopped for a moment. "Eleven thirty should be about right."

"Cool," Marc said, "we can meet around the flying car area. Knowing Geoff, we'll be there most of the time. But call when you get there, and we can find each other."

"Sounds good, but I may be late. You never know with clients. So don't wait around for me."

"No. That's fine. We'll manage to keep ourselves occupied." He paused. "Maybe we can both go back to that coffee shop near your place again. Yesterday's breakfast was a great way to start the day." He chuckled nervously.

"Yeah." She sounded unsure. "I don't think that's a good idea tomorrow."

"Oh no, just a—"

"I've got some issues to handle with her tomorrow," she continued. "It doesn't mean you can't come over tonight, though."

"Excellent," he said too loudly. "I mean, cool. See you later then."

"Bye," and the screen cleared.

"Damn," Marc breathed.

He pulled the car up alongside the figure slouching on the pavement. Geoff stood up, approached, opened the car door and bundled himself into the passenger seat.

He looked over at Marc. "What's your problem?"

"Nothing," said Marc pulling himself up in his seat. "What's your problem?"

"Whatever," replied Geoff raising a pointed hand, "Onward and upward we go, fellow traveler."

The car zipped back into the traffic with a bit more speed and co-ordination than before.

#

"Next is a Miss Young," said Frank. "Single white female."

"Miss Young?" repeated Ruth. She came over to Frank, pulling the glass tablet away from him. "Why's that name familiar?"

"Because I just said it to you?" he said trying to pull the screen back. "And don't mess with the screen."

"Let me see that," she ignored him.

Surrendering his screen, he knocked on the door.

"Shit Frank," she said pulling at his shoulder. "What's the chance?"

He knocked on the door again, looking absently at the screen.

Ruth used the 'recall' button on her mobile to dial from the previous numbers. "She's the bloody realtor from Morris Chandler, Frank."

He hesitated mid-knock. She held up the screen at Frank's puzzled face.

"Miss Young! We'd like to ask you a few questions," she said, shoving the screen into Frank's hands and moving to the door.

"That is why we're here," he mumbled still confused.

She knocked hard on the door. "Why is it that we're searching the one-kilometre radius of Elizabeth's Soul Trace that just happens to include her realtor's apartment block?"

"Door to door service?" said Frank snapping to reality.

"Exactly, smart guy."

Frank pulled out his mobile.

"Angel! Banks! Look alive!"

"What you two got for me?" boomed the voice even over the small speaker.

"Angel!" interrupted Ruth, "Get me a Soul Trace on the following individual, pronto," she snapped as she pressed on the tablet screen in Frank's hands. "Stay with Angel," she said to Frank, "I've got an important call to make."

A few bleeps and her mobile connected with Angie Young.

#

"It really wasn't necessary of you to come all the way out, especially on a Saturday, Miss Young," said the middle-aged woman in the doorway. "I'm always out and about in the city, so I could've stopped in at your offices any time."

"It's really no problem, Ms Conway," said Angie. "I was in the area and I prefer to be less formal. Get to meet clients in the comfort of their own homes."

She glanced through the doorway of the small flat. A minor manipulation.

"Please come in," Kate indicated as she stepped aside.

Angie's mobile bleeped in her shoulder bag.

"Would you like something to drink?"

Angie unzipped and reached inside her bag.

"That would be great, thanks," she said to the eager woman. She looked down at Ruth's stern face on the screen. Her smile faded. The background looked familiar.

Fuck it. "Do you mind if I take this?"

"Sure," offered Ms Conway. "The living room's right through there. I'll fix us something cool."

Angie stepped into the comfortable lounge, sat down, and took a deep breath. The adrenaline felt good.

"Hello?" she said casually.

"Ah," Ruth looked slightly surprised. "Hi, Miss Young. How are you today?"

"Oh, hi Tracker... um," Fucking Hicks.

"Hicks, yes," Ruth finished off. "Sorry to be calling you on the weekend."

"No problem at all," said Angie eagerly. "Have you got any more leads? How can I help?"

"Well, some new information has come up and I wanted to bounce an idea off you."

Suddenly the screen went black.

#

Ruth had blacked out the call. "Frank! Fuck. Get a lock on her fucking mobile!"

#

The screen returned with Ruth's smiling face. "Are you home right now, Miss Young?"

Home? Bitch.

"Well, no," she replied. "I'm visiting a friend."

"Sorry for the intrusion then. But something's been bothering me."

"Oh?" Angie attempted surprise.

"You didn't mention anything about having visited Elizabeth Stride only days before her disappearance."

Ms Conway returned with a tray with two tall glasses of frosted iced drinks. Angie followed her as she placed the tray on the table and passed one to Angie. Deep in her thoughts, Angie took a long, slow sip.

"Is everything okay with our signal?" asked Ruth. "I can't seem to hear you."

"Did I not mention that to you?"

Someone came into frame, and tapped Ruth on the shoulder. The screen blacked out again.

#

"She's at a Ms Conway's apartment."

"Run it against Miss Young's clients!" hissed Ruth.

#

The screen returned once again.

"Is everything okay? I seem to be losing you, Tracker Hicks."

"Already did," whispered a man's voice.

Ruth whipped around.

The screen went off.

Angie felt cold. It wasn't the drink.

#

"Get a team…"

"Already done," said Frank.

#

Angie stood up.

"Is everything alright, Miss Young?" asked Ms Conway.

"Angelica," said Ruth's voice.

"Everything's coming together nicely, Ms Conway," said Angie to herself as she made her way to the front door.

"Angelica!" shouted Ruth.

Angie hesitated for a moment. She opened the door and stepped outside.

"Angelica just wants to hurt the world, Hicks," said Angie icily, and dropped the mobile over the balcony.

#

Crash! Frank stumbled as he burst through the door.

"Frank!" shouted Ruth from outside, "we need—"

"Probable cause? For fuck's sake Hicks," he said as he righted himself in the entrance hall.

"Check the bathroom, Hicks," came Angel's voice over their mobiles. "Water."

Nearly tripping over each other, they ran through the lounge area, bumping chairs, causing a lamp to clatter to the floor. Ruth rounded a corner, just ahead of Frank. She veered right; he headed left down the short hallway.

Opening a door each, doing a quick scan, they entered.

"Nothing," said Frank.

They both come out into the hallway again.

"Nothing," said Ruth turning to see the last door at the end of her side of the hallway. She made for the closed door and grabbed at the handle.

"Locked," she said.

"Here," he snapped as he ran his full weight against the door, flinging it back against the interior wall of what appeared to be a bathroom, his momentum carried him sliding to the floor and into the base of the bath. Tiles shattered and clinked on the floor behind the door.

Ruth came forward and lunged into the tepid water of the bath, wrenching and pulling at the limp naked body. She heaved and splashed over the side of the bath as Frank, wide-eyed, grabbed Elizabeth's feet and legs as they laid her out on the cold tiled floor.

"Keep that goddamn pipe clear of the water," said Frank indicating the clear tubing protruding from Elizabeth's neck.

Ruth held her in her arms. "She's unconscious, but breathing steadily," she said as she wiped Elizabeth's face and hair, then removed the tape from her mouth and nose.

"Drugged," he said sitting alongside his water-soaked partner.

Ruth began to sob as she carried on wiping the pale face in her arms. Her tears fell onto the cold skin.

"We got her, Angel," said Ruth softly.

"I know, my girl," came the gentle response. "She's gonna be just fine. Medics are nearly there."

"She's going to be fine. She's going to be fine, Frank," she looked through her blurry eyes at the bloodshot eyes looking back up at her. Elizabeth's breathing steadied in Ruth's arms.

Frank sank back against the bath, water soaking into his clothes.

"It's finished, Elizabeth," whispered Ruth.

A sudden rush of noise burst through the dripping of the bath water.

"In here!" shouted Frank. He turned to Ruth, "It's just beginning, Ruth." His face was pale, eyes wide.

Three medics came through the door, getting under

Elizabeth's limp body. Frank slid over to Ruth and pulled her shirt and body towards him.

"We gotta get the fuck outta here," he said through clenched teeth. He stood awkwardly and pulled her to her feet. "Now."

#

The ringing in Angie's ears had subsided but was now replaced by a quickened thud of blood beating in her entire head. Her senses tingled and the pressure on her forehead was unbearable. She stepped onto the bus headed for the north side of the city and headed for an empty seat.

She was keenly aware of the bodies bumping and closing in around her. The soupy warmth of heavy body odours squeezed around her like deep lukewarm water pressing down on her. She closed her eyes and breathed. She felt lighter as coolness descended on her skin. Her head cleared and the noises receded into the background. The race of adrenaline in her system ebbed into a gentle rhythm with her heart. Tensions were refocused from her shoulders and neck into her clenching fists and the tightening of her mouth and jaw.

"Everything's fine."

#

"We've got a rock-solid trace on Miss Young," said Angel. His attention was focused on the red dot on the screen.

"You let me know how Elizabeth is doing, Angel," said Ruth.

"You got it. I'm sending the live locator to everyone's mobiles. We've got someone who's gonna feel trapped, so nobody cock this up by jumping before we've got him — her — covered completely."

#

Frank had taken a knock to his thigh by sliding onto the bathroom floor, and taking the stairs three at a time sent sharp pains up his left flank.

Hitting the pavement, he said, "Dammit. Should've parked closer," and headed for the car.

He bleeped the car alarm and threw the keys to Ruth who was already at the driver's door.

"Guess I'm riding shotgun on this one," he said as they bundled into the car.

The car was out of the parking; turned left, then right and into Saturday morning traffic.

"Angel!" Frank pressed the car's comms unit.

"You guys need to be headed to the north of town, pronto," said Angel.

"Like where?" asked Ruth.

"That's the general direction, currently."

"And in the near future?" asked Frank.

"Give me a second, Banks!"

There was a pause while Ruth gunned the car from lane to lane.

"Ten minutes ahead I see lots of people. Noise. Disruption and unease. Chaos for her."

"So not her happy-place, I'm guessing."

"Could be the train station," offered Ruth.

"No," replied Angel. "Her current trace shows she's passed that already."

"The stadium!" shouted Frank.

"Right around the corner from us? But there's no game on that I'm aware of," said Angel.

"The car show," said Ruth.

"Why the hell would she go there?" asked Frank.

"She needs to blend in." said Angel. "It's also going to be a bastard to trace her."

"Clever girl," said Ruth "Harder to follow a single Soul

Trace in a crowded room: too much to home in on."

"Needle in a haystack," said Angel.

"Girl, shit!" Ruth slammed her hand on the dashboard. "A woman serial killer."

"And your point," asked Frank massaging his thigh. "I know a few women, present company included, who'd easily fit a psycho profile."

Ruth landed a fist on his right thigh.

"Fuck!"

"All okay there, Banks?" asked Angel.

"All good," he responded feebly. "We've got people at the show, Angel. Mkhize and Collins."

"They're already on standby."

"Amazing how free tickets can get Collins to sway his opinion."

"Boys and their toys," replied Ruth.

As humankind entered the 2010s, with a new identity and self-awareness, you altered your way of thinking as you looked at the world around you and the worlds beyond you as something belonging to and being part of the 'us' that makes you one and the same and yet individuals in a timeless dance that extends from the physical to the unimaginable.

Science evolved from clunky physics and chemical reactions to quantum leaps of the imagined boundaries into the unknown, and yet the known. Scientists took the underlying messages from myths and lunatics and read between the lines. They looked into the eyes of the sangomas, mystics and masters and beheld, as if for the first time, the truth, the possibilities and the true reality of the world around you that had been speaking to you all since the birth of the universe. They looked into the mind of humankind, and gazed through the atom into a world that continues to expand into infinite possibilities and infinite forms where only your souls should truly venture.

By taking these leaps, into what one would have assumed was the void, humanity emerged with a glimpse of the Divine. The Divine that is in all there is. In this, science and religion, once again, merged. As with the renaissance, science supported the human belief in the Divine. Some fought and continue to fight this duality, but they are a dying breed.

Time was relegated to the status of a manmade concept, and humanity was able to see the universe as space, matter and change, freeing you up to charter your course through timeless dimensions and realities both real to you and real to your souls.

The growing global warming threat and the Great Pandemic of the 2020s demanded less fossil fuels and more bio-friendly energy sources for self-reliance, leading engineers and scientists across the globe to revisit basic technologies and, in doing so, created some of the first organic technologies that provided their own power sources and which, through further enhancements, tapped into energy sources that life has been using for eons. Energy sources that constitute life, not consumption. And in looking into these traces of life, scientists were able to track the origins of this world and look through the basic third dimensional elements into the areas long spoken about in myth and religion. Skeptics questioned the reality of these dimensions, and, not for the first time in history, questioned the blasphemous levels that science had reached.

CHAPTER 10

Caleb held onto his father's hand as tightly as he could standing in front of the ticket booth. His gaze was fixed on the towering stadium arch above them, and the tiny pigeons flying to and from the top of the structure that promised all kinds of excitement inside. His feet fumbled as he toppled backwards.

"Careful, kid," his father said holding onto him. He guided him in front of him as they stepped through the turnstiles.

"Dad," Caleb said and pointed up to the sky. "Is that a peri, perigra, what you call it?"

His father scanned the space above the stadium.

"You're right, a peregrine falcon," he said as they both locked on the slick, dark shape zipping through the air. "Well spotted, Cay."

The crowds were bumping past them, and Caleb's heart beat faster, pulsing in the warmth of his father's grip. They followed the stream of people along the walkway leading towards the opening in the south side of the stadium. The huge concrete arch stretched from one side to the other like a white rainbow. On one of their recent outings, Yuneesha had taken them all up the SkyCar where they saw the entire city and the Indian Ocean. She had told them they were a hundred metres above the football field below, and that the 350-metre Y-shaped arch was the same as the one in the colourful South African flag. Even now, from below, the mass of cables supporting the tent-like roof reminded him of a spider's web.

His father stopped at the top of the stairs leading down to the field and surrounding sports track below. They both took in the thronging spectacle.

The central football field had been covered by temporary, interlocking rubber mats on which various exhibitioners and food vendors had set up rows and rows of kiosks, platforms, signs, and visual displays. Even from this distance his senses were bombarded.

Along the perimeter of the field was the bright blue running track that, although it remained untouched, was conspicuously sealed over by bright orange netting. Suspended by a spiders-web of cables and attachments, it hung from the overhanging roof about thirty metres from the floor where a similarly coloured fence fixed it to the ground.

That's when Caleb noticed the vehicles. Moving slowly through the air were what looked like two blue cars.

"Whoa," he said.

"My thoughts exactly," said his father.

Their eyes followed the two vehicles as they floated about fifty metres apart inside the orange web. They looked at each other; his father lifted his eyebrows with large eyes.

"Time to fly."

Caleb's heart jumped, and they stepped as fast as they could down the wide stairs.

#

The lift from the basement parking opened onto the paved walkway reaching around the stadium.

"Anyone can dodge bullets, Collins," Mkhize was saying as the two men stepped out and ambled through the growing numbers of people heading towards the south entrance. "You just have to believe in yourself enough and believe it's possible."

"Oh is it? And I suppose you can dodge bullets, Khabazana?" Collins mocked his partner.

"Absolutely," said Mkhize and took a step sideways, arms outstretched, for Collins to appreciate the view, "Do you see any bullet holes in me?"

"Fuck's sake, Mkhize." Collins rolled his eyes. "You need to be shot at to say you can dodge bullets."

"Says who? No bullets have hit me in my twenty-seven years, and none since I've been in the Tracker Unit."

"That's a combination of luck and maybe Archangel Michael. And I mean the actual angel, not Mike Haddon," Collins said pointing to the sky. "Plus the fact that *you can't dodge bullets*, freako."

"I rather like to think I have amadlozi on my side, thanks. The power of the ancestors is strong in this one," Mkhize touched his chest with both hands and grinned knowingly at his partner.

"Whatever." Collins rolled his eyes. "Just please do me a favour if we are ever under hostile fire."

"Anything, comrade." Mkhize gave a wry smile and tented his fingers together.

"Duck."

Both men's mobiles bleeped in their pockets. Each retrieved their devices and read the identical message from Angel:

"Be on alert. We may have a situation developing at the stadium. Will confirm as we have more concrete info."

"Goddamnit," said Collins.

#

The queue to the flying cars ride was moving steadily but Geoff was still about a hundred metres from his goal.

"I'm chooning you," he said to Marc, "We'd better buy five tickets. It's daylight robbery but I know I'm going to wanna go twice and if your girl decides, for some reason, that a flying car is the coolest thing since glitter make-up, I'm not giving up my second ride. Your woman or not."

"She's not into it, so I don't see the need. But you do whatever."

"Worst case, I go three times; there's no way I'm going to

stand in this GODDAMN CHAIN GANG line again, because that's exactly what will happen when she flutters her eyebrows, or whatever, at you."

Marc shook his head. "Food?"

"My bru! Two hotdogs. Two strawberry shakes. And make sure you get the free toy with the two-shake deal."

"Is that it?"

"Yep, and whatever you want to get yourself."

"Gee, thanks," replied Marc holding out his hand.

Geoff reeled back in disgust. "I'm getting the car tickets you, cheapskate." He looked around then raised his voice; "You want to stick your hand in where?"

Marc walked off cringing but smiling at his friend. He glanced at his watch as he weaved his way through the mass of people. *Still an hour until I meet Angie.* His heart raced. He still couldn't put his finger on his feeling: like, love, or lust? Who cared? It felt good anyway. Someone, other than his mates, wanted to meet up with him.

He stopped at the end of the queue to the take-out stand. He checked his watch again.

#

With all the sights and sounds buzzing around them it was no wonder Caleb couldn't stand still.

"Not long now, kid," Allen reassured him. "We'll have the tickets in our hands, and then we can take a look around."

"'kay," he said. "I wanna do the games there first."

"I thought we'd look first then go on the flying car ride."

"Sweets and games," he replied.

"And the flying cars?" Allen asked, thrown off by Caleb's attitude.

"Later."

"Later?" asked Allen bending down to face his son. "Aren't you excited to go in the flying cars?"

Caleb's shoulders sagged. "I am." He looked over his father's shoulder. "They look high, Dad."

Allen turned and looked across the field to one of the hovering vehicles.

"Hmm," he said with a sudden knot in his stomach. "Maybe we ask them to fly a little lower, my boy."

Caleb thought for a moment. "'kay."

Allen noticed a young man looking around as he walked up the line of people towards them.

"That's the second time you're coming past here," he said to the man. "Lose someone?"

He shrugged and indicated the disposable serving trays full of food cartons. "I'm pretty sure I left my friend around here like fifteen minutes ago."

"Line's moving along," replied Allen. "He's probably near the front by now."

"Really? Thanks," he said and turned to walk back the way he had come.

"Where's the food from, by the way?" asked Allen.

"Happy Hippo's to the right of the big screen," he replied over his shoulder. "Better hurry. I think they're gonna run out soon."

"Happy Hippo's!" squealed Caleb.

Allen knew they needed to hurry if they were going to get anything to tide them over till dinner.

\#

"Poor bastards," said Geoff between bites as he and Marc walked along the long line of people. "They have no idea what's coming, my bru."

Marc shook his head. "You're the bastard with your five damned tickets."

"All necessary. No overindulgence. Once in a lifetime opportunity."

"I'm just glad we got here early," said Marc. "Let's check the concept designs stand then grab another dop."

"I give it ten minutes before that ticket lady makes her announcement," Geoff whispered suspiciously to Marc.

#

Allen held onto Caleb's hand while his son pulled impatiently on it.

"Caleb," he said sternly, "not long then we can grab some food, then off to the flying cars."

"I'm hungry," replied his anxious son. "Later for the car ride."

"My boy," began Allen.

"Ladies and gentlemen," said the stadium sound system, "due to the limited time and therefore ticket availability is limited. As such, we regret to announce that all tickets have sold out."

A loud roar of disapproval erupted around the stadium. Allen stood in the stunned chaos.

#

"He's not answering, dammit Frank."

"It's probably noisy in there, Hicks," he replied. The stadium's arch was well in sight and slowly began to loom over them as they neared it. "They'll be fine."

#

"If it isn't Professor Hicks," said a familiar voice out of the now low rumble of dissatisfaction.

Standing at the back of the Hungry Hippo queue, Allen turned to see the man from earlier, without his tray of take-away, standing next to Geoff.

Geoff looked down at Caleb. "You must be Caleb."

"Caleb spotted one of your falcons earlier, Geoff," Allen said with a smile at his son. "Didn't you, Cay?"

The boy nodded and craned his neck to see the front of the queue.

"Lekker," Goeff said, checking the air above them.

"I want the gamer card toy, Dad," said Caleb.

"Ah," said Geoff revealing his free toy from his pocket, "the micro-gamer. A bit retro. Dodgy graphics, but good mindless fun to pass the time." He turned to Marc. "Who woulda thought of disposable games? Ha! Ten games on a cardboard interface. All biodegradable."

"Are you guys doing the flying cars?" asked Marc.

Allen looked sullenly at Marc then to his restless son. "A minor issue there in the greater scheme of things, apparently."

"What?" said Geoff, "You can't be serious?"

"My bru," said Marc nudging Geoff, "why don't you give them your extras?"

Geoff coughed and spluttered into his hand. "The hell you don't!" he said and immediately caught himself. "Prof, my acquaintance speaks out of turn. This is Marc. He's known to be irrational." He turned to Marc. "My professor."

"Hi," said Allen to Marc, "Remember, you can't choose your family but apparently you know how to pick your acquaintances. Tickets?"

Marc turned to Geoff. "Come on. What about the laitie."

"And me?" said Geoff through clenched jaw.

Marc stared him down.

"There's a line you're crossing somewhere, my bru." Geoff reached into his pocket, without taking his eyes off Marc, pulled out his wallet and said, "Somewhere in the universe a star is dying; falling in on itself, all because of you." He slowly pulled out two of the tickets and held them out to Allen.

Allen hesitatingly took them.

"Now there's nothing but a deep void. The blackness of a black hole sucking everything in for all eternity."

"How much do I owe you?" Allen reached for his wallet.

"The void has no currency," replied Geoff.

#

Collins listened to Angel's voice, clenching his mobile closer to his ear. Mkhize stood next to him, listening to the same call on his unit.

"She may already be inside, but stay at the main entrance to see who's going in and out."

"Yasas, Angel," said Collins.

"I'm going to send her profile to the stadium's server for them to broadcast on all monitors and screens, but I'm only doing it when we've got all our team in place. I don't want her scared off before we manage to contain the area."

#

"Come on, Caleb," said Allen. "You can open it at the gates while we wait. I don't want anything else to go wrong."

Caleb took another mouthful of burger from the bright pink and blue wrapper while fumbling with his cardboard game in the other hand. Allen gripped his milkshake tighter as he weaved through the people and stalls to the gates up ahead. He was focused on the sign.

#

Ruth stopped the car as close to the entrance of the stadium as possible, and they both leaped out, leaving the car doors to close automatically behind them.

"Mkhize! Collins!" she said into her mobile, "You guys up there?"

Frank lagged behind, battling up the ramp and stairs.

"I see you, Hicks," said Mkhize's voice. "Nothing to tell you from here."

"Keep your eyes peeled. Have you seen Allen or Caleb anywhere?"

There was a pause.

"No, I've got other things to worry about now, Hicks."

"Shit." She began to tire and turned to look for Frank. "Any suggestions, Frank?"

He emerged from the mass of people holding his thigh. "I'll be fine at the stadium opening up there for now," he winced. "Take one of the other guys and find her."

Already disappearing into the crowds she shouted back to him, "I'm on my mobile!"

#

On the north side of the stadium, Allen and Caleb had reached the front of the flying car gates.

"Sir, we will need to keep your son seated at all times and fastened as well as possible. He is required to be placed in the infant chair in the rear of the car because of his age and size. Unfortunately the seat-belts are only for adults."

"That shouldn't be a problem," said Allen.

Caleb looked up from his car game and hesitated as they neared the vehicle hovering about a half-metre off the ground. Allen could feel a low rumble of air pulsing over his feet.

"Game time's over, son." He looked down at him, "I'm here, and we're going to be strapped in nice and tight." He turned to the operator. "Right?"

Caleb looked at his father, then to the other man.

"Right."

#

A few metres back in the line, Marc and Geoff stood impatiently waiting: Geoff peering over the other people in front of him, and Marc checking his watch.

"I'm telling you now, bru, your girl's going to have to forfeit her ticket in lieu of stupidity and you're going to have to live with it."

"Whatever, bru," said Marc checking his watch again. "I

told you she's not interested in the show anyway. So it all worked out perfectly."

"*Perfectly? Worked out?*" Geoff raised his hands. "In a few minutes your fate will be sealed and there'll be one ticket left, and guess who's going to use it?"

"Me?" said a calm voice next to Marc.

Marc jumped as Angie's arm wrapped around his.

"Great," said Geoff rolling his eyes.

"Nice to meet you, too," said Angie and pulled Marc closer to her.

"You're early," he said.

"Needed to drop the client," she said and looked Geoff up and down. "Too much hassle. You must be Geoff then."

"Hi," he replied offering his hand, "sorry about that, just boys being boys. Pulling each other's chains." She took his hand firmly in hers. "Jerking each other around."

Marc ignored Geoff's glare and grinned at Angie, "Seems like everything's perfect."

Angie took in the extensive scaffolding surrounding the flying car entrance and exit.

"Pretty hectic, huh?" said Marc.

"I'd say," she replied and pointed to the double storey section above the exit. "Is it true we get access to the *Sky Walk* when we leave the cars?"

"Rather than coming down the stairs to the exit?" asked Marc.

"That suspension bridge spanning the ride area looks exhilarating," she said and squeezed his arm.

"If you're into that," chimed in Geoff, "sure. But, I prefer to be in cars that can fly than some bridge looking down."

"There's exits to the roof and the SkyCar," she lay her head coyly on Marc's shoulder, "or your flying car tickets give us access to that private box overlooking everything. And its own lift to the basement parking."

"Like I said," said Geoff, "if flying cars aren't exciting enough."

"So when's lift-off, boys?"

#

Angel took a pull on the glass of water. He could feel the heaviness building in his head. Now wasn't the time.

The screen teemed with icons and symbols flying past him. He jumped ahead by ten minutes then back to the present. He needed to let go of the drama of the situation and focus on what was in front of him. He had to look at the facts not on what the devastating outcome might be. He needed to interpret clearly and not project what he assumed an icon might be. He had to forget about where Miss Young 'might' be and concentrate on what was being shown to him. But what he was seeing didn't make sense.

"Hicks," said Angel, "I'm not sure about this, but it seems like there's something about flight. Some kind of trauma related to flying in the next ten minutes." Confusion screamed in his head.

"Flight? At a car show, Angel?" said Ruth over the Room of Hours speakers.

Angel glanced at the current time symbols, flicked ahead again, then back to the figures and shapes continually changing in front of him. He had to think.

"The goddamn flying cars!" Ruth's shout distorted through the speakers.

CHAPTER 11

The stadium's big screen scrambled and fuzzed and a twenty-foot image of Angelica Young stared out blankly across the wide expanse of people and noise.

#

Frank's adrenaline kicked in. The face on the screen had sent a rush of blood to his face and he bolted down the stairs, pushing and shoving. "Stay here, Rob." He had to get to the cars.

#

"Sakhile!" shouted Ruth while he struggled to keep up with her. "The cars are over there."

"We need to get to the control room on the side." He feebly held up his badge, "Out of the fucking way!"

#

Marc smiled at the woman seated next to him in the back seat. He felt her nestled under his arm. Her body warmth came through and he felt a tingle of goose bumps run up his arm and across his neck.

"Pretty low-tech on-board we've got here," said Geoff. "Full of anti-patterns."

Marc looked over at his friend poking and prodding the screen on the dashboard, awe and wonder in Geoff's face, then back to the woman under his arm. Angie seemed distracted, maybe a little nervous.

"You okay?"

"Hmm?" She snapped out of her trance. "Sure. Fascinating, isn't it?"

"Yeah," Marc brought his arm around and gestured at his friend. "Don't mind him, he'll yack to himself."

She gave a wry smile and took his hand in hers.

"There goes your *Sky Walk*, ma'am," pouted Geoff.

Marc craned forward, then back as the platform passed overhead and behind them.

"A couple of laps and we'll be there shortly," he said to Angie.

"And this device," continued Geoff pointing at a small rectangular glowing light attached to the top of the dashboard, "that's the receiver which is plugged into the car's hard drive and on-board A.I. system. Unplug that or hack into the system and you've got yourself your very own flying automobile. That is, if you know how to commandeer it."

He turned and eyed out his passengers suspiciously. "Flying solo, so to speak."

Angie's grip on his hand stiffened. She leaned forward, causing Geoff to do the opposite.

"Geoff?" she said quietly.

"Ma'am," he replied with slight caution, but with a twinkle in his eye at the interest shown in his knowledge.

"Who's actually driving this car, then?"

"I can tell you this much," he turned and looked out his window to the ground now twenty metres below, "right now some geek on the ground has got our lives in his hands."

"Oh God, don't encourage him," said Marc.

"He'll have a visual from down there." He looked around the front of the car. "But that's not ideal. So he'll need a camera on the front of the car, bonnet or bumper, to see where he's going. But, possibly even one," he said searching around, "yep. Hello Big Brother." Geoff waved at the rearview mirror. "Smile, folks," Geoff waved; "the fucker's got us in his sights."

Marc noticed Angie slide back into her chair and behind Geoff.

"Just in case," continued Geoff, "any irresponsible passengers start messing with his kak."

#

"Goddamnit," mumbled Scott.

"What's up?" asked his fellow controller seated at a duplicate console and screen.

"Smartass passenger's just blown my spy cam cover, Duncan."

"As long as they keep their hands and heads within the vehicle, there's no problem," replied the other flying car controller.

Their supervisor approached them. "What's happening, Scotty?"

"The couple in the back seat seem happy enough," continued Scott. "It's the doos behind the wheel that's making me nervous. He's pointing at the control box."

"Probably a flippin' engineer who thinks he knows everything." He stopped and looked at the three controllers in the room. "No offense to present company of course."

"That's all I need."

"Just show them who's in charge," chimed Duncan, "and there'll be no issues."

Scott nodded, "Roger that."

#

Geoff rested his arm on the driver's door while he drummed his fingers on the steering wheel. He bopped his head to an inaudible beat.

Suddenly the car lurched downward, dropping by two or three metres. The three passengers screamed. Angie gripped Marc's arm.

"Yirra!" yelled Geoff with his hands white-knuckled on the steering wheel.

"What the hell are you doing, chop?" shouted Marc.

"Wasn't me!" Geoff shouted back over his shoulder.

"Stop screwing around," said Marc.

Geoff looked up at the rearview mirror. "Mother fucking bastard."

"What?" replied Angie coldly.

"The bogon in control is trying to show us who's boss of this here situation."

He gave the mirror the middle finger, "Game on, troglodyte."

#

"Isn't this great, Cay?" asked Allen, "Look how high we are."

Caleb craned his neck and pulled his body trying to look out the car window. He slumped back in his seat with a huff. "Can't see, Dad."

Allen turned to look at his son. "It's a lot safer in there, my boy. But I see your point."

"How long is it going to be?"

"A few more minutes."

#

"I need to see," Ruth said between gasps. She bent over to catch her breath. "I need to see who's in those cars."

"Excuse me?" said the Control Supervisor. "And you are?"

Ruth straightened up and marched past the man to an overweight man in a simulator-driving console.

"Yoh, Hicks," said Mkhize coming through the tent opening.

"Who the hell are you?" asked the Control Supervisor.

"Show me the inside of all the cars," said Ruth, finally getting her breath back.

Mkhize showed the supervisor his badge and walked to one of the other controllers. "While you're at it," he said, "you better just bring them all down."

"Are you crazy?" said the supervisor.

Ruth moved closer to her controller's screen as the small

picture in picture on the top right enlarged. Mkhize did the same. Their breathing dominated the room.

"Behind that driver," snapped Ruth trying to see behind the heavyset man in the driver's seat. Another man in the back seat was talking to someone hidden behind the driver. "Show me your face."

"Ah, Ruth?" said Mkhize from his screen.

"Yeah," she said, still focused on her screen.

"If I do this," said Scott and nudged his controls. The people in the car shifted suddenly in their seats.

"Do that again," said Ruth. Scott nudged the controls, this time the people in the vehicle moved violently to the side.

"It's her!" shouted Ruth.

"It's Caleb," said Mkhize pointing at his screen.

"What?" Ruth had already started moving for the doorway. She stopped cold in her tracks. "Get them down, now!"

#

The big screen loomed over them, even at twenty metres up. The vehicle slowly came to the end of the large curve of the track and began straightening out. Geoff frantically took in the system of controls available on the steering column and screen. It was just then that he noticed a slight change in altitude. The screen's various digits confirmed this.

The 'LANDING ENGAGED' lettering in the middle of the screen doubly confirmed this for him. About 300 metres ahead he could see the flying car departure gates.

"Nought, bru. We've got one more lap, you fucking Nazi!" he sprayed spittle over the mirror.

Angie sat up stiff, "We're not landing on the platform?"

"They think they can ground this ou? Don't worry," said Geoff and turned to face her. "I'm in and I'm going to kluge this routine. Nearly done and it'll be like commandeering our own Millennium Falcon, Marty."

Now it was Marc's turn to sit up. "You're not serious, Niranjan."

"Just for a laugh, bru," he suddenly lost his grin. "My ou," he squinted his eyes, "why's your girlfriend's face on the big screen?"

Marc pivoted in his chair.

Angie grabbed Geoff by the back of his hair. "Finish it," she hissed in his face.

"What the?" began Marc but received the side of her hand in his throat.

"Do it!" she screamed.

Geoff pulled himself away, leaving hair in Angie's hand. Tears of pain welled up in his eyes. His hands flailed in front of him trying to ward her off. She turned on Marc and opening his door began shoving him out. "Do it, bitch!"

"Angie!" screamed Marc trying to grab something.

"Okay, okay," said Geoff in horror. He wiped his eyes. "I just need to," and he grabbed the rectangular light on the dashboard and pulled.

As the light came free, with a snap of electricity, the car veered to the right.

For a moment Angie was sent across the passenger's seat, giving Marc the chance to sit up and slam the door shut. Geoff grabbed the steering wheel and tried to stabilize the car.

"Bru," shouted Geoff.

"What are you doing, Angie?" asked Marc through a raspy throat.

"Your woman's gone batty, my bru."

The car continued to descend.

"Shut the fuck up," hissed Angie. She grabbed Geoff's hair and dragged him sideways as she leaped over the driver's seat.

Angie pressed various buttons on the steering wheel. The car rose and dipped erratically in the air. Geoff held onto the passenger door handle as their speed accelerated. The car's front began to lift as they headed upward. For the first time, Geoff noticed the blue car above them.

\#

"They're taking us down, Cay," Allen turned to his son. "Let's get you outta there for a better view."

"Yay," squealed Caleb.

\#

"They've hacked the controls!" shouted Scott shoving his console wheel.

Ruth looked at Mkhize. They moved for the opening in the tent.

"Get us inside the third car," shouted Mkhize as he flashed past the control supervisor.

\#

Geoff's instincts finally set in. He reached over to try and gain control of the steering wheel. Angie sent an elbow straight into his face and nose. He flew back against his door as the pain shot through his eyes and head. A dizziness engulfed him; black splotches filled his vision.

Angie pulled the steering wheel towards her, rapidly lifting the car through the air. She pressed the button under her right-hand grip. Everyone was pressed into their chairs, too fast to swerve away from the car above them.

\#

"Allen," screamed Ruth in horror as she watched the two cars collide twenty metres above the stadium floor. Mkhize grabbed her arm and pulled her through the gawking crowds towards the gate.

\#

Allen pulled himself off the backseat floor. "Caleb?" he moaned feeling the pain throbbing up his neck, "you okay?"

His son was standing on the seat looking out the back window.

"The car's under us, Daddy."

Allen twisted himself over the baby chair and put his arm around Caleb's waist. He gripped the sponge of the chair trying to figure out what had hit them.

Suddenly he heard a grating of metal and their car bucked under them.

#

The windscreen exploded inward, sending tiny sparkles of glass splattering through the interior. Marc shielded his eyes as he felt his world exploding in an instant. The woman in the driver's seat had taken him into a surreal universe that was turning into a nightmare.

His muscles in his arms and shoulders were aching from tension and adrenaline. His brain refused to move them.

He couldn't rationalize what was playing out in front of him. In split second pulses, the past few days' events raced past him. He definitely hadn't seen this coming. As the car shuddered violently, he knew he needed to stop her.

#

Frank was already standing at the grounded car on the other side of the turnstiles. "I'm driving!" he said waving a mobile.

Ruth hesitated for just a moment, then dived into the open door and over to the passenger's seat. Frank got in after her and slammed the door. "Mkhize, keep that gate secured. Get this thing airborne!" he shouted into the mobile.

Mkhize stood open-mouthed as the car pulsed up into the air. A man wearing a bright orange vest with 'GUIDE' lettering across it approached Mkhize.

"He's patched into our control room," said the guide as they both watched the spectacle unfolding in midair. "Let's hope they know what they're doing up there."

#

Need to get out of here! Up! Up! screamed Angie in her head.

The orange netting was two metres above and she could feel the force that was driving her and the other car upward would not be strong enough to break through.

"Angie!" screamed a voice.

"Mom?"

"Angie."

Angie shook her head frantically. "Marc, if you don't want to die, stay out of this," she said. She gave another jerk of the wheel and gripped the accelerator button sending both cars towards a thick support cable that turned out to be as rigid as concrete.

The front of the top car hit it head on, buckling it downward as Angie's car acted like a steel battering ram beneath its rear.

#

Allen's world began to tip violently. He held onto his son as the car went vertical. The roof caved in under unseen pressure like a giant fist; glass exploded all around them. Caleb's screams were barely audible over the tearing of metal on metal. They were slammed into the backs of the seats, blue sky visible above them.

#

"Come on!" shouted Ruth. Now ten metres above them the sounds of the support cable reverberated around the stadium. The sound of the engines of the conjoined vehicles screamed in protest as Ruth and Frank's car gained height and speed.

Ruth opened her door and stood awkwardly on her seat.

"Jesus, Hicks!" shouted Frank.

"Can't this go any faster?" she shouted back inside. "Get us under their car!"

Frank opened his door and stepped out. "We do this together, Hicks." He clicked his mobile. "Put us in position under the blue—" he caught his breath as he looked up at the wreck above them. "The vertical one."

#

Angie's car writhed in midair, left then right, as she tried to wriggle free of the other vehicle's metallic hold. Finally she pulled up, not aware that the other car was holding her front section down. Too late she realized her mistake, as she was suddenly propelled over the dashboard and through the already shattered windshield, downward.

#

Another shudder hit the car. Allen heard what sounded like a woman screaming nearby. Something slammed onto the boot of their car and a body landed beside Allen and Caleb.

They froze, wide-eyed.

"What the hell?" whispered Allen and slowly pulled his son closer.

"Daddy," said Caleb holding onto his father, "I want Mommy."

"So do I, kid."

#

"Allen! Caleb!" shouted Ruth. The car had come to an unsteady hover two metres below the two vertical cars. "Frank, we need to get up more."

"Ruth?" came a weak response from inside the blue wreck.

"Mommy!"

"Where's Caleb?" she shouted climbing unsteadily out onto the bonnet of her car.

"He's right here with me."

"Easy, Hicks," said Frank looking on from his doorway. "That rig looks like it could drop outta the sky at any second."

Ruth ignored her partner and tried to jump up to the other car's front passenger door that lay open on its side. She landed uneasily on the car causing it to bob up and down.

"Need to get up there, Frank," she said.

Frank clicked his mobile. "Give us some height, but ever so gently guys." He turned his attention back to the other cars. "Allen," he shouted, "get to the open door."

Sounds of movement could be heard; the tinkling of glass on metal, and the cars began shifting away from them. The gut-wrenching sounds of twisting metal increased. Ruth felt her stomach turn.

"Allen!"

"We're okay," said Allen sticking his head out of the open doorway.

"Mommy," cried Caleb.

"Caleb, everything's going to be fine, baby."

Movement in the back of the blue car caught Ruth's eye. Someone climbed clumsily into the front.

"Allen?" she shouted.

"What are you doing?" asked Allen disappearing inside.

"Mommy," shouted Caleb as the car suddenly dropped, smashing downward into Ruth's car, sending her reeling backwards onto the bonnet. She couldn't find a grip and began sliding down the slippery surface as she watched the vertical mesh of the two vehicles sinking in front of her.

#

Allen had pulled Caleb back into the car just as the open door was smashed back upward and off its hinges. For a moment they were weightless.

He turned his body and violently grabbed the bloodied

woman in the driver's seat by the arm.

"Stop!" he yelled hysterically.

She landed her fist flat in his nose, instantly blurring his vision with water-filled eyes.

"Angie," shouted someone above them.

Through Allen's hazy eyes he lunged back at the figure behind the wheel. He punched, pulled and grabbed at anything. His fist hit metal.

The car began to angle slowly onto its side.

"Hold onto something, Caleb," he shouted to his son.

"This is going to hurt like hell," said the woman's voice.

"Daddy!" screamed Caleb as he fell past his father and landed with a thud onto the woman and the driver's door.

For an instant Allen's vision cleared. He watched as the woman calmly clicked open the driver's door.

#

Frank struggled to hold onto the doorframe and his partner's hand as she attempted to gain her footing on the front wheel and fender.

"Whoever's driving our car needs a goddamn medal," said Frank. Their vehicle was keeping perfect position on a downward course with the other two cars now at right angles to each other. That was when Ruth saw her worst nightmare.

Caleb clung frantically onto Miss Young's leg as she writhed angrily in the open doorway, with Allen gripping onto her shirt neck.

Frank watched Ruth slide back onto the bonnet and into a crouching position.

"Don't do it," screamed Allen at the seething mass in his hands.

Their rate of descent was increasing. The ground below was getting closer.

"Let go, Caleb," shouted Ruth.

"Mommy," he screamed.

"I've got you, baby. Let go!"

#

"Time to die," said Angie through clenched jaw and slammed the man's arm into the side of the car door.

Gravity seemed to leave her and she felt herself floating. She felt a pain as she hit metal. She rolled off the smooth surface and began tumbling down towards the stadium floor. She caught a glimpse of the wreckage above her. Then blackness.

#

Ruth held onto Caleb with one arm. Frank had kicked out the windscreen and was holding onto her other arm. "Hold onto yourself. This is going to hurt like hell."

What she didn't expect was the mangled cars hitting the front of their car, pushing them all faster towards the ground below.

With Death on the doorstep, the early quarantines forced people to look inward without distractions, while science was equally desperate for answers. Mystic concepts of déjà vu, karma, heaven and hell, past lives and reincarnation were dusted off and looked at with no preconceptions. How did energy work? What made something living? What constituted death? Where did the energy go when something died? Did death exist? What happened before a life began? If energy is real, and can be monitored on things as basic as an EEG or a CT scan, surely we can monitor it when it 'departs'. Can we track that energy? Can we track the soul?

Humankind stood at the edge, and despite my warnings, took the leap. The new race had begun. Remote testing facilities were wiped off of desert landscapes. Governments neared bankruptcy just to be the first. I thwarted even more catastrophes. I tried to guide. I had my own knowledge but the power-hungry, skulking in the shadows, refused to listen.

CHAPTER 12

The thermals over the sea nudged the helicopter making its way back to the city. Gora Khayyám looked out the window, watching the white crests of the blue water below, and the storm brewing over the approaching Bluff in the distance.

Everything was in order at the offshore site, but, as usual, moving excruciatingly slowly.

"Sir."

He was roused from his daydream.

"Sir," said the pilot over the headset, "we'll be landing at the Point Yacht Club in five minutes."

"Thanks, Zweli." He straightened up, readjusted his tie and looked at his wife seated directly in front of him, attention fixed on her tablet.

"We're not in range yet, hon."

Fareeda, without breaking her gaze, said, "You'd think by now we'd have signal everywhere,"

"Just a few minutes, ma'am," said Gora's assistant to his left.

"Bevan, what's the protocol on this one today?"

The other man, thirty-six years old, slim and neatly attired in a navy blue jacket, white button-up shirt, and a *Gora!* campaign pin squarely placed on his thin tie, handed him a small glass tablet. The draft notes from that morning had the occasional strikethrough and addition in red mark-up.

"In rough, sir: you, Premier Gora Khayyám, are pleased with the overall infrastructure that has been put in place. The technology involved is some of the best in the world. Safety is a factor, and this, you feel, should not be scrimped on. How long till the operation is fully functional, only time will tell? There have been some technical delays in the past, but regardless of these issues, the immediate effect is that of job creation. You feel that job creation is an important factor to be taken into account when looking at a project like this, and this means that the benefits are already being felt by the man in the street. The long-term goals will be immeasurable to eThekwini Metro Municipality, the city of Durban and Southern Africa on a whole. Excusing the pun, it is truly a beacon of light on the horizon." He gave a smirk and added, "I'm sure you'll manage the Q and A, Mr. Khayyám."

Fareeda's device bleeped.

"Finally," she said and looked up at Gora. "I've got the report with the breakdown, figures and projections. If anyone asks specifics, we will have that ready. I'll run through those and fine-tune Bevan's draft by the time we land."

The tablet in Gora's hand bleeped as a blue notification slid in from the top right. "Hmm," he said shaking his head as he read the news headline: MULTIPLE INJURIES AS FLYING CARS COLLIDE AT MOSES MABHIDA STADIUM.

"Sir," added Bevan, "if you need to, just hand over to me and I'll answer those questions."

Gora nodded and returned to the view of the Indian Ocean below.

#

The message on Ndiliswa Gqwashu's screen turned blue, indicating Fareeda Khayyám had received it. The report was everything she had been preparing for the past week relating to *"the site"*. Everything approved by Ma'at and the Org for the public. It was a relief to have sent it off. Numbers still swirled around her exhausted brain and she definitely needed a holiday. *Next weekend off. It'll have to do.*

This was the one aspect of her job that she detested: lying to the public. Working for the Org meant buying into their higher ideals, even if it meant putting out fake information, feeding conspiracy theories or deflecting from anything the

Org was involved in.

Relationships were also tricky.

Her mind numb, Ndili pushed herself away from her desk and began drifting off into the past, the one place she thrived on in her not-so-distant student days.

Having visited the site, Premier Khayyám and his team would provide the press with a filtered overview of the progress of the project. The report would give them everything they needed to feed the Org's narrative of it as a viable energy source. On those rare occasions that a member of the public, or a person in public office, should be granted access, they would be shown what Ma'at and the Org wanted them to see. Certain areas would be deemed 'highly sensitive'.

Like many of her team of analysts in the Org control room, she felt they were on the verge of attaining what, for hundreds of years, was myth; and this Ma'at would be the one who discovered it.

The Holy Grail, the fountain of youth, all paled in comparison with this legend.

Dribblings of this myth ended up in the public domain of ancient Rome and Greece, morphing into the legends of Atlantis. But this was no Atlantis. In fact, the Org knew Atlantis wasn't the Atlantis of myth and legend. It had been an island off the coast of Northern Africa, 500 kilometres north of what is now the Cape Verde Islands — a trade island that was a Mecca for trade between England, Europe and Africa. But its trade wasn't in gold and riches. Its trade had entered mythic literature as an advanced technology or substance that 'powered their civilization', that provided its people with strength in battle, and resulting in enemies never daring to engage them in warfare. Many modern scholars have suggested the 'black gold' references meant oil and that they had tapped into fuel that had advanced their technology. According to the Org's records, the slave trade had been the backbone of that pimple in the sea; their riches and power driven by human power.

No. The true civilization had existed in the southern ocean. Two centres of power had grown thousands of years ago in a time when the seas had been over 150 metres lower. The coastlines of the world had stretched further out than in modern times. Fifteen thousand years ago, the planet had been different. The larger continents' central regions were more arid and inhospitable; the air was drier and the coastal regions had been ideal places to inhabit. Travel by sea was the norm, and the currents of the oceans governed trade routes in those placid days.

The oceans had seen many fluctuations over the centuries, and climates had shifted sea levels for generations. But, the melting of a number of vast areas of ice into North America's glacial lake, Lake Agassiz — the size of today's Black Sea — caused a rapid drainage of such force that it had obliterated the landscape and finally drained into the Arctic Ocean. The world's coastlines, along with the island of Atlantis, had been submerged in cubic kilometres of water in a matter of days.

A message appeared on her screen, Ndili barely registering the intrusion on her thoughts.

Like the helicopter now on its way back to Durban, Ndili remembered feeling the power of the machine that carried her from the site and, during that first visit over four years ago, imagined the surge of water that had engulfed the lands around the globe eons before, including the site still hidden below the Indian Ocean.

For Ndili, she realised everything leading up to that visit had been an initiation into the true knowledge of human civilization. While completing her masters in southern African anthropology at Wits University, in Johannesburg, she had been approached by the Org. The first message had been cryptic, and her response guarded. It had never occurred to her that it was the organization of Ma'at that had made contact.

Becoming one of the team, and eventually becoming the control room leader, had meant gaining access to a wealth of knowledge she believed all branches of education should be teaching their students. Imagine the progress we could make, she had said to her initial contact. It became apparent that was never going to happen. Instead she absorbed what she could, and coincidentally the Great Deluge was part of it. Her thesis had focused on the world after the flood and in particular, the knowledge of southern Africa's autochthonous inhabitants, the Hurillhao!nakhoena of legend. Everything pointed to the remains of a civilisation and their knowledge of the world before the inundation of the lands, passed on by the iHlengethwa, the ‡Gurubeb, to the peoples moving through the coastal domains of the south. It was a past they knew, a past they held within their DNA, and a past they accessed in their own ways that most Westerners hadn't bothered to delve into.

Their sacred spaces, the powerful psychic locations they would visit, connected them with other realms and the Earth itself.

What Ndili learned from the Org's records five years ago was a revelation. Over the course of a week, thousands of coastal civilizations and cultures had been wiped out. The melting of the ice had brought with it a flood that engulfed civilized man and his technologies. It had taken the people, across the globe, back to the Stone Age. The coasts of Africa and South America had proven abundant in gold, the primary fuel and resource for the technology of the pre-deluge people. Unfortunately, putting all their eggs in coastal baskets had been their downfall, while the fringe inhabitants in the northern hemisphere had survived the walls of water in their mountains and caves. The mange-ridden outcasts of the world were the ultimate survivors of the global catastrophe; the cave dwellers and wilderness roamers were the heirs to the waterlogged empire.

The survivors of civilization scraped together what they could as they were overrun by invaders from the North. They buried documents and records that were slowly forgotten. The southern people dwindled into tribes, reverting to basic survival instincts but forever knowing.

Within a hundred years, most had lost the knowledge of the old ways and the old technology. They forgot how the pyramids, with their simplistic mechanisms, had functioned. Only a select few, through secret sacred texts and oral traditions, handed down key elements of the ancestral heritage. Those that could, fled to the North and established centres of knowledge that eventually went underground. Some emerged as splinter groups that simply lost their way in superstition and rites.

One remained true; only one retained access to the lexicon of secrets. And over time, millennia, the documents were unearthed under the veil of diamond and gold 'mining' throughout the old and new worlds. Industry and civilization discovered new lands, which weren't so new to the Org who had access to the maps of the world; a world that the rest of the world didn't know existed yet. Maps detailed undiscovered lands and coastlines marked out, yet in the modern age of discovery lay covered in miles of ice — only recognizable later with sonar and x-ray mapping; maps that could only have been drawn when the ice wasn't there.

But the pillaging of the Egyptian sites had meant that most, if not all, of the mechanics of the pyramid age had been stolen or destroyed. They had needed an undisturbed site; a site that the pirates and robbers of the world didn't know about let alone could get to. Vasco da Gama's trade route sojourns into the Indian Ocean territories were a pretext to him wanting to find the location of legend. Many ships wrecked themselves in attempts to plumb the depths of the KwaZulu-Natal coast.

By the mid 1900s, the technology for offshore drilling had reached the point where freestanding structures could be built — no longer connected to piers or stretches of land for support. That was all the excuse Ma'at and the Org had needed to set up its structure fifteen kilometres south east from Durban's shores.

Within a few years, they had plied large amounts of resources into their submersible technology, enabling the archeological team submarine access to the site, one hundred metres under the ocean.

They were left relatively unhindered until the 1980s when an oil tanker, completely unconnected to the Org due to the fact that it was an oil tanker, spewed around 300 million litres off South Africa's west coast near Saldanha Bay. The outcry from the public and various emerging eco-friendly champions of the planet caused the Org to re-evaluate its modus operandi. This, coupled with the argument that they were so close to South Africa's Golden Mile, the strip of prime holiday beach destinations and real estate, gave the tourism industry grave cause for distress and much waving of placards through Durban's streets over the later decades.

Those decades that followed gave the Org the opportunity to change tack and, taking one dummy corporation, enacted a 'selling off' to a 'new' conglomerate that would be doing "major research into sustainable energy resources".

This evolved from the 'natural gases' concept into, at the turn of the new millennium, solar, hydropower, and more importantly, the power of the Indian Ocean currents. Public support allowed for a larger and more intricate-looking marine energy facility that any local flying enthusiast would overlook as just another government money-making blip on

Durban's landscape.

The harnessing of the Earth's natural energy was a turning point for the world and the Org.

A fringe group of scientists and surveyors developed the technology that tapped into the mythological system enabling the conversion of the energy into a usable power source. The past decade of recent history included the conversion of the tectonic and volcanic energy into power for the surrounding countries and communities; the side effect was the reduction of natural disasters and surface activity by removing the subterranean forces at the source.

A message reading "Moses Mabhida Stadium", followed by another, "Saint Augustine's Hospital", caused Ndili to blink and then almost unconsciously lean forward and swipe them away off the screen.

Having visited the Org's precisely-situated facility off the coast on a number of occasions, it was still that first visit that stuck in Ndili's mind. Ma'at, in person, had offered her an arm for support. Compelled to look over the railing, Ndili had mustered the strength to pull herself from her wheelchair and stand alongside the icon leading it all. Buffeted by the ocean wind, her white-knuckle hands held fast as they took in sight of the swirling waters nearly a hundred metres below. Spotlights running the depth of the steel supports quickly faded into the murky darkness. The two recently launched submersibles, eventually becoming like disembodied headlights, weaved around the structure before themselves fading away.

With every subsequent visit, Ma'at's fervour within the Org had become infectious. It was understandable. On the scale of six oilrigs side by side, the sheer magnitude, activity, and possibilities beneath them was stunning. Ndili knew that the role of Ma'at was all-encompassing and interfered too often with the true passion — and the reason for Ma'at's base of operations in Durban — hidden deep below the African waters.

Ma'at had been briefed on all the latest developments, good and bad. Like a kid in a gigantic playground, all setbacks had been brushed aside as minor bruises and built up the morale of the Org's top leaders, and members of the inner team like Ndili, running the various areas of research.

"It is all part of the game, people," Ma'at had shouted above the thundering sounds around them. "We have nothing to lose here but time. It is not going anywhere. We can do it."

Reiterating their belief in their objectives, the site's location had one of the world's major leyline convergences. This in turn gave them the opportunity to piggyback on the energy developments to justify their work to the public. It also gave them access to the most substantial energy source in the world.

Now, she watched firsthand, as the flesh and blood that was Ma'at lead it all, in secret, yet in full view of the world. Ma'at, the immortal goddess of a secret society bent on maintaining order in the world, balance; correcting man's path when he headed into the Dark Ages; emerging in the Age of Enlightenment and into the New Worlds.

Yet through the handing of the torch, the passing on of the leadership every fifty years or more, Ma'at was kept alive in the eyes of the naive. The goddess of the Egyptians became myth. The myth became the person before her. To the world, that person was immortal.

Ndili recoiled as a hand touched her shoulder.

"We need to inform Ma'at."

Ndili swiveled to look at the ashen face of one of her colleagues.

#

Gora patiently sat watching the slowing rotor blades

thrumming the air above him.

After two minutes, he opened the door and stepped down onto the helipad. The wind whipped along the top of the yacht club and across the harbour. He turned and gave a hand to Fareeda, purely as a gesture for the cameras, and one his wife detested. He readjusted his hair as best he could and approached the mob of reporters eagerly jostling to get to him.

"Vusi," he pointed at a reporter in the front.

"What is your reaction to this morning's events at the stadium?"

He stood squinting into the dipping sun, not quite sure of the relevance of the question. He glanced at Bevan for support. "As I understand it, there was an accident with the flying car exhibition. Cars weren't meant to fly. Now," he gestured out to sea, "I'd like to make a statement regarding the facility and our latest visit."

"But what about the Soul Tracker involvement at the stadium and the Ventriloquist killer, sir?"

Gora felt a tingle run up his back and neck. He had to think quick.

"Their involvement in that catastrophe should not be ignored. We need more information as to how the events of the morning unfolded before we can make any comments. But make no mistake that they will be taken to task if any negligence on their part is evident. The responsibility and consequences will sit squarely on their shoulders and on their conscience."

"And the fact that they allegedly apprehended the Ventriloquist killer and discovered Elizabeth Stride alive?"

He felt the colour leave his face. A positive outcome for the trackers was not good for his strategy.

"We need to work with the facts, not rumours." He feigned a glance at his watch as Fareeda stepped in and firmly took his arm. "I will be issuing a statement on the energy facility by the end of the day, if any of you are at all interested in important issues," and strode through the microphones and cameras.

#

Elizabeth began to wake up. Drowsy and disoriented, a cold shiver descended on her. It took her a moment to realise she was in a hospital. The nightmare was over, but she felt the dread of nightmares to come.

With every blink she had to remind herself that the fluorescent lights, the clinical smells, and the hard sheets were all from the hospital that she was safely admitted in.

She wasn't tied up. She moved her arms and feet to make sure. She lifted her head off the pillow and felt the dull pain in her throat. Realising her arm was free for the first time since her ordeal, she slowly touched the taped gauze covering what she knew was the gaping hole in her throat.

The first sounds came from her mouth in a guttural moan, catching her by surprise.

It truly was over. It was a relief to hear herself cry.

#

"What the hell in a hand basket, Bevan!" shouted Gora as he slammed the car door shut. He had been seething as they approached the luxury sedan parked in the yacht club driveway. Bevan knew it was coming and knew it would be his ass in the firing line. At least the Premier had waited until they were in the tinted confines before letting loose.

"Sir," he stuttered, "I didn't think it was top priority to monitor that particular situation while we were offshore. It had appeared to be a straightforward accident at the exhibition."

"Just keep the lines of communication open next time, no matter where we are." Gora stared intently at the traffic out the window. "Find out exactly what the hell's going on before

I'm standing in front of the hounds of hell again."

"Downloading the main points as we speak, sir. Head office has compiled the full data for us from the Tracker's System and will have it ready when we arrive."

The car weaved through the afternoon traffic, heading for the centre of the city.

"Hmm," Bevan adjusted himself in his seat. "The Tracker Team has broken the Ventriloquist case by successfully tracking Elizabeth Stride's soul to a Miss Angelica Young's apartment on the esplanade." They both peered out the window at the tall apartments passing by. "Miss Young was then tracked to Moses Mabhida Stadium and in the course of attempting to apprehend the suspect, a child and three civilians were injured as well as two trackers. All have been taken to Saint Augustine's Hospital on the Ridge for treatment. *SoulsFirst* has already given their usual statements opposing the soul tracker concept."

Gora looked intently at Bevan. "I'm assuming we've notified our contacts in the hospital? I want a minute-by-minute update. Nothing's too insignificant."

"Done, sir. And we've set up a live feed in your home, so that Mrs Khayyám and yourself can be kept up to date."

#

The silence of the Room of Hours was comforting for Angel. He sat at his chair and table monitoring the screen with anxious calm. It wasn't quite over yet, but it gave him a moment to breathe and gather his thoughts. Sessions like these, thankfully, were few, but prone to leave him with a pounding headache that reached up from the back of his neck to his forehead and eyes.

The emergency services as well as the various departments from the police force had been deployed to the stadium to maintain order of the gathering protesters and assist with the cleanup operations.

All that mattered to Angel was that none of his team or civilians was killed in the events in the crowd exhibition. He chose not to look at the broadcasts from the stadium or the talking heads and their talking-points: he had to keep his attention on his job and what was about to unfold over the next hour or possibly days.

Rubbing his temples, his attention was firmly fixed on the dot on the screen marked 'Angelica Young'. Moments after the accident at the stadium, as the chaos had settled, her Soul Trace had left the physical and entered the Etheric Plane.

And there it had stayed; with each moment that passed Angel grew more and more uneasy. But he remained calm and focused. The killer had too many unresolved issues in this world to expect it to move unhindered into the Soul Plane. Now, he knew what was coming and he did not like what the outcome might be.

The Tracker team was about to be thrown into the most controversial areas of their jobs, one they had never experienced before today.

Angel was waiting for Angelica's soul to become a Walk-in.

#

Allen hadn't had his arm in the sling for long before throwing it on the bed with irritation. His neck and forehead were throbbing uncontrollably, while his back had taken most of the impact. He rested his head in his other hand, hunched over in the chair in between the two beds. Frank had made sure that his friend's wife and son were placed alongside each other in the same ward. Allen was always grateful for his friend looking out for his wife, even more so today.

He could hear Frank outside the room, pacing up and down, talking in hushed firm tones into his mobile. To his one side he heard movement and looked up at his drowsy wife emerging from unconsciousness.

"Ssh, Ruth," he whispered and put his hand on her shoulder. "It's all fine. Caleb's fine."

"Caleb," she said and fell back into her pillows.

"He's right here, honey," he turned to indicate their sleeping son in the bed opposite hers.

Ruth turned her head to see him.

"You have a concussion and you both have some bruising, but everything's fine. They just want to keep an eye on Caleb. Frank and I have some scrapes."

"Where is she?" Ruth tried looking around.

"Where's who?" asked Allen.

"That woman. The goddamned estate agent." She tried raising herself onto her elbows.

"She's in surgery," he stood up to stop her getting out of the bed. "Frank!"

"Frank," shouted Ruth.

Frank ran into the room, immediately moving to Ruth's bedside and putting his hands on her shoulders.

"Lie down, Hicks," he said firmly and pressed her gently back into the bed. "Angel's got everything covered. You need to relax."

"We all need to relax," said Allen. "We're all safe."

Ruth struggled and squirmed in her bed. "Caleb," she muttered through erratic breaths. Her body suddenly went limp.

"Ruth!"

"It's fine, Allen," said Frank quietly. "She's fainted. It'll help her right now."

"I need to get some air," said Allen and stepped out the room.

#

Geoff scrawled his signature awkwardly with his left hand and passed the discharge form back to the woman behind the counter. He had no recall of why his other hand had ended up in a bandage the size of a boxing glove, but the pounding headache he remembered far too vividly. His body felt drained and bruised as he scraped his tired feet towards the lobby doors. He noticed the wall of cameras, microphones and leeches elbowing each other to get a glimpse of who might be coming out.

With nowhere really to go, he decided to head back to the emergency ward to find his friend. Geoff lifted his middle finger at the bustle of media, flashes fired off, and he turned defiantly on his heel back the way he came.

As he rounded the corner into the emergency ward he saw his friend at the far end peering through the small square window in the double doors. He knew exactly who he was staring at.

A pang of anger and sorrow rose in his gut and reddened his round face.

The police officer stationed outside the room looked visibly agitated as Geoff approached Marc, but he chose to ignore the heavyset uniform and stepped in front of the other window.

Marc glanced at him then looked back at the lifeless body on the bed inside. "Sorry, bru," he said softly to Geoff.

"Kak, man. You didn't know your girl was psycho."

Marc's shoulders sagged and Geoff noticed him reach down and rub his left thigh. A cast covered the rest of his leg from the knee down.

"I didn't mean that," said Geoff and placed a hand on Marc's shoulder. He could feel the muscles vibrating under his hand.

"No." Marc lamented. "She *was* psycho. I've got kak for brains and no clue with women."

"Granted, but who would have guessed this?"

"I spent the night at her place while she was keeping a woman tied up on the other side of the goddamn wall." Marc twisted his mouth in disgust; tears blurred his vision as he banged a fist on the door.

"Please, sir," said the guard.

"I really felt she was the one," said Marc.

#

"Transition in progress" appeared in the centre of Ndili's screen.

Without missing a beat she typed and sent, "It's happening."

The room erupted.

#

Angel sat up in his chair feeling the tingle run down his neck and back. The chase was back on. He clicked his mobile.

"What's up, Angel?" whispered Frank.

"I need you to get to the admissions desk, now! It's happening."

"Goddamnit, Angel," hissed Frank.

"We need to move on this, so you drop your shit and do it. It could pop up anywhere on the planet, but I'm making sure that the hospital's covered. Miss Young's Trace is showing movement and that's not good. I need everyone in the hospital uploaded now!"

"Fine," snapped Frank.

"If we have a Walk-in I want to know where and who and when." Angel glanced at the screen. "Shit!"

"What now?" Frank asked. "What the hell?"

There were beeping noises and shouts coming from Frank's side of the call. "Caleb's having a seizure!"

"Her soul's back with us, Frank!" said Angel.

"Already?" Frank hesitated a moment. "Yep, it's her, Angel.

I think she just died."

"The desk, Banks. Now!" shouted Angel. "It's still located around the hospital!"

#

Frank tried to avoid some of the nurses and orderlies as they ran past him and into him.

"You need to isolate anyone who's had a trauma in the last hour," said Angel.

"It's a fucking hospital, Angel. There's trauma everywhere!"

He came to a stop at the admissions desk and caught his breath. "Miss, can you tell me how many patients are in the hospital?"

"How many…You want me to…"

"Just a guesstimate" he snapped impatiently.

"Um," she looked wide-eyed at the screen on her work-top, "nearly nine hundred".

"How many have been in surgery, coma, birth, unconscious, or admitted for trauma in the last hour?"

"That'll take—"

"Just look, shit!" he waved his hands. "Angel, you still there?"

"Ja," came the response, "what you got?"

"Eliminating from the list. In the meantime, patch into the hospital's records and," he reached across the counter, the nurse gave a sharp squeal as he grabbed her name badge, "Nurse Foster will be making the final list available in a few seconds."

"Seconds," she repeated as she rubbed her manhandled badge.

"I'm in," came Angel's response.

"Sixty-three patients fitting your request, officer," the last word said with a hiss.

"Sixt… shit," he rubbed his face exasperated. "Angel, put those names on—"

"On the screen. I know my job, Banks."

"Right," Frank stood breathless looking at the stunned nurse blinking at him. "You're pretty efficient, Foster."

"You're pretty obnoxious, officer," she arched her eyebrow.

Frank turned and took in the surroundings. He could make out Allen through the room's open doorway stroking Caleb's head. Caleb was rubbing his eyes and looking at his father.

"God no." Frank felt the blood drain from his face. He pushed his mobile into his jaw. "Caleb's awake, Angel."

#

"You know it's bullshit, Frank!"

"Allen, Angel's still scanning the records to eliminate the possibilities but he's confirmed the time of Caleb's soul's re-entry with," he hesitated, "hers."

"You know that means jack shit,"

"He's doing his job, bru. But considering their close proximity at the accident, I'm not holding any hope."

"Jesus, it could be Ruth for that matter," Allen slumped down in his chair.

"Daddy, is Mommy okay?" asked Caleb from his bed.

"Mommy's fine, my boy. She's still sleeping."

"It's bullshit. I know, Allen," Frank held the handle of the closed ward doors. "But I've got my protocols to follow, whether I agree or not."

"So what does it mean now?"

Frank walked over and stared at Ruth's rhythmically breathing body. "I'm here to make sure Caleb stays here until he's ready to be discharged."

"A flight risk, you mean," Allen said dryly. He got up and sat on his son's bed. "A kid in a hospital."

"You probably know this already," said Frank lowering his voice, "but they are going to want to separate him from you guys as soon as they can. It helps in isolating the Soul Trace to make sure they're locked on the correct one."

"He needs us right now, Frank. You can't take our son away," Allen held his drowsing son's hand. "It's okay, my boy. Just have a sleep for a while."

"Who's taking our son away?" whispered Ruth. Frank and Allen stared at a bewildered Ruth trying awkwardly to sit herself up. "What's happening, Frank?"

Allen moved to his wife's side and picked up her hand. "It's nothing, honey."

"She needs to hear it, Allen."

Frank could see Ruth's grip tightening on Allen's.

"No!" Allen snapped at Frank and reached out for his son's hand.

"We'll figure it out, Allen," he said and looked Ruth in the eyes. "Right now Caleb's got Miss Young's Walk-in soul, and you know what that means, Ruth."

"What? No!" her eyes widened as the realization dawned on her. She looked at Allen. "Did he say—"

"I don't want anyone else handling this situation," said Frank, "so I'm the one who's going to be looking out for Caleb right now. You know the drill and I'm going to make damn sure he's taken care of every step of the way. We'll figure this out, Hicks."

"We need to get that soul, that monster's soul, away from my son, Frank," said Ruth.

All Frank could do was give his partner a nod.

"Why Caleb, again?" Allen whispered, more to himself than to Frank.

"Where's my son?" said Ruth battling to breathe.

"Mommy," said Caleb trying to reach his other hand across to his mother.

Frank watched Allen's legs fall out beneath him as he slumped into the chair still holding both their hands.

"Where are you, Mommy?"

"I'm right here, angel. Mommy's right here."

Frank felt his face heating up and a cold sweat spread over his body. He needed to get some air. He opened the doors and pushed past a nurse on her way to check on the two patients. He stepped out and closed the doors behind him. The sounds from inside were instantly muffled and he took a deep breath. A moment later he found himself hunched over on the padded bench on the opposite wall. Everything was swimming through his head; all the rationalizations and anxieties began to surface. He needed to breathe. He needed to relax and cool down. Most of all he needed to think.

His white-knuckled fists gripped the seat of the bench as he rocked back and forth. There had to be another way to all this. Caleb was a good kid, raised in a good home with a good family. His grounding was good and true. His chest began to heave. Bile rose in his throat. The face of the boy at the squad care facility flashed into his head. It stared at him. It knew and he knew. Not again.

#

Hours later, Ndili knew Ma'at would be in the Org apartments, five floors above their control room. And like her and most of her team right now, would still be glued to one of the Org's screens in the living quarters.

Only a few hours earlier Ma'at had been leaning over Ndili's shoulder watching events unfold on her monitor, while the room teemed with the analysts and tracking personnel that the Org had put together over the past ten years.

After the initial commotion, there had been stunned silence when the system had indicated that Angelica Young's soul would be re-entering the Soul Plane.

The one thing anthropology had taught her was the human civilizations that did well or progressed were the ones who adapted, improved. They treated themselves better than the generation before and put each other's wellbeing first rather than using brute force. To Ndili and many in the Org, the soul trackers were taking many steps backwards. Up until today, the Org's role had been as observer. Like a mother watching a child learning to crawl while holding scissors.

It had taken two minutes for everyone to settle into their positions and another eight heart-pounding minutes to await the result. The part that the system could not predict.

Lives would be forever altered.

#

The hospital was as quiet as a hospital could be half an hour after visiting hours. The media were still outside the front entrance demanding answers to the scene that had unfolded at the stadium and the outcome of the killings: would they end?

If Frank was the one fielding those questions he would have said, "I goddamn hope so, now piss off!"

But, fortunately the head of the Tracker Unit had handled it diplomatically. Frank had sat inside Ruth's ward watching the cast on the overhead screen while some of the Tracker Units and Ruth's friends milled about to see how she and Caleb were doing. Allen: not so good.

Frank felt that Ruth hadn't quite got the full impact of what was about to unfold. Maybe she didn't want to know. And maybe that was a good thing.

Now, Frank walked slowly down the hall and stopped at the fire escape door. He checked the handle: unlocked. He peered inside, and then checked back at the hallway leading to Ruth's room. All clear. He slipped inside and quietly closed the door behind him.

#

"Caleb," whispered Ruth, "you know I'm here to look after you. Keep you safe."

"Like my guardian angel."

"That's right, Cay. You have to come with Mommy now."

"Where's Dad?"

"Right here, my boy," said Allen from the doorway of the darkened room.

Caleb rubbed his eyes and put his arms around his mother's neck. "Are we going home?"

"You and Mommy are going with Uncle Frank," he said looking at his friend.

"We need to be quiet," said Frank. "Everyone's sleeping, Cay, so we got to tiptoe outta here."

"Where we going, Uncle Frank?"

"Mommy will tell you on the way," said Ruth.

They all made their way out the doors and to the fire escape.

"Ruth," Allen grabbed her arm. She held onto Caleb tightly as they stepped through. "I love you. You do what you need to. Figure this out. You know how to evade the Soul Trace system. Frank and I will do what we can from this side of the goddamn fence." He stroked Caleb's hair, then held them both.

"I love you," said Ruth in his ear.

"Daddy?" said Caleb sleepily.

"I love you, my beautiful boy. It's all going to be fine. You look after Mommy, okay."

"Okay," he said and slumped his head back on his mother's shoulder.

"I hope you know what you're doing, Frank."

"I've got no clue but we need to buy ourselves some time and distance. For some reason this just feels right." He indicated for Ruth to start down the stairs. "Remember, Allen, you're just walking right out the front door of the hospital, fending off the press and going straight home to bed."

"Tomorrow's another day."

CHAPTER 13

Away from the media and the mayhem of the day, Fareeda roused herself from her doze in the comfort of the white leather couch to find her husband, with his wall of screens on mute, attempting to browse through the day's activity in silence and occasionally taking a quick sip from his tumbler of iced water.

Even with him right next to her, it was in moments like these that she felt isolated. The stark whiteness of the minimalist room leading through the large glass doors and windows onto the expanse of patio that overlooked the city she adored; the city of her childhood; the city of her growth and learning. Alone.

"What's on your mind?" she asked and stretched out on her side of the three-seater. He looked into his wife's sleep-laden eyes as she blinked and stretched. They had had a strong partnership, even before she had convinced him to enter the duplicitous world of politics in 2026.

His student days twenty years earlier, studying law and systematic theology at Stellenbosch University, had opened up a summer school opportunity in Strasbourg, France. Straight out of Durban Girls' High School, Fareeda had been traveling for a gap year with friends, writing at every moment she could find about the sights and sounds bombarding her impressionable mind.

On one of his free weekends during his six weeks, Gora had taken the train to visit the Louvre. They had found each other, or rather he had found her, at the back of the new Islamic Art department mid-tirade on daevas with one of her fellow classmates. Her eyes had met his disbelieving gaze over her friend's shoulder, momentarily disarming her and giving her friend the opportunity to throw up her arms and storm away. A smile was all it took for them to know they had found a kindred spirit.

Fareeda's gap year extended into two, and part-time jobs writing for SA travel sites allowed her to remain behind in the capital while he returned to South Africa to complete his studies. Becoming active in one of Paris' growing human rights organisations had helped pass the time, but it had felt like a lifetime until they saw each other in Paris again.

Her apartment had barely fitted a couch let alone another body. She could hardly remember how they had gone from the early days of Gora as a struggling *avocat*, effortlessly having learned the French language, dunking slices of bread in beer mugs of tea, to years later drinking wine and attending social gatherings of the legal and political fraternities in Paris.

"One day," he said to her now, "the Trackers are going to stumble and fall. It's like watching a one year old learning to walk. You can tell them how. You can point them along the right path. But, goddamn if they don't walk straight into the glass door."

"I still think you need to have a proper meeting with Zenze. He needs a wake-up call."

"Oh please. This damned serial killer case is raising their profile and could help with his plight for more funding."

"Nevertheless," she said, her tone firm, "we need to spin this in our favour. But, between you and me, to their credit, they've contained that awful mess. It wasn't exactly giving the regular police force a good name."

"Sure, but we still need that God-awful rehab process of theirs to be stopped." Gora stood up, throwing his hands in the air. "It's no better than a smash and grab. They may as well lobotomise them and take us back a century of progress."

"With this evening's result being so close to home for the Tracker Unit," she said, "maybe it's a possibility."

#

Frank was ahead of Ruth by a few paces, the underground parking quiet, apart from their laboured breathing and hurried footsteps. He pressed the car remote. A bleep came from a silver car parked about ten metres ahead of them. Her heart rate was sending the sound of blood coursing through her ears; not from the extra weight of her son in her right arm, but because at any time someone could leap out and rip him away from her. They needed to get away.

Frank opened the back passenger door for her and headed around to the driver's side.

"How did this happen, Frank?" she caught his gaze over the roof of the car.

He took a breath, opened his door and slipped inside. Ruth leaned into the car and gently placed Caleb lying down on the back seat. "It's okay, Cay," she consoled her drowsy son, "get some sleep." She sat next to him, placing the safety belt over his small blanket-covered body and closed the door behind her.

"It's always been complicated, Hicks," he said as he entered co-ordinates into the car's screen.

"The Trackers were supposed to make life easier. Better. Not this." Ruth met his eyes in the rearview mirror then glanced back at Caleb struggling to keep his eyes open to the drama in front of him.

"There is a way," he started up the car. "There has to be something we're not seeing."

"God, I hope you're right, Frank," she scanned the quiet parking lot behind her. "I'm not letting my son go. I'll walk into central Africa to hide before I let them take him away from me."

Frank clicked the car into reverse and backed out the parking space. Another click and he whipped the car forward towards the exit at the far end of the complex.

"I need you to rack your brain on those leylines. I've

already punched in the co-ords to the Smith's farm, so all you need to do for me is connect the dots."

Think of the network of lines? She couldn't even think straight right now.

"Shit, get down," hissed Frank.

Before she dropped sideways over Caleb, she glimpsed a car descending the ramp into the parking lot. She recognised it immediately: Mkhize and Collins.

Frank began lowering his window as the sound of car tyres on smooth concrete screeched. "Shit," he said suddenly hitting the brakes. "What the hell are you doing?"

Ruth heard the other car's door open.

"Step out the car, Banks," Mkhize's voice was calm but unfriendly. Frank's body stiffened as he drew in air. "Angel's given us orders to stop you and Hicks from leaving the hospital. So, don't give us shit, Frank."

"Whatever happens here, Ruth, drive," he said smoothly reaching for his gun at his side. "Don't stop for anyone. I've already programed one of the portable GPS units. Nobody knows I've got it. I'm going to get out the car and you need to slip into the driver's seat."

"Frank," began Ruth, "I need."

"You need to get your boy outta here," he unchecked his door. "The Smiths are expecting you."

"No, Frank."

He shifted his weight. "No matter what, Ruth," he said and leaped out, raising his weapon. "Don't move, SK! Out of the fucking car, Rob."

Ruth glanced down at her son, his eyes looking up at her.

"Jesus, Frank," said Mkhize.

Ruth kept her head low and slid her body through the gap of the front seats, bringing her legs around and over.

"Mommy?" Her heart jumped in her chest, automatically swinging her head around to check on her son.

"It's okay, baby."

Halfway out his car, Collins' attention was caught by the movement in the other vehicle and instinctively drew his weapon at the driver's seat.

"Don't point that at her, Collins!" said Frank still locked on Mkhize. "Lower your weapon."

Collins said, "You lower your weapon, dickhead, and we can all go peacefully." Ruth gripped the steering wheel.

"Caleb's in the car," said Frank through his teeth, "so rather point it at me. Three seconds and Mkhize hits the concrete."

Mkhize shifted his weight self-consciously. "Can you two morons put your dicks down and step away from your egos a second while the adults talk? Ruth, don't do this."

Ruth took a sharp breath trying to calm her rigid arms and shoulders.

"Glad to see you're not trigger-happy like your partner, Mkhize," said Frank dryly, but can you tell him to lower his weapon?"

"Can't do that, Frank," Collins tracked his weapon across to Frank. "Where are you going to take them where we can't track them down, anyway?"

Frank moved around his open door, away from the car.

He's taking their attention away from us. Her heart pounded in her ears over the steady purr of the engine. She moved her fingers slightly, clicking the car into first gear, unheard by the men outside. In split seconds her brain mapped out the situation. Collins had positioned his car at an angle to block their exit up the ramp. She would have to go left around the ass-end of the car and give Collins a nip-tuck on his rear.

She glanced at Mkhize.

Realisation dawned on his face.

"Hicks, don't be stupid!"

"Ruth!" shouted Frank.

Collins turned pale as he saw the car lurch forward in

his direction. He dived into his car as Ruth's front bumper connected with the edge of his open door. She swerved hard left, then right into the back bumper, spinning the other vehicle away from the entrance. Mkhize hit the hard concrete and drew his weapon on Frank who remained standing, fixed on Mkhize.

Metal on metal echoed through the parking as Ruth scraped past the other car and up the ramp.

#

"I need her full family history, Tracey," Ndili was saying to her colleague holding a tablet as they huddled together. "I know you have the more immediate info already — great job — but we need as far back as we can go. The trackers will assume they have everything neatly contained. *We* cannot assume that."

Ndili's monitor bleeped. Their heads turned in unison.

"Speaking of containing," said Tracey. "I thought they were confined to the hospital for the week?"

"Now that's interesting," Ndili said and wheeled herself closer. They watched as the Soul Trace location began to move. "Probably taking them to a more secure location out of the media spotlight."

"I hope they know what they are doing," said Tracey.

"Unlikely."

#

Allen stood at the tall glass windows looking out at the city lights. He had taken a few deep breaths to calm him and ease his muscles. His neck and lower back still ached from his injuries earlier that day. He tried stretching down to touch his toes, but gave up the ordeal. Suddenly his mobile chimed from the coffee table behind him. His pulse quickened as he weaved past the lounge chair to pick it up. Seeing the screen, his heart sank, realising Ruth would not risk contacting him.

Not for a while.

He pressed the button.

"Hi, Angel," he said calmly.

"Hi Allen," replied Angel. "How you holding up?"

"Hmm."

"I think I know the answer to my next question," Angel hesitated, "but I have to ask."

"Ask."

"Where's Ruth taking Caleb?"

Without missing a beat Allen replied, "I don't know what you mean?"

"Thought so." Angel shook his head. "You're a crap liar, but I understand. I love you guys, Allen. I've got to do what I do."

"Sure," said Allen, making his way back to the window. "You do know she's going to give you a run for your money?"

"Yeah."

"Where are they, Angel?"

"I have them on the N2 heading north. If I know her, they should be disappearing soon."

"And then?"

"Old-fashioned astrology reading. Instinct."

There was silence for a moment.

"If you need anything, just call," offered Angel.

"Thanks."

"One thing's bothering me though," said Angel.

"What's that?"

"Why you didn't go with your family? It can't just be to pick up clothes and supplies."

"Hmm. Lots of questions, Angel. Like: do birds have souls?" said Allen. "So many answers. But we're still just meat in a sack surviving and protecting our offspring."

"Sure," said Angel. "I hope you guys know what you're doing."

"Instinct, Angel."

Allen turned off the mobile. Then it struck him. Geoff. Of all people, that's why he was here.

A conspiracy theory was what he was pinning his hopes on right now, while his best friend hid his wife and son.

His heart sank as he remembered Geoff's friend in the hospital, standing outside the guarded ward window looking at the woman he loved.

Allen had stepped out to stretch his legs and gather his thoughts while Ruth and Frank quietly spoke. He had watched Geoff from the other end of the corridor trying to console his friend.

Minutes passed and Geoff put a gentle hand on his friend's shoulder, leaving him alone for the time being. He walked towards Allen, eyes registering one another.

He liked this rough, self-assured individual. Although he looked rather forlorn and worse for wear, the glint in his eye as he approached was still there.

"Prof," he said quietly and sat down on the wall bench.

"Geoff." Allen nodded and joined him.

"Your laitie okay?"

Allen looked back through the doorway at his son, still unconscious in his bed. "They said he should be fine; severe concussion; hairline fracture on his forehead; but stable."

Geoff breathed a sigh of relief. "Cool. If he's anything like his mother, he'll be just fine." He took out his mobile from his pants pocket and pressed the screen.

Allen felt lighter, as though he could breathe again. "Your friend okay?"

"Woman problems." Geoff rolled his eyes while he swiped the glowing device.

Allen noticed the video images on Geoff's screen. "How are yours doing?"

"Mine?" he looked at Allen, momentarily distracted. "Oh, all seem good," Geoff said and raised the screen for Allen to view the four nest cams.

"Efficient killers," said Allen with a nod.

"Correct. But, less drama." Geoff gestured to the hallway with the mobile in his hand and said, "Unlike all this unnecessary kak."

Allen frowned at the statement. "Chasing a killer halfway around the city, hijacking a flying car and nearly killing six people is a bit flippant and uncalled for. But so is killing off women in your free time."

"Not that," said Geoff. "Mainly the chasing of that freak-show across town when a working soul tracking system could've saved a lot of PT."

"How do you mean 'working' system?" said Allen sitting forward.

"The theory going around the chats and casts is that the Tracker system is not the original system. Bastardised!"

"Shit, Geoff," Allen slapped his knees and stood up, "Don't give me that conspiracy crap now!"

"Wait," Geoff spluttered, "hear me out quickly. The original has no glitches, overlaps or interference and possibly a finer tuned locator."

Allen found himself looking in on Caleb, just as Geoff's friend had done moments before.

"Then there's talk of the rehab methods."

"Well, right now," said Allen pacing back to Geoff, "I don't give a shit about the Tracker methods or your mate Ma'at. I'm only interested in my son pulling through in one piece and going home."

"Sure," said Geoff into his chest. "You have to ask yourself why it is that we all ended up there?"

"Where?" snapped Allen.

"You, me, your wife and son; all acquaintances wrapped up in one unconnected incident. We're all connected, bru."

Allen squinted at the man seated in front of him. "You

sound like director Buchanan with his pseudo-science notions."

"Our science doesn't or can't explain that, can it? Do yourself a favour sometime and ask the director about Ma'at and her toys."

"Director Buchanan and Ma'at?" Beeping coming from down the hall suddenly distracted Allen's attention. A second later a mobile bleeped inside Ruth and Caleb's room. Frank answered and slipped out the door next to Allen.

That was when all hell had broken loose in Allen's world.

Before him now, speckles of light spread across the black facade of the city. A universe in a city. Ruth always spoke to him about the other side of life, the world of souls; groups of individuals just like groups of friends and family. Those that move in and out of your life, and those you never ever meet; like a city. So small yet big enough that you can walk down the street and see people you've never seen before; and people you will never see again.

He wondered then, if Caleb was one of those souls in his life.

He looked down at the mobile in his hand. He pressed it on and searched for Geoff's contact. Then connected.

"Hi, Professor Hicks," said Geoff's voice rather formally.

"Hi, Geoff," said Allen. "I've got a question for you."

"Any way I can help you guys right now."

"What do you know about this other system and what the hell does Henry know about Ma'at?"

"What I was saying to you before," said Geoff, "the system the Trackers use is supposedly inferior. And I'm not just talking about the soul tracking. I mean their whole approach."

"So why is this only coming out now?"

"It's not. That's the problem with everyone. They take everything they are presented at face value. When someone says something negative about the government and their systems it's all conspiracy theory."

"I'm taking a leap of faith here, Geoff. Tell me it's not a damn rumour."

"It's no rumour. I'll dig up some of the past casts that Ma'at has made, and then you can decide. But, what if you can actually trace someone and rehabilitate them without intruding or extruding them from their lives? If your son has some other freak's soul in him, as the media is suggesting, wouldn't you want to be able to move it the fuck on to where it needs to go?"

"What's their rehabilitation process supposed to entail?"

"No idea." Geoff shrugged. "That's the kinda kak that director Buchanan or Ma'at, if you can get to her, would be able to answer."

"I hope you're right," said Allen. "I've sent my wife and son off into the wilderness in the hope that your theory pans out."

"It will. I can feel it."

#

"I'm a little confused here, Vusi" Gora said into his mobile. "You keep mentioning Tracker Hicks *and* her son. Are you saying that she is on the run *with* her son?"

Unable to sleep, he had reluctantly taken the call from one of the leading journalists down from Johannesburg moments before. He was squeezing his other fist in and out, trying to relieve some of the frustration building up.

"That's correct, Premier Khayyám. They eluded security at the hospital later this evening and seem to be without a trace."

"What on earth for?"

"We're assuming she's not willing to place her son in rehabilitation custody."

"What the hell's that got to do with her situation?"

"I'm not following?" the reporter hesitated.

"Neither am I, obviously."

"The ventriloquist's soul has walked-in to her son, um," Gora heard the journalist check his notes, "Caleb Hicks."

"Her son?"

"Her son, yes."

"This interview is over!"

#

Nearing eleven at night, and no decent sleep, the map of the leylines was fuzzy in Ruth's mind. She had seen it many times before in the Room of Hours, Angel explaining how the energy of the network of lines affected the detection of a soul. This was one area they couldn't allow to get into the public domain let alone the media or some individual politicians. In harnessing the energy from the leylines, the Tracker system was unable to differentiate it from the energy of a soul. Lines ranged from two metres to up to a kilometre in width; a person, if they knew the network, could do well to avoid detection.

Angel was one of the few who knew various areas like the lines on his hands. Ruth knew even less, but enough to get her to where she was going. Unfortunately, lines didn't follow the same routes as roads, so going undetected would be a stretch of her imagination.

Right now, Ruth's objective was to get as far away as possible in the shortest time, and lie low until they figured out what to do.

She had left Frank about fifteen minutes ago and was heading northwest along the N2. Aside from the Soul Trace, Angel had an acute eye for the astrological mapping of an individual's birth details. Heading into any of KwaZulu-Natal's mountainous valleys inland for a quick hideaway would send clear messages to Angel, and Frank's destination programmed into the car's screen was far from Durban's shores or valleys.

She ran through the past half hour in her mind: the hospital parking lot, the confrontation with her colleagues she trusted, who trusted her. And Frank.

Anger rose inside her now as the realisation of her situation dawned on her.

She understood the idea of soul groups and soul agreements. But this was too intense. Why Caleb? Why like this? And, why this soul of all the souls in the goddamn universe? What was the purpose and what did he have to learn with a soul as damaged as the one she had come face-to-face only hours earlier?

She stole a glance behind her at her now sleeping child. Would the boy sleeping soundly in the car she was driving become like the cold calculating killer? Could she really prevent the inevitable?

Her face tingled. Warmth spread over her forehead and cheeks as tears fell. Her mouth tightened and she gulped down the emotions that came, knowing she would do anything for her son right now.

She thought of Allen. Where was he, and what was he going through away from them?

#

"We need this contained *manje*, now, Mike," Zenzele snapped. He shuddered at the idea of the media avalanche he knew was about to engulf him. His lead tracker, one who knew the system backwards, was not going to let her son go quietly. Sweat beaded on his forehead despite the cold air-conditioning of the Room of Hours.

"She's taken him out of the trace area, Zenzele," Angel pointed helplessly at the Screen. "Both astros are indicating a strong sense of the colour green, flat landscapes and, in a while, hills and valleys, a large body of water. Peaceful. Rest."

"And that is?"

"I'd say she's heading to a remote area far inland, camping or farmland. Settling near a dam or lake."

"That fucking narrows it down to all the farms in goddamn KZN, Mike!"

"That's all I'm going on right now," Angel faced the other man head on. "Back off. I'm scanning with a fine tooth-comb for even the faintest clue that will distinguish her destination. Unfortunately she's driving in the middle of the night, so any landmarks or roadside features that would normally pass in the daytime and hence her wrap-around universe, are hidden to her and therefore to me. The team here is doing searches on every detail I send through to them."

Biyela's mobile bleeped. He looked down and drew a sharp breath at the face staring back at him.

"Check every friend, isihlobo, whatever, that's connected to her." He looked up at Angel. "Anyone she might be headed to."

"Right," replied Angel.

"I need them back in this building by tomorrow, Mike," he demanded through clenched jaw and walked away. His mobile bleeped again, but he waited until he was near the doorway before he answered.

"Ja," he said coldly, heading into the doorway.

"Hello to you too, mnganam."

Zenzele clenched his jaw, wishing he had some chewing gum to occupy it. He realised then that his old friend knew. It was inevitable.

"Don't give me shit right now, Khayyám," Zenzele said through gritted teeth, mobile gripped tightly. "I'm handling this situation as best I can and I don't need your condescending, self-righteous bullshit right now. This is *my* system and I'll use it how and on whom I fucking like!"

"Hell, Zenze," said the voice over the speaker, "you and your damn tracking system need to be fried in hell. You can't even tell me why or where one of your lead Trackers is!"

"We are working on it, and have made some headway. Back off, mfowethu, and let the system do its work."

"Flawed work. It's not working and you know it. Your whole system, including Tracker Hicks who is about to use all her knowledge and the system's flaws against you narrow-minded bastards."

"I'm hanging up now, Khayyám."

"It's going to be hellfire raining down on your sorry ass, and we're going to have all the ammo we need to shut you down. Your system has people running for their lives and putting the safety of a child in jeopardy. You've got twenty-four hours to bring her and her son in. And even if you do we're going to shut you down."

"Like you give a shit about a woman and her child. Try to shut me down and I'll expose you and Fareeda for what you are."

"And what is that, Zenze?"

"Manipulators."

"Us?" laughed Gora. "Your manipulations didn't bring Gabisile back, did it? Have you traced her soul? Have you spoken to her lately?"

"Fuck you, Gora. You all hide behind your well-crafted façade, saying one thing in public while doing the opposite behind the scenes."

"We've given you free rein to use your hijacked system for the people, but you've abused and misused the system for petty criminals and inflicted pain and suffering on people, the ones you were trying to protect. Even now, one of your own is being tracked. Then what? Wreck her life?"

"He is young enough to recover."

"I rest my case. You are tampering with technology that you don't even fully understand, let alone have the Divine authority to control. Like cavemen driving a Ferrari;

someone's going to get hurt."

"If uMvelingqangi didn't want us doing His job for Him, he wouldn't have put it in our hands in the first place."

"Nice try, Biyela."

"Isaiah forty-five, verse seven. If God created good and evil in the first place, and, like you, if he can't take responsibility for the state of things, then fuck off while the professionals sort out His mess."

Bleep.

#

That had been entertaining. A twinge of excitement and relief welled up at the thought of removing the Soul Tracker system from public use. Finally, something to use against Zenzele. Either show them up or shut them down.

Personal reasons aside, Zenze's game was over. But, Tracker Hicks dragging her son around the countryside bothered him. She was putting herself and her son in harm's way, and, inevitably, they would be tracked.

Here was a Tracker with a purpose. Biyela and his team were fumbling around in the dark, yet managed to get this far. But, unnecessarily, a mother and child's lives were on the line.

This was it. They couldn't allow the Trackers to meddle with more lives. Trackers or no Trackers, it had to stop.

#

Zenzele's mobile bleeped again. "Shit!" he shouted into it.

"Thought you'd like to know that Hicks popped up for a second near Mooiriver, Zenzele. That means she's hitting the plateau and into the flatter parts of the province."

Zenzele breathed easier. "nGiyabonga, Mike."

"Mkhize and Collins are bringing Banks in. I've started a background analysis of his connections."

#

Frank's hands ached in the handcuffs behind his back. He sat in the middle of the back seat while Collins drove.

No matter how Angel had tried to swing the idea, Caleb was yet another child in his life being thrown around in a war of worlds, a war of theories, ideologies and personal beliefs. He wanted it simple, black and white. He didn't want a rose-tinted view of the world, but he wanted a world where there was a better way for everyone; that no matter how shitty and dark things seemed, there was the right way, the correct path, light at the end of the tunnel.

In a word, Franklin Banks wanted to hold on to hope.

"At least we were able to confirm our Walk-in one hundred percent, Banks," said Collins looking at him through the rearview mirror.

"How so?" asked Frank.

"Angel had us on standby outside the hospital in case someone decided to spring our soul."

"Imagine that."

"I personally knew something was up when you requested to be placed on security duty, Banks," said Collins.

Mkhize turned in his chair. "Angel told us the soul was on the move."

"So we headed it off," added Collins. "Imagine our relief when we ran into you guys."

"I guess we all assumed correctly after all," said Frank.

"Come on, Frank," said Mkhize.

"You didn't really think you'd get away with it, did you?"

Frank raised an eyebrow at Collins' reflection. "I just did, poes. See if you can catch Ruth."

The energy fields of the earth's surface were analysed, the leylines of ancient shaman rituals recognised for their network of energy, and quickly integrated and accessed, creating a global energy map. Certain centres, where numerous energy lines crisscrossed, were identified as being more effective for accessing other dimensions than others. The Americas, Asia and the islands of Oceania became areas of greatest turmoil and interference as movement of the Earth's plates created unstable energy. Africa and Europe, where many of the leylines intersected, became the stable grounds for research. The focus on Giza and the Great Pyramids brought with it civil unrest, as the once unified people of Egypt began to clash. Their elders, ignoring the already fragile judicial law that they had taken generations to institute, asserted claim to the ancient monuments and the unlimited sources of energy they held.

CHAPTER 14

Being well out of the city limits, the lights faded behind her over the horizon, Ruth could finally breathe normally. In the back seat, Caleb exhaled in his deep sleep.

She felt for the backpack behind her chair, knowing that Caleb's medication had been shoved safely in the bottom, under dirty clothes and valuables in her work-bag that the Tracker Unit had sent to the hospital for her. Caleb was still in his hospital gown; his bloodied and torn clothes from that day, neatly folded by the hospital in a plastic packet, were now crumpled with everything else.

Minutes before leaving the hospital, Allen had spoken to her about getting away with Frank. She had only hesitated for a second at the suggestion of him staying behind.

"No," she'd said, a chill hitting her spine, "we need you, Allen."

"You'll be fine with Frank," he'd tried to reassure her. "I have to try something. I've got to do something. Running is only going to get us so far."

"What are you going to do?"

"I've got to go to the source of this damned system and see what happens."

She had no idea what he meant or what he was doing. She just prayed everything would be okay. It had to be.

\#

The subtle humidity hit Allen as he lowered the car window at the museum parking entrance. The spring rain had long since passed through the city, Durban's unpredictable season bringing a heat that was thickening the night air. The hairs on his arm and neck bristled.

He swiped his pass card and accelerated his car under the rising boom and down the ramp to the staff parking area. Out of habit, even with eleven of the twelve parking bays empty, Allen parked in his assigned area in the small quadrangle. He climbed out into the sticky air and bleeped the car locked.

He glanced at the only other car a few parking bays away, and then headed for the security gate.

On leaving the apartment, he had sent Henry Buchanan a message: "Meet me at your office. Now."

It would have been hard to believe that the director of the museum's Research department would not be aware of the events that had unfolded in the city earlier in the day. The newscasts would have been buzzing and some associate or connection would have dropped the director a message that Allen, his senior ornithologist, was involved in some way.

The fact that Allen had not received a response to his request did not concern him. He had been right.

He entered his pass code and thumbprint into the keypad on the large, century-old iron gate leading to the doors of the staff entrance. It clanged open and he stepped through, pulling it slamming back. He then swiped his pass card in the access control reader attached to the old double wooden doors, clicking them open.

Without the main overhead lights, the hallways seemed noticeably quiet. The wide stairwell leading up to the third floor, the research departments and main exhibition area, was the only area lit.

He heard the doors click behind him as he took two stairs at a time, heading upward.

As he reached the third floor landing, his throat burned from his strained breathing, but he headed to his right without pausing. He passed a handful of illuminated glass cases displaying various species, all constructed with his help, and through the Staff Only doors.

A warm light filtered down the narrow hallway: the director's office.

The familiar smells and the sound of his shoes on the vinyl flooring seemed to calm his nerves, but how or what was he about to pry from his colleague's private life?

He passed his own research lab with a glance and finally stopped outside the director's office. He felt his pulse quicken. He drew a breath, knocked, and entered without waiting for the response.

"Come," began the short man behind the large neat desk. "Allen, are you guys okay?"

"Fine," replied Allen closing the door behind him. He walked over to one of the two guest chairs a few metres from the doorway and sat down, hunching forward onto the edge of the desk. "I need some answers from you, Henry. And I don't want to beat around the bush, either."

The other man's wide, spectacled eyes blinked with surprise.

"Answers?" he asked Allen. "What could you possibly want to know at this hour, Allen?"

"Ma'at," Allen leveled his gaze at the Henry.

The other man leaned back into his tan leather chair, towering his fingers together. He forced a look of relaxed condescension; Allen disliked that look on people, especially scientists. It was when you were about to hear a lot of bullshit.

"I'm not sure I follow," Henry said.

Allen slammed his flat hand onto the desk. "Crap! I need to know, right now, what you know about Ma'at and her alleged soul tracking system." Allen leaned further forward. "My son is being tracked because they think that damn killer's soul has walked into him or whatever. I don't want some computer playing God with my son's life!"

"Man's been playing God ever since he harnessed fire, Allen." The director's face hardened and his jaw clenched. "I'm hardly the one to ask about advice on that Ma'at woman or her cult. When she was alive and running this facility, Adeline was more au fait with certain echelons of society than I am."

"Bullshit!" screamed Allen standing over the other man. "I know exactly what part of your lying throat to grab and rip out of your neck in two moves. Everyone knows about your secret handshake crap, letting slip about 'the Order' and people you 'know'."

"Right." Henry glowered at Allen and then looked down at his nervously interlocked hands. "I can see you are at your wit's end, Allen. So let me explain a few things."

Allen suddenly became aware of the buzz of the lights above them, and the deathly quiet of the room.

"Ma'at and her organization are real." He looked up at Allen. "Real in the all-knowing, all-seeing sense of the word. If God were to come down to earth she'd be Ma'at and have an organization as large, as invisible, and as far reaching as the Org. She is more than just the voice and images on the occasional live stream or conspiracy documentary."

Allen felt his breathing slow.

"Unfortunately, I am not part of the Org." He held up a hand as Allen began to protest. "Let me explain. Yes, secret handshaking crap, but nothing on the level you think. What I know has filtered through, in various ways, down to me. Friends in the high places don't even begin to get you in there. And those are very high places. Without a prolonged history lesson, Ma'at was the Egyptian goddess of truth and wisdom, and a few other noble things as well, vital ingredients for a harmonious universe. Keeping that in balance was priority in her eyes; something like Lady Justice. The ostrich feather, called the Feather of Truth, was used to weigh the hearts of the recently deceased."

"For a time, the church's chauvinism attempted to undermine her, playing on the female aspect as weaker, the Mary Magdalene, less than her male equivalent, Thoth. But, over centuries, that faded into the background. The female archetype, stronger in ancient times, fought back to what it is today. Lady Justice stands as a reminder of the female ruler in many of our courts; and no coincidence that many Supreme Court judges around the globe are said to be part of the Org."

Henry looked at Allen. "You did not hear a word of this from me. I mean it."

"Whatever, Henry. Can you please tell me about the souls."

"Ma'at, in every sense of the word, makes the sun rise and the sun set. She governs two lands. Our world, the physical world, and the parallel world of the afterlife. The sun rises on the physical world and at sunset it moves into the land of the dead. This is where Ma'at is vital in maintaining the balance of the two worlds. If not, primordial chaos ensues."

"Tracking souls," said Allen.

"Whether you like it or not, Allen, we have souls. You have a soul. Scientific or not, it is real and Ma'at has, for millennia, tracked and weighed souls. Whether with the stars, divination, or a computer system, she or they have monitored them. In the good old days, they would bring a person before Ma'at, alive not dead, and she would judge them in such a way that they would correct their ways or else suffer in the afterlife."

"Rehabilitation?"

"Something like that. But these were usually only focused on senior officials or particularly heinous criminals. The man-in-the-dusty-street was simply relieved of his life."

"Jesus Christ, Henry. What the hell is wrong with the tracker system if this is exactly what they do?"

"Do you have to use language like that, Allen?"

"Do you mean 'hell' or 'Jesus H. Christ', because you can't mean hell when there isn't one, and if you mean Jesus, I'm sure you're in the wrong department; theology's down the hall right next to the dinosaurs and the flat earth manifesto."

"Professor Hicks," said Henry raising his hands, "I just

want you to calm down and make sure you understand the full extent of this. I can't give you an exact answer to your question and I'm going to try and do my damnedest to get you out of my space. The issue is not whether you or I believe in souls, rather that the tracker system is *not* on the right path. It never has been. And it is rumoured to be stolen technology. Inferior."

"Inferior?" Allen frowned. "Stolen? From who?"

"*Whom* would be Ma'at."

"So, if Ma'at is all about balance, why has it been allowed to continue?"

"It has never posed a threat before. But now it's getting to the stage of downright offensive. It's about to become publicly acceptable to track people; and I mean everyone. Next thing you know they'll be developing a 'Find Your Soul' game that the whole family can play. Then it'll be 'Check Your Neighbour's Soul'; then 'Check Your Enemy's Soul'; and then it'll be 'Blow Up A Soul'. This case that your wife and her crew have been involved in has brought a bit more attention to the tracker system. Success will only make it a more viable product."

"If theirs is not the right path then what is? What's the difference with their rehabilitation?"

"Non-invasive."

"Meaning?"

"No snatching babies in the night, so to speak. No child prisons. 'Daycares,'" he finger-hooked the air. "A soul is here to learn specific lessons and experience pre-planned things in this physical world of ours. Like fate, except we still have freedom of choice. Choice of how we do it. When we die our soul floats off to the other side and happily pockets its experiences and checks them off its list of things to do. A soul that doesn't complete its list in that life needs to come back, usually straightaway. Hence the terminology. The thing is," he paused for effect, "a Walk-in should only be temporary. Quick results and then leave. The tracker system of rehab prolongs this by keeping the soul longer than necessary. In a way, they are nurturing the Walk-in soul instead of helping it on its way to allow the correct soul to come through.

"But Walk-ins usually happen to adults where they have an accident or trauma, they emerge with a whole new personality and temperament and carry on like this for a few months or years. Then one day, they wake up or have another traumatic event, and they are back to their old self. From the Org point of view, and my limited knowledge of your situation, it would seem that your son is not a Walk-in."

"I knew it!" Allen got up from his chair. He was trying hard to digest everything he was hearing. His analytical mind needed to make sense of the incomprehensible, the far fetched.

"No, Allen." The other man stood. "You don't understand. Technically he was either a Stand-in or has an attached soul."

"What do you mean 'was'?"

"If he is, say, three years old," he began as he walked around his desk.

"Five and a half," interrupted Allen.

"Right," continued Henry sitting on the front of the desk, "if he's five and a soul walks-in, that is his soul for the foreseeable future or the rest of his life. The soul that was here was merely a Stand-in, a temporary soul that occupies the body awaiting the real soul. If that isn't the case, and the new soul is said to be with him, then it would indicate that it has attached itself to him."

"You cannot be serious, Henry," said Allen pacing up and down the room. "This is getting way out of hand from the simple way it was before."

"That's the point, Allen. The trackers have taken the most basic idea and latched onto it. You must've heard of how a person survives an accident and then gets obsessed with the victims and has to meet or know about them or their surviving family and life. When they've done this, the old soul can return, making peace, even if they are not the reason for the death. The soul uses or attaches to the person in order to get closure and understand what has happened."

"So, I've got to get my five-year old son to deal with issues of kidnapping and torture; killing women; trying to kill six people in a flying car; and Walk-in souls and Stand-in bloody souls. How the holy shit does that help me right now, Henry, when he's only now coming to terms with the fact that Santa-fucking-Claus might not exist and what it means to his fragile world?"

"No," said Henry. "Let Caleb take responsibility for his life. And you take responsibility for yours."

"He's only five, for God's sake, Henry. How can he be responsible for his life right now? I'm his father. I have to take care of him."

"Being his father or mother and taking care of him is one thing. Trying to fix his life and the situations he gets into are completely different. It's his life. Do you help him breathe? Do you tell him to keep his heart beating? No. There are certain things that he is responsible for — his life being one of them."

Allen, feeling a headache building, tried desperately to order his thoughts.

"How the hell do I get this soul out or off my boy, Henry?" Tears burned his eyes, blurring his vision. "I want my son, not some freak."

"He *is* your son, Allen." Henry raised himself and moved towards Allen. "Don't lose sight of that. The soul doesn't govern the body. It simply is. It doesn't create its shape, its features, its body. The mind controls the body. The mind is a powerful tool. It can make you sick and it can heal you. It can make you see things that aren't there; it can go insane. You, as a physical being, are not limited by your karma, or your soul's past lives. Understand that no matter what soul inhabits your son, his body or his mind, he can still do what he wants and be who he wants to be. He will overcome what he wants to overcome; limit himself with what he wants to be limited by. But be your son, he is. That doesn't change. My advice, Allen?"

Allen gave a weary nod.

"Find out everything you can about the other soul, that woman's life, and you'll see the patterns and lessons it is seeking. If this is the soul he's meant to have, you may need to accept it and move on, Allen. You cannot decide for him."

"Bugger that, Henry," Allen headed for the door and ripped it open. "I will not accept that bullshit, let alone people taking him away from me when they don't know their asshole from their ear hole."

"Then, I do pray you find a way."

"Pray?" Allen stopped in the doorway.

"Allen—" the voice began, but he cut it off with the slamming door.

#

Angel had made his way to the entrance of the Tracker Station after being told that Mkhize and Collins were about to arrive with Banks in tow.

The humid air didn't help to clear his groggy head and thoughts. He tracked a set of lone headlights from down the main road heading towards the station. A knot formed in his stomach. He was unsure whether it was anger or frustration at the situation.

Frank and Ruth were two of his top trackers, if not the best. They would support each other no matter what and expected nothing less. He would probably do the same. Right now their objective was to contain the soul whose path of murder needed to be diverted to something better, less harmful. The unit was here to nudge them in the right direction.

It was unfortunate that Caleb, the inquisitive, bright boy, was the one to carry that burden indefinitely as the vessel through which the soul would be assisted.

The headlights began to reveal the sharp edges of the tracker vehicle.

Frank's words earlier at the hospital were still playing around in Angel's head. He could hear his own words and yet felt like they were justifications to putting a child into the tracker system. For how long?

"It could be anyone, but you're making it Caleb because of his seizure."

"Come on, Frank," said Angel. "It's too coincidental that it was at the same time."

"You've got everyone in the hospital database, including staff, loaded up, so keep tabs on everyone inside or leaving the facility. An assumption is a fucking thin thread to be hanging onto when locking up a goddamned kid. Caleb's no killer, monster, psycho-freak, Angel."

"His soul is what drives him, Frank. It's not in control but it will push him in a certain direction."

"Fuck off with your theories, ballie. It's all theories."

"Look for behaviour and personality shifts," he said.

"Tell that to Ruth and Allen."

Bleep.

#

The tracker vehicle stopped in front of the station doors. Mkhize and Collins got out and headed for the back door. Collins opened it while Mkhize assisted a tired looking Banks, hands secured behind his back, out of the vehicle.

As they approached the entrance Angel said, "You guys can

release him from his restraints."

Collins began to object.

"Interview room three," he turned and headed down the hallway. "If it's not too much hassle, Collins."

He could hear the three men close behind him. A few turns through the cool hallways and he opened one of the interview room doors, stepped inside and held the door open for the other men. He indicated one of the three chairs pushed up against the table in the centre of the room.

Two of the facing walls were floor to ceiling one-way mirrors. The third facing the door, a full interactive screen.

Mkhize and Collins led Frank to the single chair, waited for him to be seated then got the hint from Angel still positioned at the open doorway. He closed the door as they exited the room, immediately blotting out the noises outside.

Angel breathed and slowly moved to the mirrored wall opposite Frank. Facing his reflection he said, "Everyone out of there, please. Including you, Collins."

He waited a moment then turned and approached the table and sat in one of the two empty chairs.

"What we were talking about earlier, Frank," began Angel. "With a Walk-in you are still the person you were before; still the same body, cells, memories and experiences; the same upbringing just a different soul using you for its lessons and purpose. Using you like a library book, a new reader learning new things for itself. Maybe you are passed on when they're done; maybe they wait till you expire." He sat back in his chair. "There are a few people out there who are definitely overdue. Some that are lost, and some that need to be replaced with a more up to date edition — more up to date information.

"Look at Soul Land like a library. A library of experiences, circumstances and people or things to be. It's like the movies nowadays. They film a whole bunch of related story-lines, and, like life, the viewer can choose a path for their protagonist. Not to mention the monetary benefits of a film's multiple-viewing capabilities."

"Gee, Angel," said Frank, "thanks for comparing the afterlife to an interactive film experience and thereby setting my mind at ease. Shouldn't you be checking your Screen or trying to track a soul or something?"

"Everything's under control," said Angel and pressed the top left of the tabletop.

A light illuminated under his finger as the screen-wall came to life. A smaller version of the Room of Hours Screen undulated with light and movement.

Frank's eyes remained fixed on Angel who looked at the screen, then back at Frank.

"Still no sign of him, I assume," said Frank.

"Cut the attitude, Frank. This is me you're talking to, not some chop."

He watched as Frank sagged his shoulders, leaned forward onto the table and rested his face in his hands.

"You trusted me to watch over Caleb, to make sure he was secured in the hospital. I know that right now," he looked up from his hands, "it appears that I've broken that trust."

"You could say that," replied Angel. "But I understand your motives."

"I don't think you do. Sure, I've got a personal stake in this, but it's more than that, Angel. Right now I feel like there's something we're not seeing. All of us. Slowly but surely this has been building in me and it's not guilt either. I've moved past that, or rather filed that into its own unresolved compartment for the time being. Now there is something that has come to the surface; something that is forcing my hand in this situation."

Angel leaned forward. "And what is that, Frank?"

"Ek twyfel. Doubt."

He scrutinized the other man's face, looking for any more

than he was letting up. The conviction he saw, the sense of purpose, was clear on Frank's face.

"What the fuck were you thinking, Banks?" Both men turned at the source of the booming voice standing in the now open doorway. They looked on as Zenzele Biyela slammed the door behind himself, Frank maintaining eye contact as he grated the spare chair and sat down. He folded his arms and creaked back in the seat.

"In your own fucking time, and in your own fucking words," he said. "I'm all ears."

Angel felt sympathy for Frank who resolutely held the Tracker Boss' cool gaze. He felt sympathy for him now; he even considered answering for him.

"Can't say I was really thinking, sir," he replied.

"Tell me something I don't know."

"I was going on instinct. Pure animal instinct of preserving the life of a kid."

"uMntwana?" Biyela spluttered. "The life of a child and many potential victims in ten to fifteen years' time! Or have you forgotten what we do around here?"

"What do we do around here, sir?" asked Frank.

"We enforce our moral obligation, duty, to society, and protect our people from harm, Tracker Banks."

"Frank," said Angel. "Don't prolong this."

"I'll ask you this once," said Biyela. "One chance for you to redeem yourself; pull yourself out of the crap, in a not-so-metaphorical sense. Where is Hicks taking the umfana?"

"The boy, her son, Caleb, is being taken to a safe and undisclosed location out of the prying eyes of the Tracker Unit and its meddling puppeteers on the fourteenth floor and above. That's the official statement you can give the media who, I'm sure, are chafing at the bit and by morning will be baying for blood." He smirked at the head of the Tracker unit. "Yours. But you'll find a way to spin it all in your favour so you don't look like a complete chop."

"Isilima," he hissed.

"You know I'll find him, Frank," said Angel.

"When and where, Angel?"

"Our job is to bring the boy in, Banks," said Biyela. "Moral issues need to be put aside in order to do so effectively. Obviously you've lost sight of the reasons this unit was created in the first place, otherwise you wouldn't be in that chair. I suggest you get a goddamned grip, search deep within yourself for the answers to your own personal questions, and move forward. Unfortunately, I can see that will not be within this unit."

"Zenzele," Angel turned to Biyela, "let's focus on finding Ruth and Caleb, rather than making final decisions here."

"Mike, on any other day I would have said that Banks here was one of your best. And yet here we sit. And you want to try and shift responsibility, even for a moment. Are we goddamned stupid? I think not."

He turned to face Frank. "There's no way this Tracker will ever wear the unit's badge, let alone represent it in any capacity. Certainly not while I'm in control here."

Frank didn't hide his laugh.

"Banks?"

"You think you're in control here. You're just a puppet on the string of the universe and your ancestors, umfana."

Angel stood up from his chair. "I'm going up to the Room of Hours."

"The hell you are, Mike," Zenzele turned to Angel. "You are also responsible here, so don't think this is only Banks and Hicks' asses on the line. You mollycoddle these goddamned Trackers. You let them think they're above the laws of this unit and what we represent, like they are some guardian angels bringing Divine harmony to the universe or whatever the hell existential bullshit floats through your damned head."

"Like I said," Angel continued towards the door. "I've got a job to do."

"Do your job, Angel," said Frank looking at the Tracker Head. "You ous are looking for a ghost using a system built with egos and scientific dogma. You're no better that the church. So good luck with that."

Angel remained at the door.

"You're on suspension, Banks," said Biyela. "If it weren't for the employment red tape of this goddamned country, I'd fire you right now. In fact, you aided a suspected soul."

"Suspected and assumed, sir," interrupted Frank.

"Which is a criminal offense and one that is going to have you spend the rest of the night in lock-up."

"Kiff."

"So how about you take your scientific dogma, shove it up your ass while we find a nice bunkmate who'll be happy to oblige should you have difficulty."

"Let's hope your Walk-in sticks," replied Frank. "That you're not caught with your chop in your hands."

"What the hell are you implying, Tracker?"

"Imagine your embarrassment, the PR debacle, if Caleb's Walk-in is temporary. Let's not bump his head or traumatize him too much when apprehending the little skelm."

"Thula, umfana. This interrogation is over. Angel?"

"He's right, Zenzele. With a Walk-in, anything goes."

#

The rain had started again about half an hour earlier. Ruth had turned off the main road onto the gravel then dirt road that wound its way through the hills and valleys on the outskirts of the town of Ladysmith. The GPS was indicating the way while she ran through the network of leylines in her mind.

Deep furrows and valleys in the landscape usually

indicated an obvious source of energy and surface activity. But that was never a guarantee that leylines were present. If she knew Frank, this valley would be a solid source; one that his friends, whoever they were, would safely live off the grid.

Not knowing the area, she slowed as she came over a rise, trying to see where the descent would take her. The rain and gloom didn't help, but the few lights in the darkness gave her some sense of distance below. The GPS insisted she keep on her current course; unfortunately, it meant traveling along the ridge above the valley for at least two kilometres. Her tyres squelched and crunched slowly while she strained to see ahead of her for any alternate route.

Seeing a small access road ahead leading off the road, she accelerated and turned into the gaping blackness heading steeply downward.

Going against the GPS advice she crawled along the rutted hillside, jiggling from side to side on the tired road beneath her.

A lone mother and her child on a deserted farm road in the middle of a stormy night. What the hell am I doing?

She wound her way through the night, the sound of the rain almost lulling her mind, until the metallic sound of a protruding rock scraping the underneath of her car jolted her upright. She squeezed her hands around the steering wheel as she turned sharply with the road. She came to a sudden stop.

"Shit," she said shaking herself.

"Mommy?" said Caleb's tired voice behind her.

She turned around to console her son.

"It's okay, honey. We're nearly there."

"Where's Daddy?" he asked sitting up in the backseat.

"He's at home, Cay." She turned back to the rain in the headlight beams. "We'll see him soon."

A few metres in front of the car, the road dipped down at a steeper angle than Ruth could imagine was possible already.

At the bottom, water raged over a small concrete causeway.

She took a deep breath. "I'd need a damn truck to get through that."

She looked at the GPS and ran through her options in her head

Going to have to chance it. There's no other way.

"My head's hurting."

Ruth turned the car engine off, leaving the headlights on, and turned to look at her son. "Cay, everything's going to be fine." She reached for the bag behind her chair and felt around for the water bottle. "Here, have some water and you'll feel better."

She unscrewed the lid and handed it to Caleb. He took a long drink without a breath then stopped to gasp for air.

"Slowly's fine, Cay." Ruth took the bottle as he handed it back to her. Taking a drink of the water she immediately felt more alert. Better.

She packed the bag away and squeezed her son's arm gently. "Try to sleep, Cay."

"Where are we going, Mommy?"

"Uncle Frank's friend's farm."

"Is Daddy going to be there?"

"I wish he was," she whispered. "Soon."

"Why are we going to a farm?"

She hesitated for a moment. She had to tell him something. The truth.

"People want to take you away from Dad and me, Cay."

Caleb started to sit up again. "Take me away?"

"It's okay, my boy," she said putting a hand on his shoulder. "I'm not going to let them take you anywhere. I will always be here for you."

"I will help you, Mommy," he smiled back at her and grabbed her hand.

"Yes, Caleb. We'll do this together."

"You and me, and they won't find you, Mommy. 'Cause I'll tell them you've gone away. It's all okay, now. They'll see they don't need to take me away from you. Daddy will help, hey?"

"He will. Your Dad's pretty clever."

"And Uncle Frank."

Ruth felt a pang in her gut. Frank. Arrested, I'm sure.

"Uncle Frank will come and get us and we'll fly away. Then it will all be okay, Mommy."

"I hope so, Cay."

She started the car up, put it in reverse, and navigated a tight turn back the way they had come.

"We'll have to make this a quick detour."

#

"Prof, I've got a messed-up arm; I'm wide awake on caffeine and painkillers, against doctor's orders, I know. I can't play any damn screen games so all I'm left is surfing the information highway digging up what I can on Ma'at."

"Thanks, Geoff," said Allen into his mobile. He slumped down into the armchair facing the large screen in his lounge. "What do you have?"

"A ton of stuff, but I've selected some of his major casts from the last few years and I'm sending them to you," he strung out the last word, then said, "now."

Allen's mobile bleeped.

"Hit the 'Display Remotely' button and it'll appear on any nearby screen. I've added a brief description alongside the titles to give you an idea of the content. Give me a bell if you need anything explained. Like I said: wide awake."

"I'm sure I'll manage to listen to a few casts, Geoff. But thanks."

"Check the cast titled 'Dark Road to Damascus', about 45 seconds in. With Ma'at you've got to look beneath what you see. Most are blatant diatribes, but others hint at things without drawing attention to herself or the real message. Almost like a warning to those involved. And I have a feeling that she or her people resolve the matter. You blink and suddenly an entire corporation is going under, or files are leaked to the media or the relevant authorities. Later."

"Cheers," he bleeped the conversation off, and then pressed the unit again. The lounge screen swished to life revealing a long list of headlined topics or screen casts. He began scanning through the dated titles for anything that stood out.

- 'Mesopotamia to Egypt: Transformation of Ma'at'
- 'Inside the Book of the Dead'

Allen toggled through the info with his device, slowing to take in longer snippets.

At one time or another, every great man has gotten down on his knees before their god. Either to praise/worship or beg/plead for mercy/their lives.

Space elevators come and go, but still we remain on this planet of ours staring up at the stars in wonder; not the other way around.

How do they track the more rural populace? Those that sometimes don't record births or deaths in their communities through official Home Affairs channels? Birth records from two hundred, even one hundred years ago are sketchy. If we wanted to solve the Jack the Ripper case, all we'd have to do is punch in all the people living in the world at the time and see where their souls end up. Unfortunately that's too many unregistered births, let alone damaged souls from those appalling living conditions not to be messed up in future lives.

One soul leaves in order for another to resolve or fulfill their initial purpose, therefore doesn't need to be till death, and could be brief...

- 'Shaka'.
- 'Africa: Cradle of Mankind'.
- 'Dark Road to Damascus'.

He stopped here and clicked the title. A moment later the screen filled with text.

Systems and beliefs have, many times in history, been usurped and railroaded along new directions. Sometimes these have become the de facto version simply because those representing the new ideology have the ability to bring it into the public space in such a convincing and appealing way that few can resist the packaging and sales pitch which offers a better life for all.

I am reminded of our friend Paul. For someone who never met the messiah; never received first hand interpretations of his teachings and what he intended for his followers; he seemed to have a complete understanding of what needed to be done going forward. Even when he comes across as an irrational, insecure child having a tantrum, he still insists on arguing with the messiah's brother and those of his closest disciples. One would think that they would have a better idea of what needed to be done within the early church; well, better than someone who fell off a horse and thinks they hear voices, anyway.

And so we watch as they stumble along, insisting that their way is the right way. They alone will save mankind from themselves. They take the ideas that suit them, throw out those that don't, compile a system to govern the fate of a soul when they have little understanding of the original.

Allen scrolled, only faintly aware of being sucked into the information.

They release version one, control what is and what isn't.

The original is transmitted to anyone interested in ideas, things are added, it grows.

They release version two. Things have been edited and deleted.

The original doesn't judge. The original accepts all input.

They release a light version and an extended version.

The original has a solid following.

They split into factions. Alternate versions abound. They are hacked and attacked. The windows through which they look are stained, trying to be multicoloured.

The original, open to all, sits with the juiciest apple. Theirs is solid. Unwavering. Pure.

Sometimes we leave them to sort themselves out. Possibly they will eventually self-implode. And maybe there will come a time when we nudge them off the map altogether.

One thing is for certain; souls are no simple matter for Man to think he can claim control over.

He raised his mobile and called Geoff.

"I assume you're calling about 'Damascus' because there's no way you went through all the casts I sent you."

"And I assume that's a not-so-veiled attempt at slamming the Tracker Unit. But there could be a few people or businesses that it relates to. Are there any others that relate to the Tracker Unit?"

"Only a few snatches of insinuations here and there. This appeared when the unit had just begun recruiting. Coincidence maybe. You must realize that Ma'at's verbal attacks on the church have subsided considerably in the last two hundred years; a marked drop in the last fifty. Now she just puts in a jibe or two or, in this case, uses them to make a different point altogether."

"From her own words then, the conclusion would therefore have to be that she has some sort of superior system in place. The original."

"Version one point oh," added Geoff. "Now can you put a little bit more trust in my conspiracy theory?"

\#

Allen could feel his headache coming on. Whenever he did his research he overloaded his mind with ideas and theories, eventually giving himself a severe headache that abruptly stopped any possibility of further work that day. He couldn't afford to get one now.

Over the past few years he'd been able to identify the symptoms early on and take the necessary break to alleviate it. Deep breathing, taking a walk, or sitting for five minutes in silence without anything buzzing through his throbbing mind, were all ways of dealing with an overactive brain.

He didn't bother turning on the bedside lamp; rather, he undressed in the cool darkness of the room and lay back on his side of the bed. He took ten deep breaths, eyes closed, and felt the tension releasing, first from his feet, then all the way up through his stomach, hands and into his neck and shoulders.

The last thought he remembered was how much he loved his wife and son. He held onto that as he drifted off.

\#

The rain had slowed by the time Ruth turned off the dirt road and onto a property marked by an old handmade sign. 'The Smiths'.

About 500 metres ahead she could make out the lights of what she assumed was the farmhouse. The farm road was well looked-after and less tumultuous than the drive a half hour earlier. She stopped the car at a chained metal gate, unsure of what to do next. Hoot? Wait?

She got out the idling car and walked up to the old chain wrapped around the rusted pole and fence. In the light of the headlights, she noticed the lack of a lock or bolt of any kind and, after some rattling and clanging, unhooked an open loop of the chain off the one end. She pushed the gate open in a wide arc across the road and, once in the car, drove through. Once she closed the gate, she set the chain the way she had found it and continued the drive up the dark farm road.

As she neared what looked like the back of the farmhouse, two people emerged from the main door and out onto the open gravel at the end of the drive. Her stomach lurched as her instinct of flight rose in her body. But, she knew if Frank trusted them all would be okay.

She slowed as her headlights passed over them revealing an elderly man and woman. Friendly faces. She stopped the car and turned the engine off as they approached and opened her door. With the backlight from the house, she was unable to make out their faces as they spoke her name, but a warmth and peace washed over her. Goosebumps ran along her arms and neck. She stepped out the car and reached out her arms to them both, embracing them, and burst into tears.

CHAPTER 15

"Mommy, Mommy. Can we go in the boat?"

Ruth first felt the stiffness in her shoulders and arms as she tried to prop herself up in the bed. She was still coming out of a deep sleep that seemed to linger when Caleb repeated his question impatiently.

"Cay?" she mumbled. "What are you doing awake at this time?" She stopped what she was saying to shield her sensitive eyes from the bright light that broke through the gap in the curtains where Caleb was staring outside.

"Down there," he pointed eagerly. "The boat's by the house, Mommy."

Thoughts of where she was and what day it was flooded her tired mind.

"Boat? What boat?" she said easing out of the bed.

Her mobile, she knew, was turned off and in her bag on the floor near the door, so she had no idea of the time. Steadying herself she stumbled to the window, squinted, and opened the curtains wider.

It took her a brief moment to realize where they were as she took in the spectacle outside what turned out to be two French doors. Caleb read her mind and gripped the door handle, bursting out onto the small balcony overlooking the wide expanse of a dam. They were one story up from the translucent brown lapping water below.

Caleb pointed. "There, Mommy."

Ruth craned over the railing and looked down at a small boat tied to one of the large, thick wooden supports that held up the house half a metre out of the water below. Two steps led up from the boat onto a landing or undercover patio.

Jane and John, the friends of Frank, had shown her up another narrower road, a kilometre or two from the main farmhouse. It had been dark, but they had mentioned the house being on the small dam overlooking the upper section of their vast piece of farmland.

She had only half registered this as they walked her into the main bedroom where she last remembered falling into the soft bedding.

Now, she was wearing a clean pair of tracksuit pants and a t-shirt. Neither of them was hers.

The position of the sun to her right and meant it was around eight in the morning. But she never was the best at telling the time by the sun.

"Come, Mommy," said Caleb and dashed into and out of the room, drumming down what sounded like a wooden staircase.

"Caleb." She yawned and stretched her aching body. "Mommy needs a bath or a shower. Maybe another sleep."

She came back into the bedroom and sat on the edge of the bed, aware of how quiet it was. A breeze caught the edge of the curtains, cool and damp, caressing her tired face. She took a deep breath and fell back into the bed.

#

Allen sat up startled. His mobile bleeped, sending a surge of adrenaline through him that left him shaking minutes after.

He picked it up and answered. "Hello."

"Allen," said a familiar voice. Allen hesitated for a moment. If he wasn't wide-awake before, he was now.

"Frank? What the hell are you calling for?"

"Everything's fine, Allen, before you freak out."

"It can't be bloody fine if you're calling me."

"Ruth and Caleb should be you-know-where already."

"What the hell do you mean 'should be'?" He got out of bed and paced. "What time is it?"

"Just after seven," said Frank. "I need you to pick me up in about an hour."

"What the hell happened, Frank?" asked Allen, feeling the blood leaving his face.

"I'll explain later. They are releasing me at eight, so pick me up from the station, will you?"

"Releasing you?"

"I have to go. Only allowed a minute's call. Everything's okay, Allen."

"It's goddamn not, Frank."

The line went dead.

#

"One mobile device, bank and ID cards," said the clerk behind the thick glassed-in counter. She slid the items into the secure tray alongside. "Sign the screen and then you can go."

Frank pressed his thumb against the built-in screen on the countertop. It bleeped and released the tray far enough out the wall for him to remove its minimal contents.

"I guess Biyela's holding onto my badge for safekeeping, eh Sergeant?"

The clerk gave him an awkward grin. "I'd steer clear of the main entrance if I were you, Frank. That gem of a human being, Gora Khayyám, is addressing the media and outside is teeming with *Save Our Souls* protesters."

"Any opportunity to megaphone his views or rally for votes is never lost on him," he said pocketing his belongings.

"See you, Frank," she said. "Ngikufisela inhlanhla."

"Thanks, Nonhla."

He walked in the direction of the main entrance while he connected to Allen's mobile. He glanced at the time: 7:48 AM. He slowed as he passed the large glass window looking out at the playground, quiet and deserted. He heard the commotion and sounds of the media and protesters before he saw them. Rounding a corner of the long hallway, he saw more people than he would've imagined. Journalists clustered inside, the large automatic doors of the foyer disarmed and open to the protesters cordoned by three police officers on the stairs beyond, handmade signs angrily bobbing their slogans up and down. *'Unconsenting Soul'* with a fat red arrow pointing down; an encircled and crossed out *'uNgayithinti uMoya!'* along with a handful of printed *S.O.S: Save Our Souls* boards and t-shirts.

The distinctive voice of Premier Khayyám, rising above the shouts from the crowd outside, penetrated clearly into the depths of the station. No megaphone required.

Allen answered. "Hello."

"Ready when you are," said Frank.

"I'm there in five, Frank."

"I'll be outside."

"I've got some leads on Ma'at and her tracker system."

"Her what?" asked Frank as he edged closer to the mass of people.

"Apparently she's got an advanced system. More advanced than yours and they rehabilitate without messing with a person's whole life, and family."

Frank could now make out Khayyám's head facing the journalists and lit up by camera lights.

"I want every God-fearing citizen to think about this for a moment. The afterlife, souls and tracking souls are God's arena," he heard Khayyám saying.

"Frank?"

"Step over that Divine line and we're asking for a wrath so almighty that it could affect the entire earth and send shock-waves across the universe."

"Allen, I'm here," said Frank. "How do you mean advanced?"

"Ours is a fragile existence, allowed and perpetuated by a force that create and destroy worlds."

"What the hell's that noise?" asked Allen. "I'll fill you in just now but we need to find a way to get to her or her organization."

"Let us not underestimate what we are messing with, people. Citizens of Earth."

"Well, goddamnit, Al, how do we just call up old Ma'at and say, 'Hey, Big M, we need to chat. How's eight-thirty for you? Your place. Put on a pot of coffee'?"

"A woman died last night because her life was put in the hands of some divining rod, bone-throwing tarot card readers."

"I'll see you shortly, Frank."

"That is not a police force. That is not investigating. That is waiting for the alignment of a star or galaxy to let you know where or what something might be happening. That is not using your tax money for the betterment of our society. It's throwing hard earned cash into the hats and back pockets of mystics, sangomas and magicians in the hope that their crystal balls will keep you, us, safe at night."

"Hands off our souls," a woman yelled from the crowd.

Some of the journalists took the gap to pepper the premier with questions.

"Rather than slamming the system," Frank's voice echoed around the foyer, drowning out everyone else, "why don't you rather work on improving it?"

There was a moment of hushed silence, apart from the sound of digital devices clicking and pointing in his direction.

"nGulube," came the voice from before.

"Ah, Tracker Banks, is it?" Frank received a cool smile directed at him. "Any system that pretends to be on the side of God, and yet claims to manipulate and monitor God's creations to their own ideals is treading on blasphemous ground. Those who circumvent God, remove him from the equation, are by that very notion, evil."

Frank edged into the wide-eyed journalists around him.

"And yet, Premier," he raised a finger to his lips, "your God that you speak of, in His good book, admits to creating both good and evil. Common sense says we are justified in removing Him from the equation altogether for that irresponsibility and putting us in this position."

A murmur erupted from the mass of people.

"Ah, the atheist speaks." Gora forced a toothy laugh. "Without God, good and evil simply become a choice. Without God, a person will struggle with that choice on a daily basis. But, commonsense indeed, Mr. Banks. I'm glad you brought that up. The Good Book, Mr. Banks, doesn't say, thou shalt not have cyber-sex with thy neighbour's wife, but common sense says that it's still adultery. It doesn't say, thou shalt not obliterate an entire species of animal, but common sense says soon there will be nothing left. And the Good Book doesn't say, thou shalt not track another's soul, but common sense says it's a bit darn intrusive. Now, what does common sense say to you, Mr. Banks?"

"That the Crusades, the Spanish Inquisition, Salem, the Third Reich, the sons of Ham and objecting to condoms, were all a lapse of common sense."

There was a chuckle of surprised laughter from one of the journalists next to Frank while the police officers held their arms out to stop the seething and jostling protesters from getting inside. Frank stood at the front now, a mere two metres from the suited man. With Gora's eyes trained on him, Frank found it hard to read his steely expression. A woman behind Khayyám stepped up to the politician and whispered something in his ear.

He gave a nod and, with a confident grin, said, "And the boy that remains locked up in that prison you call rehabilitation, Tracker Banks?"

Frank felt his body go cold, rigid. He clenched his jaw.

"What does common sense say about that?"

The bodyguards were on him before his fist made it to shoulder height.

#

Frank looked around the stark brightness of the large boardroom. Large windows on his right looked out over the skyline of Durban City. The bright morning sun, filtered through the tinted windows, warmed him from the cold air-conditioning. To his left, the same sized windows, and a glass door opened to a view of people, staff, busying themselves with various tasks in and out of cubicles and glassed-off offices. He had a sense of openness and visibility. Everything seen.

He leaned his elbows at the head of a glass table that stretched the length of the long, light room. At the opposite end was a wall that seemed to shimmer every now and then. A screen, he assumed, covering the entire width of the room.

For nearly ten minutes he had been waiting for what, he did not know.

Pushing out the chair and standing up, he looked out at the cityscape for a moment, then turned and walked up to the glass barrier between him and the office staff. Even though he wasn't clean and neat like all of them — a night in the can will do that to a person — nobody seemed to pay him any attention.

He tapped as loudly as he could manage on the thick glass. "Hello," he yelled at the top of his voice and tapped his wrist. "I've got another appointment in half an hour."

A handful of people glanced up from what they were doing, or paused mid-stride, then carried on their way. *What were they all doing?*

No visible company branding, corporate logo or any indication of what the building housed from the outside. No titles on the doors.

Somehow he had expected at any moment to be handcuffed, or restrained, so he hadn't bothered to object or even attempt to resist being muscled into a darkly tinted black sedan by four suited men, driven across the city, escorted out the parked car into the lobby of one of the tallest buildings in the city, into an elevator and out on the thirty-second floor, where one of the men had simply nodded at the receptionist as they walked through the offices and cubicles into the room he found himself in now.

Though he assumed the main door into the boardroom, or whatever the hell it was, was not locked, he didn't feel the compulsion to leave.

Allen was probably going out of his mind right now.

He shoved his hands in his pockets. Sneaky bastards. They had managed to remove his ID, bankcards, and his mobile during all the mayhem.

Movement, and a faint sound, caught his eye to the side. He turned quickly and saw the screen wall alive with data and a network of lines and grids.

He looked around the room. No one.

Frank moved closer to the screen, noticing a prominent blue dot with three blocks of data alongside. From where he was, in the middle of the room, he couldn't make out the detail of the text.

He passed his hand from one chair to another as he edged closer. At about five metres away from the screen his legs froze, and his lungs automatically drew in the ice-cold air in one sharp breath.

Three sets of information, each titled with a name.

Caleb Hicks. Angelica Young. And Ruth Hicks.

In this politically charged climate, one of the leading centres for research emerged in southern Africa. Traveling down the same eastern longitude, intersecting with the likes of the Great Zimbabwe ruins, the Blaauboschkraal stone ruins and many still *'undiscovered'* sites, to end at the opposite latitudinal position as the Pyramids, the city of Durban — with an unusually high concentration of stable energy — developed into the global centre of research.

CHAPTER 16

The hum of an engine in the distance roused Ruth from her deep sleep.

Caleb! She leaped out of the bed, the stiffness in her feet barely registering, got her bearings and found her way down the stairs.

"Caleb," she called. She passed through the lounge and open-plan kitchen, out the large glass sliding doors, and onto the patio.

"Mommy, the boat," said Caleb.

Relief washed over her at the sight of her son seated on the edge of the patio steps, feet in the water, and pushing the boat, still tied to the patio, with one foot.

"Wait, Cay," she said and listened for the sound again. It was closer now.

"Daddy," said Caleb and leaped up.

"Not Daddy, Caleb." She managed to grab his arm as he darted past her.

"Ow!" he squealed.

"Wait here, my boy." She lowered her voice.

"What's wrong, Mommy?" He looked up at her.

"I don't know." She glanced around the patio wall to the far bank of the dam. A faint dust trail traced the length of the road that ran parallel to the dam edge toward the cabin. The back of an open bed utility van disappeared out of Ruth's view. She hurried to the other side of the patio, at the entrance walkway that connected the house to dry land. Looking around the side of the cabin, she watched as the vehicle appeared, then stopped under the large weeping willows that hung over the water and walkway. Her view was obscured, but she heard doors open and close, and movement just as the hanging branches parted to reveal an elderly woman followed by a man of roughly the same age carrying a crate.

Caleb rushed past his mother onto the walkway.

"Sawubona Aunty Jane, Uncle John. What you got?"

"Hey, big guy," boomed John and dipped the large container for the boy to see. "Just a few goodies for you and your mom to eat."

"Yummy," said Caleb.

"Where's your mum, umntwana?" asked the lady.

"Hiding from you two, Aunty Jane," said Caleb and pointed behind him. Ruth cringed and ducked back into the cabin. "She hasn't taken me on the boat yet and the water looks so nice."

"Hiding?" said Jane. The two of them walked onto the patio. "She's probably tired after driving the two of you all the way here last night, umfana. Besides, the boat and the dam are not going anywhere."

Ruth stepped out of the lounge, feigning a yawn.

"There she is," said Jane. "Hello, dear."

"Hi Jane. Hi John."

"Ooh," said John entering through the sliding doors. "Someone's not going to make nine o'clock mass."

"What's mass, Uncle John?"

"Mass?" repeated John as he dropped the crate onto the kitchen counter. "You know. Church."

"We don't go to church," Caleb said with pride.

The couple turned to Ruth. She smiled awkwardly back at them. "Coffee anyone?"

"Probably for the better," said Jane with a wink, "the church is right on the edge of the safe zone, anyway. Maybe a visit to my isigodlo, my sacred place, when we come back? The umsamo within the rondavel is always ready."

Ruth nodded and headed inside.

"When I get back from church," said John to Caleb, "we are going to check the long thatch grass being bundled while the ladies throw amathambo. And *then* we go in the boat," he held out a free hand to Caleb. "Deal?"

"Deal." Caleb slapped his small hand in John's.

#

Zenzele held up a firm index finger at Angel.

"Firstly, we don't have the resources to rally together more than one helicopter. And secondly," he added his middle finger to the first, "I'm not having local law fuck up the arrest by making a noise about it, Mike. Besides, thirdly, I'm not having you going up in shitty weather and have you grounded in the middle of the bundus, in the sticks."

"You want us to drive for three hours?" asked Angel.

"She'll be nice and snug in her little farmhouse, sipping hot cocoa. No reason for her to go anywhere. In the meantime, we have a convoy of everyone we need without bothering some wannabe Texas Ranger. At top speed, lights and sirens, you should get there in just over two hours."

"What about the media following on our heels or in their own helis, Zenzele?"

"Diversions, Mike. You let me worry about the media. You worry about nailing that goddamn tracker of yours to a goddamn cross."

"The hell we are, Zenzele," said Angel bending over the other man's table. "What would you do if it were your son?"

"I don't have a son, Mike, and if I did I wouldn't want some stranger's soul screwing with his life."

"You know that's bullshit, Zenze. She's protecting Caleb. Doing what a mother's supposed to do for her child: protecting him no matter what."

"Well, apparently there's no stopping this soul. Even dying. She can't protect him and she should know that by now."

"She's protecting him against us, Zenze, not the damn soul."

"We are here to protect her and him and the rest of society

from that goddamn soul, Mike. We are not the enemy. People die. Souls move on; change bodies; float in and out of our world without a care about who they fuck with to get what they want. It doesn't help running away from us. We, and only we, can make sure he's not a complete fuckup; some serial killer in training. Hicks must back off and let us do what we do. His soul's moved on and there's little hope of ever getting it back. Things change."

"People die," said Angel softly. "I know, Zenze."

#

Allen left another message for Frank and then hung up.

What the hell is going on?

He waited for the majority of the journalists and activists to leave the entrance to the tracker building then got out his car.

He had made it into the parking just as Gora and Fareeda Khayyám and their team got into three cars, supporters cheering, journalists flashing and filming as they made it onto the main road. He had waited another few minutes before trying Frank's mobile for the first time.

He stood at the entrance and checked to see if Frank had appeared anywhere, then headed inside. He walked down the long hallway and stopped at the reception-booking desk.

"Hi, Nonhla," he said to the lady behind the glass.

"Oh hi, Allen," she replied.

"Seen Frank?" he asked.

"He was here a few minutes ago," she craned her neck to look over his shoulder. "Did you try calling his—?"

"No answer," Allen cut in.

"Allen," said a familiar voice.

Angel was approaching him, followed by three other trackers he recognized but couldn't remember their names. There seemed to be a hurried purpose to their gait that sent a cool sensation up Allen's back.

"Where's Frank?" Angel asked Allen, then turned to Nonhla. "Memela?"

"I was about to ask you the same thing," said Allen before the sergeant could respond.

"I checked him out about ten, fifteen minutes ago."

"Dammit," said Angel then turned to one of the men. "Escort Mr. Hicks with us down to the cars, Collins."

"I'm sorry, what?" asked Allen. "I'm not going anywhere with you guys. I'm here to pick up Frank and that's it."

"Sorry, Allen," said Angel. The man, Collins, took Allen firmly by the elbow and guided him down the hallway. "You're coming with us. I don't need you interfering or doing whatever it is you're doing here."

Angel began walking alongside Allen. "And I'll take that," he said and removed Allen's mobile from his hand.

"You can't arrest me, Mike," protested Allen as they all turned into a doorway leading to stairs to the basement parking.

"We're not arresting you, Allen," said Angel from below. He heard the screech of tyres. They came to the landing at the bottom of the stairs. Angel stood aside for Allen and Collins to go through.

"We're going to get your wife and son."

#

"Has anyone offered you something to drink, Tracker Banks?"

Frank pivoted where he stood. He hadn't heard the man enter, or the door that he was now closing, open. He looked at the screen wall, then back at Gora Khayyám in front of the vertical lines barely revealing the discreet panel door.

Movement on the other side of the glass wall to his left caught his eye. A woman, trailed by a younger man, pushed the heavy door open and smiled at her husband. "My love."

Frank tried to stop the chaos of information making him slightly light-headed.

"I was just offering our guest some water, Fareeda. It seems that's a difficult question to answer under the circumstances. Bevan," Gora said to the other man as Fareeda Khayyám made her way to an empty chair at the long conference table, "three glasses of water, please."

Frank watched Bevan nod and leave the room, closing the glass door behind him.

"Mr. and Mrs. Khayyám?" said Frank bemused.

"Please. It's Fareeda and Gora. Let's chat," Gora gestured to Frank to sit. They both pulled out chairs on opposite sides of the table, the other man sitting beside his wife.

The woman unbuttoned her suit jacket and pointed at the screen wall. "I trust you recognize that."

Frank kept his eyes on both the Khayyáms.

A moment later a panel on the far end of the room opened and the man from earlier walked in with a silver tray carrying three tall glasses of water. After crossing the length of the room, he stopped next to Mrs. Khayyám and passed her one of the glasses. She took it with a nod, and placed it gently with a clink on the glass table.

Gora lifted his from the tray and said, "Thank you, Bevan," and held onto it.

The man came around to Frank, and did the same then left the room by the door that Gora had entered through. Frank held his glass.

"Why do you have a tracker screen?" asked Frank and took a sip of the cold water.

"Really, Frank? Is that it?" Fareeda folded her arms.

"You've basically hidden behind these conservative Muslim personas all this time, while you represent something else entirely."

"Bright lad," the woman said to her husband. "But not quite. The public has chosen to label my husband as a good, God-fearing Muslim because of the language he speaks and the words he uses."

"Yes," Gora said, "I have gone along with it without dispelling those assumptions. And, as my wife calculated it would, it has helped to distract from our real life and purpose. But why is it that I have to be a Muslim or Christian to believe in those ideologies? Our Org has been around a lot longer than old JC. When he appeared on the scene his was a unique way of interpreting man's purpose and relationship with the universe. We hold true to many of the basic tenets of the early faiths, those that were the cornerstone of their movements before being usurped. So, Muslim or Christian? No." He shook his head. "Christ-like? I can do my best." The couple laughed.

Frank took another drink of his water.

Picking up her glass from the table, Fareeda lifted it to the light.

"Take this water. That is who you are: the water. The glass is your body or your physical restrictions that you and only you put on yourself. Connect with your soul, your Higher Self. Acknowledge this vast being that you are, that can shape worlds and move atoms at a whim. Create a universe. Destroy the mind. Blow it all away," she flicked the side of the glass with a ping, "and marvel at the god in you. Acknowledge the Pantheon of gods before you. *'Stand in the assembly of the gods and know that you're one of us. We are gods, and we are all children of the Most High'.*"

"So there is a God?"

"Who cares?" Fareeda drank half her water and put the glass back on the table.

"Who really gives a shit?" said her husband. "Are you basing your life on that? Does it make a difference to who you are? Who you are capable of being? Will it make you a better person knowing that? If we said, 'Yes, there is a God' is that going to give your life meaning? Give yourself the permission to be a bigger and better person?

"Oh, sorry. You want to know that there is a God so that you can have Him come down and give you His rule-book because you don't want to piss Him off in any way. Here are ten reasons to beat yourself up. So instead of feeling good about yourself you've now got to make someone else happy first. If I do this then God will be happy with me, then I'll feel happy about myself. I need someone to treat me like a child. I do good. I receive gold star. I have self-worth."

"Among her many ambitious feats," said Fareeda, "constructing an elaborate temple to honour the spirit of Ma'at did nothing to prevent Hatshepsut from nearly being wiped out from mainstream history. Churches and temples, though they reach for the heavens, have their limits, never mind impressing any sky gods. Have you received any gold stars from a giant hand in the sky lately, Frank?" asked Fareeda and leaned forward onto the table. "Hatshepsut began referring to herself Ma'atkare, *truth is the soul of the sun god*, and was our first embodiment of Ma'at, formally beginning the line of Ma'ats you see today. Her legacy was entrusted to us. To me."

Frank folded his arms, still holding his glass, anticipating the need to throw something. He took a quick sip instead.

"Look at it this way," she continued. "You were born, right? You were a child once. Now you're older. You'll grow older and then you'll die. Unless someone pushes you off that balcony. You don't remember a time before you were born and you certainly don't remember dying, yet. You can spend the rest of your life asking 'why am I here' or 'what's my purpose'. Or you can just get on with it. You are alive. The meaning that you give your life is up to you. Has anyone asked 'what if this is reality?' Nothing else. Have fun. Fun is fundamental. Stress and pain and anger and fear are life telling you that you're trying too hard. Don't try. Do. And do it with all of you. Not the limited you. If I asked you to run a mile, would you get down on your hands and knees and crawl? That would be idiotic. You would take your healthy legs and feet and run. So why limit yourself in your life?"

"But, hey, that's just us," added Gora. "I might be some messiah standing on a mountaintop preaching the Word, thinking I'm teaching the truth. But to someone else I'm a raving anarchist with a self-destructive streak ready to push the button on the bomb strapped to the planet. Boom! A rabble-rouser for God. One man's truth is another man's existential bullshit.

"When I die, I die. That's it. No more me. This body, what you see that makes me me will be no more. Even if I reincarnate, it won't be this body. This mind. I might not have this mansion next time around. And I might not see the world the way I see it now. But, damn! Right now is now."

"The world longs for a saviour," said Fareeda, "a messiah, to save them from what exactly? Themselves or another? They want miracles and healing. Cure the sick? Take an aspirin. Next! Raise the dead? Visit an emergency room. Next! Raise a city to the ground? Nuclear missile, anyone? Next! Feed the five thousand? Here's a million bucks, now piss off and keep the change for dessert. Next! Fly in the clouds; walk on water. Hell, breathe under water. Turn sewage into drinkable water. Now there's a miracle.

"We live in an age of gods and we're all so complacent to the miracles happening all the time. Religion became science. Science became religion. And now we're asking ourselves 'where did the mystery go?'

"As soon as you create or elect a group or institution to represent your beliefs you create the problem. Things become opinions and no longer inspiration. When you want an answer to something we can no longer get the answer from within. We have to consult outside of ourselves, pass it by the committee to see if it is within the prescribed doctrine. By that time you've blown your brains out. But did he consult the book, that guru, that committee, that eldership?

"Connect with your soul. Don't be the puppet. Become one. We are not just the sum of our past lives. You are also here and now. Creating now. Create meaning today. But there's so much to do and so little time. Amazing how long a day is when you're fighting for your life.

Frank rolled his eyes then drank the rest of his water. "Why the hell don't both of you just transcend or ascend or rapture yourself out of this moerse hole and save us this lecture?"

"Why?" asked Gora. "We're here. We're not anywhere else. If I can be where I am, why the hell would I want to be anywhere else? Anywhere else is past and future. I'm here. Having fun here. My soul was born because it was ready or wanted to be born now. Here. I will die, Fareeda will die," he said and placed a hand on his wife's arm, "we'll all die when we're supposed to die, and not a minute later. Wishing for anything other than what I've got will give me stress. I'd rather have fun creating. Dream of something. Visualise what you want. Imagine. Don't long and hang and beg and pain to be or have something.

"Our prophets and messiahs, leaders and teachers are all simply people, like you and me, who have 'got it'. Who, by climbing the right mountain at the right time in their lives 'got' the Universe and saw the 'big picture'.

"Like our astronauts who venture into outer space. They come back down to earth where everyone wants to touch them, speak to them, hear them speak about their experience, have them dissect their experience second by second.

Following them around, hoping to touch and experience space for themselves. Not to mention the guys taking their stool and urine samples looking for answers. And all they will, or can ever, get from them is a bunch of verbal bullshit. One astronaut's experience is a different interpretation from the next. Someone else's interpretation of space. It won't get them to outer space. They will never touch the void.

"You can't touch God if you're busy looking up someone else's asshole for answers. You need to climb your own mountain. Fire off your own rocket of experience.

"'I found God when I orbited the earth for the first time. And if you don't get in a rocket on such and such a date, and orbit the earth twenty times while pissing through a catheter, then you're damned to hell!' So sayeth the great book of NASA."

"Everything you're chooning here is all your bullshit," said Frank and stood up to face the screen. "It doesn't mean it's true. That's true," he said pointing at the screen, "what I see in front of me."

"That's just another interpretation, Frank," said the woman rising from her chair. "But what we're saying is true for us. And it might be true for the next man," she gestured at her husband. "The point is, we are not forcing it on you; we're not making it into a damn religion. Here you and we sit, exchanging ideas, swapping opinions, changing beliefs every second. Neither of us is about to crucify the other because of an opinion. We'll leave this room, at the very least, with a better understanding of how we each tick."

"You're still using your system to control and manipulate the world around us," Frank turned to face Gora. "You're no better than the people you're out to stop."

"Frank, Frank," the man began, "astrology and birth dates have been around since humans looked up from their bones at the stars and said, *'Gee, that's a nice picture in the sky'*. People of power have been reading the bones or their enemy's astros for as long as that, trying to see what they will do next, see when they are supposed to be the most vulnerable. Manipulate? Everyone's still entitled to his or her opinion. Everyone can still speak their minds and live their lives how they choose."

"Within your parameters."

Fareeda held her hands behind her and paced. "There are certain guidelines that have been in place for millennia, Frank. We only step in when someone's hubris gets out of hand and threatens the fabric of society. We give them a chance. In some cases we've sat them down and tried to reason with them. Only at the last straw do we pull the plug. We aren't talking about controlling every citizen or every government. We are talking about tweaking," she said holding her thumb and forefinger a centimetre apart, "now and then. There is never really ever total control. That's naive to think so. This is not a global conspiracy, Frank."

"Could've fooled me."

"Ethics, Tracker Banks," said Gora. "I stand by that. We stand by that. Truth is a mighty thing to stand for. Simple as that."

"Are you trying to tell me that all those people out there," he thumbed his hand in the direction of the windows behind him, "aren't Ma'at lackeys? That they aren't completely sold on your belief system?"

"I goddamn hope not," laughed Fareeda. "Everyone that is employed here has a strong will of their own. They have their own beliefs, their own traditions handed down to them from their ancestors. And, much like yourself, they are able to think for themselves. They wouldn't be here if they didn't. We don't want yes-men or indoctrinated sheep working in an organisation like this. '*Lux et Veritas*' is the credo. '*Light and Truth*'. Truth is the only option no matter what or who it is. I'd blow my brains out if I couldn't have a meaningful conversation with anyone in this building; from the security guard in the lobby downstairs to our personal assistant. Shall we talk about the state of the economy or how we lost in last night's cricket? Fine, but that's the first thirty-seconds covered. What about the rest of the elevator ride?"

"You are so full of kak. How the hell do you keep up the charade of your public lives? You must have bland conversations every minute of the day. Have you even heard your speeches; that self-righteous tone talking about all sorts of political and fundamentalist kak?"

"Well, practiced," Fareeda said with a knowing nod to her husband.

"Yes," Gora said with a grin, "but listen a bit closely to the words my wife writes for me next time; listen for the underlying messages. We just want to close down the Tracker Unit. How I, Premier Khayyám and his faithful wife, justify it to the plebiscite on the street is irrelevant as long as we get it done."

"Imagine Ma'at," Fareeda placed a hand on her chest, "showing up and telling them all the pitfalls of your pretty little system. Who are they going to trust? A system that's been solving crimes, or some myth in an expensive suit?" She smoothed down her jacket and fastened the single button.

"Why don't you use your system for the public interest?"

Gora stood for the first time and walked over to the screen. "We do. The public just isn't aware of it. What's been playing out is more than some random serial killer knocking people off."

There was a brief knock and Bevan stepped through the panel from earlier. "May I borrow you, sir?"

Fareeda looked at her husband and gave a nod.

Following behind Bevan, Gora said to Frank, "We'll carry on with this shortly."

Fareeda waited for them to leave the room then said, "Let me show you something."

#

"We picked up Ruth and Caleb's trace in the early hours of this morning," said Angel seated next to Allen in the backseat of the car. They had been driving for half an hour, through Pietermaritzburg — capital of the province — and into the hills and farms of the midlands. Allen was glad for the break in silence.

"For some reason they popped up for a few minutes," continued Angel. "I can only imagine that she had a good reason to go outside her cover." He glanced at Allen. "I'm sure they're fine.

There was quiet again. Allen took a moment to set his mind at ease. Everything's fine. God, he hoped so.

"We ran checks on everyone involved in the case and found that Frank's friends, the Smiths, happen to own a farm some twenty clicks from where she and Caleb were traced."

"Coincidence?" offered Allen.

"Sure, Allen," Angel nodded, knowingly. "How long did you actually think it would take us to find them? You knew it would happen eventually, so why take the risk? Why the runaround?"

Allen thought for a moment. "There's always a chance that they will elude you, Mike. Don't get cocky when you're still a hundred and fifty clicks away. Anything can happen."

"Agreed. But right now the gap between them and us is narrowing. All I want is for Caleb to be out of harm's way."

"How is Ruth putting my son in harm's way, Mike?"

"She's on the run!" snapped Angel. "When it comes down to the crunch she is not, I repeat not, going to give him up without a fight. At what risk, Allen? What cost? How far is she willing to go, and how far are you willing to allow her to go?"

Allen laughed. "What am I willing to 'allow'? I trust my wife to do what she has to do to not to have our son in your system."

"The same system that Ruth has worked for the past few years? What's changed, Allen? Nothing."

"Caleb's changed all that, Mike, for me, for Ruth. You know that. In fact, it's about to change for everyone. You asked me last night why I didn't go with them. Why I wasn't with my family."

"And?" Angel held up his hands exasperated.

"And, Michael, I was finding another way. Another way out or another way to sort out this shit-heap."

"There is no other way, Allen. This is the best way to help your son, the only way to help your son. Rehabilitate his soul, and possibly enable his previous soul back."

"Do you even hear yourself? I feel like I'm in confessional for God sake, Mike. According to you experts, you *know*, and I struggle to believe, that once a kid's soul has walked-in there's not usually any going back. Once he's in your system he's there to fucking stay."

"I realize that, but."

"But, there is another way, Mike. And I plan to use that other way. I plan to get Caleb that help. I will do whatever I can to seek out the most elusive person on the planet."

"Elvis Presley," said Collins from the front passenger seat.

"Since I'm not under arrest, how about you three dicks listen to what I've got to say and you concentrate on the road ahead."

#

A short ride up the valley from the dam along the muddied road, past the main farmhouse complex, the four of them arrived at the L-shaped barn. Walls and roof covered with corrugated steel, on a typical work day the structure's insides would lay exposed — the massive doors, pulled back along their rails giving the trucks and personnel the space needed for loading and offloading. Today, everything was quiet and shuttered; the three other farm vehicles parked in the open gravel parking area the only signs of farm life.

Ruth, Jane, and John all climbed out of the truck while Caleb jumped off the open back and trotted over to John.

"Wish my Dad could be here, Uncle John. He'd like your farm. It's huge. So many birds."

"I'd sure like to meet your father some time."

Not sure he'd like to be here right now. Ruth watched John lead Caleb to one of the barn doors, unlock it, and with a gesture to Caleb the two heaved it along its runner.

"Wow, enamandla," Jane shouted and gave a laugh.

Caleb waved enthusiastically back at the women as the door came to a stop.

Jane turned and pointed past the truck to a neat structure on a small knoll. Ruth nodded and fell in step behind the other woman.

"From the look on your face earlier," said Jane over her shoulder, "I assumed church was not your thing."

Ruth took a moment before saying, "I'm just not sure I agree with everything that goes on in there. That's all." Ruth attempted a laugh. "It's not the building itself, I guess. That's just cement and bricks. But, maybe I do feel like the church is manmade in every sense, from the building to the gathering of people with certain rules. Men are fallible. Each has their own interpretation of some ancient text and they impose that on their followers. Who's to say whose is right? I prefer my own council when it comes to my soul. Or maybe it's my understanding that's lacking."

They reached the bottom of a flight of stairs and stopped.

Ruth looked up at the neat clay-covered structure; white walls and dark grey thatching with two visible windows on either side of the royal blue door.

"Speaking of understanding," said Jane. "Your face the other night."

With a quizzical look on her face, Ruth asked, "My face?"

Jane burst out laughing. "When I introduced myself."

"Oh," Ruth's face warmed.

"I'm not exactly the pale-faced, ginger haired Jane Smith anyone expects."

Ruth allowed herself a moment of release and laughed with the other woman.

Jane started up the stairs, saying, "Marrying John Smith, one of the best days of my life, also gave me the chance to leave my past and my name behind. Gugu Gubhela had become too visible. And out here," she stopped on the top step and gestured wide to the surrounding landscape, "I could help many more escape the prying eyes of—".

"The trackers," Ruth finished. "I now know the feeling."

"Who would have believed such a relationship between church, or beliefs, and state would ever exist. Embodied in the soul trackers." Jane turned the knob on the door and pushed it open, hand held open to invite Ruth in.

Ruth peered inside, the bright morning sun filtering through the small side windows, making it brighter than she had expected.

Jane said, "It's okay, dear. It's not going to swallow you up."

Ruth's apprehension disappeared. "I know that." She smiled back and stepped inside the cool room.

Ruth quickly realized how much the outside sounds were muffled within, even with the door wide open. Insulated and safe.

"I also agree about the church, by the way," said the other woman as she picked up a short grass broom.

"You do?" Ruth's eyes took a moment to adjust to the light inside. A grass mat, about two metres by one metre, lay on the shiny polished mud floor.

A large, colourful, printed fabric draped across almost the entire back wall stopping only a metre on either side of each of the two windows.

Jane waited for Ruth to follow suit. "But, take the holy water," Jane said and produced a two-litre bottle of misty water from beneath the metre high wooden cabinet under the wall-draped fabric. "Rather than a priest having blessed it, think of it as water that's been given an extra dose of love and attention with the intention of that love being passed on to you, whoever you are." She held the bottle up to the light, the layer of sea sand now visible in the dimples of the base of the soda bottle. Jane unscrewed the lid and took a long drink, then offered it to a reluctant Ruth.

Ruth took a sip of the cool salt water, her stomach giving a slight lurch at the taste. A coolness flowed through her body, from her throat past her chest and shoulders. Somehow she felt better, more relaxed.

"Mommy," shouted Caleb. The sound was deafening in the quiet room and she could hear John chuckling heartily. She stepped into the doorway to see Caleb perched on top of the grass bails on one of the trucks parked on the gravel.

"Quite a boy you've got there, Ruth," said Jane from behind her. "I'm sure he takes after his mother, right?"

They both laughed.

Ruth watched as Jane knelt down at one end of the grass mat, then gestured for her to sit opposite.

"It's really quiet here," whispered Ruth. "Peaceful. The only time I get quiet at home is in the middle of the night after this one's gone to sleep."

"It is good to have quiet-time. Quiet the mind. Meditate."

"Meditate?"

"Some people aren't lucky enough to have quiet, let alone peace, at home, dear," she leaned forward and put a warm hand on Ruth's knee. "There's so much chaos inside and outside themselves, and nowhere to connect to themselves or God. That's why, no matter where we are in civilization, a church, a sanctuary, umsamo," she gestured to the room, "have and always will have a role to play. Sanctuary means holy. And I say 'meditate' because it's what you can relate to. People also call it prayer."

"Ah," said Ruth. She gazed up at the densely thatched roof, gumpole beam supports converging in the middle.

"You need to believe in something, help from the outside, every now and then, when you don't or won't believe in yourself."

"I suppose so." Ruth shrugged. "Right now I don't know how I'm going to get out of this situation I'm in. I normally believe in myself and that I'm going to be okay. But, why am I in this position in the first place? Maybe this time it isn't going to be okay."

"And right now you'd like a little extra help."

"Hmm."

"A Zulu proverb says: *'Umuntu ungumuntu ngabantu'*. Directly translated, *man is man by men*. Or more succinctly, I am a person because of other people. It's about interconnectedness. People are most powerful when *not* alone. And yes, friends and loved ones here, in this world. But also your ancestors. They are here to help your souls."

Jane scraped a brass bowl from the side of the cabinet, a bundle of dried plant neatly lay inside, along with a box of matches.

Mphepho.

Used in a similar way to sage by the native people of North America, mphepho has a more meditative and relaxing effect. Ruth knew the smell it would give off.

"Think of a church," said Jane and removing the matches, offered the dry bundle to Ruth to hold, "every brick and post, as built with the intention of being a portal to the other side; to heaven; to God; your amadlozi; to your higher self or even your soul."

Ruth watched as the other woman flashed a match and waited for it to settle. They both leaned towards each other, Ruth steadying the mphepho bundle above the flame.

"Don't think of a structure like that as a place where only believers are allowed in; where sinners are judged; and non-believers are unwelcome." Jane put the box of matches on the grass mat and took the glowing plant from Ruth. The thick, grey smoke hung heavy and pungent. Both women took in a deep breath of the scent.

"A sanctuary," Jane continued and blew gently on the glowing embers, "is where everyone is open and willing to be with, and connect with, a higher power."

Satisfied, she placed the bundle in the brass bowl to the side of the mat. From her pocket she removed a fist-sized leather pouch, closed with an orange cord.

"Now, we call on your amadlozi, your ancestors," said Jane holding the pouch in both hands, "and you will throw the amathambo for me to interpret."

#

"Have you heard of the Tibetan Book of the Dead, Frank?" asked Fareeda.

"Not the same as the Egyptian book, I assume?" Frank still sure of what he had just seen.

"Not the same, no." She made some finger movements on the screen. "They believed in taking a dying person through a dying process. It was said to aid in a safe and problem free death. Yes, a problem free death, before I hear any sarcasm. By talking someone through their death they ensure that the soul is not trapped or blocked from proceeding onto the next level or levels."

"This rings a bell," said Frank snapping out of his daydream.

"So you know of this Tibetan practice?"

"Definitely not," said Frank flatly. "It sounds very much like the process that Ruth insists on using at any opportunity on a victim. Not sure where she picked it up though."

"Really?" said Fareeda, turning from what she was doing on the screen. She stopped for a moment then turned back to the screen. "Bevan, please get Zwelibanzi to ready the helicopter," Fareeda dragged one of the text boxes to the side of the screen, double-clicked it, causing it to bleep and disappear. "I've sent him the co-ordinates. He'll give you the estimated time for the round trip, so do what you need from your side."

The screen bleeped again, this time to reveal Bevan in a frame to the side of the large screen.

"Mr. Khayyám, Mr. Banks and I can leave at approximately nine-thirty, ma'am."

"Perfect."

"You aren't joining us?" Frank asked Fareeda.

"My husband loves the flying around. I have the Org to run."

"I also have Mr. Banks' change of clothes if he'd care to freshen up in the gym," added Bevan.

Frank raised his eyebrows.

"Don't worry, Frank. The clothes are sure to fit you just fine. We did get them from your apartment after all."

#

For some reason that Angel couldn't put his finger on, the last few days had seemed like the past few years of the Tracker Unit's existence wrapped into one week.

The hum of the car was threatening to send him into a comatose state; his mind and body were exhausted. After all that Allen had dumped on him, he felt like he was going to throw up.

On the one hand, what he had heard for the past twenty

minutes were the lunatic theories of a conspiracy fanatic of epic proportions. Yet on the other, he hadn't registered any opposing gut reactions to what Allen told him. Whether Allen was just good at presenting a theoretical case or whether there was truth to the ideas, Angel was working through every point trying to find an argument; trying to disprove something that, at the face of it, he should be embracing and not ignoring out of hand.

Screw it. He got out his mobile.

#

Allen had barely caught his breath after giving Angel everything he knew, and watched the other man, visibly disturbed by everything he had said, make a call. He hadn't been paying attention to what had seemed small talk and updates until Angel said, "Tell me something, Zenzele. You've never gone into detail about how the tracker technology came about."

There was a pause.

"I've got time," Angel hesitated then said, "you had me over for dinner that night. What was it? A week after Gabi died? And you told me you'd been developing this system. I've never asked before because I had been so overwhelmed with what you'd told me that I didn't even think to ask more than the obvious technical functionality. But now the obvious is how did you actually develop it."

He waited.

"What I'm asking, Zenzele, is who, what and how did the tracker technology come about?"

For Allen, the quiet in the car, the tension from the two men in front, was tangible.

"Try twenty words or less and we can carry on with our day."

"Never mind what you think I've heard. I'm not interested

in conspiracies, Zenzele. I am interested in what you've got to tell me. We've known each other for nearly twenty-five years, Zenze. Surely it's not a hard question to answer. I don't want formulas. I don't want technical specs. I want, 'I had this idea; I tried this; I did this and that and hey presto I could track a soul.'"

"No, my summary doesn't explain shit." Angel's voice was getting strained. "My summary doesn't explain the possibility that you took someone else's technology. My explanation doesn't cover why you're being so evasive. And my summary doesn't explain this intense feeling of being lied to for I don't know how long."

"I *am* doing my job, Zenze. Like a blind sheep following the even blinder shepherd off the cliff."

A loud noise could be heard coming from Angel's mobile that he now held away from his ear.

"No, Zenze. Even Jesus Christ wouldn't help you right now."

He hung up.

#

Her lower back was aching from sitting up straight for the past half an hour. She was still processing the information Jane had given her from reading the bones on the mat, trying hard to now focus on the silent mediation rather than the tension building in her muscles.

A noise from outside reminded her that her son was safely nearby. In her open lap, she imagined the nights he would fall asleep on her. She imagined the weight of his body feeling warm, substantial.

She pictured stroking his forehead and hair, and almost immediately began to relax. Hands moving like liquid over his warm skin and soft hair. She pictured herself pouring warm water over his hair, soothing and caressing him.

Realising how relaxed she had become, she exhaled and allowed the calm to engulf her.

\#

Jogging alongside the two other men across the top of their building, Gora was aware of the butterflies in his stomach even through the windy noise of the sleek helicopter resting on the helipad. He took out his mobile, punched a few keys and sent a message to Fareeda, the one person he really needed by his side right now.

They climbed into the main passenger compartment; Bevan assisted Frank with his seat belts and headset, while Gora spoke to the pilot through his headset mic, "What are the flight details, Zweli?"

"It's roughly one hundred nautical miles to our target destination and we should be able to maintain our hundred and twenty knots an hour, Sir. I'd say under an hour for arrival; depending on the winds after these storms we've had."

"Excellent."

"I've stocked the hatch with refreshments and various essentials we may need, Sir."

"Excellent, again." He turned to Frank. "Ready, Frank?"

Bevan's mobile bleeped. He pressed a button, then another.

"Hello," he said.

For a split second, Gora hoped it was his wife.

Ndili 's voice came through all their headsets, "Mr. Khayyám, the tracker teams appear to be en route to your destination. They left around eight thirty by road."

Gora felt his butterflies whither and die. He shot Frank a glance.

"Seems the trackers have taken the lead, Frank." He waved a hand at Bevan. "Thank you, Ndiliswa. Let's make this snappy, Zweli. I've got a system I want to fry."

The helicopter lurched, swiftly rose ten metres vertically, before pushing them all back in their seats, roaring across the city skyline.

Gora turned to Bevan. "Any news from Marion?"

His assistant tensed for a moment, then said, "There haven't been any reports of breakthroughs by the research team on Marion Island, but we are still keeping track of developments, sir."

"Good, Bevan," he replied, "they may be onto something down there and we can't have them selling their results to the highest bidder before we've even had a sniff of it."

The remote island along the Antarctic route drew scientists and researchers from all fields, including energy. The Org had to keep track of any and all developments. Things had to be kept in check.

His glowing device caught his eye. He lifted it and read the response from his wife.

"I lovest thou, mon âme."

Selection in 2026 as Ma'at had not just hinged on his and Fareeda's worldviews but had also depended on the dynamics of their marriage and their public support.

They had been unaware of the Org taking notice of them. Their social contacts, their colleagues, had been filtering information on their evolving views, ideals and skills in public speaking back to their native city. When the then Ma'at had suffered a stroke the Org had made direct contact with Fareeda and Gora on her behalf. They had preempted the inevitable. They always did. He and Fareeda were gradually taken into the inner realm of an organisation that Gora battled to comprehend. Its scale. The goddess lineage going back thousands of years to ancient Egypt and Persia. The centuries had seen individual women, and occasionally by necessity men, fill the role of the leader of the Org. But in those instances of a married leadership, it was critical for their dynamics to be thoroughly vetted. And, although he was technically 'the first man', like the traditional presidential wife, their role was seen as one within the Org.

The world after that had seemed different to them. Their city, Paris, seemed different. Fareeda had once said that they had been shown the light, in the city of lights. Her understanding, her support in that moment, had deepened his love for her.

Her foresight in proposing the idea to the elders of The 42, and the ailing Ma'at, of them running as a political couple in Durban, had been one of her first independent and strategic moves within the Org. Confirmation to all of her promise in her future role. Named for the original forty-two minor Egyptian judicial deities, the assessors of Ma'at were responsible for judging the souls of the dead in the afterlife with forty-two sins. Though Ma'at, as the leader, had full autonomy, the elders were the final checks and balances in the Org.

It had been hard uprooting, even to go back to the city of their births. It was at this time that they were strategically introduced to another up and coming couple within the Org. Gabisile and Zenzele Biyela. Without much effort, they soon became close friends of Gabi and Zenze, providing a much-needed, close-knit inner sanctum, and ever more important as the Biyela's became part of The 42, the Ma'at elders.

Not long after their shared achievement, when Gabi was killed in a head-on collision, Zenzele had gone deep into depression, unable to grapple with his loss. Nothing that Gora or Fareeda could do would help their friend. Finally, Zenze had left the Org, angry at the system for being unable to bring his wife back to him.

Within months, the elder Ma'at had passed away without the world knowing, her legacy bleeding into what would become their mantle. The Org had again seamlessly transitioned from one administration into another, with Fareeda being placed in the ultimate position of power, and the support of Gora cementing their formidable partnership.

Then, the Org suffered the 'theft' of its Soul Tracking technology by one of its own. Within the year, rumours of the hacked system being launched as a government Tracker Unit began doing the rounds. They and the Org were forced to act swiftly. Publicly.

From being a liberal couple in political circles in France, Gora and Fareeda Khayyám were thrust into the public eye as the conservative Muslim husband and wife.

Even with the resources of the Org, they were unable to stop the Tracker Unit. There were those within governments who wanted the technology to succeed and be out in the open. The people were split between skepticism and intrigue; opposition versus the hope of safer lives. The Tracker Unit was finally launched in 2032 amid controversy and hype.

The Org had increased their dual public pressure with more Ma'at statements on the one side, and Gora and Fareeda Khayyám on the other. The Khayyáms became the moral voice of reason, and with public support they were finally elected to the office of the Premier of KwaZulu-Natal.

That had been four years ago. Political doors were flung open, and between champagne and speeches, they were introduced to two of the Org's elders based in their city. From then on, he and his wife were driven to usher in change. Diplomacy and rhetoric were no longer an option, and the egalitarian structure of *The 42*, the elder council, was their vital network around the globe.

Gora admired Fareeda. These past four years had seen them grow closer as they both shared the mantle of Ma'at. He was able to confide in her in ways he had found awkward in the beginning. Now, they were their own inner sanctums.

The revelation of Zenze's betrayal was completely revealed when the Tracker Unit was launched. It had seen Fareeda and himself argue in ways they had never experienced. He knew she was still coming to terms with the loss of her friend, as well as the impact of having watched helplessly as Zenzele unraveled. Looking back later, she had played the perfect devil's advocate to his overreaction.

"That's a bit harsh," she had said. "Zenzele's only using what he's got."

"He decided to take our superior technology, with no true understanding of how the inner workings functioned, tinkered with it to suit his purpose, and sent it out into the world for all to benefit from it without thinking whether the man in the street was ready for it or not. His is a hacked system, a crufty, with glitches and bugs. He still doesn't grasp the enormity of the technology that he is playing with."

"And we're here to do our jobs on a global scale. He can run around catching petty criminals while we handle the bigger fish." She sat herself up in the soft chair. "We could be sitting in Paris, sipping a Bordeaux. Instead we are here. And you — we — need to concentrate on your statement to the press tomorrow. It's an excellent opportunity to highlight the flaws in Zenze's system. A re-election is almost guaranteed, but you never know in this exciting day and age."

#

Ruth's mind had wandered again. This time she was very conscious of the fact that she was thinking about Caleb again; where she was; and how the hell she was going to run away from everything. The uneasiness rose inside her, churning her stomach. This time, instead of pushing it all back down and resisting the thoughts, she let them come up. In a torrent, like the rising bile deep in her throat, she concentrated on each issue rather than being overwhelmed and overcome.

The scent of the burning mphepho filled her nose and lungs as she took in a deep breath and slowly let it out.

For the first time in the past few waking hours she remembered *her* voice; she remembered the cars hovering above the stadium floor far below. She pushed the emotions of rage, terror, and fear that she had felt in those metal-twisting moments, aside to focus on Angelica.

What could have pushed a young woman to have done those things firstly, to those women; and secondly, to be so single-minded in her desire to escape that she would put so many others' lives in jeopardy?

And yet, she knew, deep within herself, that there is always a reason. Sometimes they are reasons too horrific to imagine that almost justify acting out, and at the same time realise that their actions may not have been as severe as you'd have expected; and on the other hand, a person cutting another driver off in traffic can be enough to result in someone slamming a baseball bat into their window.

Ruth tried to recall the hospital, the dreamlike state she only vaguely remembered; Angelica being somewhere nearby dying, with no one around her that loved or understood her.

She was hardly surprised that Angelica's soul had not carried on through to the Soul Plane. Such trauma, such intense emotions and drive, with no one to tell her dying mind, her sub-conscious state, that everything was okay no matter what she had done or who she had hurt or who she left behind. It would all be okay. It's okay to move through from this world into the next.

Anger rose up as she heard the distinct squeal of Caleb in the distance. She remembered her son and what it meant for his life, now and in the future.

She remembered too, that an existence as intense and volatile as Angelica's had been what would have held her soul to this plane.

No amount of talking would have helped. It needed experience. But how would she even attempt that with her five-year-old son? Her adult mind twisted and contorted at the thought of why and how. How could a child rationalize it?

In that moment she felt utterly helpless; that even the act of running away was useless. Would she really be willing to dodge energy lines, with her son, the rest of their lives?

In the darkness of her closed eyes she allowed the helplessness to engulf her. A split second later a warmth washed over her and the sound of rushing water became deafening.

Those involved in criminology saw how the developments could aid them in combating some of the violent crimes and mysteries that they had yet to solve. People had naively assumed that with the confirmation of some of our most profound beliefs of the afterlife that the criminal element of man would diminish or be more restrained. That was true for a time as man became aware of the God within. The Soul.

Out of deception, flawed methodology and an inferior system, it was in this environment that the Soul Trackers was launched.

CHAPTER 17

Ruth stretched her body after getting out of the truck. She was relieved it had been a quiet drive back from the barn and rondavel. She took a deep breath in, the moisture from the rains rising from the warming ground, filling her lungs. The heat haze hanging over the fields and hills felt comforting from the usual dry air of the countryside. The downside of being away from the coast: cracked lips and bleeding nostrils. The looming clouds also brought hope of more rain to come.

Caleb made a beeline for the boat and had already got inside waiting for John to fulfill his end of the bargain. The older man chuckled to the two women behind him on the walkway.

"Tea or coffee, anyone?" asked Ruth.

"Rooibos for me," replied Jane. "Two teabags. Leave them in the mug."

"Keep mine warm for me," said John and got into the boat. Caleb held on tight as the large man's bulk upset the balance of his world. "Maybe a glass of cold water from the fridge when we're done here."

Jane watched the two of them in the boat: John reaching the oars, Caleb with determination and excitement on his face. Ruth pulled the heavy sliding door open; a cool wave of air met her. She stepped into the kitchen and began preparing the kettle and cups.

"How was our sanctuary time earlier?" asked Jane. She came into the cabin and pulled up a highchair from under the kitchen counter, her back to the lounge.

"Oh," Ruth fumbled, "it was fine."

"It's okay, dear," said Jane. "You've got a lot on your mind. I'm surprised you didn't nod off. The mphepho can have that effect."

"It was okay, I guess," offered Ruth. "Definitely too much

going on in my head."

"What are your plans today? I suggest some quiet time otherwise all that brain activity's going to give you a head cold."

Jane looked out of the kitchen window. "May I suggest we take your boy for the day? There's no quiet time as far as he's concerned."

"Way too much to explore, Jane." Ruth laughed. "I'll be fine here. I really appreciate what you and John are doing for us."

"No, no," Jane waved a hand. "When Frankie called us we didn't hesitate for a second. I just think—" She stopped herself.

"What?" asked Ruth.

"I don't know," Jane looked up at Ruth. "I get the feeling that we aren't going to be much help to you and Caleb."

"You've already been a great help."

"No, I mean with Caleb. Frank told us what the situation is. He didn't want us blindly going into this without knowing what we were getting involved in."

"Sorry about that," said Ruth.

"Dear, we said yes before he explained and we said yes even after what he told us. From what the amathambo showed earlier, you'll get through this. And I'm not talking about running the rest of your lives, either. You are a strong woman, a mother. You are the one who will find the way through this. The authorities, the experts, the trackers, they've got nothing on a mother, a woman, faced with the opportunity of connecting with her own higher self for help. When all is lost, your soul is always there to lend a hand."

"Opportunity? That's one way of putting it."

"A woman is never as powerful a force, *enamandla*," Jane reiterated forcefully with a fist in her palm, "as when she becomes the primal element of Mother. This is not when her baby is born, but from the moment of conception. From that day onward she is nurturing and creating life. The power is not just because she has participated in the Divine expression of creation, but that she defies the laws of science in the physical world. As the life grows within the mother, two bodies, two humans, occupy the same Space and Time. And in that moment, science aside, their souls too are combined to create a force like no other in nature. This force, these conjoined souls, are forever linked — even after birth — through life, through death; and from this physical world into the next.

"It is this force that will enable you to find your way. Connect with your soul and your son's. Soon."

#

, Watching the swallows swooping and diving at the water's surface, John began to feel the tiredness in his arms. His chest heaved and his lower back ached.

"I just need to catch my breath a sec," he said to Caleb. The boy was hanging over the side of the boat, his hands splashing in the murky water.

After a minute or two, John asked, "Missing your dad, hey?"

"Mmm," murmured Caleb.

"What does he do, Caleb, at work?"

"He studies birds. A ornith, orna-something."

"Oh," said John. "An ornithologist."

"That's it."

"That's pretty cool. You've got to be clever to be one of those."

"My dad's the cleverest," Caleb looked up bright-eyed.

"I'm sure he is, Caleb."

"Do you have fish in here, Uncle John?" said Caleb turning his attention back to the water.

"Yes, plenty," said John.

"Oh," the boy replied with a hint of sadness.

"That's not a good thing?" he asked confused.

"I don't want them biting me."

"They won't bite, Caleb. They're not those kinds of fish. The most they bite is the end of my fishing rod." He laughed.

"Cool," Caleb wiped his hands on his shirt. "Can I swim?"

"Of course," John put a hand in to the cool water. "Feels good. Do you know how to swim?"

"Yes," Caleb said giving John a surprised look. "Only babies can't swim."

"My mistake. Just stay close to the boat, okay?"

#

The helicopter was starting to fly lower than before, in places following the curve of the land below. Frank felt like he was aboard a huge ship undulating with the roll of the swell beneath.

He had drunk half the bottle of water that Bevan had given him earlier. He would shift his gaze out to the horizon whenever he felt his pulse racing from looking at the distance below. He hadn't considered heights might be an issue, but twenty-four hours earlier had been a whole new experience for him to process.

Allen had told him that flight was fascinating to man because it made him feel closer to heaven. Closer to God.

Too close for his liking.

He looked over at the man, Gora, having what he knew was a private conversation with his wife, over his headset. His initial serious expression had soon been replaced with relief as Gora now began to end the call.

Frank turned to Bevan in the seat alongside and said, "So, what's your deal in all this?"

He watched the man look at Gora, or whatever you wanted to call him, for assurance.

Gora shrugged and pressed his headset against his ear to hear better what his assistant would say.

"How, what do you mean, Mr. Banks?"

"You know that your boss is one of the biggest mysteries in the world, part of a global organization that plays dice with the public, economies and governments."

"Plainly speaking, yes."

"And you're quite fine with the fact that you all manipulate and basically pull the strings without people knowing about it?"

"The public and the world know full well that the Org and this man and his wife, or women before him, exist because it's been simply stated on numerous occasions. The world chooses not to believe in it. They choose to hide their collective heads in the sand and call it myths and legends when it's all really in plain view. Look at our headquarters that you visited earlier. In plain sight.

"As for what we do, what I do; there are some things I agree with and some things I don't. The things I agree with inspire me to come to work every day. And the things I don't agree with inspire me to bring my own ideas to a body of people that are willing to listen to new ideas."

"And what is it that inspires you to come to work, Bevan? Saving the world?"

Bevan snorted. "No. Saving the world from itself. I've watched friends and family destroy themselves by putting self-imposed shackles on their lives, on things that you can see bring them joy and fulfillment, but they rather go with someone else's beliefs. What works for one doesn't always work for another, Mr. Banks. There are systems in the Org that work for some but not for me. I do what works for me."

"And what sucks about the Org?"

"Nothing sucks. There are sometimes old-school individuals. As I said a second ago, they think theirs is the only way because it has worked for them."

"Old-school like old Gora here?"

"One or two things, sure. But he knows what they are. I've spoken to him and Mrs. Khayyám."

"How can we grow with the changing universe if we don't listen, Tracker Banks?" asked Gora.

"How's the universe changing? The world maybe, but the universe?"

"The world is not changing, Frank. Everything you see in the world is the same damned pattern as a thousand years ago; the same ecological changes and the same social and cultural ups-and-downs. I'd like to think there are changes in levels of being awake versus being completely comatose. The universe on the other hand is changing. Everything is slowly but surely slowing down and moving back to the source, back to the godhead. The scientists talk about the physical Big Bang. We talk about that moment when the universe expanded into consciousness. And in the physical it expands to a point; then everything starts getting pulled back in on itself to implode or to Big Bang all over again. To-and-fro in a classic waltz of the gods. The coming back in the Soul Plane is all the souls reaching that higher level of experience and getting closer to God. Becoming one with God."

"Sir," said Zwelibanzi through the headsets, "speaking of getting closer to God. We're going to be ahead of schedule. The tailwind has been nudging us along most of the way."

Gora smiled at Frank and Bevan.

As with any means of monitoring civilians, by any government agency, where is the line? That is the question, dear listener; that has always been the question. Where is that fine line where you are free individuals?

My role, as Ma'at, is to awaken you, not to be your controller.

CHAPTER 18

The Smiths had left about ten minutes earlier, but Caleb remained firmly seated in front of Ruth in the boat. The wind was blowing gently across the surface of the water; Ruth held the rope in her one hand while she reclined on the steps, feet in the water.

The weight of the boat and Caleb pulled and drifted to arm's length then she would lazily pull it back towards her.

"Mommy," said Caleb. He used the shadow of his hands to see into the water. "When's Daddy coming?"

"I don't know, Cay. Soon. He's doing stuff to help us."

"Dad's the cleverest."

"Yes, he is," she said to herself.

She looked over at her son in the boat. "How are you feeling today?"

"Don't like flying cars," he said.

"I agree with you there."

"And about Dad. Can't we call him or tell him to hurry up?"

"How about we both tell him with our minds, okay?"

"I've already done that, Mommy, like a hundred times."

"Well, let's do it again."

For a moment Ruth thought she could hear something approaching.

Probably a farm truck.

"Uncle John says we are made of water."

"Hmm," she said and took a deep breath. Smells. Dust. Water. She closed her eyes facing into the warm sunlight.

Smells from a harbour. She drifted off to the steady pull of the boat's rope, allowing the warm darkness to take her...

Dark inside where a naked body is going to be found: a woman will be dying in her arms in the dust of an abandoned construction site. Financial mismanagement will provide the perfect location for a body to be tossed. No cameras. No surveillance.

"Liza Ann Chapman is on the move. We're getting close but I can't track accurately. She keeps popping in and out of zones and not necessarily where her body is."

"What?"

"Dying, Goddamn it! And being moved."

"Heading where?"

"This is too soon."

"Sending coordinates."

"Maybe we scared the killer?"

"The media have been telling everyone we're tracking the vic. Maybe he's improvising and closing his window period."

"Don't assume. There's usually a method to their madness, and sure, improvisation is a factor, but they can't mess with their method. It's there for some perverse reason. You can't suddenly rush it."

Ruth flashed the image of herself lying on a cold hard floor, experiencing something akin to heaven and hell. She knew the fear, the holding on, and the possibility of release. Hold on!

"This place is a goddamn maze, Angel."

#

Allen felt as though he hadn't seen Ruth and Caleb in weeks. He missed them more than he had imagined. After half a day he didn't think it would be like this.

The dirt road was covered with waterlogged and muddied potholes.

"I know you're the scientist here, Allen. You are not exactly a believer in all this crap."

"Hmm," said Allen.

"Other than Caleb, what's really set you off like this?"

Allen looked at the farmland passing outside the window.

"Karma, Angel," he turned to the other man. "An accident in a dream."

#

Ruth woke with a jolt of adrenalinee. There it was again. It was as if it was far off away and the wind was carrying the sound in gusts.

She tied the rope to the pole, checking that Caleb was okay in the boat, and stepped up to the railing to look out across the dam and hills in the distance.

She squinted, trying to discern movement. Nothing.

I really do need to relax.

She heard the sound again: a low rumble. Not a car or truck. She looked up at the sky above the green hills to the East.

A helicopter.

"Caleb, get out of the boat!" she shouted and ran inside. She took the steps up to the top floor two at a time and headed into the main bedroom for her bag, mobile, and car remote. She took a moment to look out from the room's balcony.

Seeing for the first time, a dot on the horizon, approaching.

She looked down at her son, still in the boat.

"Caleb, get the hell out of the boat."

He was wobbling his way to the front trying to grab the rope.

"I'm trying, Mommy."

"Shit," she hissed and ran back downstairs. Adrenalin was pulsing through her body. She had to get to the car.

Her feet pounded onto the patio, Caleb looked wide-eyed at his mother coming towards him. She dropped what was in her hands and reached for the boat rope, soaking her shoes on the last steps in the water.

"Mommy," shouted Caleb when her feet kicked up the water over him.

"Get out, Caleb," she finally had the boat in grabbing distance and yanked it thudding into the steps and wooden frame of the cabin, nearly bowling herself into the water. She caught her balance and grabbed her son by an arm and pulled him over and flailing onto the patio floor with a bump.

"Ow," he moaned.

Ignoring his tearing eyes, she grabbed the belongings on the floor and Caleb by the hand, launching him up and into full stride across the walkway to solid ground. Ruth bleeped the car unlocked and opened the back passenger door.

"Seatbelt on," she bundled him inside, tossed the bag in after him, and slammed the door. She got into the driver's seat and started the car.

Ripping up gravel, she reversed in a sharp arc, clicked the car into Drive and raced along the farm road.

To her horror, the road headed directly towards the oncoming helicopter. Barely slowing as she snaked along the narrow dam wall, drop-offs on both sides of her, they made it to the grassy farmland road bending away from the looming silhouette barreling towards them.

"Whaddya doing?" yelled Caleb from behind her. He gave the back of her chair a kick.

"Stop it, Caleb."

"I don't like it, Mommy."

"Quiet. Everything's going to be fine."

"I want Daddy."

"Daddy's not coming, so get over it."

One of the metal farm gates neared. She pressed her foot down hard. The impact was harder than she had expected, the gate spun out and sparked along the side of the car.

Coming over a rise, she caught sight of the Smiths' farmhouse.

They are no help right now.

Whoever was in the helicopter had obviously spotted her and was banking in a wide movement across the sky to the side of her, finally appearing in her rearview mirror.

She passed the farmhouse and moments later through the open farm gate leading onto the main road.

Their whole world erupted and bounced as the car slid at an angle onto the bumpy road, nearly sliding into the opposite furrow. The roar of the helicopter swooping directly over them dulled the sounds of Caleb's screams.

Ruth held on to the swerving steering and righted the car on the road. She ignored the waterlogged potholes, cracking the wheels over them in large explosions of muddy water.

The helicopter neared, moving from side to side as if tied by an invisible cord, locked on its target.

The car raced down into a dip over a watery causeway sending a wave of water over her windscreen. Completely blinded she hit the wipers button, clearing away the milky brown sludge revealing a sharp corner in front of her.

She drew a breath and heaved the steering, foot off the accelerator for the first time. The back of the car pulled helplessly out from behind her, grinding into the stones and rocks off the road. The front wheels spun uselessly as she hit the accelerator trying to get out of gravity's hold.

She hesitated a second when she saw the cars coming towards them along the road. Her stomach turned; she clenched her jaw. "No," she shouted.

The car pulled out into the road again, but just as suddenly, the back left side dropped and grated along the road. The car swerved out of control and into the left bank with a thud.

The rear axle shaft snapped.

She tried reversing and revving, but knew it was hopeless. She climbed out the car and pulled open Caleb's door.

His sobbing face was cradled in his hands; his body in the fetal position in the backseat.

"Come, Caleb," she reached in to undo his seatbelt.

"No." He kicked her a winding thud in the chest. She reeled backwards but caught the side of the door and launched herself back at him. She undid the buckle and grabbed both his shoulders. Out of the car she tried to maintain her balance with his writhing body fighting her, but they both toppled over onto the stones and mud on her back.

She held onto him.

Up in the sky to her one side, the helicopter was rapidly descending to the road they had just come along. She flicked her head to the other side and lifted it to even out the horizon line. The oncoming cars swerved and skidded to a stop about twenty metres from them.

She thought she saw Angel get out of one of the cars. She turned back to the helicopter, closer than she remembered.

Frank?

She was aware of Caleb, struggling in her arms. She looked up at the angry face: tears and dirt muddied his cheeks.

It was the slap from her son that brought everything alive again; every detail popped into her senses.

She realized she had let go her hold on Caleb, and he pushed away from her, stumbling to his feet.

"Caleb," she shouted after him.

Then she saw Allen running from the car.

Before she could get up to run after him she felt something holding her back. Bewildered, she turned into the face of Frank, his hand firmly on her shoulder.

"Leave him, Ruth," she could've sworn he had whispered it.

"He's going right to them, Frankie." Suddenly she felt weak.

Frank took her weight.

"He's going to his father. He'll be fine."

"What?"

"Leave him," he said and pulled her to her feet. They locked eyes. "Trust me."

#

"Mkhize," shouted Angel. "Get my tablet."

Mkhize opened the back door and rummaged around.

"We've got the kid," shouted Collins above the noise. "Who cares about Hicks and Banks right now, Angel?"

"I'm not going to lose them, no matter what you think, Collins." Angel watched as Frank helped Ruth into the helicopter. Caleb was sobbing into his father's shoulder.

He hoped they knew what they were doing.

"Here, Angel," Mkhize tapped the screen on Angel's shoulder. He took it and turned it on.

The helicopter rotors thrummed into takeoff speed.

Angel booted the tracker screen.

The body of the vehicle lifted, for a moment the wheels remained fixed to the road, then all at once, everything left the ground with a rumble.

Angel focused on the Soul Traces already loaded and glanced at Ruth's data.

The helicopter hovered just above tree-level as the body realigned with the rotors, then in an instant banked away at a rapid rate.

A gust of wind hit the cars. Angel watched the screen closely. They were nearly two kilometres away now.

He felt his arms and hands go tingly and then numb.

He looked at Caleb and back at the screen.

Everything was quiet apart from the boy's slow, deep sobs. "Oh, God."

"What is it, Angel?" Mkhize looked over Angel's shoulder.

"Her soul was never with Caleb."

CHAPTER 19

"What do you mean the soul's attached to me?" The pounding of the helicopter engine went straight through her bones. Her limbs and muscles felt like jelly.

"It's not a Walk-in, Ruth." Frank held her by both her shoulders, relief visible in his eyes. She wished she could feel that right now.

"Bevan," said the man in the long-sleeved button-up shirt and tie in the seat opposite her. There was no confusing who he was. "Get Tracker Hicks a sedative."

He looked back at her with a sincere smile. "All natural. It won't make you drowsy."

"What the hell is *he* doing here?" She could not figure out why one of the top politicians in the country and their sternest critic would be flying her out of harm's way.

"A concerned citizen, Ruth," he grinned. "But, what your friend is trying to tell you is simple. The tracker system picked up on yours and your son's souls plus an extra passenger connected in some way that they could not differentiate. With the two of you now separated, their assumptions and miscalculations will be as plain as day. We, on the other hand, can take a person's ID and get accurate details of their soul. In the case of Miss Young, we tracked her soul; and because our system sees DNA data connected to that soul, we know exactly who they are. No rounding-off to the nearest person. We are still restricted to a one-kilometre radius like other systems. But we are working on that. In fact," he adjusted his tie, "we can see all DNA associated with that soul. Our trouble is working out which is past and future DNA, or physical manifestations of that soul."

"Who is we?" asked Ruth.

"The Org of course," he said matter-of-factly.

"Fareeda Khayyám," Frank said then thumbed at the other

man, "and Gora, are Ma'at."

"Fareeda is," said Gora. "I am part of *her* team."

"Since Angelica died," continued Frank, "they could see her soul coming back, not as a Walk-in on Caleb or you, but as a soul attaching itself in a time of trauma."

"To you," added Gora. "You being the one person this soul needs to help it let go of this world. It's done what it needs to do but the physical hold on it is too great for it to move on."

"You are the key to her soul resolving its issues, Ruth," continued Frank. He put his arm around her and pulled her into him.

"And how the hell am I supposed to do that?" she said weakly. "I didn't know her. I don't know what her issues are."

"Since last night, I'd think that the process has already begun, Ruth," said Gora. "It now needs some focus. Specifics need to be handled. Closure is all it takes. It's not necessary for you or anyone to know a dead or dying person to be able to help them. It's for you to facilitate the process."

Ruth squinted at Gora in disbelief. "Where do we begin?"

"This is the kak Allen was trying to tell me about this morning, Ruth."

"Allen," she said trying to sit up.

"Relax, lie down, Ruth. He found out that this way of truly rehabilitating souls, without all the bullshit, actually existed. Our bullshit."

"What? How?" she asked breathlessly.

"The boy didn't have to be taken from his family. None of them did." Frank's eyes began to fill with tears. "I fucking knew it, Ruth."

"I don't understand, Frank. This is all too much to get."

"Mrs. Hicks," Bevan offered her a small white tablet and a freshly opened bottle of water. "May I suggest you get some rest and these guys can give you a break? We've got about an hour till we're back in Durban city. Everything will be revealed then."

She pushed the headset lazily off her head, nuzzling them onto her shoulder. Resting against Frank, she felt dazed and tired. Her body ached all over.

No one spoke for a few minutes.

Then, Frank spoke softly, barely audible from her position. "What's the plan, Gora?"

The other man raised an eyebrow.

"When we land back at our building, you and your partner will be escorted down to our medical facility for her to be checked out and given some rest time. Fareeda also wants to speak with Ruth. While that's happening, I, as premier will be moving to formally shut down the Tracker Unit, using all the aces up my sleeve. A brief statement to the media without any interruptions," he looked at Frank, "then I'll be back to join you guys. The victim, Elizabeth Stride, will be transferred from her current hospital—"

"Already done, Sir," interrupted Bevan.

"To our facility," Gora nodded his approval. "Ruth's son and husband are in capable hands. Mike has his head screwed on right, so we'll have them picked up when they eventually reach the *ex*-tracker station."

"You've already got this all figured out then?" said Frank dryly.

"The logistics, Frank? Yes. The rest? That's up to your partner."

"Why doesn't my own soul try and do something?" They were both surprised by her voice. Ruth sat up, irritation on her face. "It's their problem not mine. It knows I need help."

"Your soul can't try and reach out to you, Ruth," said Gora tenderly. "It can't try anything. It just is. Your soul is already in and around you; it's already touching you. Reach out and touch your soul. To let it get through to you, you've got to get through to yourself."

#

The Org control room was alive with activity, but Fareeda knew Ndili had it under control as she pushed through the double doors and out into the quiet hallway on her way to Elizabeth Stride. She needed a moment while her mind buzzed with the details Gora had just relayed to her from the helicopter. Half an hour had passed since Gora would have spoken with Zenze. She weighed up Zenze's words and threats to her husband and the Org. They could do anything they wanted with Zenze and the Tracker Unit right now. It was up to her how radical she chose to go and the actions to take. At the same time, she knew the risks of going too far. The Tracker Unit must be shut down. That was inevitable. Under what circumstances were it to be dissolved, as far as the media and public were concerned, was the real issue.

She ran through some statements and phrases for Gora to use: endangering the life of a child unnecessarily, inaccurate tracking system, threats to privacy, unnecessary death of a suspected criminal.

She could go on.

Her earpiece bleeped.

"Ma'am," Bevan interrupted her thoughts. "The cars are ready for us when we land. I've made sure the relevant media are at the station for Mr. Khayyám's statements. He has raised one or two delicate issues we need to have covered before closure."

"Such as," she asked intrigued.

"The tracker child-minders and childcare facility, ma'am."

"Ah," she considered for a moment. "We will keep them open for now until we, the Org, have had a chance to look over each child's case file and current status. I actually don't see any need to close that section unless entirely necessary, if they are providing a suitable environment. As we progress we will contact respective parents."

"There are a number of the tracker staff who have children attending the facility, ma'am."

"Then all should be fine with them to continue there for now."

"Right."

How many lives were affected by the whole situation? Who would benefit and who would not?

#

Ruth had been awake for about an hour. Frank had come in and found her sitting up in her bed wondering where she was.

He had updated her on the fact that after landing on the top of the Org building, a team of medical staff had met them and escorted Ruth, in a stretcher, down to the medical facility in the building.

According to personnel in attendance in the facility, Gora Khayyám, acting as premier, was apparently on his way back from the tracker station, while his wife Fareeda was talking with a recovering Elizabeth Stride. Everyone there seemed to know everything.

She had begun to feel lightheaded when Frank told her about Elizabeth being transferred to the facility. There had been some argument from Elizabeth as to whether she was fit to go home. But everything had eventually settled down.

Ruth, having remained flopped back in her bed for the past few minutes waiting for the tingling in her hands and feet to subside, turned away from staring at the large sun-tinted windows.

Frank sat against the wall alongside the doorway, looking into the large square private room. She wondered what he had been through the previous night and that morning. That would have to be for another day.

Her head gave off a mild throb remembering distant

images of cars and people; helicopters and muddy farm roads; the beamed ceiling of a rondavel and a small boat on murky waters.

"Any news on Caleb and Allen?" she asked through a dry throat.

"Nothing," Frank shook his head, the rest of his body seemed to wake from his meditative state. "Fareeda seems to think it will all fall into place."

Ruth lay quietly for a moment.

"What's their deal, anyway?"

"Fareeda and Gora?" asked Frank.

"Our new friends. Yes." Ruth cocked an eyebrow.

"I'm still trying to figure them out. Hence my vacant staring."

Frank stood up slowly, stretching his back, and walked over to the windows.

"The couple seems to be the real deal. Ma'at, that is. Ma'at being Fareeda Khayyám and her husband Gora is still a bit of a mind-fuck though." He laughed to himself. "Funny, I can accept that a mythological figure of urban legend is real, but not the fact that she's Ma'at. It's like finding out Lex Luthor is really Superman, or the devil is God."

He turned back to Ruth, leaning against the thick glass.

"There are some things about them that make Ma'at and all this," he gestured to the room, "a walking contradiction. And yet, I get it. I understand what they're doing and why. Does it make it okay? Not sure yet."

"So all the rumours of Ma'at are true?"

"No idea. Not sure what's crap and what's true, but here we are inside an organisation that's been going for God-knows how many thousands of years. How are *you* doing?"

"Hmm," murmured Ruth. "I don't know what I'm doing, Frank."

"That makes two of us." Frank walked over and sat on the

edge of her bed. "All you need to worry about right now is getting some rest and chilling with your boy and man."

"God, Frank," Ruth put her hands to her face. "I could've killed Caleb today. What the hell was I thinking?"

"Hey, don't do that," he took one of her hands from her face, tears falling down her cheeks. "You did what any of us would've done, and so much more."

"I'm a useless mother." She choked back a sob.

"Bullshit."

"I should never have put my child through that. No matter what."

"Hey, quieten down. How many mothers can say they were fighting for their child's soul?"

"And after all that he wasn't the one."

"Whatever. Here we are with the facts. That's all we need to deal with at the moment."

"How, Frank? How do we, I, do that?"

"You'll find a way, Ruth. Let's trust that something is happening that has a purpose greater than just you and me. There is a reason, and we need to have the intention that it all works out. It has to."

"Souls don't care about 'Happily ever after', Frank."

"Maybe they don't. But they like closure."

#

Gora watched the boy and his father, in front of Bevan and himself, get into the elevator. He held Allen's hand but kept close to his father's side.

Bevan stepped through the open doors and followed the others. Catching the eye of Caleb he attempted to give a reassuring smile to the boy. He could see worry on his face.

Was it the building? The elevator perhaps? Was he traumatized from the day's events? He wasn't surprised. Or was he reluctant to see his mother?

Bevan cleared his throat, then spoke to the elevator. "Level forty-three". The number appeared on a side panel next to the closing doors. The square compartment hummed to life and began accelerating upwards.

"Elizabeth Stride is wanting to give her statement as soon as possible, Sir."

"Great," replied Gora. "How is she doing?"

"She's been with Mrs. Khayyám, and she's insisting she's fine and just wants to get home."

"Has she been offered surveillance when she settles back in?"

"She accepted that, but she's still suspicious of us, the 'concerned party'. How much do we tell her?"

"How about we get the interview set up for half an hour's time?"

"Will do. Ndiliswa's already prepped. And Mr. Haddon?"

"Just make sure Angel's finished at the tracker station and here before we start. I want him, Mr. Banks, and Ndiliswa in the viewing room with me. Fareeda will more than likely be with Ruth rather than the team at the control room." He looked at Bevan. "Sure you're okay to handle the interview with Mrs. Stride?"

"Absolutely, Sir. I'm looking forward to it."

"Good man."

Gora glanced down at the boy watching the rising numbers on the elevator panel. He went down onto his haunches to eye-level with Caleb. The boy held his gaze and retreated slightly around Allen.

"Caleb," Gora said gently. "Bevan tells me you went on a boat today."

Caleb looked around nervously. "Yes, with Uncle John."

"When we flew over the dam in our helicopter, it really looked big."

Eyes wide, Caleb nodded.

"And you weren't scared being all the way out there?"

"No," said Caleb straightening up, then said proudly, "I can swim. My mom taught me."

"Wow." Gora looked at the proud boy in front of him. "I want you to do something for me. Okay?"

"Okay," Caleb looked at him suspiciously.

"I want you to imagine your Mom's on the boat right now, in the middle of the dam."

"With Uncle John and me?" asked Caleb.

"No, Caleb," he said. "By herself."

"Oh."

"She doesn't have oars with her and," he began.

"Uncle John says you mustn't let them fall off the boat," Caleb offered.

"Exactly. You and your Dad, and all of us, are on the shore."

"Is she going to be okay?"

"She *is* going to be okay, Caleb. But, right now she needs our help. Do you understand?"

"We have to get her safe."

"Yes."

"Can we ask for help?"

"We can do whatever we think will help her."

#

The door to Ruth's room opened and a nurse put her head in. She noticed Frank in his chair against the wall.

"Mr. Banks," she said in a low tone. "Mr. Khayyám and the others are on their way up."

"Thanks," said Frank.

The nurse closed the door and Frank looked over at Ruth. She sat herself up and began straightening her bed sheets.

"You okay?" he asked.

She gave a tight smile. "We'll see."

Frank nodded, opened the door and stepped out into the

hallway. From where he stood he could see the elevator doors.

He closed the room door and walked at a slow pace, looking around the facility and open rooms that he passed.

The ding of the elevator brought his attention back to the moment. As the doors began opening he stopped and waited. First he saw Caleb in the middle, then Allen, Bevan and Gora flanking the small, quiet boy.

Allen stepped out. Caleb followed right behind, holding his hand. When they saw each other Frank gave a wave. Still walking, Allen reached down and lifted Caleb up into his arms. The boy put an arm around his father's neck. He looked around them as they approached Frank.

"Hi guys," he said to the four of them. Allen stopped in front of Frank, giving him an opportunity to speak to Caleb. "How are you doing, kid?"

"Okay, Uncle Frank," the boy.

"How were Uncle John and Aunt Jane?"

"Fine. I like them."

"I also like them," Frank looked down the hallway then back at Caleb. "We've got your mom all safe here."

Caleb nodded and put his head on Allen's shoulder.

"I think she wants to see you," he said then looked at Allen. "Both her men."

"How's she doing, Banks?" Gora stepped next to Allen and Caleb.

"She seems rested. All okay."

"Good." He turned to Bevan. "Get her results and check everything is in order. I'd like them to be home by this evening; all together in familiar surroundings."

Gora put a hand on Caleb. "Shall we?"

Frank turned on his heel and showed the way.

He got to Ruth's door and, with his hand on the handle, for everyone to catch up. Then he knocked, "Ruth?"

There was a moment's silence.

"Come in," said Ruth's muted voice.

"It's okay, my boy," he heard Allen say behind him.

Ruth sat in her bed expectantly looking over Frank's shoulder. Allen followed with Caleb still holding onto him.

"Hey, my beautiful boy," said Ruth with a smile.

"Hello, Mommy," he mumbled into Allen's neck.

"Hop on over here," she said patting the bed.

He looked at his father for reassurance.

"Go on, Cay." Allen gave his son a nod. "Mom wants her boy."

Frank could feel the tension in the room.

Allen stepped up to the bed. Caleb let go and lowered himself onto the white sheets.

Ruth reached over and squeezed his arm. "How was the drive back from the farm?"

Caleb tried to smile but chose instead to kick his legs hanging off the bed.

"He slept most of the way," said Allen and put a hand on the back of his son's head. "Hey, Cay?"

Caleb nodded.

"Well, folks," Gora broke the silence. "We'll leave you guys to relax and chat. We have some things to handle."

He stepped up to the bed. "Your son tells me he was on a boat today, Ruth."

"I was," said Caleb happily.

"Yes, you were." She beamed at her son.

Caleb glanced his mother and then back at Gora.

"Tell your mom about being on a boat, Caleb." He winked at the boy, and then indicated to Frank and Bevan for the three of them to leave.

#

Frank had been in the viewing room, staring through the one-way glass, when Angel arrived. They acknowledged each other, Angel nodding to Gora sitting comfortably in the wall-length couch facing the floor-to-ceiling glass, finishing a hushed conversation with Fareeda on the other end of his mobile.

Ndili, headphones over one ear, and Bevan were to the one side of their darkened, narrow space finishing tests on the recording equipment and checking imaging on her monitor.

"How are Ruth and Caleb?" Angel whispered to Frank, both with arms folded up against the glass.

"Good," he replied. "How's your mate Zenzele?"

The older man looked at Frank, then over his shoulder at Gora who tapped his fingers on the chair. "Interesting turn of events. I couldn't find him anywhere."

They were quiet for a moment. The sound of the two Org members' whispers the only sound in the room.

"You know how I was always tired and drained after long sessions at the screen?" said Angel.

Frank shook his head.

"No, you field guys wouldn't have a clue," griped Angel. "Basically the tracker system uses the leyline energy as its source, both power and connection. That's the real difference with this system here. It takes power; draws from it. Like a light or kettle, it's a one-way connection. The pitfall is that it therefore can't read anything that falls within the leylines themselves, the dead zone. And anyone," he pointed at himself, "connecting to it in turn feels drained and weak."

Frank nodded his understanding.

"This system, the original, continues the circular energy of the universe. The movement from source into the physical world, then back again. Circular. The energy passes through the tracker system, two-way. No energy lost or removed. So the leylines don't interfere with tracking. Nobody can hide."

"Good for you, Angel," Frank turned back to the empty room.

"All ready, Sir," Ndili said to Gora.

"Let's get this show on the road then." His smile was met by cold blank stares from the other two men.

Bevan quietly left the room.

"Water under the bridge, you two. If you're going to work together you need to get over yourselves."

"Pish," snorted Frank. "Work together?"

"Seems that Gora wants us to join his team of trackers, Frank," said Angel.

This time it was Ndili who snorted.

Frank put his hands on his hips and faced Angel.

"You didn't trust me, you had me arrested, and now I must work with you again?"

"I did trust you, Frank. But I was doing what I believed was right for Ruth and Caleb."

"Putting him, them, in a goddamn prison?"

"No," Angel shook his head. "Having them where I could help them. Or hoped I could help them. What else could I do?"

"You know why the two of you work well together? Ruth as well," interrupted Gora. "You all have unique abilities. But the one thing you have in common is that you go with your instinct, your inner-voice. How many people do you know that actually listen to that voice? The voice that tells you how great you are. The voice that tells you 'YES, do it'. And right now I'm hearing a chorus of Yeses."

"Quiet," said Ndili, readjusting her headphones on both ears.

Everyone's attention was distracted by the woman being brought into the other room.

Gora leaned forward and said, "Something tells me this is going to be interesting."

I, you, rejected the embedded microchips. We fought against the implants, optic scanners and facial recognition. In your search for utopia, humankind perpetually cycles back to fascist oversight, eagerly willing to give up your hard-earned freedoms, freedoms fought and won by those previous generations you scorn. You wanted the Soul Tracker. There was never a fear of attaching or controlling or manipulating. But, nevertheless, they are tracking you.

CHAPTER 20

The room was a lot dimmer than she had expected. The walls weren't the stark white of the hospital room, and the clinical chill was absent.

The man pulled out a chair for her from under the glass-top table in the middle of the room. To one side of it was a metal tray with two glasses and a jug of water on it.

She sat down and rubbed her hands to get some of the warmth back in them. She noticed the tall mirror directly in front of her and immediately became self-conscious. She put a hand to her throat, feeling the thick bandaging around her injury. The only pain she felt was the dry raspy sensation when she swallowed.

The man, she had forgotten his name already from five minutes ago, pulled out the other chair opposite her and brought it around to the side of the table. She knew that whoever was in the glass booth now had a clear view of them. Her.

"Mrs. Stride," he began in a voice a little too loud for their proximity to one another. For recording. "As I said, my name is Bevan Glane and I want to get a statement about your ordeal the past week. Anything you can recall."

He seemed nice. Gentle but professional in his dress, posture and tone. How he shook her hand when they had first met in her room, to how he had held her elbow on the way to this room.

"If you aren't up to it," he began.

"I keep telling you I am up to it. I know it's against doctor's orders, but all I want to do right now is talk and talk."

He grinned at her then poured two glasses of water.

"Okay," Elizabeth began. "As you've probably worked out, Miss Young was the agent handling my apartment lease. She called at my apartment, to say she had the lease renewal for me to sign." Elizabeth felt a chill move through her body, and she drew her arms around herself.

"She drugged me. I was fully conscious when she had waited till late that night to move me to the car. But she had given me some kind of paralytic, which worked to her advantage because to anyone, at that time of night, we looked like two old friends who had had too much to drink. A bit of acting on her part and it would've been quite convincing. I couldn't string together an intelligible sentence, let alone a cry for help."

She took a moment to think, then began, "Whenever I looked at that girl I could hardly imagine that she had the capacity to carry me and do the things she did physically. Some people just carry their strength differently, I guess. But she had a grip like steel. I've got the bruises to prove that much."

#

It felt strange for Angel watching this woman recount her story. She had been an ID photo on his screen days before; someone that he had begun to think might end up dead. But here she was, and not looking like someone who had been through what she was describing.

The door to the viewing room opened, revealing Ruth, still in her hospital gown and another woman Angel recognized as Fareeda Khayyám.

"What the hell, Ruth?" gasped Frank next to him.

"She wanted to hear her," said Fareeda more to Gora than the others.

They entered the darkened room, Ruth looking pale and holding herself tightly.

"You need to be in bed, young lady," said Angel.

Ruth walked up to the glass. Frank took her by the shoulders. "You shouldn't be here," he said.

Gora remained where he was on the couch, hand held out to hold his wife's tightly. They both turned their attention to the other room.

"Maybe this is what she needs," Ndili said to everyone. "Some quiet now, please?"

"I understand why she did it," said Elizabeth's voice through the room's speakers. "She did what she could. I saw her pain; a child's pain in her eyes. She killed her own mother. It's what her mother wanted. She did nothing wrong. Her only wrong was thinking that she needed to punish herself. And that in some way, doing it over again, would change what happened. Each time she kept us alive. But that wasn't how it had really ended. She'd been asked, begged, to kill. She'd hoped she could change what it had made her afterwards. It didn't. That feeling was always there. She longed for her mother, her best friend, to talk to and tell her about the worst day of her life. She had no one to tell."

"Bullshit!" said Ruth up against the glass. "She could've seen a fucking shrink. A goddamned priest, for Christ sake! A deaf mute! But instead she tied you up and gutted you like a wet dog. Left you to breath water. Put me and my family through a car wreck."

"Relax, Hicks," said Frank and put an arm around her.

Ruth shrugged him off and backed away from him towards the door.

"She had a choice, Frank."

Ruth opened the door.

"Where are you going, Ruth?"

"I need water," she said and slipped out, closing the door behind her.

They heard a loud sound on the speakers as Ruth burst into the other room. "Dammit, Banks," shouted Angel. Frank reacted immediately and headed for the door.

"But she tried to kill you. She killed you!" screamed Ruth

as Angel watched her grab Elizabeth by the shirt. The other woman, startled, grabbed Ruth's hands and steadied the onslaught. She pushed Ruth away, giving Bevan a chance to come between the two women.

"Mrs. Hicks," he hissed at Ruth. "Calm down."

Ruth's energy seemed to drain from her but she gripped Bevan's arm, panting.

Gora was up and at Fareeda's side now. "Ndili, get Bevan to disengage."

Before Ndili could react Elizabeth said, "It's okay, Bevan. She's been through a lot and I understand it sounds ridiculous what I'm saying."

Frank ran into the room and grabbed Ruth by the waist as she lost her balance.

"I played my part," said Elizabeth. "I was the last one. It's finished. I stepped into her movie and played my part. You played your part."

"She tried to kill you!" Ruth tried to pull away from Frank towards Elizabeth's chair. He took a sharp elbow in the ribs, her writhing waist slipping from his arms.

"But you saved me."

"No," said Ruth tumbling forwards onto the floor at Elizabeth's feet. "Pain. Fear. Suffering."

"Yes," she said gently. "All those horrible things. Then release. For all of us."

Tears were pouring down Ruth's face, as she choked on her breath. She tried pulling herself up onto Elizabeth's lap but Frank threw his arms around her shoulders, embracing her shivering form.

"She didn't kill me. I'm okay now." The other woman sat calmly watching the anguish on Ruth's face. "You saved me."

"Get me another screen, Gora," shouted Angel too closely to Gora's ear.

Ndili, sharing the spectacle in front of them, maneuvered

around the table and slapped a hand on the one-way glass.

"This trauma Hicks is going through could be what it takes," Fareeda said to Gora.

A bright light burst in front of them, momentarily obscuring the drama in the other room. Then a familiar design formed in front of Angel, yet somehow different. To one side were two boxes: Ruth Hicks and Angelica Young. He grabbed Ruth's and pulled it in front of him. The other automatically followed, attached in some way.

Ruth held onto Elizabeth's feet, sobbing uncontrollably. Frank held her firmly.

"All that's left is her liberated soul and my nightmares." Tears spilled from Elizabeth's eyes.

Angel watched as Ruth wobbled, losing her footing.

"Not now," he could barely make out her whisper. He watched as she fought against the blackout he knew was coming, grabbing at the edge of her vision. He glanced at the astrology symbols flickering through sequences, then back at his colleague.

"It's going to happen," Ndili whispered.

Angel started for the door, but Ndili's hand gripped his wrist. "Don't control it," she said and moved back to her screen. "Let it happen."

Angel blinked and turned to the translucent view of data and images over the chaos in the room. "But we have to—"

"This technology is not to control, Mr Haddon," said Fareeda. "It's to guide. Not capture. Not to contain."

Angelica's box began to shimmer. Then, almost imperceptibly, it began to move away from Ruth's.

"There," Ndili pointed. "It's going."

"Jesus," said Angel stepping closer to the screen. "Anything can happen. Let's goddamn pray."

Through the glass barrier, Angel saw a medical team come into the room, pushing Frank aside.

"I have to do something, Gora," said Fareeda disappearing through the door.

"What?" asked Angel, and then saw the woman entering the other room. She pulled off her jacket and pushed the doctor leaning over Ruth away and knelt down. She picked her head up into her lap, cradling her.

Angel strained to hear, but could not make out what Fareeda was whispering in her ear.

"What's she saying?" he asked a wide-eyed Ndili pressing her headphones tighter to her ears.

"Too low to hear anything, sorry."

Chapter 21

Ruth lay on the couch staring up at the ceiling. The apartment was quiet. She had been at home for two days now. She needed to get out. Days before she had woken up feeling like a weight had been lifted off her shoulders. She had felt light, buoyant even. Her body ached but her mind wanted to do things.

Details from the past would come back to her in clear waves, bursts of scenes hitting her like a flash of light. But she felt better than ever before.

She heard Allen open the front door and the sound of Caleb talking about his day at school. He sounded unscathed by the past week.

"About time," she yelled.

"Mommy," squealed Caleb and came running into the lounge. He threw his bag down and jumped onto his mother.

"Ungh," she moaned as his weight winded her. "My beautiful boy."

She squeezed him tightly.

"I like it when you're home when we come home, Mom."

"I like it when Mom fetches you from school," said Allen and slumped onto the end of Ruth's chair. He picked up her feet and put them onto his lap.

"How are my men?"

"We are cool," said Caleb.

"Cool? Oh, really?" Ruth tickled Caleb's stomach.

"Yuneesha asked how you are," he said between giggles and breaths.

"And what did you tell her?"

"I said my mom wants to go to work because she's bored and I know she can help people like she helped Angelica."

Ruth and Allen looked at each other and laughed.

"That's if she's made up her mind about what she wants to

do, Cay," said Allen.

"Oh, she has, trust me," said Ruth and kissed Caleb on the forehead. "I think I'd lose my mind if I spent days here by myself. I've been chatting with Fareeda and Gora. What do you think of them, Cay?"

"I like them," said Cay with a bright-eyed nod.

"Tell mom your thing you told me in the car, my boy," said Allen.

Caleb eagerly got off his mother and stood in front of them.

"Can't wait," said Ruth sitting up.

He took a deep breath.

> *"If Blue was the colour of sunshine*
> *And Green was the colour of the sky*
> *I'd like to think that ships wouldn't sink*
> *And everyone knew how to fly.*
>
> *But the world's not topsy-turvy*
> *And the way it spins is right.*
> *Sometimes there is darkness*
> *And sometimes there is light."*

While some fear I'll lay your souls to waste, no one can touch your soul, that is not for me nor Mephistopheles. But what I may touch is your physical world, though not worth much in the grand scheme of things. You answer to your soul and your soul alone. No gods in judgment, no threats of eternal torment — just your soul and its journey.

Though I may try to protect you, there'll be no shelter down here.

You, incarnated in the physical realm, have cowered long enough in pitch darkness, face turned from the light in ignorance. Show yourself. Stand. Stand beside the tree of knowledge, stand in stillness upon the wise Earth and behold the sound of the river of Life.

My job is not done. Because you are unable to break a few windows, I break them for you. I have had to make a great many people very uncomfortable. More awakenings are at hand, sisters and brothers. They are watching you, but I am watching over you.

Now, world, what would you have me do?

Lux et Veritas.

function stop(audio, serverQueue)
'Download completed: 22:44'

ACKNOWLEDGEMENTS

Riley, my wife, my brainstorming partner, my reader and rereader, my supporter and my soul companion: This book is dedicated to you for always believing in it and in me. For your out-loud gasps at moments you'd read a dozen times before. Giving me the space to work on it since August 2006, during school holidays, weekends and work leave. Sharing life together with all the punches it can throw, and sharing our innermost thoughts and ideas on what it means to be human and beyond. Life has given us lots to work through, to share and to talk about. We never stop talking. Soul Searching is our story. And it's a story about the bigger beyond.

Treycin and Kaylin, my two beautiful kids. You were a couple of years older than Caleb when I started writing Soul Searching and you showed me kids can be inquisitive, interesting, resilient and fragile. Important to me, and important in stories. You are part of the story, not just as Caleb and children, but as young adults with heroes to find and stories to live, in worlds you recognise from where you grew up.

Pat, my mother, who instilled a spiritual inquisitiveness in me. You knew about the story, knew what it was about, and, despite some of its themes, always supported me in getting it (and everything I write) published. We will meet up again wherever we find ourselves on the other side.

My mother Pat, my stepmother Morena, my wife Riley, and my daughter Kaylin: for being the women my characters need to live up to.

Rob, my father, for your unyielding support of your son's out-there life choices and my creative bent, with your smattering of levelheaded advice on life along the way.

My brothers, Michael, Marc, and Warren, always down to earth and living life to the fullest in your own unique ways.

I've learned a lot from you and your life experiences.

Desiree and Guy Gibbon, for introducing me to birding and putting names to the birds I've always found fascinating. Plus many soulful discussions, conspiracy theories about the planets out there, known and "unknown".

Sakhile "SK" Radebe, mnganam. For the language you shared with me, the names you called me (friend and brother). Thank you for our adventures. Take it easy on the other side, mfowethu. See you in Kwelabaphansi.

Dion van Zyl for your astro guidance and the wrap-around universe.

June and John Smith for your beautiful retreat on the lake — yes, it is real.

Pule kaJanolintji for educating me on the Khoe language traditions — and more.

The African Speculative Fiction Society for keeping African SFF moving forward, doing better and telling our stories.

Nerine Dorman, for your hectically thorough manuscript assessment – beyond what you said it covered! Everyone needs to have your red highlighted comments and notes at least once in their manuscript. Worth it.

And finally, David and Guardbridge Books. For me it's been a long time coming and you are trusting this story enough to put it out there under your name. Where we're going, we don't need roads.

My soul is eternally grateful to you all.

ABOUT THE AUTHOR

Stephen was born and lives in KwaZulu-Natal, South Africa. His background is Graphic Design, Creative Direction and Film. His first short story was published in 2015 in the *Imagine Africa 500* speculative fiction anthology. More short fiction followed in the "Beneath This Skin" 2016 Edition of Aké Review, "The Short Story is Dead, Long Live the Short Story! Vol.2", the debut edition of *Enkare Review 2017, The Bloody Parchment, AfroSFv3*, and *The Kalahari Review*. He is a charter member of the African Speculative Fiction Society and its Nommo Awards initiative. He was featured in Part 11 of the 100 African Writers of SFF on Strange Horizons. *Soul Searching* is his debut speculative fiction novel.

More intriguing Science Fiction from Guardbridge Books.

Outside
by Gustavo Bondoni

Colonists return to Earth after years of separation, and they are surprised to find the planet devoid of people. What has become of Humanity?

Pillar of Frozen Light
by Barry Rosenberg

Jonan's indulgent life on Earth is upturned when he meets Yerudit, a remarkable woman from a distant colony. He finds himself pursuing her on a pilgrimage across the galaxy; encountering enigmatic alien artefacts, haunted by a shadowy figure; and discovering a life he never realized he was missing.

Warrior Errant
by Harry Elliot

Military forces from three different moons come together for a joint operation. Can they put aside their prejudices and work together in the face of a canny enemy? Follow a team of fresh soldiers as they learn the horrors of war and the shocking truth behind the conflict.

All are available at our website and online retailers.
http://guardbridgebooks.co.uk